MY BELOVED PRISONER

The wild and tempestuous peasant daughter of
a slain Saxon lord, Alana of Brynwald
bravely resists the brutal Norman invaders—
but fears the mysterious specter who haunts her
dreams. And now he stands before her—
tall and strong as an oak . . . terrifying yet strangely
exciting. The dark knight of her visions has
come to claim her as his prize.

MY LORD CONQUEROR

By rights, Merrick of Normandy should
shun the serpent-tongued beauty who wishes
him dead. But Alana's sensuous fire
draws him to her—and burns him to his warrior
soul. It is he who is lord and she the captive.
Yet Merrick can never claim true victory until
the proud Saxon maid shares his passion—
and embraces him as master of her heart.

SAMANTHA JAMES

MY LORD CONQUEROR

An Avon Romantic Treasure

AVON BOOKS
An Imprint of HarperCollinsPublishers

This is a work of fiction. Names, characters, places, and incidents are products of the author's imagination or are used fictitiously and are not to be construed as real. Any resemblance to actual events, locales, organizations, or persons, living or dead, is entirely coincidental.

AVON BOOKS
An Imprint of HarperCollins*Publishers*
10 East 53rd Street
New York, New York 10022-5299

Copyright © 1995 by Sandra Kleinschmit
Inside cover author photo by Almquist Studios
Library of Congress Catalog Card Number: 94-96273
ISBN: 0-380-77548-4
www.avonromance.com

First Avon Books printing: March 1995

Avon Trademark Reg. U.S. Pat. Off. and in Other Countries, Marca Registrada, Hecho en U.S.A.
HarperCollins® is a trademark of HarperCollins Publishers Inc.

Printed in the U.S.A.

10 9 8 7 6 5 4 3

Prologue

England 1066

It was doom foretold.

The sign appeared but days after Easter . . . a shattering light that streaked across a night-dark sky, a silvery trail of fire in its wake. The light came yet again the next night, and for six nights thereafter.

The people of England, from the king to his advisers to the lowliest villein in the village, trembled in fear. For the blaze of light was an omen, a warning from heaven, a sign of God's wrath . . . an ominous prediction of the future.

An army came, but it was not what the English expected. This one came from the north—the Danes. Yea, and the battle was well fought and truly won . . .

The days passed into weeks, the weeks into months. The summer—and their fears—began to wane. Winter approached. But for some the threat of disaster remained, for there were those who still believed that the battle was

1

not yet won, that the light that had blazed
across the sky foretold but one thing . . .

Doom for England.

Mayhap they were right.

For soon *they* came . . . From across the Channel like a vicious tempest from the sea . . . Hun-
dreds of ships. Thousands of men. They
swarmed across the land like a vile pestilence,
for they were a breed apart, these Normans.
Onward they marched, onward to Hastings,
leaving behind them a wake of destruction and
ruin. And it was there that Harold of England
met William of Normandy . . .

'Twas a battle destined to be lost.

For the English were no match against the
Normans, who fought with swords aloft and
hearts afire. Bold and fearless they were, war-
riors like their Viking ancestors; fierce and
indomitable, they were ceaseless in their pur-
suit of plunder and war.

For these were the conquerors, the men who
forever changed the fate of a nation . . .

And the life of one woman.

Chapter 1

⁓ꙨꙨ⁓

*A*ll around was a darkness such as she had never known. Blacker than the deepest pits of hell. Shadows shifted and loomed, darting back and forth, in and out, as if to snatch at her with greedy, grasping fingers . . .

She could feel . . . something. Something evil. A sense of danger that loomed all around, as heavy and thick and depthless as the shadows.

The wind rose in fury, wailing and howling. Lightning crashed across the heavens, a blaze of rending light. Thunder roared across the land, shaking the very ground beneath her feet. Great pools of blood splotched the earth. The air was rife with the sickening stench of gore and destruction.

Then she was running. Over the shriek of the wind, her pulse roared in her ears. Footsteps trampled the earth just behind her.

Blindly she ran, besieged by darkness. Beset by danger. By those horrible shadows that lurked all around. The specter of death loomed close at hand. Pressing in on her. Smothering her so that she could scarcely breathe . . .

But all at once there arose before her a hulk-

3

*ing shadow. From out of the shadows they
came . . . Man and beast. Knight and destrier.*

*He sat atop the great black steed, armed and
mailed. For one single, frozen moment, he was dark
and faceless, his features hidden behind a cone-
shaped helmet. Behind him, lightning ripped the
sky apart; it was as if he were cast in silver.*

*Slowly he raised his helm. A jolt tore through
her. His expression was utterly fierce, pale and
glittering and cold as frost; it stabbed into her like
the point of a spear. Then slowly he raised his arm.
Clasped in one gauntleted hand was a gleaming
sword. He raised it high, his weapon poised for the
space of a heartbeat. Then it sliced down . . . down
to pierce her breast . . .*

"Alana! By the Rood, girl, what ails you?
If you do not cease this screeching, you will
surely wake your poor dead mother!"

The voice was scratchy as a hair shirt, dry
and raspy with age, yet it was a familiar one.
Alana of Brynwald reached for it almost desperately as she surfaced through filmy layers
of darkness. She awoke trembling, the shrill of
still another scream curdled in her breast.

For a moment she lay huddled there, her
cheek pressed into her lumpy straw pallet, her
fingers clutching the thin woolen blanket to
her chin. Her surroundings were slow to pen-
etrate her muddled senses. Little by little reality seeped in. Only then did her terror begin
to abate.

She was here, in the tiny cottage where she
had spent her childhood and grown to womanhood. Dawns tepid light slowly penetrated

through the single shuttered window, allowing her to glimpse the furrowed cheeks of the white-bearded man who bent over her.

Her breath left her in a trembling rush. No sword had pricked her breast. There was no dark knight before her who sought to relieve her of her life's blood. She was alive . . . *alive*. But the dream, that horrible, horrible dream . . .

The dream had come yet again.

Aubrey eased back on his haunches, wincing just a little. Beneath the frayed and ragged wool of his tunic, his shoulders were hunched and thin. His hair hung to his shoulders, as white as his beard. Deep lines scored his cheeks and brow, but his eyes were keenly sharp—with both concern and speculation.

"You gave these old bones a fright, child. I heard your cries inside my hut."

Alana said nothing. She pushed aside the tattered blanket and eased herself to her knees on the damp, cold earth of the cottage, tucking her slender legs beneath her.

Aubrey watched her, his shaggy brows drawn together. She willed her hand not to tremble as she smoothed her hair. Like polished silver and gold it was, a ripple of moonglow shining down the narrow lines of her back to her hips. She had learned to say nothing of these strange dreams that plagued her in the dead of night. Far too often she had been the brunt of the villagers' scorn and laughter, taunts and ridicule.

But it was not as though Aubrey was like

any of the other villagers, nor had it ever been so. Even now, though his hands were gnarled and his years so advanced, 'twas said he was the finest tanner south of the Humber. And indeed, now that her mother Edwyna was gone, the old man was dearer to her than any other, even— may God forgive her!—her own sister.

Like her mother, Aubrey had not ridiculed the strange visions that had haunted her since her childhood years. Nearly all had come to pass. Yet something stopped her from speaking freely about them. How could she tell him? Aware that Aubrey still studied her, she lowered her gaze.

She'd had dreams before, many a time, many a night. Of strangers. Of those in the village. But she had never dreamed of herself. And now Alana knew only that never before had she been afraid for *herself* . . .

Never until now.

The dark knight. Who was he . . . or *what* was he? Alana did not know. Yet she sensed that he was her enemy, that he was a threat unlike any other. Why it was so, Alana could not say. But she feared this dark knight as nothing before . . .

Nay, she thought, drawing on all her strength. *Nay!* She did not want to think of that horrid dream. She did not want to think of *him*.

A small bundle of fur slipped onto her lap— Cedric, the cat who had shadowed her mother for years and now shadowed her. Her fingers twined through thick, yellow fur. She bowed her head low, unwilling to let Aubrey glimpse her distress. The old man would stew and worry, and she would not have that on her conscience.

"Please," she murmured. "You know I would never offend you. I would speak of it if I could. But I cannot. 'Tis nothing, this I swear. So do not trouble yourself any further."

The old man narrowed his eyes. "Then why do you shiver?"

For the first time she allowed a faint smile to curve her lips. "'Tis a cold November morn," she returned lightly. "Why else would I shiver?"

Aubrey's thin hand balled into a fist. "Bloody Norman bastards!" he muttered. "They steal our wood so that we can scarcely cook or warm our weary limbs. They steal the crops that we labored long and hard to reap. By the time the winter is finished the villagers of Brynwald will be half-starved." He choked back his anger. "Indeed, if any of us should last so long!"

With that he hobbled from the cottage. Alana shooed Cedric from her lap and arose. Like the rest of the villagers, her dwelling was a simple one. The floor was of hard, trampled earth. A small trestle table and two wooden stools sat before the hearth. She washed quickly from a wooden pail of water, then she braided her hair into a single long rope down her back. Next she wound a long strip of hide around each slender foot; her boots had fallen apart months ago. Her stomach rumbled hungrily, but she did not break the morning fast. She and Aubrey had shared most of her meager store of food last eve. There was only a small hunk of bread left and no more.

Nearly a sennight had passed since Brynwald had been taken by the Normans. The soft line of her lips curled. Aubrey was right. They called themselves Normans. But they were called bastards by those they conquered.

Dark was the day, and wretched were the people, for the English were a humble race, mostly farmers here in these northern climes of the land. But there had been no stopping the raiders from across the Channel . . . They seized their livestock, their food. Their villages were razed as the Normans plundered and warred. Their peace had been shattered, their lands and lives invaded.

For a long moment she stood in the crooked little doorway, her eyes drawn toward Brynwald Keep. High atop a craggy bluff it stood, surrounded by a wooden palisade, overlooking the churning waters of the North Sea. Though the sprawling keep had been her father's home, it had never been Alana's home. Nay, her place was not at Brynwald, though she was indeed the daughter of Kerwain, the lord of Brynwald.

A stark, wrenching pain crept into her heart, for Kerwain was no more. He had died beneath a Norman sword—and so had his wife Rowena. But there had been no word of Sybil. Alana took that as a sign that her sister had survived the fray. She prayed it was so . . .

Like the rest of the villagers, Alana had scarce ventured out since that first brutal assault. The air had been thick with smoke and the acrid smell of burning thatch. Hair-raising screams shrilled throughout three long days and nights. Even now, the sound of hoofbeats was enough to send the villagers of Brynwald scrambling for the safety of their huts.

Before they had lived in fear of God. Now they lived in fear of the Normans.

But she could not cower here forever. She must see that she and Aubrey had food to eat.

Squaring her shoulders, she took up her bow and arrow from where it hung upon the wall, then slipped a quiver of arrows over the shoulder of her bliaud. When she stepped from the doorway, she spied Aubrey hobbling toward her from across the village clearing. He frowned when he saw the bow in her hands.

"Alana, you cannot mean to go out hunting!"

"We must have food," she said simply.

"But the Normans have ordered that we stay in the village," he argued.

"And I would remind you again, Aubrey, we must have food."

Shaggy brows drew across the bridge of his nose. "And what about the Normans?" he demanded.

Soft lips curled in a faint smile. "Ah," she said lightly. "Perchance my arrow shall take aim at bigger, hardier game—a Norman soldier, mayhap!"

Aubrey did not find such jests amusing. He shook his head and glowered at her. Alana smiled slightly, and they set out.

Near the village pasture they passed the ale-wife and her daughters, but they did not deign to speak to the mismatched pair, only cast them a dark and wary glance. Aubrey scowled at the trio. "Pay them no heed," he said gruffly. "They are foolish and ignorant."

Alana said nothing. Her mother had been the village healer and had taught her all she knew of the arts of herbs and healing. But in the months since her mother had passed on, the villagers oft refused her willingness to treat their ailments. They spoke to her only when they could not avoid it.

She kept her chin high, yet a telltale bitterness bled onto her soul. Though she had long been treated so, she would never grow used to it. She had been branded different by virtue of birth, for she was the lord's bastard daughter; but she had also been branded different by something beyond her control—the visions that came to her unbidden . . . unwanted. Oh, Alana understood why they disliked her, for they were a superstitious people. They saw the hand of God and the devil in any and all things.

Even now, while the cursed Normans ravaged their lives—her life as well!—she remained an outsider. Her heart cried out at such injustice. She was *not* the devil's daughter. Why could they not see that she was no different than they, save for these bloody dreams. Nay, 'twas little wonder that she had grown to hate these cursed dreams . . .

Now more than ever.

Though the day was cloudy and dreary, no rain had yet to fall. But the earth was damp and wet, and so the sound of their footsteps was masked. Though her progress through the forest was slowed by Aubrey's presence at her side, her efforts were fruitful. By noontide she carried two skinned hares in a pouch over her shoulder.

Aubrey was tiring. He leaned heavily on his staff of ash. And she could hear it in the way his breathing had hastened to a rattle in his chest. Though at first he stubbornly refused, Alana insisted they rest. She stopped near a huge stump of fallen oak and urged him to seat himself. She settled down next to him, letting her bow and quiver of arrows slide to the mossy ground. From the pocket in her skirts she fished out the hunk of bread. Together they shared it.

When she had finished, she brushed the stray bread crumbs from her bliaud. "Aubrey," she spoke his name quietly. "Do you think I should go to Brynwald Keep?"

Aubrey twisted his head around to stare at her. "The keep! For what purpose?"

Folding her hands in her lap, she did not look at him as she spoke. "There has been much bloodshed these past days. I would know that Sybil is alive and unharmed."

Aubrey's tone betrayed his alarm. "Alana, 'tis not safe! The Normans are butchers, all of them. And who knows what harm would befall you were you to enter that den of thieves? Surely if Sybil were dead, there would have been some word."

Alana shook her head and slowly raised her gaze to his. "But what if she is sick? Alive but hurt? Aubrey, despite all, she is my sister."

Aubrey scoffed openly. "Do you think she spares a thought for you? I think not!"

But Alana was staunchly determined. "You cannot know that. Nor can I."

Aubry shook his head. "Would she come to your aid if she thought you injured? Nay! Indeed, she *has* not."

"Aubrey, I cannot speak for her. I know only what is in my heart. And we are bound by blood—"

"The very blood that has kept you apart these many years!"

For a moment Alana said nothing, for alas, what could she say? Aubrey was right. She and Sybil did not know each other well, for Sybil's mother Rowena had done all she could to prevent such a thing. Rowena had made no secret of the fact that she did not want her daughter tainted by her husband's by-blow.

"Your father would have been well put to leave your mother be." Aubrey slammed his staff upon the ground. "He loved your mother but refused to marry the daughter of a peasant. Instead he chose another that she might bring him lands aplenty and coin to his purse. Yet even then he would not free her. Many was the time I thought he should give her the chance to leave, to marry another."

"She would never have left," Alana said softly. "She loved him." A wistful sadness flitted across Alana's features. "They could not be together. Yet they could not be apart."

"He was selfish, thinking only of his pleasures. That is why he clung to your mother." Aubrey grimaced. "But married to one such as that hag Rowena, who could blame him?"

Alana's breath caught. She laid a hand on his sleeve. "Aubrey," she said, her voice very low. "You speak of the dead."

He snorted. "I speak the truth!"

Alana swallowed a pang of guilt. Faith, but such thoughts had burned in her mind countless times before. She was sorry that Rowena had died, yet if she were honest with herself, she could feel no sorrow. But Sybil had lost both mother *and* father in the same day. Closing her eyes, Alana bowed her head low and prayed for all of them. Her father. Sybil. Rowena. For herself and her sins. For while she had loved her father well and true . . . she had also hated him for what he'd done to her mother . . . and to her.

She rose, her footsteps making little sound as she walked to the middle of the clearing. "I do not know what to do," she whispered, hugging herself like a child, despising herself for feeling very much like one. "I-I am afraid for myself. Yet I am afraid for Sybil, and I could not forgive myself if she needed me and I did naught to help her."

Aubrey stroked the length of his beard. He sighed. "You are much like your mother, Alana. You look for the good in others, no matter what . . . ah, if only they would do the same for you! But I would urge you not to act too hastily. The Normans—'tis said they are born of hell. And the one who has taken Brynwald for his own . . . They say his name is Merrick. They say he is spawn of the devil— a warrior 'twould as soon sever a man's head from his body as look at him. Indeed, methinks he is every bit as despicable as the duke he serves!" Aubrey paused, stroking his beard. "We do not know what vileness they plot. And so we must be ever on our guard—"

But Aubrey was not allowed to finish. Harsh, grating laughter filled the air.

"Well spoken, old man. But I fear your warning comes too late."

Alana half-turned. Her blood seemed to freeze in her veins as, one by one, half a dozen mounted riders came to line the boundary of the clearing between herself and Aubrey. Her dream of only that morning came back to fill her mind . . . *Perchance my arrow shall take aim at bigger, hardier game—a Norman soldier, mayhap.* But such was not to be, for it seemed *they* were the ones who had been snared instead . . .

By Norman soldiers.

They stared at her with leering eyes, all six

of them mounted upon their great, dark horses. Hungry-looking as wolves, they were; she felt as if *she* were the meal they would feast upon.

Her gaze darted toward her bow and quiver of arrows, there upon the ground next to Aubrey. Both fury and despair raced through her; there was no hope of reaching it, for any one of them would be upon her in an instant.

"What, would you put an arrow in my heart, wench? Ah, but I would do the same to you— though not with my arrow." He grinned. "And not in your heart."

The one who had spoken dismounted. From beneath his helm, glittering black eyes raked over her, lingering on the gentle thrust of her breasts beneath the thin wool of her bliaud. Oh, but she wished she possessed a mantle— not to shelter her from winter's chill, though— nay, rather to hide her from this lout's prying gaze. Yet it was not fear, but anger that rushed to the fore as he leaped to the ground.

"I am Raoul," he announced in thickly accented English. "Who are you, girl? And why are you alone in the forest with naught but this old man to protect you?"

Alana lifted her chin and glared at him. By all the saints, she'd rot in hell before she would deign to answer this wretch from across the sea.

He persisted. "Who is he, eh? Your father, mayhap?"

Alana's lip curled. "'Tis none of your affair who he is. And 'tis none of your affair what I do in this forest."

"It is when the new lord of Brynwald has ordered that you Saxons remain in the village. You are from the village, aren't you?"

"Aye, but—"

"Then I would say it is very much our affair."

Aubrey had risen to his feet. His voice rang out strongly. "Leave the girl be, Norman."

The man called Raoul ignored Aubrey. Instead he crossed the clearing to stand before Alana. "A Saxon with spirit—I like that, girl, I like that."

So close, Alana saw that he was young, with dark, aristocratic features. But there was a glint in his eyes that sent a warning all through her. And the way he stared at her made her skin crawl.

He spread his hands and smiled. "I think he is not your father, girl. But never say he is your husband!"

There was a burst of laughter from his companions. "Then mayhap she's looking for more livelier sport in bed!"

Another gave a gritty laugh. "And little wonder, for no doubt his manhood is as withered as his skin!"

Alana nearly choked on her fury. "Stop it, all of you! He is neither my father nor my husband. But he is a man I love dearly, so leave him be, you Norman pigs!"

"Alana! Say no more, their words will not hurt me!"

Raoul's eyes came back to rest on Alana. "Ah. Does he protect her? Or does she protect him?" He reached out and caught a handful of golden hair in his fist. Wrapping it around his hand, he gave a tug. When Alana resisted, his expression turned savage.

"Come here, bitch!" He gave a vicious jerk. Alana could not withhold the startled yelp of pain that broke from her lips.

Aubrey's face turned a mottled red. "Leave her be, you bastards!" He started forward. But he hadn't gone more than a step before one of the mounted Normans smote him full on the back of the head with a blow from the flat side of his sword. Aubrey pitched forward without a sound.

"Aubrey! Oh, Aubrey!" Alarm rent her breast.

She tried to twist away, but her captor had seized her by the waist. Alana went wild then. Twisting. Scratching. Kicking. She clawed at his face and felt her nails rip into his cheek. He gave a vile curse and grabbed for her hair. Somehow Alana managed to wrench free. Desperate to reach Aubrey, she gave flight across the clearing. Behind her, gritty laughter rang out.

"What say you, men? Shall we each have a turn at her?"

"Think she could take two of us at once?"

Shock ran through her like wildfire. For the first time it struck her what they truly intended. They would use her. Rape her violently. Over and over again, mayhap . . .

She fell on her knees beside Aubrey's prone form. When she touched his shoulder he gave a low moan. Praise the saints, he was alive!

"Aubrey! Aubrey, oh please, you must rise. We must flee before it is too late."

The man called Raoul had reached her. "Come here, wench," he said sharply.

Alana leaped up and spun around. She flung out her arm and smacked him full upon the face. The back of her hand stung but she cared not, nor did she care for the rage that contorted his features.

"Leave us alone, you Norman bastard!"

He swore. "By God, wench, you will be silent or I will silence you!"

He drew back his hand to strike her. Alana saw that his fist was closed and braced herself for the impact. But the blow she expected did not fall.

It was odd, really. It was then that she realized yet another knight had entered their midst.

God in heaven. Her mind screamed her terror, even as a strangled sound climbed high in her throat. For it was him . . .

The man from her dream.

Chapter 2

There was among the Normans a man named Merrick. In the prime of youth and vitality, he was tall and well-muscled, as strong as the mightiest oak. Like most Normans, he had been bred to be a soldier, trained in the arts of war since he was a boy. And Merrick learned his lessons well—to wield sword and lance among the best in the land—to ride and hunt and fight. Although he was the son of the Count of d'Aville, he would never inherit, for he was the youngest; indeed, he had five elder brothers and two sisters.

And so, for what lands would come to him, he must fight. What rewards might come his way, he must earn. Proud and indomitable, he was a man who would make his own destiny. 'Twas for that very reason he took up arms with Duke William, who promised vast estates in return for victory; Merrick was determined to carve out his domain in this land across the Channel . . . in England.

And it was to the north, along the sea, that

William sent his fiercest knight; there Merrick battled long and hard against the lord of Brynwald—battled and won.

Now Brynwald was Merrick's . . . and so it would remain.

Merrick was also wise enough to recognize that although the English had laid down their arms, they had yet to subdue their enmity. Mayhap it was their Saxon pride—or mayhap it was merely stupidity. No matter the reason, Merrick was well aware it would be a long time yet before they would surrender their loyalty.

Indeed, the scene before him now but supplied proof of the same. He'd heard the shouts, the shrillness of a scream, and knew well what he might find. So it was that Merrick was not surprised at the sight of his soldiers surrounding a Saxon wench. They were men, not milkmaids, and lusty ones, at that. That they had trapped the wench troubled him not, for such was the way of war. Nay, he would not have deprived them of their sport.

But that was before he'd seen her.

Merrick was a man who knew well the charms of a comely maid, and this one was certainly that. She wore no wimple; her hair was glorious, the color of shimmering pale gold; it fell down her back clear past her hips in a braid as thick as his wrist. Despite the strips of hide that bound her feet and the shabby clothing she wore, he knew she was lovely beyond measure, for her profile promised only sweetness and youth. Yet when their eyes met, her gaze locked on his as if he were the devil himself. Indeed, he could have sworn she was terrified of him . . .

He nudged his mount forward. He did not stop until he was but a few paces distant. "What is amiss here?"

It was Raoul who answered. "We found this girl and the old man here, where they do not belong." He would have reached for her elbow, but she rounded on him fiercely.

She stamped one ragged foot. "What would you have us do?" she cried. "Aubrey and I were hungry, as are all of the villagers!" She pointed to the bag with the dead game. "We left the village only to hunt, and there you will find the two hares for our evening meal."

Raoul's lip curled. "The old man does not look as if he could hold a bow, much less shoot an arrow straight and true."

She tossed her head and said coldly. " 'Twas I who shot the hares. And if I'd had my bow in my hand when you came upon us, I vow you'd be as dead as those hares."

Raoul's expression tightened. Before he could say a word, Merrick laughed. "The wench does not seem to favor you, Raoul." While Raoul's dark features grew flushed, Merrick glanced at the old man. "Is he dead?"

This time it was another burly knight who spoke. "Nay, milord. The blow was meant only to silence him."

"That is good." Merrick gave an approving nod. "I would avoid needless bloodshed whenever possible."

He transferred his gaze to the girl.

"You are from the village?"

She made no answer, but her delicate chin notched higher. She stared at him with burning eyes.

A dark brow arched high. Her defiance, silent or no, rankled. "Since you do not deny it, then I can only assume that you are. Just as I must also assume you were fully aware of my order that the villagers were to keep to the village."

At last she deigned to speak. "Why?" Her voice rang out as clear as a summer morn. "Why should we? Are we prisoners then?"

Merrick's jaw clenched. Clearly he had been mistaken, for it was not terror that glazed her eyes. It was hatred, pure and unwavering. "Nay, you are not prisoners. But for now, 'tis best that you keep close to the village. 'Tis the best way—the only way—to preserve the peace."

"Peace?" Mockery lay deep and biting in her tone. "My lord, how can there be peace when you allow no freedom?"

His eyes narrowed. He spoke easily, his tone belying the sizzle of anger that seared his veins. "You know nothing of me, Saxon, save the country of my birth. Yet if you could, you would do me grievous harm, would you not?"

Her tone held the fervency of a prayer. "If I could, by God, so I would!"

He merely regarded her in silent speculation, his steel-gloved hands crossed loosely before him on the saddle. "Would you, now," he mused. "For what reason, might I ask?"

"I need no reason other than that you are a Norman swine!"

"A swine?" His lips twisted into a tortured smile. "Then why do you stare at me as if I were some apparition from Hell?"

"Perhaps 'tis because you are!"

"A Norman swine. An apparition from Hell. Which is it, girl?"

She surveyed him in ill-disguised hostility. "My lord, I think you are a swine from Hell . . . and much, much more."

Merrick's smile withered. His eyes narrowed. He studied her dispassionately. "Who are you?" he asked abruptly.

She straightened her shoulders, her spine so stiff it appeared it might splinter in two. "I will tell you nothing, Norman. Not my name, nor anything else. Not until I know yours!"

Up close, she was even more exquisite, Merrick decided in the back of his mind. Young, yes, yet not so very young . . . But sweet?

He smiled tightly. "I hide nothing from you, Saxon. I am Merrick. The keep on the bluff is now mine. The land on which you stand is now mine."

Hidden fire seemed to alight inside her then. The soft line of her lip curled in disdain. "So you are Merrick. Lord of the manor. Lord of the Norman pigs. Well, I tell you this, Merrick of Normandy. You are naught but what you are, a swine who belongs in the pen with the rest of the sows!"

For an instant Merrick could scarcely believe his ears. Such audacity—and from a peasant yet!—was not to be endured. Sheer fury hardened within him. By God, she was either a fool, or very, very brave . . .

In truth, Alana was neither. She was frightened half-out of her wits. What madness possessed her that she would dare taunt this knight who haunted her dreams?

He sat his mount with arrogant pride, a powerful figure garbed wholly in black. A mantle of wool swept across his shoulders, emphasizing their width. Unlike his Norman brethren, his hair was not tonsured; it swept heavy and dark along his head, like the sky at blackest midnight. But unlike the English, most of whom wore beards, he was clean-shaven, the line of his jaw square and ruthless. His skin was bronzed from wind and sun, like worn leather.

A low murmur went up among his men. With but a look, he commanded silence. And as the silence ripened, so did Alana's unease. She watched as he dismounted, clearly taking his time, making her wait for she knew not what, the beast! And all the while, not once did he take his eyes from hers. They were like pale blue frost, those eyes. He approached with silent footsteps, possessed of a surefooted grace.

Alana fought against the urge to run screaming into the forest, for he seemed bigger than ever. It was not her imagination that proclaimed his shoulders broad as a sword was long. And he was taller than any man she'd ever seen, taller even than Radburn, one of her father's most valued men-at-arms.

He stopped before her, so close her feet were planted squarely between his. He touched her nowhere, yet he was so close she could feel the rise and fall of his massive chest with every breath he drew.

She didn't move, though instinct clamored she do just that. Deep within her breast, she knew that her father had not shown weakness in battle despite this fierce opponent. Nor, she decided with perhaps more valiance than prudence, would she.

Though she was inwardly quaking, boldly she met his regard.

"Thrice now, you have called me a swine." Softly though he spoke, there was no disguising the edge in his tone—nor the threat he now posed. "By God, woman, I have killed many a man for much less. And you *will* call me lord, Saxon. This I promise. By God, this I vow."

A reckless daring arose to the fore.

"I will call you what you are, a Norman dog!" she cried. "You speak of peace. Yet you Normans know nothing of peace, only of war and killing! You are thieves, all of you. Thieves of land. Of lives. And I will not obey you, Norman. Nor will I obey your law. I spit upon you, all of you!"

Only when the deed was done did Alana realize she had gone too far. Only then, as he slowly wiped the spittle from his cheek, did it strike her how incredibly rash she had been . . .

He seized her with such startling quickness that she cried out. Belatedly she recognized the violence in his features—oh, but she had spoken unwisely once again! He needed no weapon to slay her; he had only to wrap his fingers about her throat and squeeze the breath from her body. It struck her then . . . his hold was not brutal, yet there was no mercy in it either.

"I did wonder," he said softly, "if you were truly so brave. Or merely foolish." He paused. "It seems I have my answer."

Sheer panic wedged in Alana's breast. She pounded against his chest. "Let me go!"

"Not yet, Saxon. 'Twas you who started this game we play"—a hard smile creased his lips—"but I will see it ended, this I promise you."

Slowly he released her. "Mayhap I should cut out your tongue, Saxon." His gaze swept over her with brazen insolence, lingering on the thrust of her breasts beneath her bliaud, and then the secret feminine place where her thighs met. 'Twas as if he saw all that lay hidden beneath her clothing.

He smiled, a smile she knew instinctively did not bode well for her. "Or perhaps," he said softly, "there is another way to silence that lovely mouth of yours."

Raucous laughter ensued. His men warmed to their lord and his intentions.

"A juicy morsel, she is!"

"Give her a taste of a Norman blade, milord!" jeered one.

"Put her on her knees, where she belongs!" added another.

"Ah, and just think where her mouth would be then!"

The men roared.

Alana's face burned painfully. Though they spoke in French, her father had taught her well. Even if she had not understood, their leering grins bespoke far more than she was wont to know.

And all the while, Merrick of Normandy's gaze had yet to leave hers. "Leave us," he said to his men. "Take the old man back to the village, then return to the keep."

Alana watched anxiously as two men dragged Aubrey to his feet. Relief washed through as she saw that he appeared unhurt, though he was clearly groggy and dazed. After all the soldiers had dispersed, she pressed her lips together to keep them from trembling. She remained where she was, frightened and uncertain, her arms wound around her body, as if she might defend herself thusly. But there was no escaping his gaze.

And she had the awful sensation there was no escaping *him*.

She swallowed her terror. "Why did you tell them to leave?" Her voice was but a breath.

He smiled—a demon's smile, to be sure! "Perhaps I will finish what my men would surely have begun, were it not for my timely arrival."

Alana's mind flew like the wind across the
seas. The men in the village had said no woman was safe from the ravening Normans. That
very first day, at the edge of the pasture, she
had seen a burly Norman rising from between
the bloodied thighs of Hawise, the dairyman's
eldest daughter.

She shuddered. "Nay," she said faintly. "You
cannot mean to—"

"'Tis just the two of us, Saxon. You could
not fight me."

Mayhap he was right. Mayhap she *should*
not fight him. Yet she knew she would.

She hesitated but an instant, then tried to
dart past him. He caught her easily. Steel-
gloved hands around her waist, he swung her
around.

She tried to pummel his chest. Everything
within her rebelled against him. "Nay! You
will not touch me!"

Her blows fell like twigs against his shoulders. He tumbled her backward to the mossy
ground. Husky laughter rushed past her cheek.
"Saxon, I touch you now."

And alas, it was true. Alana was shocked
to feel the weight of his body full and heavy
upon hers. His chest crushed the softness of
her breasts. The battle-forged hardness of
muscled thighs lay hard and taut against
her own. From breast to belly to the tips
of her toes, there was nowhere they did not
touch.

His hands like iron manacles, he forced her
arms back so that they lay on either side of her

head. "We are the conquerors, Saxon. Surrender to me, your Norman lord."

"Nay!" she cried. "I will not surrender. *We* will not surrender! We will fight until you are driven back to your Norman shores."

The grip on her wrists tightened ever so slightly. "And who would be the victor in our battle here and now? Norman or Saxon?"

Alana gritted her teeth and sought to buck him off. He was immovable, like a stone above her. She screamed her rage. "You may have beaten us now, Norman, but we will rise against you and then *we* will be the conquerors."

He laughed. The bastard, he laughed!

Alana went wild then, seeking to kick him, to free her hands that she might shove him away. But her struggles were in vain. He had only to press his chest against hers until she lay gasping and still.

"I ask again. Who is the victor now, girl? Norman or Saxon?"

Perilously near tears, she denied him yet again with a wordless shake of her head. A glimmer of anger flashed across his face. Above all else, she was aware of the power of his body, the strength of his will. She closed her eyes, fearful of the form his retaliation might take.

But he said not a word. He made not a move. Alana opened her eyes to find him watching her, an odd expression on his face. She went utterly still as he released her hands, only to strip the gloves from his own.

A roughened fingertip scaled the length of her throat, then skimmed the parted fullness of her lip—as lightly as a feather. Then it dipped low and down the arch of her neck till it rested there at the neckline of her bliaud. She was stunned that he would touch her so, for she was half-afraid he might tear the clothes from her body and take her then and there as the soldier had ravished Hawise.

Yet this was more a caress. Her mind began to churn so that she could scarcely think. So close to him, he was more frightening than ever. His jaw was square and rugged, his mouth harshly carved below the jutting blade of his nose. His eyes were startlingly light against the darkness of his skin, a pale translucent blue. But there was no cold in those eyes, not now. There was only a glittering heat that made her go hot inside, then icy cold.

Her heart leaped, apace with her pulse. His gaze had fallen to her mouth; she could feel the moist heat of his breath upon her cheek. Surely he would not kiss her, she thought in panic. *Nay, surely not . . .*

"You are the victor," she cried. "You, Norman, not I!"

A terrified sound escaped her. Certain he would ravage her mouth with his, she twisted her face away.

He rolled away and got to his feet. "You offend me," he said with a twist of his lips. "You would admit defeat rather than suffer a mere kiss?"

Alana scrambled to her feet. Her chin came up at his mockery. "A kiss from a Norman" —she made no effort to hide the bite in her tone—"indeed, a Norman swi—"

The fierceness in his expression stopped her dead. "Do not say it," he growled, "for I vow this time you'll live to regret it."

She did already, Alana thought shakily. He stared at her challengingly, as if he expected some scathing retort. When such was not forthcoming, he turned away.

Alana surveyed him warily. Her hand slid inside the fullness of her sleeve, where her dagger was strapped to her arm. She had not forgotten it, but there had been no time to use it. It would have been futile to try against Raoul, with so many others present to thwart her. A shiver wracked her as she thought of her dream—it seemed impossible that the dark knight was here before her now! Ah, but Merrick was no demon in disguise. No specter of the shadows. He was but a man, flesh and bone and blood . . .

She slipped the blade from its berth. Clutching the finely honed handle in her palm, she hid it behind her in her skirts. Her mind raced; her mouth grew dry. Could she do this? Mother of Christ, she truly had no desire to kill this man. But if she could wound him, she might be able to flee.

She waited until he bent to retrieve his gloves from the ground. His back to her; it spun through her mind there would be no better time.

But Merrick spied the glint of steel from the corner of his eye. With the reflexes of a warrior, he whirled just as she raised her hand, poised to strike.

He caught her by the hand. His fingers closed about her wrist with merciless intent. She fought him more fiercely than ever; they tumbled to the ground once more. For the second time in as many minutes, he lay heavily atop her form.

His grip was unrelenting. He squeezed until her grasp began to loosen, then he snatched the dagger from her palm. Her regard was scorching, her outrage forged as deeply as his own.

He'd meant to teach her a lesson here, and by God, so he would. She would not be free of him so quickly—or so easily. If she would not yield her anger, so be it, but she would yield to him nonetheless.

"Curse you," she burst out. "Curse you to Hell, Norman!"

A dark anger swept over Merrick. His anger burst into flames. In fury and frustration he stabbed the blade into the earth beside her head.

By God, the wench had just sealed her fate.

Chapter 3

"**O**n your feet, Saxon."

His eyes were as cold as the seas. His tone brooked no denial. Alana gingerly obeyed. Her knees were quaking so unbearably she feared she could not stand. The leashed violence she sensed in him frightened her beyond measure. What was it Aubrey had said? *They say he is a warrior 'twould as soon sever a man's head from his body as look at him.* Alana shivered. Gauging his mood this very moment, she could well believe it.

He bent low to retrieve the dagger, this time taking care not to turn his back on her. He weighed it in his palm, running his thumb over the bejeweled hilt. He slipped it into his belt, then leveled on her a gaze of blistering intensity.

"You talk about the thieving Normans. But perhaps 'tis you who are the thief. Who did you steal this blade from, Saxon?"

Alana maintained her silence. 'Twould do no good to tell him. He would only brand her a liar.

His jaw clenched. "Were I you, Saxon, I would test my temper no further. Now tell me—whose is this dagger?"

Alana knotted her hands together to still their trembling. Summoning her courage, she lifted her chin. "'Tis mine," she stated coolly. "'Twas given me by my father."

"Your father!" He gave a shout of laughter. "Lady, you would take me for a fool of the highest order. The dagger could only belong to a man or woman of some wealth."

"Aye," she agreed heatedly. "My father!"

"Kindly enlighten me, then. Who is your father?"

Alana clamped her lips together.

He swore beneath his breath. "The truth, Saxon, and I would have it now!"

"Surely you would know him, Norman." Her tone was scathing. "The lord of Brynwald died beneath your sword."

"What! Do you mean to say your father was Kerwain?"

"Aye!"

"Your father died in battle, aye. But he did not die beneath my sword." His eyes scraped over her. "And I have seen Kerwain's daughter for myself. She did not wear tattered hides to bind her feet, but boots of the softest leather. Her bliaud was not little more than rags, but cloth of the finest weave."

Alana straightened her spine, painfully aware of her wretched appearance. "I am no thief," she said feelingly. "You asked for truth. I gave you truth. 'Tis none of my concern if you refuse to recognize it!" Somehow she mustered what little pride and dignity she'd managed to retain. "And now, Norman, will you grant me leave to return to the village?"

"Nay, Saxon, I will not."

Alana had already half-turned. Startled, her gaze flew back to his.

"You heard me well and true. You may not return to the village."

Alana fixed wide eyes upon his face. He was well pleased with himself; she could see it in his half-smile.

"Nay," he went on. "Instead you will come with me."

Alana's mouth was dry as parchment. Her lips scarcely moved. "Where?" she whispered.

"Why, to Brynwald."

"Brynwald!" She could not hide her shock. "For what purpose?"

He smiled then, a thoroughly dangerous smile. Alana's hand went to her throat. A staggering horror shot through her. He meant to punish her for her insolence, she thought vaguely. She knew it as surely as night followed day.

"Perhaps you will scrub floors. Help the servants in the kitchen. Tend the animals in their pens. Why, you might even serve my knights"— his wicked smile widened still further— "in their nightly pursuits."

Tears of fury glazed her eyes. "Nay! I-I will not be your slave!"

"There is no disgrace in servitude."

"There is disgrace in serving you!"

His jaw clenched hard. "Indeed," he said coldly. "How so?"

"You are a Norman!"

"Aye, I am a Norman. A Norman who is now your lord and conqueror. Accept it, or live to regret it."

Bitterly she cried out her despair. "Have I no choice in this?"

His tone was arrogant through and through. "A choice? Of a certainty, wench. *My* choice."

So he said . . . and so it was.

As Alana soon discovered, he was not a man to trifle with. He commanded that she walk before him. He followed close behind, high upon his warhorse, a black steed who pranced and pawed the air, as devilish looking as his master. They had nearly breached the edge of the forest when the notion took root . . . Nearby was a place where the trees grew low and thick in number, so thick that man or woman might dart between them, but such a feat with horse and rider was impossible. Hope flowered within her breast. If she could flee . . .

She soon wished she had not.

He caught her with consummate ease, snatching her high onto the saddle before him. Alana fought a surge of panic, for she had never learned to ride. And though she strained to hold herself stiffly that they might not touch, he would not allow it. His arm hard about her waist, he dragged her back against him, so close she could feel his every breath as if it were her own.

It was near vespertide when they arrived at Brynwald Keep. Passing through the wooden palisade, he did not stop until they were well within the walls of the keep. The moment he brought his warhorse to a halt, Alana managed to slide to the ground. She fell heavily, scraping her hands and bruising her knees, but she cared not. All she wanted was to be free of his hated touch.

Despair rode heavy on her heart. Only this morn she had told Aubrey she wished to come to Brynwald, that she might assure herself Sybil was safe and well. But not like this, never like this . . .

She shivered, though not from the chill of the air. She couldn't help but recall her dream. She prayed it was a vision that would not come to pass, that it was not a vision of the future—*her* future . . .

Yet she had fallen into the hands of the very man she feared above all others . . . and all through her own folly.

With a start she realized Merrick had dismounted. She felt his eyes upon her like the prick of a knife. He tossed his reins into the hand of a thin youth. The lad possessed the same dark hair and winged brows—his son, mayhap? The question had no more than hurtled through her brain than strong fingers grasped her elbow.

"This way, Saxon."

He led her across the muddy yard. Horses and Norman soldiers milled about, though she glimpsed several faces she recognized

—the stablemaster and the laundress, and a few others as well. None deigned to look her way. With hunched shoulders and downcast eyes, the atmosphere was subdued and severe. There was none of the good natured jostling that would have been present but a sennight past. What laughter there was came from the Normans.

Glancing to the side, she saw several knights openly leering. One elbowed another; he whispered something and the knight let out a gust of laughter. Alana's cheeks burned. She dared not look at Merrick. No doubt they thought she had lain with him.

He nudged her up the steps that led into the hall. There a blazing fire burned in the hearth at the far end. Still more knights gathered at the trestled table that dominated the length of the hall, and against the benches lining the walls.

It was then she spied Sybil. She was just about to head through the doorway that led to the kitchens, housed in a separate building from the great hall. Alana gave nary a thought or care to the man at her side, but darted across the floor.

"Sybil!" she cried. "Sybil!"

Sybil spun around. Disbelief flitted across her features.

"Alana! Whatever—"

"Oh, Sybil!" Alana embraced her fiercely. "I was so worried about you! I did not know if you were alive or dead!"

Sybil opened her mouth but before she

could say more, a shadow fell over them. Alana knew, even before she turned, who had stepped behind her. Her spine rigid, she turned to face him.

He ignored her and addressed himself to Sybil. "You are acquainted with this wench?"

Sybil dropped her eyes. "Yea, milord. This is Alana."

His gaze now rested on Alana. "So her name is Alana." A half-smile curled his mouth. "Well, my lady, my knights caught her hunting in the forest though the villagers had been ordered to keep to their huts. She would surely have slain me had I not divested her of her dagger in the nick of time. Then she told me an outrageous tale—that it was given her by Kerwain, that she is his daughter."

Though Alana longed to lash out that it was true, she pressed her lips together. Let Sybil tell him. Mayhap then he would believe her.

Sybil bit her lip. For the longest time she said nothing. Her uncertainty made Alana glance at her sharply, for this was so very unlike her. And indeed, it struck her that for once Sybil was not so very haughty. Her ivory cheeks were smudged with dirt, her wimple slightly askew. Spots of grease darkened the front of her bliaud. Wisps of hair emerged from her braid. Never had Alana seen her so untidy.

"Milord," she said at last, "'tis no tale. She is my half-sister, the elder by two months."

Merrick's brow darkened. "The elder by two months! How can this be?"

"Kerwain sired both of us. But my mother was Rowena, who died in the fray. Alana's mother was Edwyna, a peasant from the village. Alana was not raised here in the keep as I was."

Once again Alana felt the probe of those icy blue eyes. She met his gaze cleanly, making no effort to hide her smoldering disdain.

A dark brow rose high. "So you are not legitimate issue."

Now it seemed Sybil was only too anxious to speak. "Nay, milord. She is not."

He held her gaze a moment longer. Alana held her breath, for though his eyes did not free her, his expression betrayed no hint of his thoughts. At last he gave a curt nod. "Go with your sister and see that you make yourself useful," he ordered. "I will decide your fate later."

It was in Alana's mind to disobey flagrantly, to deny him to the fullest. Oh, but he was an arrogant beast! And though 'twas not in her nature to be so surly, she could not help it. They seemed to strike sparks off one another. But she sensed she had tested his patience to the limit, and might not be so lucky again. She spun around, though not without a last, challenging glare.

In the kitchens, preparations for the evening meal were underway. Sybil handed her a knife, and they began chopping cabbages and onions. Smoke from the fire pits hung thick in the air. Alana peered through the haze at her sister.

"They say he has made slaves out of all

those who survived," she said, her voice very low.

Sybil sighed. "'Tis true," she admitted. "He captured those who would have fled. We were given a choice—serve him or be imprisoned."

"And what of you?"

Sybil's golden brown eyes fell. "I was given the same choice," she said quietly.

Alana cried her outrage. "But you are the lord's daughter!"

Sybil shook her head. "He is lord now and I have little choice but to obey," she said sadly. "None of us do. The Normans will not be ousted. 'Tis said that Duke William has taken all of England for his own and proclaimed himself king."

Sybil was far more accepting of her fate than Alana had expected. Alana peered at her suspiciously. "He has beaten you, hasn't he? Oh, the wretch! Sybil, I will—"

"Nay, Alana, he has not. Indeed, he has told me that when his sister Genevieve arrives from Normandy, I will no longer toil in the kitchens as I do now. I will then serve as her maid."

Alana sniffed disdainfully. 'Twas impossible not to notice Sybil's chafed, reddened hands. Sybil was not used to hard work, as she was. A lady's maid would surely have an easier time of it.

"Why must you wait? Why can you not serve his wife?"

Sleek, dark hair fell forward, shielding the small, secret smile that crept across Sybil's lips. "He has no wife."

"But . . . I saw a lad who must surely be his son, for he had the same winged brows—"

"His nephew Simon. He fosters as Merrick's squire. Merrick's sister Genevieve is the boy's mother."

After that, they both turned back to their work. But though her hands were busy, an aching heaviness tugged at Alana's heart. And yet, some small measure of comfort filled her heart. Her father had now joined her mother to live with the angels above; mayhap they were together in heaven as they could not be on this earth. And though she mourned her father's death, at least Sybil was alive.

And while there was life, there was hope.

The next hours passed in a blur. The Normans took their supper and the sisters served them. Alana made countless trips from the kitchens to the hall bearing great platters of food and ale. Her arms and shoulders ached from the weight; Sybil looked just as drained.

The Normans were a thoroughly unruly lot. She tried to dodge the greedy, grasping fingers that tugged at her skirts and bosom yet was not always successful. She longed to slap their hands away, yet she did not dare for fear of finding herself clubbed to the floor. She had watched in horror as one poor girl spilled a tray of sweetmeats at the feet of a burly soldier and suffered that very fate. Alana gritted her teeth and sought to ignore them.

The night grew old and torches burned low. She was on her way to fetch more ale when her elbow was firmly seized. She found herself spun around nearly full circle. With a gasp she recognized the knight she had first encountered in the forest—Raoul.

Gleaming black eyes roamed her face and body, brash and bold. His regard made her skin crawl. "Tell me, my lovely one. Did Merrick please you?"

She strained to free herself. "Let me be!"

He caught her narrow waist and tugged her close. "'Tis whispered by all the Norman maids that he's endowed like an ox—and with the stamina of one, too! 'Tis why they swoon at his feet. Ah, but I would have pleased you far better, had you let me."

Alana could not help it. Her gaze veered straight to Merrick, who sat at the high table. He was staring straight at them, the slant of his mouth grim and unsmiling. Glancing back over his shoulder to see where her gaze resided, Raoul scowled. When he realized their exchange had not gone unobserved, he freed her, but not before he pinched her arm. "We shall see, eh?"

With a sigh of relief, Alana scurried away. As the night marched forward, she cast more than several anxious glances toward Merrick, but he paid her no heed. As for the Normans, their appetite for food was exceeded only by their greed for drink. Yet little by little the roar of voices and boisterous laughter that filled the air began to thin. At length, many of the Normans stumbled away. Others lay slumped at the table or sprawled on the benches that lined the walls. Drunken snores filled the air.

Alana paused, slowly lowering a pitcher of ale to the table. It struck her then . . .

She had not seen Merrick for some time now. There was no one to see. No one who would know should they choose to leave . . .

Sybil came up to her, smothering a yawn. "We need not stay any longer. I've been given a pallet in the servants' quarters belowstairs," she said with a grimace. "You may take the one next to me."

"You are right," Alana whispered in an odd voice. "We need not stay any longer."

Sybil glanced at her sharply.

She seized her sister's hands. "Sybil, there is no one to see if we should choose to flee this keep! No doubt the sentries are as sotted as the rest of these men." Excitement gathered ripe and full in the pit of her belly. "We can escape from the Normans—from Merrick! There is no better time than now!"

Sybil's gaze swept the hall. "Merrick is not here," Alana said with a shake of her head. "No doubt he's gone to seek his bed."

But Sybil was uncertain. "Alana," she began. "I am not certain that—"

"Sybil, think! Do you want to remain a slave forever?"

A brief spasm of pain flickered over Sybil's face. "Nay, but . . . Oh, mayhap you are right."

"I am, Sybil. But we cannot delay any longer."

"But—where would we go?"

"It does not matter! Perhaps to York. Oh, don't you see? I would free you of this

Norman's yoke—I would free *us*. Now hurry. By the time they awaken, we must be long gone."

Hope flared in Sybil's dark eyes. She nodded. "They took most of my belongings," she said quickly, "but I managed to hide several trinkets in my pallet. If we can spare but a moment, I will fetch them. We may need to barter them later."

Together they hurried down the narrow, winding stairway. Most of the servants were long since abed. Sybil weaved her way to the back of the damp, dank room toward her pallet. While she hunted for her treasures, Alana waited in the passageway outside.

Soon she appeared. "I am ready," she announced breathlessly.

Alana tugged her forward. "You lead the way," she whispered. "You know the keep better than I."

The hall was dark and shadowed; the last embers of the fire burned low. Those within slept the sleep of the dead. Still, Alana cast a worried eye over her shoulder. Luck was with them, for no one followed. Her heart pounded. Her breathing hastened. The wide arched doorway to the yard was but a few paces distant. They were almost there . . .

All at once Sybil stopped short. Alana caught herself from barreling into her in the nick of time. She made a sound of dismay. "Sybil, do not stop! We must hurry—"

"I think not, Saxon. Nay, I think the two of

you will go nowhere this night—or any other night, for that matter."

Alana froze. The beat of her heart grew silent and still. Bitterly she bit back a cry of frustration. God in heaven, it was him—Merrick!

He filled the doorway, his booted feet braced wide. Bareheaded though he was, the top of his head nearly touched the timbers. Alana's mouth went dry as parchment. His eyes were steely blue and glittering; it was as if the very fires of Hades leaped within their depths.

"I am curious, ladies. Whose plan was this?"

Sybil was only too willing to give up her sister. "'Twas her idea, milord. I would never have done so were it not for her!"

"She is right," Alana said quickly. "Do not blame her."

His lips tightened to a thin line. He spoke but one word to Sybil. "Go."

Sybil fled as if the hounds of Hell snapped at her heels. Though Alana longed to fly along with her, she remained where she was, secretly quaking inside. She had tried to escape him, and no doubt Merrick would not take such a thing lightly.

"So. You brew trouble already. Tell me, did you truly think to flee?"

The mildness of his tone did not hide his anger. Alana's chin climbed high. By God, she would show no fear, not before him, nor any other Norman.

"Yes!"

"You could flee to the ends of the earth, and I would find you, Saxon."

"And what then, Norman?"

His eyes darkened. "And then," he stated grimly, "you would wish that I had not."

A chill ran through her. Alana did not doubt it. His tone, like his expression, was utterly unyielding.

In that instant, she hated him as she had never hated anyone, for his arrogance knew no bounds. "I tell you now, Norman, I will not grovel and beg for mercy, for I know you would have none!"

"Mercy?" His tone was cutting. "Lady, you live. Your sister lives. There are many among your people who live. Only those who raised their blades against us died. And I tell you, Saxon, that your fate—and your sister's—could be far worse. You might find yourself beneath a master far more cruel than I."

When Alana made no reply, he smiled tightly. "Your eyes smolder, Saxon. If you could slay me with them, I do believe I would even now lie cold in my grave. 'Tis a good thing you no longer have your dagger."

A surge of recklessness shot through her. "Then know this, Norman. You *stole* my dagger but I am also well skilled with bow and arrow."

He merely inclined his dark head. "A warning," he acknowledged coolly. "Well, here is one for you, Saxon. I will tolerate no further attempts to escape me. Should that occur, I promise—nay, I *vow* you will regret it."

Alana bristled. *Damn* his Norman hide! If he meant to kill her, why did he prolong her torment?

"Damn you," she said fervently. "Why couldn't you have stayed in Normandy? If not for you, my father might still be alive!"

His jaw clamped tight. "I understand that you mourn him, Saxon, yet many of my people died as well. All is not as it was before, and it will never be so again. 'Tis just as I told you this morn. We are the conquerors and you the conquered. That is the way of the world, and the ways of men. You must accept us or risk more bloodshed."

"Accept you? Never!" she cried. "So if you would kill me, then do it now!"

He laughed as if she'd said something vastly amusing. "I think not, Saxon, for we are not finished, you and I. And I can think of many more pleasurable things to do to you than kill you."

He moved then, walking in a slow circle around and around her, until at last he stood before her. They were so close—*too* close. Her heart leaped wildly as he stood there unmoving. And all the while his eyes took brazen liberties no other man had dared. It was as if he stripped her utterly bare . . .

A horrified inevitability filled her mind. She knew then, she knew what he intended . . . When next he touched her, it would not be with just the stroke of his eyes. Nay, 'twould be with the power of his hands.

Her own had grown icy cold. Hiding them in her skirts, she swallowed a sick feeling. Somehow she managed to force words past the stranglehold in her throat. "Please," she whispered. "What do you want of me?"

He smiled as if he knew her every thought, her every fear. "I think you already know, Saxon."

Her fingers clutched her skirts. "Nay," she said faintly. "You cannot—"

That devil's smile widened ever so slightly. "But I can," he said softly, "for I have claimed Brynwald Keep. I claim all that Kerwain once held. And now . . . now I will claim you, Saxon."

Chapter 4

He was angry, and fiercely so. Alana sensed it with all she possessed. And though he hid it well, she knew that he despised her. What was it Raoul had said? His grating voice echoed in her mind. *Endowed like an ox—and with the stamina of one . . .*

Waves of alarm shot through her. Icy fingers of dread crawled up her spine. To lie with this fierce, angry Norman . . . He would not be gentle. She could still feel the imprint of his body hard and heavy upon hers. Images of Hawise, bleeding and broken, flashed through her mind. How could she stand it . . .

Yet how could she stop him?

To run would be futile. Her first two attempts had taught her so. Yet what choice did she have?

She spun around and bolted. But he was quick, so agile he caught her easily, his arm hard and strong as he whirled her around.

Alana's cry was a blistering curse. "Leave me be, you cursed Norman!" Her fists flashed out toward his chest, but she struck not a single blow. Instead she felt herself tossed upon one broad shoulder like a sack of grain. He strode forward, taking the winding stairway abovestairs two at a time. Alana's head whirled; his shoulder drove the very breath from her lungs with every step. She was giddy and light-headed when at last she was lowered to her feet once more. Blindly she flung out a hand to steady herself. Not until her fingers closed around masculine, hair-roughened forearms did she realize she had reached for him—her tormentor yet! She snatched her hands back as if she'd been burned.

His laughter stung. Straightening her spine, she glared at him, then deliberately turned her face aside. A huge bed strewn with furs dominated the opposite wall. A dull shield and wicked looking sword lay propped in the corner. The chamber was utterly masculine . . . utterly his. With a sinking flutter she realized he had brought her to his bedchamber.

A roaring fire had been lit in the hearth. Struggling hard to maintain her composure, Alana instinctively moved closer to its warmth.

She whirled when she heard a bolt slam down across the wide oaken door. A jolt went through her as she saw that Merrick had turned back to her. He surveyed her with hands braced against his hips, his posture so arrogantly masterful that she felt a sizzle of anger all through her.

Through some miracle she managed to raise

her chin bravely. "Have you not had your fill
of unwilling Saxon maids, Norman?"

His slow-growing smile was maddening.
"Did you know me better, you would know
I've no need to take by force what can be won
with honeyed words and lips—and indeed,
with far more pleasure."

Alana's lip curled. "Ah, yes. Raoul told me
how all the Norman maids swoon at your
feet. But if indeed I should do so, know this,
Norman—'twill be in disgust."

His smile remained, but his eyes had gone
utterly cold. Still, when he spoke, his tone was
almost pleasant. "Lady, were I you, I would
consider what course you pursue. For indeed,
I might well be tempted to show you how very
wrong you are. Indeed, it might prove quite a
challenge to show you what untruth you dare
speak."

He was right. She didn't realize that to
taunt him was to tempt him. Nervously she
moistened her mouth with the tip of her
tongue. Wisely, Alana said nothing. Warily
she watched as he crossed to a small square
table across from the hearth. A flask of wine
had been placed there, and he poured a generous measure into a chalice. He picked it up
and drank deeply. As he lowered it, he wiped
his mouth with the back of his hand, staring
across at her all the while.

In truth, Alana was thoroughly unnerved.
Her father had been a kind, soft-spoken man;
he was firm when the occasion demanded it,
but never cruel. And though the men in the

village were sometimes coarse and irrever-
ent, they were farmers, not soldiers. But
Merrick . . . he was a warrior through and
through. She sensed a hardness in him—a
ruthlessness that was somehow frightening.

Slowly he approached her. Alana stiffened
as he came near. He did not stop until they
stood but a breath apart. A faint alarm seized
her then, for she was struck anew by his size.
He was so tall her head scarcely reached his
shoulder. The level of her gaze rested squarely
in the center of his chest. He made her feel
small and feeble—and helpless in a way she
liked not at all.

"I would make certain I understand, Saxon.
If you were to find yourself locked fast in my
embrace, you would feel only disgust?"

Her chin came up. He stood so close she was
forced to tilt her head to meet his gaze. "Aye!"
she said heatedly.

He raised a brow. "Let us be honest, Saxon. I
am not so very ill-favored. Indeed, I am scarcely a leper. Why, there are many who find me
quite appealing."

Alana gasped. Oh, but she had never encountered a man so boastful! She spoke unthinking-
ly—and quite recklessly. "You say you are no
leper. Well, I say you are no prize either!"

The makings of a smile dallied about that
hard mouth. "Ah," he said lightly, "but I suspect you may well be a treasure indeed. So
come now. 'Twas but a kiss I craved earlier.
'Tis but a kiss I ask now."

"Ask?" she cried in outrage. "'Tis not in

your nature to ask, nor even to demand. You Normans take what you would have. And 'tis not a kiss you seek but far more! Well, know this, Norman. I will not have you. Do you hear, I-I will not have you!"

Their gazes tangled furiously. His lips hardened into a grim line. His eyes blazed blue fire. Yet to Alana's surprise, he said nothing. She gave a silent sigh of relief when he retreated back to the table. There he reached again for his chalice, then turned back to her. His words were not what she expected.

"The war is over," he said easily. "William will bring peace to the land. I suggest we put aside our enmity as well." He raised the chalice high in a mock salute. "To Normans. To Saxons. To a union of the two ... indeed, a coupling methinks should begin this night."

Alana gaped. Oh, but he was cruel to taunt her so, and when she thought his mood had eased ... She could not help it. Her eyes skipped to the door.

He smiled—oh, a demon's smile, in every way!

Alana swallowed, her mouth as dry as parchment. She could feel the heat of the fire, warm upon her back. Yet in all her days, she could not think when she had been so utterly cold inside, as if her veins were rivers of ice.

Then all at once he was there before her. She jerked as strong hands descended upon her shoulders. Alana stood like a captive doe, waiting for she knew not what.

His cold whisper touched her cheek. "I am

a man of patience, Saxon, but you test mine sorely."

His smile had vanished. His jaw might have been hewn of oak; his expression was hard and unyielding. She made a curt, jerky movement, as if to wrench herself away.

His hands slid swiftly down to clamp around her hips. "Be still," he hissed.

Alana's heart leaped to her throat, for the air was suddenly seething. He held her fast, yet though she was bound tight within his embrace, there was naught of hurt in the way he held her. Yet she hated the way his eyes raked boldly over her, as if he stripped her naked . . . With naught but the touch of his eyes he leisurely sampled what his hands would soon claim.

His touch seemed to burn her flesh, both inside and out. Those devil hands swept up the incline of her ribs . . . and lingered. Her breath came in sharply, for his thumbs hovered there, at the swelling peaks of her breasts. Did he touch her nipples—or was it but her imagination? Hot shame roiled within her.

She made a choked sound low in her throat, a plea of desperation. "Do not do this," she whispered. "Please do not."

If anything, his expression grew ever more hard. The arms tight around her back were suddenly like iron manacles. He spoke through lips that barely moved. "You will not run from me again, Saxon."

His gaze was starkly commanding. Shaken beyond anything she had ever experienced before, Alana found herself incapable of speech, of even moving. But alas, he mistook her silence for rebellion.

He gave her a little shake. "Are you afraid of me, Saxon?"

"Nay!" she cried.

The word emerged quickly enough. But her eyes gave the lie to her claim. They were huge, wide and dark, endless pools of deep green. Merrick felt his anger recede, only to be replaced by something else, something far different . . .

It was impossible to touch her like this and feel nothing. He found it no hardship at all to see beyond her ragged clothing to her beauty. Her lips were parted, as softly pink and moist as an English rose. Desire pierced his middle like the shaft of an arrow. All that was hotly primitive and male surged high within him. He was acutely aware of the feel of her in his arms. She was so slight his fingertips nearly touched at the base of her spine. So small. Almost defenseless . . .

Grimly he reminded himself that for all she was poor and ragged, the wench was scarcely humble. Nay, she was far too proud for her own good.

Oh, he knew he would not take her, not now. But it gave him a measure of satisfaction that *she* did not know that. He smiled as he saw the fear leap high in her eyes. Though she sought to mask it swiftly, her efforts were in vain.

Ever so slightly, his grip on her waist tightened. "You say you will not have me. Well, I say this, Saxon. If I so chose, you would even now lie beneath me. You know that, don't you?"

She did not dally this time. "Aye," she said jerkily.

He released her. "As it were, I am weary and would seek my bed for the night. Were I you, I should do the same." With that, he picked up a pile of furs from the bed and tossed them at her.

Alana caught them instinctively, still uncertain what he expected of her. He paid her no heed, but proceeded to tug his tunic over his head—it fell to a careless heap at his feet. She stared numbly as she caught sight of his chest, wide and covered with dense, dark curls. Now his hands were busy unlacing the leather thongs that cross-gartered his chausses. She bit back a gasp. Sweet Jesu, surely he would not strip naked! But it appeared he would not stop . . .

Nor did he.

Her jaw had gone utterly slack. His waist was incredibly narrow, his arms were corded and lean. As he bent and peeled hose and drawers from his legs, his back was one long arc of sleek bronzed flesh. It flitted through her mind that his body was one of both power and grace. He straightened then, affording her a glimpse of brazen male virility.

Her heart seemed to stop. He turned and crawled into the bed. Her breath tumbled out in a rush.

He rose up on an elbow. "You're welcome to take your place beside me in this bed. I'm feeling generous tonight, and so I will leave the choice to you, Saxon."

Only then did Alana realize she still stood mutely, the pile of furs clutched in her arms . . . A tide of heat and color crept into her cheeks; she was thoroughly embarrassed that she'd been caught staring so openly.

But at his words, she spun around and dropped to the floor, her heart apounding. There before the hearth she curled herself into a ball and dragged a fur over her head. From across the chamber came a burst of low, masculine laughter.

Then all was quiet.

Alana trembled and shivered, though the chamber was warm and not at all chill. Desperately she sought to calm the throbbing tempo of her heart. She was still aghast at the obvious—that Merrick had chosen to let her be. Oh, but she had been so convinced he had brought her to his chamber to make quick work of her ravishment!

Instead he had granted her a reprieve. Why, she did not know. Nor, she decided shakily, did she care to know or even guess, for she was not yet ready to discount his threat to do the very same! What was it Aubrey had said of him? *They say he is spawn of the devil—a warrior 'twould as soon sever a man's head from his body as look at him.*

It was not in Alana's nature to trust easily—and Merrick her enemy yet! She warned herself to be cautious. Aye, he had not yet revealed the demon he surely was. But she did not trust him. She *dare* not trust him.

So it was that his presence across the room lent her no ease, and such thoughts would not cease. They twisted and turned throughout her mind like an aimless path. And though she thought to sleep not a wink, soon her body relaxed. And sleep she did, quite deeply . . . and dreamlessly.

A watery sunshine seeped through the shutters when Alana awoke the next morning. She lay there a moment, assailed by an odd sense of the unfamiliar. Then all else fled beneath the keen onslaught of memory. With a gasp she lurched to her knees, still clutching a fur to her breast.

Her haste was for naught, for she found herself quite alone. Arising rather stiffly, she rubbed the ache in her back, casting a disgruntled glance at the bed as she did so. Of course the lofty wretch had claimed the comforts of a soft mattress for his own, even as he had claimed Brynwald for his own. Yet perhaps she could count herself lucky—a cold stone floor was far preferable to sharing a bed with that Norman beast!

She smoothed her clothes, then attended her personal needs. After washing from a small basin, she shook her hair free, then combed through it with her fingers. She did not braid it again, but tugged it over her shoulder and left it free. She paused, uncertain what Merrick expected of her. She was heartily glad he was not present, and in truth had no desire to seek him out. She had no desire to anger him if her presence was demanded elsewhere; nor did she want him to think she cowered here in his chamber. Her mind so inclined, she was about to venture without when the portal opened.

Merrick stood outlined in the doorway, a tall and powerful frame garbed in dark wool. Alana instinctively stepped back as he stepped within.

He wasted no time looking her up and down. "Ah, you are awake and just in time, too." His tone was as hearty as his smile—and just as false. "Why, I began to think you intended to laze abed throughout the day."

Alana was just about to let loose a scathing retort when he stepped aside. A tall, lanky youth followed him in, the one she had seen yesterday who resembled Merrick so strikingly—his nephew, Simon. Folding her hands before her, she watched as the lad crossed the floor to place a tray of food atop the table. Though she smiled faintly at him as he passed, he paid her no heed.

When the boy had gone, Merrick gestured to the tray. "I thought you might be hungry, Saxon."

Alana hesitated. There was a generous hunk of bread on the tray, the aroma of which made her mouth water. In addition, there was a small wedge of cheese. Sharp pangs of hunger knotted her belly, reminding her that she'd had very little to eat in the last day. Sybil had passed her a hunk of mutton last eve, but she'd been so nervous she could eat but a small portion, and instead had fed it to the mongrels who roamed the hall.

But she eyed Merrick warily, for she could think of no earthly reason why he should think of her needs . . . or perhaps she had found the reason after all.

"You are right, Norman. I *am* hungry. But I cannot help but wonder what I must give in return for this meal."

His eyes flickered, as if she had caught him off guard. But then he smiled, that dangerous smile she was coming to know far too well. "Mayhap a better question would be this, Saxon . . . what *would* you give?"

His gaze fell to her breasts. Alana resisted the urge to cover her breasts with her hands, for she knew the thinness of her bliaud hid little of her shape. Her face flamed even as her spine stiffened.

He laughed. "A pity, Saxon, for I see the prospect distresses you."

"Distress?" Her chin tipped high while her blow struck low. "Make no mistake, Norman. 'Tis disgust and naught else!"

His smile withered. For just an instant, his expression tightened in displeasure. Yet when he spoke his tone was oh-so-pleasant. "I can see the night has only sharpened your tongue. Mayhap your mood would be far more agreeable were you to break your fast."

Her gaze had shifted to the tray. She was not

aware that he noted very keenly the longing in her eyes she could not quite hide.

He gently grasped her elbow and pulled her forward. Tearing off a hunk of bread and slicing a wedge of cheese with his dagger, he set it on a small wooden trencher and placed it directly before her. "Eat," he said gruffly. "I am not such a brute as you think that I would seize you while you avail yourself of the sustenance you need so sorely."

Alana flushed. Though always slender, she had never been quite so thin as she was now. She sat on the chair he pushed over for her. Placing her fingertips on the edge of the trencher, she cast a tentative glance at him from beneath her lashes.

"There is more than enough for both of us," she murmured. "I would share it—"

He shook his head. "There is no need. Eat your fill and think no more of it."

His tone was brusque, yet not so very unkind. Still, she was vastly relieved when he turned his back on her and moved to replenish the fire. Chewing on a doughy crust of bread, she watched him as he retreated across the chamber. Light flooded in as he threw the shutters wide. He remained there, his back to her, and eventually she forgot him entirely as she assuaged her hunger.

He approached just as she finished. Flustered to find him so near, Alana scooted the trencher back onto the tray and arose. To her surprise, Merrick extended a hand for it.

"I will take it back to the kitchens," she

said quickly. "No doubt they have need of me—"

But once again he shook his head. "You may help serve the evening meal. For now, you may do as you please." His features turned stern. "But do not leave the keep," he warned, "for I promise you—"

Whatever feelings of softness she might have felt for him were destroyed in that instant. "Never tell me," she said bitterly. "I will regret it, will I not?"

His smile was brittle. At the door he gave her a slight bow. "It pleases me that we understand each other so well, Saxon."

Alana clamped her jaw shut. She slapped the table with her palm as soon as he was gone. Her mood was no longer tame. "It pleases him," she echoed furiously. Oh, but he was an arrogant, selfish bastard—just like the master he served!

It was some time before the spate of temper eased. She paced the length of the chamber and back, time and again. The soft line of her mouth was mutinous when at length she came to a halt before the window. There she looked out upon the courtyard.

Gradually she became aware of all that went on below her. In a keep as large as Brynwald there would always be a need for rushlights, and in the center of the yard a handful of women were so engrossed. Some peeled rushes, which were then passed on to others to be soaked in fat before being bound into place. Near the stables several horses were being led back into their stalls.

But all at once there was a flurry of activity. Near the gate a handful of Norman soldiers rushed forward, shouting and pointing. From the look of them, they clearly thought the intruder a menace. Alana caught sight of a drab brown tunic, then shaggy gray hair and stooped shoulders. A strangled cry broke from her lips.

For the man now surrounded by angry Norman soldiers was none other than Aubrey.

Chapter 5

S econds later she was outside in the yard, intent on weaving and darting her way through the crowd that had begun to gather. A cluster of soldiers had started toward Aubrey.

Her head was bare, as were her feet. Her hair flew out behind her like a banner of sunlit gold. Stones and twigs cut into the soles of her feet. She paid no heed but forged on like a knight at full tilt.

"Hold, old man!" shouted one of the Normans.

She could hear Aubrey, his voice vibrating with rage. "You will not stop me, man, nor will your army. I will see the girl Alana, brought here by your fiendish lord Merrick!"

With that he took his staff and swiped at the ankles of the nearest soldier. The man's legs buckled beneath him.

Alana's heart jumped in horror, for the soldier was back on his feet in a thrice—and this time with sword in hand. "Nay!" she screamed at the top of her lungs. "Leave him be! Leave him be, I tell you!"

Her chest was heaving when at last she reached the outer ranks of the circle that had gathered. She darted a swift glance at Aubrey. Praise God, he appeared unharmed, save for a bruise on his temple.

"Who are you, girl?" asked one burly soldier.

"I am the one he seeks," she said breathlessly. "I am Alana."

"He swore to kill us all," the man continued stubbornly. "We will not tolerate such threats from a Saxon. He must be punished.

Sheer fury flamed in her eyes. "Do not dare! If any of you lay a hand on him, I vow I'll see that you burn in Hell!"

A low murmur went up. Several of the Saxons present crossed themselves, a gesture that did not go unnoticed by the Normans.

Nor was it unnoticed by Alana. In a flash it came to her. This time—aye, this time—her curse might well mean salvation for Aubrey.

Slowly she raised her chin. Her gaze swept the crowd. "If you do not believe me, just ask those here." She pointed to a raw-boned laundress. "Ask her. And him." She pointed to the pantler's assistant.

The laundress wasted no time nodding her agreement. "'Tis true," the woman said in a rush. "Cursed she was, though she be the daughter of our lord. And from the time she was a wee one yet!"

"Aye," chimed yet another. "A witch, she is. Everyone knows it."

The Norman soldiers were nervous. A number of them had even fallen back several steps. Gathering herself in hand, Alana prayed that God would forgive her her deception.

"You see?" she went on with a boldness she was far from feeling. "Now I suggest you let the old man go. Else I will turn you all into goats, the lot of you!"

A low murmur went up. The Normans glanced at each other uneasily. There was not a man among them who would dare challenge her further.

"Aye," she went on brashly. "Mayhap I will do it anyway—and your Norman lord along with the rest of you!"

"Indeed," came a grim voice from behind her. "That might prove quite interesting, Saxon."

It was Merrick. Alana's heart plummeted. She had the awful sensation Merrick would not be so easily daunted as his men.

And alas, she was right. He gestured to the nearest soldier. "Take the old man to the hall and await my order."

Alana's blood seemed to freeze in her veins. Somehow that had an ominous ring to it. Then even that thought was wrenched from her mind, for all at once his hand was on her elbow, like a clamp of iron. Though she struggled and twisted, he was determined—and far stronger than she. He dragged her toward the hall and up the stairs, all the way into his chamber. He thrust her inside and slammed the door shut.

Alana stood frozen there in the center of the room. His arms were folded across his chest.

His posture was no less than threatening. The vice-like hold of his eyes entrapped her, as surely as chains. She was afraid to move, just as afraid not to.

She had displeased him yet again. There could be no doubt, for his expression was dark as a thundercloud.

"Trouble follows you like a storm from the sea, Saxon." His voice was as cutting as his eyes. "I begin to wish I had left you in the forest."

He spun around and would have strode away. "Wait!" she cried. "What will you do with Aubrey?"

He turned. His face was a mask of stone.

Her hands twisted nervously in her skirts. "You will not harm him, will you? He has done nothing."

His eyes narrowed. "I am not beholden to you, Saxon. Nor do I see the need to answer to you."

Panic leaped in her breast, for his expression was so very forbidding. Alana did not move. With her eyes she mutely pleaded. "Please, I must know. Truly, he meant no harm."

He said nothing.

A hot ache burned her throat. "You asked this morn what I would give. I had no answer then. But if you let Aubrey go free, I-I will offer myself to your mercy."

Still he did not speak. Alana moistened her lips. "Did you not hear me, Norman? Do what you will with me—whatever you will."

"Mercy? And what if I have none?"

"Then I am doomed," she whispered. There was a stark, wrenching pain in her heart. Mayhap she was already . . .

And alas, he scorned her. With words. With scorching blue fire in his eyes. "So soon you forget," he mocked. "You cannot bargain, Saxon, for you have nothing to bargain *with*. I will do whatever I wish, *when*ever I wish. You are already at my mercy—and so you will remain. And do not fool yourself into thinking I will let this pass. Make no mistake, Saxon, I will deal with you later."

With that he was gone. Alana stood motionless but an instant. She ran to the door and tried to open it. A cry of sheer fury broke from her throat. She collapsed on the floor in a flood of angry tears. The lout had locked her in!

It was much later when she heard the sound of the bolt being slid from its berth. Alana glanced up from where she'd been sitting at the table, her forehead braced upon her arms. The door creaked open slowly. The lad Simon stood there, a tray in his hands, but he did not enter.

He extended the tray. "After you've eaten, my lady, my lord wishes your presence in the hall, to help serve the evening meal," he informed her, his tone coolly formal.

My lady. At any other time, Alana might have giggled. But as it was, a melancholy weariness dragged upon her heart. She summoned a faint smile and arose. "Thank you, Simon." She took the tray from him, thinking that the boy would indeed grow to be a fine, handsome young man, as handsome as his uncle . . . The thought brought her up short. Merrick . . . handsome? Sweet heaven, but her mind turned in the strangest ways!

She scarcely tasted the meal he'd brought, yet she forced herself to eat. She did not dally, but made her way down the stairs and into the smoky kitchens. She had scarcely entered when Sybil spotted her. Her sister wasted no time presenting herself in front of Alana.

She heaved her arms on her hips and fixed her with a glare. "There you are!" she snapped. "Do you know the whole of the keep knows what you did today? No doubt they will soon call me the devil's daughter as well, and all because you are my half-sister! But 'tis well known 'twas your mother who gave you the devil's curse."

Devil's daughter . . . the devil's curse. Alana's even temper began to fray. "Say what you will about me, Sybil," she said with flashing eyes. "As for my mother, you know as well as I she possessed the kindest soul in the village. So say no more about her."

Sybil sniffed indignantly. "Or what? What will you do, Alana? Turn me into a goat as well?"

Sister, you need no help on that score, Alana decided crossly, then was immediately ashamed of her pettiness. 'Twas not at all like her to be spiteful. But just as she would have sought to ease the mood wrought by the exchange, Sybil snatched up a tray and spun around.

A needle of hurt sliced deep. Oh, Alana told herself she shouldn't allow her sister's deliberate cruelty to bother her so. Countless times she had seen Rowena treat her mother with the very same callousness. And so it was that she was not surprised when Sybil pointedly ignored her throughout the evening.

Again Alana made innumerable trips between the kitchens and the hall, bearing great platters of food and pitchers of ale. The crowd was only slightly less boisterous than the previous eve. More than once she found herself the object of whispers and guarded glances. At least now, no one dared pinch her breasts and grasp at her buttocks as they had done last eve.

But then there was Merrick. Sybil served him, thank the Lord. Yet time and again, she felt his piercing regard. His gaze drilled into her back like the points of a hundred tiny daggers. His promise rang in her ears. *Make no mistake, Saxon, I will deal with you later.* The very thought made her belly tighten in dread. She'd heard tales of the Normans and their vicious nature. Indeed, she'd seen it firsthand in the village.

At the very least, he would have her thrashed. Or perhaps he would do it himself. He might even cut out her tongue . . . She dared not think of what form his punishment might take.

But whatever it was, she was certain he wouldn't allow her to go unscathed, as he had last night.

It was very late when a scraggly line of Saxons entered the hall. Alana's heart went out to them, for she sensed their weariness both in body and spirit. But there was one in particular . . . His clothing was tattered and blood-spattered. Chains fettered his feet and hands. Awareness sharpened her vision.

The man was Radburn, stoutest and bravest of her father's men-at-arms. Of noble upbringing, his father was an earl in the south of England.

Relief flooded her, for it had saddened her greatly to think that he, too, had been killed by the Normans. A poignant memory sent her spinning back in time, for she had grown to womanhood with girlish dreams of a husband and babies . . . Aye, dreams of this very man had filled her mind—and her heart.

He was so tall. So strong. So brave. Deep within her, Alana had known how very foolish were such fanciful notions. Yet still she had worshiped Radburn from afar. He was ever kind and ever considerate in those brief moments when they chanced to meet. And once—*once*—she had caught him looking at her with something different in his eyes. Something wonderful. But it was not until she had seen him with a rich widow from York that reality struck a killing blow.

And Alana knew . . . It did not matter that her father was Kerwain of Brynwald. A man such as he would have naught to do with a bastard—a baseborn peasant.

Soon the Normans began to empty the hall. Quickly Alana's gaze swept around. Radburn was there, slumped against the outer wall. Darting a hasty glance to either side, she sneaked a leg of mutton from one of the tables and hid it in the folds of her bliaud. Her pace hastened as she crossed the floor.

His head came up just as she reached him. Surprise lit his face. "Alana!"

Alana dropped to her knees and wordlessly handed him the haunch. She did not mind that he spared her no thanks. The way he bit greedily into the juicy flesh clearly bespoke his hunger. She kept her silence as he ate. When he'd finished, he tossed the bone to the hounds and wiped his fingers on his tunic.

She couldn't take her eyes from his face. One entire side was red and swollen, a mass of bruises and cuts. Her hand stretched toward him. "How—"

"'Tis nothing," he said with a dry smile that made him visibly wince. "A sennight and it will be gone."

Her lips pressed together indignantly. There were no words to vent her fury.

His chains clanged together as he touched her hand. "I saw your father fall," he said gently. There was a small pause. "Alana, I know not what to say except . . . he died bravely."

Sudden, startling tears glazed her vision. Radburn patted her hand awkwardly. "Alana—"

She dashed away the moisture from her cheek. "I'm all right. 'Tis just that I—oh, I hate that the Normans are here. I hate what they have done. Our lives will never be the same!"

"I know." He squeezed her fingers. "We must accept them, Alana, for we cannot beat them. But at least we are alive." His gaze caught hers. Alana sensed he would have said more, but all at once she realized they were not alone. Merrick had stepped close. He stood there, his hands behind his back, his features as drawn and tight as she had yet to see them.

His gaze flickered over her. "You should not be here, Saxon."

"Pray tell, why not? I do not shirk my duties," she snapped.

"Indeed," he said curtly. "Well, your duties for the night are not yet over. I require your presence at once in my chamber."

Hot color stained her cheeks. Alana was furious that he would shame her so, and in front of one of her own people yet!

The line of his jaw was tense—so very tense—but she did not care. "I will be along shortly—"

"Nay, Saxon. You will come with me now." He hauled her to her feet.

Alana's teeth came together so tightly her jaw hurt. "Stop!" she hissed.

"Nay, lady, I will *not* stop. And I warn you now—say no more, for I will not allow you to make a spectacle of yourself yet again." Already he had begun to propel her toward the stairway. There was no give in either his voice or his touch. His fingers dug unmercifully into her soft flesh. She tried to jerk free, but to no avail.

He marched her down the corridor. Undulating shadows from the rushlights mounted on the walls preceded their way. Once they were locked within his chamber, it was readily apparent his dark mood had not eased.

"I am curious, Saxon. The man in the hall . . . is he your lover?"

Alana gaped. Her *lover*! "Nay!" she gasped. "But even if he were, 'tis none of your affair!"

"I disagree, Saxon. It is most certainly my affair, for it's just as I told you earlier. I am your lord and conqueror and you are mine."

Alana still smarted with humiliation. "Why is he chained?" she demanded.

"He is a dangerous man."

"Dangerous?" She cried her outrage. "He's been beaten!"

"You are a woman," he growled. "You know little of the fire that heats a man's blood during battle. When he was taken prisoner he fought like a wild boar. My men did what was necessary to subdue him. Take heart, Saxon, for he is lucky to be alive. When we are certain he presents no further danger and is ready to accept me as his new lord, his chains will be removed."

"Aubrey presented no danger to your men. Yet no doubt they took great pleasure in beating him, too." To her horror, there was a betraying wobble in her voice. She despised the tears that threatened yet she could not help it. With an effort she blinked them back.

"Aubrey was sent back to his hut, Saxon. Alive *and* unharmed." Merrick was furious that she thought him so callous. Yet she was not the only one, for indeed, every Saxon he'd thus encountered was convinced he was a monster!

"You, Saxon," he went on, "are as much a warrior as any of your father's men. You would fight me, though you carry no sword or armor. Indeed, 'twould appear you never tire of battle. Only you do battle with your tongue. Tell me, is that why they call you witch?"

Oh, but she longed to screech at him for all she was worth. Instead she struggled for a calm she was far from feeling. "Aye," she stated daringly. "Mayhap you should be wary, Norman. Mayhap I will put a curse on *you*."

He smiled, his eyes locked upon hers. "It would seem you are many things, Saxon. A great huntress. A dreaded witch. At times you possess an air about you, such as a great lady of the keep. Well, you may have fooled my men with your foolish tales, wench. But you do not strike fear into my heart."

"And you do not strike fear into mine, Norman!"

His smile was maddening; it continued to dally about his lips. "No? Fear can be a powerful ally, Saxon. You've learned that, I think. You threatened to turn my men into goats. You used their fear against them. 'Twould seem to me we are far more alike than you are wont to believe."

As he spoke, he came close . . . ever closer.

Alana's heart began to pound. Her pulse began to flutter. He did not stop until her feet lay squarely between his own. She could not stifle the sensation of being trapped . . . trapped and wholly helpless.

She could not tear her gaze from his face. His jaw was hewn in stone. His eyes were pure ice, yet within was a fiery glitter. It struck her then . . . his mood was dangerous. *He* was dangerous. If he wanted, he could snap her in two like the brittlest twig.

Oh, but she regretted the taunts she had flung so carelessly! "You are still angry," she said jerkily. "Wh—what else could I do? Aubrey is an old man. He did not come to seek trouble. He came to see if I was alive and well. And I—I could not allow your soldiers to hurt a harmless old man."

For a moment Merrick said nothing. He wondered what she would say if she were aware he secretly admired her bravery. In his mind's eye he saw her, standing there in her bare feet, so proudly defiant. Yet he could not countenance her behavior, for he suspected she would but test him further.

His hands came up to cup her shoulders. She jumped at his touch, as if to tear herself away, but he held her fast. She was acutely aware of the power in his grip.

"I can feel you trembling, Saxon. You are defiant, yet you are not without fear. So tell me. Just what is it you expect me to do?"

"I know what you will do," she stated baldly. "You will punish me."

"Ah." A wickedly arched brow arose. "And how do you think I will punish you?"

She gave a tiny shake of her head. "You know," she whispered.

"I do not. What do you think I will do?"

"You will . . . take me." It came out in a frenzied rush.

"Take you?"

She closed her eyes and shuddered. "Aye," she said faintly. "You will—take me to your bed."

For the space of a heartbeat, Merrick stared. Were he not so insulted, he might have been vastly amused. The women he took to his bed found pleasure, not pain. But here was one who clearly thought his possession an act to be endured—and with the utmost horror, from the look of her. But when next her eyes opened, they were full of blistering hatred.

Nor, it seemed, would she come willingly.

He was suddenly filled with a black rage. She thought him such a beast; mayhap it was time he acted one.

He flicked a hand at the shoulder of her bliaud. "These clothes offend me, Saxon. Remove them."

The delicate line of her jaw fell open, then it closed with a snap. "I-I cannot! I will not!"

"And I say you will, lady." He was as grim as she was stubborn.

"And if I do not? Will you beat me the way your men beat Radburn?"

Merrick gritted his teeth. "By God, wench, you tempt me sorely. And you *will* do as I say. Because I ask it. Nay, because I command it."

"Nay—"

"You deny me the pleasure of your body—" Ruthlessly he squelched the denial that sprang to her lips. "Aye, you did. You do, and well you know. 'Please', you said. 'Please do not.' Well, you may withhold your body but you will not withhold the sight of it from me."

Her lips trembled. She had to force the words around the knot in her throat. "God will judge you, Norman."

"God? Ah, coming from you, that is rich. My men think you a witch, and you Saxons think me the devil himself. Quite a match, is it not? But for now, Saxon, your clothing—and be quick about it, lady."

There was that in his tone that demanded she heed him. Slowly, stiffly, she bent, pulling the garters from her knees, and then her hose. Her bliaud came next, and all too soon her threadbare chemise. Her hands were shaking as she threw aside that final barrier, until at last she stood naked before him. Naked . . . and ashamed.

There was no escaping the touch of those crystalline eyes. For timeless seconds he looked his fill, a scalding exploration that left no part of her untouched. In all her days, none but her mother had ever seen her so exposed. She closed her eyes, shamed beyond anything she had ever known.

He smiled.

"What would you say, Saxon, were I to ask that you do the same to me?"

Her eyes flew open. "What!" she gasped out. "Undress you?"

"Aye."

Some sound escaped her, she knew not what. The thought of stripping the clothes from his warrior's body, skimming her hands along his muscled flesh . . . Her stomach clenched oddly. She shivered, unaware that her hands came up to shield the softly rounded curves of her breasts.

"No? Another time, then." She was shocked to feel his knuckles against the fiery heat of her cheeks. "You will bend to me, Saxon," he said softly. "For now I would demand a kiss only."

"A kiss? You do not fool me," she cried softly. "You will do what you will—"

"Ah, but if I were to take you now, you would but martyr yourself. You would be the wounded one, and I the great despoiler."

"Is that not what you are?" It was her turn to quote him. " 'We are the conquerors, and you the conquered.' Those were your words, Norman. And I—I *hate* you for them."

He ignored this last. "And I am pleased you remember, sweet witch. But for now, I would claim the kiss we've yet to share."

There was no time to protest, no time to even *think*. Strong arms locked hard around her back. His mouth captured hers. She was caught full and tight against him, so close her legs were caught tight between the iron length of his. Struggle was impossible. Her breasts were crushed against the soft wool of his tunic. Her hands were fisted against his chest, trapped between their bodies. She did not fight him, for she knew she could not win.

Sheer panic kept her frozen in place, and then something else, something she had never expected. But one thought scattered through her brain as his lips claimed bold, blatant possession of hers.

She had thought the feel of his mouth upon hers would be abhorrent, as he was abhorrent. His lips were not cold and hard, as he was cold and hard. His kiss was not brutal and harsh, as he was brutal and harsh. Yet even as there was nothing soft about the man, there was something soft about his kiss.

Lean fingers plunged through the tumbled waves of her hair, tilting her face to his. His lips were like a scorching brand against hers. He commanded, aye, even as he demanded. He guided, even as he sought, his lips warm and firm, irresistibly compelling.

Alana could not help it. All at once she was caught up in the moment, caught up in *him*.

Warm breath filled her mouth—*his* breath. She should have been shocked; indeed, some small part of her was struck dumb by this, her first kiss. Yet indeed, she cared not, for there was a part of her that longed for it to go on and on. . .

Time was meaningless. She lost all sense of where she was, of who *he* was. Over and over again he kissed her, darkly passionate, impossibly sweet. She could feel the slight roughness of his cheek against her tender skin, yet it was not at all displeasing. His scent swirled all about her, woodsy and oddly pleasant.

A jolt tore through her as his tongue touched hers; she felt it like a dart of purest flame, and then he was exploring the honeyed interior of her mouth with a breath-stealing thoroughness that pushed all rational thought from her mind.

There was a strange pounding in her ears—the wayward beat of her heart, she realized vaguely. It was as if she were melting, her limbs like hot wax. Her head began to spin. She could do naught but cling to him weakly.

The pressure of his arms about her back loosened subtly. Slowly he lifted his mouth from hers. It took an instant before Alana was able to focus clearly. When she did, it was to find him staring down at her.

His gaze had dropped to her mouth, damp and moist from his kiss. With his thumb he traced the pouting fullness of her lower lip. "And do you detest me now, sweet witch?"

She turned her face aside. "Aye," she said quickly. But it was a feeble sound, a token denial, and they both knew it.

Her eyes slid away. She hated the triumph etched on his dark features. Her response to his kiss had pleased him, pleased him mightily, and she despised herself for her weakness. She shivered, crossing her arms over her breasts;

she had completely forgotten her nakedness until now.

His grip tightened on her shoulders, but only for an instant. So it was that she did not see the frown that lined his brow.

"You are cold, Saxon. 'Tis time to seek your bed."

Cold? Alana was suddenly awash in amazement. How could she be cold, when the heat of shame stained the whole of her body from the inside out?

She made as if to resume the previous night's berth near the hearth, but again his voice rapped out sharply. "Nay, Saxon, not there." She was bodily turned and shoved gently toward his bed.

Oh, but she longed to screech at him that she would not share his bed. Yet she did not dare, for she had no wish to provoke him further. Her pride was sorely stung already, and she knew it would not end here. Her movements quick and jerky, she pushed back the furs and slid within, her face the color of the dawn.

Merrick had just tugged his tunic over his head. Tossing his clothing aside, he gave an impatient oath and climbed in beside her, now as naked as she.

"What nonsense is this, Saxon? I would save you from another night on the cold stone floor. Yet you would act as though I wound your very soul, when in truth I but think of your pleasure."

Her fingers clutched the furs to her breast. "I

will find no pleasure in this bed," she choked out.

An odd smile crept across his lips. "Just as you found no pleasure in my kiss?"

In that instant she hated him, hated him with a scorching passion that blinded her to all caution. "I felt nothing," she stated heatedly. "Do you hear me, Norman? I felt nothing, for you *are* nothing!"

His arrogant smile did not waver. "Were I you, lady, I would be wary, for you tempt me. You tempt me sorely to prove that you lie, which I would do, I'm sure, with a great deal of pleasure—on my part *and* yours. And I do not think you want that, do you, Saxon?"

She glared at him. "God rot your soul," she said fervently. "If that is what you intend, I would rather you just . . . just take me and be done with it!"

"Would you now?" He gave a husky laugh. "In time, sweet witch. In time. Perhaps on the morrow, eh? Perhaps not. Oh, you need not worry," he added when her eyes flew wide, "for I will spare you this night. But hear me, Saxon, and hear me well, for it seems you are a stubborn wench indeed."

Alana shrank back as he leaned close, but there was no escaping him. He reached her easily, running a single fingertip across the fragile span of her collarbone. His expression had gone utterly unyielding, utterly intent.

"Aye, I will take you," he went on, and alas, the seduction was wiped clean from his voice. "You will not know when. You will not know where. But you will be mine—indeed you are already mine. Were I you, I'd not forget it."

It was both a warning—and a promise.

With that he rolled over and turned his back to her. Her mouth dry with an ashen dread, Alana stared at the width of his bare shoulders gleaming in the firelight. He spoke no more, and indeed, there was no need.

You will be mine, Saxon—indeed you are already mine.

She knew then, she knew what he intended . . . He did not spare her out of mercy or kindness. Only now did she begin to truly understand him.

He'd said he would possess her, and so he would. Alana did not doubt it. But he would make her wait. Wondering what the night might bring. Not knowing when . . . Oh, but he was cruel as the devil from whom 'twas said he was sprung!

Her fingers twined in the sheet. She stared blindly at the shadows flickering on the ceiling. Bitterness forged a burning ache in her breast.

Aye, he had come. He had conquered. The battles he fought were over.

But hers had just begun.

Chapter 6

For Alana it was the longest night of her life.

The taste of fear was like ashes in her mouth. At first she was convinced that Merrick was merely out to trick her by pretending to sleep. She was certain he would reach for her at any moment, that he would do as he promised and take her, willing or no. Even when she came to realize he did indeed sleep, she lay stiffly, afraid to move, certain that the slightest movement might wake him and stir his anger—even worse, his desire.

The moon had begun to fall and the night nearly spent before she finally slipped into a restless sleep.

It seemed she had just closed her eyes when she felt him leave the bed. She had lain huddled on her side the night through, as far from him as she could get. Now, though her eyes were closed, her every sense was quiveringly alert. She could hear him moving about the chamber, stirring the fire and coaxing it to life, the rustle of clothes and weapons.

Then all was silent.

"Saxon."

Alana froze. The voice was soft as swans-down . . . and came from directly above her.

He gave a low, husky laugh. Warm fingertips traced the slope of one bare shoulder. "You do not fool me, Saxon. I know you do not sleep."

Alana did not share his good humor. She screwed her eyes shut and directed a most fervent prayer heavenward that he would leave. But alas, God was otherwise engaged, for the next thing she knew, the mattress dipped low.

"Come to me, Saxon," came his whisper.

Alana flounced to her back, her eyes open now and glaring at him with blistering intent. "I will not—" she began furiously.

He bent low and smiled, that arrogant smile she was coming to despise. "Ah, but you will. Have you not learned that yet?"

With a cry she shoved at his chest. But alas, his arms slid around her and brought her close—so very close she could feel the rise and fall of his chest. What protest she would have made was never to be. With the pressure of his body full upon hers, he held her in place. Alana could not move; she could scarce-ly even breathe. Though that harshly carved mouth still curved in a smile, his eyes held an oddly hungry light. She had one burning glimpse of his features before his head came down.

But he did not plunder her mouth, as she thought he might. A strangled cry caught deep in her chest. His mouth brushed past the delicate curve of her jaw. Hot lips traveled down the arch of her throat and lingered there, where her pulse had begun to beat the driving rhythm of a drum.

He released her hands, yet she scarcely noticed. The furs were brushed aside, baring her to his gaze . . . and aye, his hands. She stiffened when the heel of his hand brushed the peak of one nipple. Once. Twice. Again. Her heart was pounding so that she feared it might burst clear from its berth within her chest. Her eyes flew wide when he proceeded to kiss the rounded swell of each breast.

And then his mouth was on hers again. Leisurely he tasted her, as if he possessed all the time in the world. Her breath came in jagged spurts when at last he raised his head.

He was no longer smiling. He bestowed on her a long, slow look, one that was far beyond her experience to decipher.

And so were his words. "You make it difficult to leave this bed, Saxon."

With that he climbed from the bed. Alana snatched the furs up over her nakedness and hurriedly averted her gaze as he strode unashamedly before her. He left the chamber soon after, but not before he'd wrung from her another kiss . . . and another unwilling response.

She shivered, for now that he had gone, the bed seemed absurdly cold though the fire he had stoked now roared in the hearth. Unbidden, her fingers crept up to her lips. The feel of him was still with her. The smell of him was still strong about her.

With a weary sigh she arose and dressed, determined to put all thoughts of Merrick of Normandy from her mind. Sybil was already in the kitchens when she arrived. There was a fresh catch of fish from the sea, and she quickly joined the task at hand. Beside her, Sybil was sullen and had little to say. Alana's heart bled for Sybil's plight, for she had not been born to a life of such work. Yet she knew of no way to change all that had happened . . . Mayhap Radburn had been right, she acknowledged tiredly. The Normans could not be beaten, and so they must accept them.

She did not see Merrick again until nightfall.

And alas, once they were alone in his chamber, the events that followed were but a repeat of the night before. Thinking he did not see, she slipped into bed, still clad in her chemise. Oh, but a foolish notion was that, for it seemed he saw everything! The line of his mouth tight with displeasure, he tugged the garment from her body and flung it aside. "Now you know better," was all he said.

Soon a sennight had passed. Yet when darkness crept over the earth, he made no move to claim her, to possess her as he'd promised he would.

Alana was not fooled. Aye, she knew what he was about. He would torture her, torment her with this wretched waiting and wondering! She had dared to challenge him, to defy him, and now he would tame her. He would teach her that he was master, that she was subject to his every whim and will.

He allowed her no privacy. He allowed her no shame.

For he touched her where he pleased. Whenever he pleased. Time and again his eyes dwelled upon her as she served the evening meal, dark and gleaming. Time and again his vow echoed through her brain, though she willed it not, though she wanted it not.

You will be mine, Saxon—indeed you are already mine.

Only last eve he had pulled her close, the furred darkness of his chest flush against her spine, a muscled thigh thrust between her own. They lay together like lovers, though lovers they were not; his arm was tight about her waist, his hand warm and familiar upon her belly.

Then, to her everlasting embarrassment, she awoke to find her nose buried in the bristly dark hairs on his chest. Even worse, to find him regarding her with lazy amusement.

He ran his finger down the tip of her nose. "Tonight, sweet witch," he had whispered. "Tonight."

An awful dread seized hold of her. In the cold light of the dawn, she realized . . . She could never accept the Normans—she could never accept *him*. Most certainly not in the way he intended! It came to her then, an idea sown in desperation.

She must flee, before it was too late.

She did not pray for an answer, for salvation. Indeed, her prayers had done little these past days. Nay, she dare not bow to a heavenly force. If she was to escape from Merrick, she could rely on no one but herself. And—oh! but God might strike her dead, she dared not trust in Sybil. She bit her lip, recalling that first night when she had thought to escape. Sybil had been only too eager to point an accusing finger. Sister or not, Alana sensed Sybil would go to any length to protect herself, no matter the cost to another.

It was a sobering thought. Yet Alana knew that Sybil was far from helpless. She was well able to fend for herself. And indeed, it was not Sybil he had threatened to bed.

The opportunity to flee came far sooner than Alana expected. That very day, in fact. She overheard one of the pantler's assistants say that Merrick had gone out on horseback this morn and was not expected back until nightfall—the mighty lord out surveying all he had wrested from another, she reflected scathingly.

But then her mind began to race. She could scarcely contain her excitement. For the first time a frail hope flared brightly in her chest.

Shortly after noontide, the servants took a short rest in order to eat. Alana did not seek an empty corner like the others; when no one was looking she slipped a loaf of wheaten bread and a large hunk of cheese into a linen cloth. Her hands weren't entirely steady as she tied the ends together, then grabbed a horn of ale. No one said a word as she slipped out a kitchen door.

Her head held high, she crossed the yard and marched toward the open pasture that led to the village, as if she had nothing to hide. The day was overcast, yet here and there a watery sunshine crept through the clouds. She shivered a little against the damp chill, for she had no mantle to warm her. But she continued on, for she would not allow a little discomfort to sway her from her course. And indeed, she was almost free . . .

"Hold there!" A Norman whose girth nearly exceeded his width blocked her way. He wasted no time looking her up and down. "I know who you are, lady. And my lord Merrick gave no instructions that I should let you leave."

"No doubt he didn't tell you *not* to let me leave either," she challenged boldly. Her breath tumbled to a standstill. She prayed she was right. But when the soldier said nothing, she tossed her head and held up her pouch, "The cook told me I was to take his meal to him near the village."

It appeared the guard was not ready to take her at her word. He took the pouch and poked through one of the folds with a grimy finger. Though he seemed satisfied with what he saw, he remained unconvinced.

"It seems odd my lord did not tell me." Beneath his noseguard, he peered down at her.

"That I do not know," Alana answered. "But I do know he will be most displeased that I am delayed. Aye, I'd say his wrath will be great indeed should he learn you kept me from my task. As will mine," she added pointedly.

She regarded him unblinkingly. The guard paled and thrust the pouch back into her hands. "Go then," he muttered. "And be quick about it."

Alana could have shouted her joy. Instead she hurried away as fast as she was able. It was indeed the village where she directed her steps. As she walked, she glanced from side to side, searching for any sign of horses and Norman soldiers.

She passed a few herdsmen along the rutted path to the village, but they paid her no heed. She planned to stop at her mother's cottage as well to gather up her mother's herbs and remedies; if nothing else, perhaps she might sell them for the coin they would bring. But first she must see to Aubrey.

Once in the village, she veered straight toward the old man's hut.

Aubrey sat near the fire, his gnarled hands stretched toward the flames. His head swung in startled surprise as she rushed through the doorway.

"Alana!"

She fell to her knees beside him. "Oh, praise God you are safe!" she cried. "We must leave, Aubrey. We must leave now before it is too late!"

"Leave?" Bleary eyes searched her face. "For where, child?"

She tugged at his arm. "It does not matter where. London perhaps, for I can stay at Brynwald no longer . . . nay, I *will* not! I must leave, and you must come with me!"

He shook his head. "Alana," he said gently, "I have spent my life here. Do what you must, but I cannot leave."

"Aubrey, you must!"

"Nay, Alana. I cannot."

"Aubrey, you do not understand! I must flee. I must flee *him*."

"Merrick of Normandy?"

"Aye!"

He stroked his wizened cheeks. "Why? He has not harmed you, has he?"

"Not in the way that you think." Oh, how could she explain? She could hardly confess what he would inevitably do, not to Aubrey! The shame was simply too much to bear. She wrung her hands, and added, "But he will be the death of me yet!"

Aubrey smiled slightly. "Death will be at my door far sooner than yours, Alana."

She shook her head wildly. Her breath came jerkily. "If I stay, something terrible will happen. I know it!"

The old man pursed his lips. "How? How can you know this?"

"Because I dreamed of him, that's why! I dreamed of him, and never have my dreams led me astray, Aubrey. You know this better than any other. I dreamed of death and darkness and blood." She was half-crying now. "And he was there, Aubrey, *he was there*!"

Aubrey sighed. "Alana, at first I, too, was convinced Merrick of Normandy was the monster all claimed him to be. But he has sent food from the keep for me daily. Only yesterday he delivered it into mine own hands. He asked if there was aught else that I needed. And when I asked after you, he said you possessed a most hearty dislike of all things Norman, most especially him. But he told me you were well." He laid a hand on her shining head. "And you are, child. I can see it. So calm yourself. There are storms to be weathered, but your fears are for naught. I know it, Alana. I *feel* it."

Alana stared at him, her stomach churning. Could it be his mind was no longer clear? Yet one thing was very clear—Aubrey would not listen.

And he would not be coming with her.

Her heart wrenched as she watched him struggle to rise. "I must rest," he murmured. "Come back when I am not so very weary."

Springing to her feet, she helped him to his pallet against the wall. Never had he seemed so—so very old! So frail and weak.

In that instant, her heart was surely breaking. How could she stay at Brynwald? Aubrey might believe Merrick of Normandy posed no threat to her, but she knew better. She'd heard the deed threatened from his own lips yet! And then there was her dream, that horrible dream . . .

The ache in her chest was nearly unbearable. She seized Aubrey's hand where it lay upon his sunken chest. Tears stood out in her eyes as she brought it to her lips. "You will be in my prayers with every breath I take," she whispered. "God keep you, Aubrey . . . God keep you."

*   *   *

Even as Alana ran south toward the village,
Merrick rode in to Brynwald from the north. He
tossed his reins to Simon, vastly irritated that
of late his attention was oft not on his duties,
but on the blond, beauteous Saxon wench
who even now laid claim to his thoughts.
Mayhap, he thought darkly, she was Satan's
handmaiden after all. For in truth, she was a
temptation no sane man could resist.

The servants in the kitchen flung their heads
up and stared wide-eyed as he entered their
midst moments later. He did not see Alana,
and all shook their heads when he asked
where she was. It was Sybil who finally
answered. She stood behind him just outside
the doorway.

"I've not seen her since before the noonday
meal, my lord." She smiled slyly. "No doubt
she's off hiding somewhere and won't come
out until her share of work has already been
done. A beating might make her less inclined
toward laziness."

From the back of the kitchen came a loud
guffaw. "Is it Alana you speak of, lady?
Sounds much more like yourself, if you
ask me."

Sybil glared at the offender with venom in
her eyes. "Well, no one did," she snapped.

Merrick raised a brow when she then proceeded to grace him with a wide, sweet smile.
He contemplated the seductive sway of her
hips as she brushed by him. She was every
bit as comely as her sister, yet most assuredly

she did naught to stir his passions. A pity, he decided with a stab of black humor, for he suspected Sybil would have given him far less trouble than her sister.

But Alana was not in the hall or his chamber. Indeed, she was nowhere to be found.

A gnawing suspicion had begun to grow. He strode into the yard and ordered his mount saddled, then beckoned to several of his men. As he waited, his gaze again swept the yard, searching for a slender form and hair the color of pale moonlight. It was then he noticed one of his men striding toward him, along with the guard Gerard who'd been posted at the rutted track that led to the village. Gerard stepped up before him, wearing a rather sickly expression.

"My lord." He cleared his throat. "I understand you seek the Saxon wench Alana."

"I do," was all he said.

Gerard shuffled his feet. "My lord, she passed by not long ago. She carried bread, cheese and ale, and said she'd been instructed to take the meal to you near the village."

Merrick made a sound of disgust. "Have you no sense, man? If I'd issued such an order, I'd have made certain you knew it!"

The man swallowed. "My lord," he pleaded, "I did wonder what she was about. But she claimed your wrath—and hers as well—would be great if I delayed her. And the way she looked at me . . ." He paled all over again. "My lord, I feared it might be the evil eye, for we all know she is a witch—"

"She is no witch," Merrick said grimly, "but a woman far more clever than you, it would seem." He snatched the reins of his steed from Simon. "You are relieved of your post. I'll have no spineless cowards like you under my command."

A moment later he and a small party of his men thundered toward the village.

Merrick did not doubt that Alana was attempting to escape him. She was no fool, either, he suspected. He was certain she would take to the forest and seek refuge rather than follow along the cliffs by the sea; she could be spotted far too easily there. But he decided to check the village first, for he didn't worry that she might be well ahead of him. Even if she were, he had the advantage, for he was on horseback and she was on foot.

He and his men were nearly there when he spotted several farmers. "You, there," he called out, reining his steed to an abrupt halt. "The girl Alana . . . where is her hut?"

One of the men pointed far afield. "There at the end of the pasture," he shouted.

Merrick gestured one of his men forward. "The rest of you go to the old man Aubrey and see if she is there," he instructed. "If not, search all the villagers' huts."

Seconds later, he leaped from his mount. Sheer determination marked every line of his body as he strode toward the tiny, thatch-roofed cottage. He flung the door wide, full of restless impatience.

Inside, Alana froze.

An eerie foreboding raised the hair on the back of her neck. She knew, even before she turned, who was there.

His massive frame completely filled the doorway, his shoulders so wide they completely blotted out the tepid sunlight. He said not a word, yet the fierceness of his expression bespoke his displeasure all too keenly. As the silence grew ever stronger, her unease sharpened.

He stepped within the cottage. Slowly he closed the door behind him.

Time stood still.

His voice, when at last it came, was almost absurdly quiet . . . deadly quiet, she soon realized.

"I warned you, Saxon, that I would tolerate no further attempts to escape me."

Sheer instinct prompted her denial. "Oh, but I did not—"

"Do not lie to me!"

She stumbled back, as if she'd been struck. The deerskin pouch in which she'd stuffed her mother's earthenware jars dropped to the dirt floor. It spun through her mind that he needed no weapons. With but the sound of his voice, the touch of his eyes, he could easily flay a man alive.

"I told you, Saxon, not to run from me again. I told you that you would regret it." A step brought him closer, another closer still. "And now you will," he added softly.

Alana blanched.

She whirled and snatched a knife from the table. But alas, though she was quick, he possessed the lightning reflexes of a warrior. She had no chance even to raise it. He was upon her in a flash, seizing it and throwing it into a cobwebbed corner.

Harsh laughter rushed past her ear. Terror clutched at her insides. In all her days, Alana had never heard a sound so terrible. "That trick did not work before, Saxon. What made you think it would work now?"

His eyes afire, he wrenched her to him with a force that ripped the breath from her lungs.

"Let me be!" she cried.

In answer he whirled her in a circle. The next thing she knew she lay sprawled on her pallet. His body followed hers down.

Fear of a kind that was unknown to her burst within her. "No!" she screamed. "Why are you doing this?"

His eyes were burning torches of fiery blue. "You violated my order."

"And now you would violate me? No, I tell you. *No!*"

"I merely take what belongs to me." The slash of his mouth above her was grim, so very grim. "And aye, I do believe 'tis well past time."

She strained to be free of his weight but it was no use. In desperation she hammered her fists against his shoulders. He caught her wrists in his hand and held them fast to his chest. With his free hand he clamped the back of her head.

His kiss was raw and hungry and greedy, a kiss that tasted of bruising lust, filled with the fervor of unrestrained passion. Her lips parted helplessly before the angry demand in his. His tongue dove swift and deep . . . but a prelude to an invasion of a deeper kind.

She was half-numb with fright and lack of air by the time he raised his head. His expression was harsh, his eyes glittering and terrible to behold. He leaned back, tearing off his tunic. Stunned into immobility, her gaze dropped to his chest, dark and wide and awesomely masculine.

Then once again he rose over her, against her. In shock she felt her bliaud wrenched to her waist. A jagged sound of anguish wedged in her throat, for his hands were on the drawstring of his braies now.

"Nay." She managed but a single, strangled word. "*Nay!*"

"Yes," he said from between clenched teeth. "Yes!"

Alana squeezed her eyes shut, awash with humiliation. She could feel his manhood, hard and fiery-hot against the softness of her flesh. She sought to clamp her legs shut against him, but alas, he was there between them. With naught but the pressure of his knees he pried her thighs wide. She gave a half-sob, for now she lay naked and open and vulnerable to him.

But the onslaught she expected did not happen.

In that split second when he would have driven home, there was a flurry of movement

from behind him, like an arrow flung from
aloft. Alana's eyes flew open even as his entire
body jerked. A spasm of fury twisted his lips.
He was on his feet in an instant.

Stunned, Alana raised herself up on an
elbow. She stared at the bloody furrows in
his shoulder. Merrick appeared to have forgotten her. His head was tipped back. Even
as they watched, a small, scraggly yellow body
bounded to the rafters high above their heads.
It was Cedric, she realized dimly . . . Her cat
had leaped upon Merrick's shoulders.

Scowling blackly, he bent low and grabbed
his tunic, jerking it over his head. Alana
remained where she was, trembling and shak-
en, afraid to move, for the very air around him
seemed to thunder and roar. Finally she half-
rose, tugging her bliaud over her nakedness.

She was not forgotten for long. With both
hands he dragged her to her feet. Her lips still
throbbed from his possession. His expression
was dark and dangerous, his features forged
into an iron-hard mask of determination. She
couldn't look away as he pulled her crudely
into the vice of his thighs.

"I was prepared to give you time to accept
me. But no more. We will finish what we
started here, Saxon. This I promise. By God,
this I vow."

His voice was stripped free of all tolerance.
Oh, but she had been a fool to think she could
escape him! He would not allow her to go
unpunished. And this time—sweet heaven,
this time there would be no mercy.

His fingers encircled her wrist, a shackle of steel. He tugged her toward the doorway. By some miracle, Alana managed to snatch up the pouch in which she'd stuffed her mother's herbs.

She hugged it tight to her breast while he dragged her outside. Several of his men waited there, mounted on horseback. Merrick grabbed the reins of his steed, then gestured to the cottage.

"Burn it," he said with glacial calm. "Burn it to the ground."

Chapter 7

~~~∽∽~~~

He didn't allow her to walk, though Alana would gladly have welcomed the chance. Instead he lifted her before him on the saddle. High atop the great black warhorse, Alana battled a rising panic, for the creature flung his proud head around and nipped at her shin. With a gasp she shrank back, in her fear unmindful of the man behind her.

A steely forearm tightened around her waist. "Be still," he hissed.

All the way back to Brynwald, she couldn't decide which one she hated more, the beast beneath her or the one at her back.

Once they were back in the yard at Brynwald, he reined the horse to a halt and lightly dismounted. Without preamble he reached for her. A hard arm about her waist, he plucked her from the saddle. Yet her feet had scarcely touched the ground than he released her, so quickly she lost her footing and staggered against him. Instinctively she caught hold of the front of his tunic—a mistake, that! Her gaze immediately rushed upward to his, only to find him regarding her with thinly veiled distaste. In horror she realized she still clutched his tunic. A hot tide of color stained her cheeks as she hurriedly righted herself.

He turned and gestured to his nephew. "Simon," he said when the lad appeared before him. "Escort the lady to my chamber and remain with her. She is to see no one, nor will she be allowed to leave on her own. Is that understood?"

"Aye, Uncle." The boy inclined his head. "My lady?" Knowing she had no choice, Alana followed him to the bedchamber. A cozy fire burned in the hearth, but despite its warmth, she felt chilled to the bone. She shivered, unaware that Simon had noticed. In silence she looked on as the boy stirred the fire and heaved another log onto the flames. To her surprise, he did not withdraw but turned to face her.

"I cannot think why you should be so foolish as to flee," he stated bluntly.

Such directness caught Alana wholly off guard. Her gaze flew to his face. He regarded her every bit as severely as his uncle.

Alana blinked, for what could she say? She could hardly speak of Merrick's plans for her. For all that Simon was almost as tall as some men, he was still a boy. "You would not understand," she said with a faint shake of her head.

Simon studied her still. "You think he is cruel, don't you?"

"Cruel?" She gave a short laugh. "My father is dead, and his wife as well, slain by his men. My sister has been reduced to a servant. Battle rages across the land, and no doubt countless others lie cold in their graves. You Normans take our land and our freedom. Now I would ask you, Simon, do you truly expect me to fall on my knees and give thanks to your uncle? I think not."

There was a faint flicker in the boy's eyes. " 'Tis true that some men make great sport of killing—"

"Aye, and you would know, wouldn't you?" Her words were heated and biting. "Isn't that what you Normans do best?"

He stood a bit stiffly. "Aye, 'tis what we do best, for we are a fighting breed, like our Viking forebears. A knight must be prepared, for who among us knows when the next battle will come? As for the battle here, my uncle slew only those who would have slain him. And do not forget, 'twas your father who first engaged the battle, lady."

"He defended his land. His home!"

"And Merrick but did his duty to his liege, Duke William. The English say we make war for no reason. But 'twas your own King Edward, upon his death, who promised England to William. Earl Harold was but a usurper. Duke William had no choice but to take England by sword and lance, when by all rights there should have been no need. 'Twas a matter of honor . . . and duty."

Honor. Duty. It was on the tip of her tongue to snap that his countrymen knew little of either. But she was coming to realize it was but a waste of breath and spirit to argue with these Normans, even one so young as Simon.

Simon gave her a long, slow look. "My uncle is a man who values loyalty and trust above all else, lady. When he gives his word, he will not forsake it. And when another gives their word to him, he expects no less. I would remember this were I you."

Her lips compressed. She would say no more, for what was the use? Instead she turned and moved to take the chair before the fire. She felt Simon's watchful gaze but ignored it. Instead she tugged her fingers through the tangles in her hair, which had come loose in her struggle with Merrick. She sighed and bent her head, suddenly weary beyond measure.

The afternoon dragged. Alana was not inclined toward further speech, and neither was Simon. She ate the food that was brought later, though she had little appetite. When she'd finished, he moved to the door and waited. It was time for the evening meal in the hall.

Merrick was not yet there when she entered the cavernous room. But she knew the moment he arrived, for she felt the weight of his stare like the prick of a dagger. He walked on to the high table, and when Sybil moved to serve him, Alana breathed a sigh of relief. Yet when she deigned to glance his way some time later, she realized he watched her still, grim and unsmiling. Her heart jolted, then set up a wild clamoring. Deliberately she turned her back, seeking desperately to put him out of mind as well as sight.

But the evening was still young. The night was yet to come. And she could not bear to think what might happen once they were alone. What surely *would* happen . . .

Some time later she paused to wipe her hands on a rag. Her gaze scanned the far wall where she'd seen Radburn last eve. Her brow furrowed, for there was no sign of him. And then, alas—her eyes caught Merrick's.

An odd feeling knotted her belly. From across the hall he beckoned to her. Alana hesitated. It spun through her mind to turn aside, to pretend she hadn't seen him. But after all that had happened today, she was not so brave as she might have wished.

Her legs felt wooden as she moved across to stand before him. He did not rise when she reached him, but remained seated. Even then, he radiated a power and presence that reminded her all too keenly of his strength. Long, dark fingers curled around a goblet of dull silver. A muscled leg stretched out before him.

His expression was granite-hard. "You search for someone, Saxon . . . who?"

Alana returned his gaze but said nothing.

He was undaunted. "Your lover again?"

Something sparked inside Alana. "If you mean Radburn, he is not!"

"So his name is Radburn. Well, Saxon, for your sake, I hope that you do not lie to me."

There was no denying the challenge inherent in his tone. Alana decided it wise to ignore it, for she sensed his present mood was dangerous. Masking her unease, she peered into his goblet. "Your ale is near gone. I will fetch more—"

"Nay, Saxon." Hard fingers caught at her hand. "Sit," he commanded.

Alana's heart leaped. "Sit? But I cannot think why—"

"Why else, Saxon?" His smile was maddening, his eyes pure frost. "I would have you near to gaze upon your beauty."

"To torment me, more like!" she muttered under her breath. Yet even as she spoke, those hard fingers curled more tightly about her own, and he was drawing her down—down—to sit on her knees before him.

The hall was noisy, yet she heard nothing. Scalding shame poured through her. She was no fool. She knew what he was about. He meant for her to feel like a pawn, and so she did. His booty. His possession. Her chest ached from holding back her tears.

Soon he began to toy absently with her hair. Alana wished fervently she had taken the time to braid it; she felt absurdly bound to him, as if he held her to him like a chain. Again and again his fingers slid through the silken strands. A burning resentment simmered in her veins, for it was somehow altogether too intimate, almost as intimate as the crush of his mouth upon hers.

Just then there was a loud crash and a sharp cry from across the hall. Sybil had fallen. The heavy platter she carried went flying. Rivers of ale seeped everywhere. Alana half-rose, her only thought to help her sister.

But Merrick's fingers curling around her arm waylaid her. "No," he said.

Alana turned wide, dark eyes to his. "Please," she said very low. "Let me go to her. She is unused to such hardship."

"She will learn," was all he said.

Alana's breath came in sharply. "She will learn? Is this forever to be her fate then? To attend your men? To serve ale and wine and food?"

Merrick's lips tightened; he did not speak.

"I find it odd you say nothing, Norman." In truth, Alana was secretly appalled at her daring. "Did you not tell Sybil when your sister arrived from Normandy she would no longer be forced to serve your men like this?" Scorn lay heavy in her tone. "Is this how you Normans keep your word?"

His gaze, cool and remote, rested upon her upturned face. "So quick to plead for your sister," he murmured. A devilish brow rose high. "I wonder that you do not worry for your own fate instead, Saxon."

His power was uncanny, she thought darkly. With naught but the touch of his voice, he could cut like a blade. Alana's vision shifted to her knees. She linked her hands together on her lap that he would not glimpse their unsteadiness. Though her lips trembled, she made no effort to conceal the bitter bite from her tone. "You promised no mercy, Norman. And so I expect none."

All at once the air came alive with a seething tension. He wrapped her hair around his fist so that she was forced to tip her head back. And when she did, she was caught fast in a web of steely blue fire. "Were you to beseech sweetly, or implore gently, I might be inclined to prove myself a generous lord indeed." His eyes were no longer icy cold, but heated and searing. They fell to her mouth and settled there. "Would you?" he asked softly.

She stared at him through eyes that stung painfully. Desperately she sought to still the frenzied beat of her heart. This time it was she who said nothing. She would neither beg nor bargain with this arrogant knave!

"No?" With a harsh laugh, he released her. "I thought not. So be it, then." He leaned back. "Await me in my chamber, Saxon. I will be along soon."

Alana needed no further urging. She picked up her skirts and ran across the hall.

But before she could mount even the first stair, her arm was caught. She was spun bodily around. Her cry of protest withered when she saw it was Sybil.

It was readily apparent her sister was in a temper. "I should have known you would find a way to be free of the toil the rest of us must endure," she spat. "You are a sluggard, Alana."

Alana shook her head. "Nay, 'tis not that at all, Sybil. I know you are angry that I did not come to aid you, but Merrick . . . he wouldn't allow it—"

"Merrick! Ah, I understand only too well, sister. You cast your witch's spells on him, the way your mother did with Father. Well, best enjoy it whilst you can, Alana, for he is a devil. No doubt he will find another whore to replace you soon enough."

"Oh!" Alana was both furious and hurt. "You cannot think I want this. I want nothing from him—nothing! And I am not his whore, Sybil. Indeed he has not yet . . ." She stopped and her cheeks went fiery red. All at once she was acutely embarrassed at what she'd been about to divulge.

Sybil planted her hands on her hips. Her expression was a cross between incredulous and suspicious. "Do you mean to say you haven't lain with him yet?"

Alana's cheeks went fiery red. "Lord, no," she said with a shudder.

Sybil tried to disguise her sly smile. "Then you are wise to be wary," she said suddenly. "I've heard some of his soldiers talking. They say his prick is enormous. As thick as a man's wrist and half as long as his sword. Why, surely he is a monster, to be fashioned so . . ."

Alana was stunned, mortified and wholly taken aback at Sybil's crudity. Lord knew Edwyna had tried to shelter her as best she could, however living in the village, Alana had been exposed to all manner of speech by the village men. But never in her days had she heard a woman speak thusly—and Sybil a lady yet!

Sybil's chin climbed high when at last she gleaned Alana's horrified expression. "I only repeat what I heard." She defended herself staunchly. "That's what they said, I swear on the grave of our father."

Alana was still too shocked to say a word.

Unbeknownst to her, Sybil relished a secret satisfaction. "Aye," she said sweetly. "You are wise to be wary, Alana. But mayhap you will be lucky, eh? If you do not please him, mayhap he will turn his favors to another. Indeed, I shall pray it will be so." She patted Alana's shoulder before departing.

Alana climbed the stairs slowly, unable to put aside Sybil's words. *Enormous . . . thick as a man's wrist . . . half as long as his sword*. A sickening dread churned low in her belly. She told herself Sybil had been trying to frighten her, for what she said was simply not possible. Surely Merrick couldn't be so very different from other men . . . or could he?

So preoccupied was she that she did not see the shadowy figure that stepped out before her until it was too late. She barreled nearly full tilt into a solid form. She was righted by a pair of hands that reached out and grasped her shoulders. Her breath caught as she recognized Raoul.

She tried to step back, but he would not allow it. His fingers dug into her soft flesh.

Alana battled a faint alarm. Merrick's chamber was but a few footsteps down the passageway. If she could break free and run . . .

"Oh, no," he said with a faint smirk. "You will go nowhere, Alana."

Alana struggled for calm. "Release me," she said evenly.

His regard was leering. "Do not be so impatient. We have much in common, you and I."

Her back went rigid as stone. "Are you braver than your fellow soldiers? I told them I would turn them into goats, and that's what will happen to you if you don't let me go."

Such bravado did little good. He merely smiled, a smile that turned her blood to ice. "Were you possessed of such power, you'd already have done so to free yourself. There would have been no need to run from Merrick. Or mayhap you should run to me instead. I would treat you far better than he."

He caught her up hard against him, his hold ruthless. His lips drew back over his teeth in a wolfish parody of a smile. His head began to lower. Hot breath struck her cheek. Gleaming black eyes swam before her face. She turned aside to avoid the kiss he would force upon her, striking wildly at his chest.

"No!" she cried. "*No!*"

"Scream all you want, girl." His laugh was grating. "Merrick is not here to save you now."

"Ah, but he is. And it would appear that the lady still does not favor you, Raoul."

It was Merrick. Raoul cursed roundly and let her go. Alana staggered slightly, her knees weakened by sheer relief. Oh, it made no sense that her tormentor should be her salvation, yet in that moment Alana could hardly deny she welcomed his presence as never before.

"Alana."

Her gaze swung to Merrick's features, partially hidden in shadow. It struck her that this was the first time he had used her name.

"Yes?" She was still breathless from her struggle.

"I would speak with Raoul alone."

Alana needed no further explanation, nor further prodding for that matter. She turned and bolted down the passageway.

Once the two men were alone, silence abounded, a silence borne of a curious tension. Merrick stood with his hands linked behind his back. He said nothing. Only the frigid scope of his eyes bespoke his displeasure.

Not so with Raoul. An easy smile twisted his lips. "What would you have me say, Merrick? She is a tasty morsel, eh? And 'tis hardly the first time we've had an eye for the same maid. Besides, you've yet to take her to your bed."

Merrick's eyes narrowed. "How do you know?"

Raoul shrugged. "I overheard the wench tell her sister." He spread his hands wide. "So if you cannot handle her, my lord, of a certainty I shall—"

"Do not lay a hand on the girl again lest you wish to lose it." Merrick's tone was silky smooth. "I would hate to see your sword arm useless, Raoul. Do I make myself clear?"

Raoul's smile slipped a bit. He nodded.

"Excellent," Merrick murmured. "The girl is not fair game for you or any of the others. Make certain they know it as well."

Raoul nodded and left. Merrick watched as he disappeared into the shadows, then he turned and strode toward his chamber.

Alana was sitting before the fire when Merrick walked in. At his entrance, she jumped up. He stood unmoving just inside the entrance, his expression wholly unreadable, eyes locked upon hers. And as the silence ripened between them, so did her unease.

She shifted nervously. There was a sharpness about him that boded ill. "What is it?" she asked, her tone very low. "Why do you stare at me so?"

For an instant she thought he would not reply. Then he said slowly, "You cause trouble in ways I'd not expected, Saxon."

She wet her lips, still uneasy. "What do you mean?"

"Only this. From now on, you will not serve the others. You will serve only me."

Her breath caught. "What! Don't you have enough Saxon slaves to do your bidding?"

He approached her, until they stood but a breath apart. The merest hint of a smile grazed his mouth, but his eyes were cold. "You misunderstand me, lady. For indeed, I've decided your duties shall change."

Alana stared at him. An awful suspicion began to take root in her mind. "What!" she said faintly. "Never say you want me to—"

"I can see you take my meaning. You will serve me, Saxon, and me alone. You will do whatever I wish. Whene'er I wish."

For an instant she could only regard him in stunned incredulity. But fast on its heels came a raging fury. "Do you think I do not know what you are about? You do this only to spite me for trying to leave!"

He ran a fingertip down the delicate slope of her jaw. "Nay," he said softly. "I do this to please me. And please me you will, lady."

"I'd rather you locked me away never to see the dawn again," she said bitterly.

"Oh, now that I do not doubt. And indeed, I wonder that I do not do just that. You are a temptation, Saxon, and I admit, I was foolish to think this would not happen. You see, I watched my men tonight . . . I watched my men watch *you*."

Her lips parted in surprise. "Nay," she said faintly. "You are wrong—"

"I am not. They undressed you with their eyes. They covet you for their own. But I alone will have what they covet. I will not share you—and they will know it."

"What of me? What about my wishes?" she burst out. "And you wonder why I would seek to leave here! By God, I would ally myself with the devil himself, for I'd rather have anyone, anyone but you, Norman!"

He smiled tightly. "Even Raoul?"

Raoul. The very mention of his name made her skin crawl. Yet in that instant she hated Merrick far more, hated him for his mockery.

Most of all, she hated him for the power he wielded over her.

He raised a brow. "No, then. I thought not." His hands came down on her shoulders, disturbingly warm and strong.

"Aye," he said again. "You will serve me, Saxon. In any way I choose. In every way I choose. And you will begin this night." His tone was soft, so soft a shiver danced down her spine—delight or fear? "You will begin even now," he whispered.

She was drawn close against his chest—so close the beat of her heart seemed not her own. There was a subtle tightening of his hands on her shoulders. His dark head bent low, blotting out the light. Her eyes fluttered shut. She braced herself inwardly, conscious of a strange inner trembling. It was then that the oddest notion took hold. Surely she didn't want him to kiss her. Surely not . . .

But his lips never touched hers. There came a violent pounding on the door.

"My lord," someone shouted. "Come quickly. Your nephew Simon . . . I fear he is dying!"

Chapter 8

Raoul's mood was vicious as he walked away from Merrick. Someday, he decided furiously, someday Merrick would not be the all-powerful lord. Yes, he vowed, someday the tables would be turned . . .

He hadn't gone more than a few steps when a rustle of movement snared his attention. His head whipped around. There, hidden in the shadows of an open doorway, was Alana's half-sister. She tried to step back when she realized she'd been discovered, but Raoul was too quick. With a growl of rage he wrenched her forward.

"Curse you, wench, I know what you are about! Do you spy on them—or me?" he demanded.

Sybil's eyes flashed. "Mayhap I should ask the same of you!"

Raoul's jaw thrust forward. He did not refute her.

Sybil tossed her head. "Aye, I saw you in the hall when I was with Alana. You lurked below the stairs, listening to all we said." She smiled sly. "Indeed, Raoul, 'twould seem we have much in common."

She eyed him boldly, her hands braced on generous hips. She paid no heed to the way her bliaud stretched taut over her breasts, clearly displaying their rounded shape. "Mayhap more than you think," he muttered.

She did not flinch from his blatant regard, but met and matched it with her own. *Here was one who well realized her power over men—and no doubt used it to her every advantage*, he thought. An admirable trait, he decided vaguely, though he was hardly wont to let a woman exert such control over him. Nay, he would far rather admire her in other, more pleasurable ways.

A primitive lust had already begun to boil within him. His eyes glinted. The two were sisters, not so alike in appearance, but both were beauties nonetheless. His desire had been piqued by the proud, haughty one, whom he still wanted. But he would settle for this one . . .

He snatched a candle from an iron spike mounted on the wall. Quickly he scanned the chamber behind her. Neither weapons nor trunks lined the walls. No one would be returning here to spend the night.

Sybil cried out when he grasped her arm and pulled her within. Raoul whirled on her.

I've seen the way you look at Merrick. You want him," Rauol growled. "And I want her. So let us make do with each other in the meantime."

With that he seized her in a bone-crushing embrace. His mouth ravaged hers in a kiss of bruising intensity.

"Stop," she gasped when she was at last able to break away. "I do not fight you."

He raised his head and raked her with a burning gaze. "And why not, wench? Do you not despise the Normans as your sister does?"

Her eyes gleamed. "Nay," she answered. "Indeed, what does it matter that you are Norman? You are handsome and well muscled"—her gaze swept down his body—"and well endowed from the feel of it."

His grip on her eased ever so slightly. "Methinks you are not as cold as your sister, wench," he muttered.

Sybil laughed, a low, sultry sound. "I give you a solemn vow here and now, Raoul. I will please you far more than she."

He allowed her to wiggle from his arms. Displaying no embarrassment whatsoever, she let her bliaud slip from her shoulders. Her chemise followed and then she was naked.

He stared with avid boldness. Her breasts were jutting and white and full, crowned with huge dark nipples. Dark curls grew lush and thick at the juncture of her thighs. With burning eyes he watched as she smiled and tipped her head back. Her gaze never leaving his, she licked the tips of her fingers, then slid them slowly around her nipples, leaving them shiny wet and erect.

Her eyes half-closed. Raoul's hand fumbled with his braies as she played with her breasts.

His hand closed around his rod, pulsing and stiff. He began to work his hand forward and back. His blood pounded. His breath came harsh and fast.

Sybil paused in her self-ministrations. His prick seemed to swell and grow and thicken beneath her very eyes. She grew hot all over, especially there in the secret place between her thighs. In an instant, she was there before him, naked and on her knees. She licked her lips.

"Let me," she whispered. "Let me."

Raoul cast back his head and groaned. With deft, sure hands and hot, wet mouth she brought him to the brink of heaven.

"Enough," he growled. He dragged her up and to her feet then took her mouth in a ravening kiss. She met him openly. Eagerly. Her hands slid into his braies to smooth sleek, hard flanks, even as his fingers slid through damp, dark curls to her woman's mound.

"Tell me, wench," he rasped. "Are you as wet there as you are here?" His mouth opened on hers. Their tongues dueled wildly.

Her legs parted in invitation. Boldly he stroked hot, pink flesh fairly weeping with dew.

Her head arched back. A seductive smile curved her lips. "I've always wondered . . . do you Normans do it differently?"

His head jerked up. His eyes were glittering.

Her smile widened. "Show me, Norman," she invited. "Show me your prowess with your lance of steel . . ."

In answer he gripped her buttocks. Bracing his legs wide and lifting her high, he brought her fiercely down on his engorged manhood, impaling her hard and deep. Spasms of ecstasy shook her. She clutched at his arms and moaned deep in her chest, a keening sound of rapture.

Their coupling was wild and savage. They didn't make it to the bed, or even to the table. There were no further words. There was only panting and groaning, the sounds of mutual lust.

Simon was indeed sick, and deathly so, from the look of him. His skin was pasty white. He writhed on the floor in agony.

Merrick knelt beside him. "Simon." His voice was hoarse with concern. "My God, boy, what ails you?"

Simon's features were a mask of pure anguish. "My belly," he gasped. "There are . . . swords in my belly." He gazed pleadingly upward. "Help me, Uncle . . . I pray you . . . help me."

Never in his life had Merrick experienced such helplessness. An acrid fear clutched his insides. He was half-afraid his man was right—that Simon might die.

No . . . no! He could not let that happen. Genevieve had entrusted her only son to his care. He could not fail her . . . he could not fail Simon!

His mind tumbled and churned. They had

brought no physician with them from Normandy. Indeed, there was no one to whom they could turn . . . His mind screamed. How could this have happened? *How*? A fleeting notion took hold . . .

"Take the boy to the bedchamber across from mine," he barked out. He whirled and retraced his steps.

Alana jumped when the door crashed open. She rose, clasping her hands before her. "How is he?" she asked quickly. "How is Simon?"

"Mayhap you are the one to tell me, lady." Merrick spoke from between clenched teeth.

Alana stared at him. Her mouth went dry, for his countenance was terrible to behold. The very air around him seemed to sizzle and burn.

She gave a tiny shake of her head. "I-I do not know what you mean," she said uneasily.

A vivid curse filled the air. "You choose to play the innocent but I will know the truth, lady." Alana cried out as he seized her arm and proceeded to march her across the hall. Her head was still spinning when he stopped beside a narrow bed. She drew a sharp breath as she looked down at Simon.

Beside her Merrick was taut with fury. "He was with you most of the day, Saxon. And someone heard the two of you arguing. So did you do this? Did you cast some witch's spell over him that he might sicken and die?"

Outrage came later. For now, Alana was only hurt that he could think her so cruel. "Nay!" she cried. "God's blood, he is only a boy—"

"A Norman, lady. And you've made your feelings toward us quite clear."

Alana stared down at Simon. 'Twas clear the boy was in dire straits. He clutched his knees to his chest. He moaned almost constantly. She touched his forehead. His skin was hot as fire, yet moist and clammy, beaded with sweat.

She shook her head wildly. "I would never harm him," she whispered. "He is just a boy . . . I could never harm anyone!"

Merrick made a sound of disgust and spun around.

Alana ran after him. "Wait!" she cried, snagging his elbow. "I-I can help him, if only you will let me."

"You?" His lips curled. He made no secret of his doubt.

"Aye! My mother was the village healer. I helped her countless times over the years, from the time I was a child."

He said nothing, merely stared down at her with narrowed eyes.

"Ask Sybil, if you don't believe me. Ask any of the villagers. They would have naught to do with me after she was gone, but as God is my witness, she taught me all she knew of herbs and potions." Her fingers trembled where they lay on his forearm. Beneath her fingertips, his muscles were knotted and tense.

Still he made no answer. "Please." With her eyes she pleaded with him. With words she beseeched him. "I would help Simon, if only you would let me." She held her breath and waited.

Just when she thought he would refuse, he spoke. "No tricks, Saxon," he warned harshly. "You will heal him. Else you will pay the price."

Alana nodded. A chill went through her as she turned away, for Merrick appeared utterly ruthless, utterly demanding. She returned to the bedside, her mind working furiously. Her mother had taught her well, but it was just as she claimed—her skills had seen little use. She prayed that she might remember . . . And she prayed that Simon would live.

Else she might very well die.

Perchance some force from on high had been looking out for her that day. Alana gave thanks that she'd had the foresight to rescue the pouch with her mother's herbs. Simon burned with fever, yet shook with chills from head to toe. Pain wracked his entire body. He thrashed wildly, his limbs scarcely at rest. She prepared a tea to help ease the cramping in his belly. Merrick lurked just behind her shoulder, ever watchful, ever on guard. He made her so nervous she nearly spilled the goblet in which she'd poured the steaming brew.

She took a deep breath and turned to face him. "Must you watch me so?"

He folded powerful arms across his chest. "I watch you to make certain you do not poison him."

Alana held fast to her temper. "I do not poison him. I would give him something to ease the cramps in his belly."

"Indeed." He stepped close and sniffed. "It smells most foul, Saxon."

Her eyes were snapping. "If it will ease your mind, Norman, I will drink it first."

He said neither yea nor nay, so Alana took a generous sip of the tea. After a moment, he gave a terse nod. "Proceed, then."

Gritting her teeth, Alana turned her back on him, resolving to forget Merrick's presence. Nor was it difficult, for Simon's condition grew steadily worse. At first he could keep nothing down. His fever rose ever higher, hot as fire. At first she suspected he'd eaten food that mayhap had been spoiled. Yet no one else had sickened. More than once, it crossed her mind that perchance Merrick was not wrong after all. Mayhap someone *had* poisoned him . . .

She spent the whole of the second night bathing him with cool water, from head to toe. He was barely conscious and could ingest neither food nor water. The cramps in his belly were still ferocious. His breathing was fast and labored. His lips grew chapped, his skin withered like parchment.

Alana became desperate. Her mother had oft warned her that such signs were dangerous. She could help him, if only he could drink! In sudden decisiveness, she took a reed and thrust it into the tea. By holding a finger over the top, she was able to draw the liquid into the reed and then dribble it into the corner of his mouth. Her patience unending, she sat there hour upon hour, praying he swallowed enough of the brew to ease the pains in his belly.

For three long days she stood vigil at his bedside. Merrick often hovered near. Knowing he examined her every move made it difficult to concentrate. Several times he commanded she leave, that someone else might take her place. Alana curtly refused. No doubt he thought she could not save the boy, but she would prove to him she hadn't lied, no matter what!

Her efforts were rewarded by the evening of the third day. Simon's fever broke. His breathing was almost normal. He fell into a deep, untroubled sleep.

Alana knew instinctively that the crisis had passed. The relief that flooded her was immense. Merrick had gone to the hall for the evening meal. Numb with fatigue, she decided to lay her head down, just for a bit. Faith, but she couldn't remember when she had been so tired! She would rest, just for a moment . . .

That was how Merrick found her. She sat on a low stool near the bedside, slumped forward. She was sleeping, he realized.

He moved across to the bedside, taking care to be quiet. His gaze slid to Simon. His regard sharpened, for Simon's color appeared almost normal—and he seemed to be slumbering peacefully. Touching the boy's forehead, he breathed a heartfelt sigh of relief. Praise God, Simon's fever was gone!

His eyes returned to Alana and lingered. Despite his efforts to harden his heart, there was something oddly vulnerable in her pose.

Her cheek rested atop one hand; the other lay curled in a small fist amidst the rumpled linen sheet.

"Saxon." The sound was but a breath of air. He paused, experiencing a rare moment of indecision, then he lightly shook her shoulder. "Saxon," he said again, more loudly this time. Still she didn't stir.

She was exhausted, he realized grimly, and little wonder. She had refused to let anyone else tend Simon—never had he encountered such stubbornness in a wench! His thoughts were tinged with both exasperation and a grudging respect. Nay, he couldn't fault her care of Simon. Indeed, if not for her, Simon might even now lay cold in his grave.

He strode belowstairs to summon a maid to sit with Simon, then he returned to the chamber. He hesitated, then bent low to gather her in his arms. Faith! but she weighed scarcely more than a child!

In his chamber, he pulled back the furs and lowered her gently to the bed. He made short work of unwinding the hides that bound her feet, flinging them to the floor, his mouth tight with disapproval. He did not stop there but continued his task, easing her bliaud from her shoulders and down her body. Her chemise came next; it was so worn in places it was nearly sheer, he noted grimly. Though his hands displayed far more care than haste, his last tug caused a rent in the linen he knew could not be repaired.

There was an odd tightening in his gut. She

lay before him, naked and wondrously so—like a feast provided for his sole pleasure. Merrick would not have called himself a man had he spurned the temptation roused by such a vision of loveliness. He could count each curve of her ribs, yet she had gained some flesh in the little time she'd spent with him.

Her chest rose and fell with every breath. Her breasts were small but sweetly curved, tipped with nipples the color of pale pink roses. Her belly was flat and concave. Dark gold fleece crowned the treasure between her thighs. Despite her slenderness, there was a soft, womanly roundness to her that roused all that was raw and hungry and male in him. Her skin was pale and umblemished. He knew that if he were to touch her, she would feel like warm, rich silk. Blood rushed hot and thick to his loins, pooling there until he swelled taut and rigid as marble.

Merrick could not help himself. Her mouth was soft and full and slightly parted, moist as a morning dew; it was as if she were begging to be well and thoroughly kissed. Suddenly that was exactly what he longed to do— kiss her into oblivion. Taste for himself her unguarded response. Bury his rod inside her, deep and hard as he slaked his passion . . .

With the tip of a finger he traced one deep pink circle, the gentlest caress. Beneath his fingers the peak hardened to a tight little bud. The glint in his eye bespoke his satisfaction. Even in sleep, she responded to him. Defy him she would—fight him to the very end—yet her body was not so immune to him as she would pretend.

A faint smile rimmed his mouth. If she knew he saw her thus—touched her thus—he would bear the sting of her fiery tongue. A dark resolve slipped over him then.

He would not lay a hand on her this night. Nay, not a finger. For he wanted her awake. He wanted to watch her as he brought her to climax. He wanted to hear her moan her passion into his mouth, feel her flesh clamp tight and hot about his own.

Beating down his regret, he stripped. But when he would have pinched out the candle flame, he caught the glint of dark gold eyes gleaming at him from beneath the chair.

It was her cat—the cat whose claw marks even now striped his shoulder.

He strode across the floor and threw open the door. Grabbing his tunic, he whipped it toward the animal. "Begone with you!" he muttered. "Now, you wretched creature!"

With a hiss and swish of his tail, the cat leaped from his hiding place and ran through the door.

Pacified at last, he crawled into bed beside Alana. Sweeping the hair from her brow, he pulled her close and closed his eyes. Soon he joined her in slumber.

Not so with Alana.

She was exhausted, weary in every way. But while sleep came easily and for a time numbed the whole of her body and mind, it did not

remain a healing balm for long. Deep in the
murky abyss in which she sought refuge, her
restless mind gave her no peace. A dark side
of the spirit slipped over her. Aye, and the
dream, the dream she so dreaded . . .

It came yet again.

The same . . . yet different.

*She was close to the sea, so very close. The briny
scent stung her nostrils; the bracing force of the
wind whipped her hair and skirts. The sound of
the surf pounded in her ears. Her vision was filled
by the dark outline of sea and sky.*

*But all at once the smell of the sea became the
stench of death, cloying and sickening. Twisting
images and shapes shifted and loomed and circled in
every direction; darkness caved in, closing around
her so that she could scarcely draw breath. Desperate
to escape, she began to run, as if she were beset by
demons and devils. Yea, and mayhap 'twas true,
for he was there again.*

*He sat upon his warhorse, huge and dark. Beneath
his helm, his eyes glittered. Terror turned her blood
to ice. His sword was held high above his head.
Even as she stood paralyzed in fear, that massive
blade swung down . . .*

*She could not move. She could only scream, and
scream and scream . . .*

"Saxon! Awaken now. You are safe . . . do
you hear me, girl? You are safe . . ."

Safe? Oh, she recognized that voice. She recognized the strength of those arms swept tight
around her back. In some distant part of her
mind, she knew she had awakened. The light
from a candle wavered at the bedside. But her

frenzied mind could neither accept nor comprehend such comfort—and from him yet!

Nay, she thought faintly, she would never be safe. In that shattering instant, she knew only that Merrick was all that she feared . . . *everything* that she feared.

"Don't touch me. I tell you, do not touch me!" With a strangled sob she broke his hold and scrambled back against the wall, clutching a pile of furs to her breast.

His lips pressed together. "What madness is this that you shrink from me so? 'Twas just a dream, do you hear? Dreams are not real, they cannot hurt you."

Alana shook her head wildly. "You are wrong. 'Tis not just a dream. This will happen. I tell you *this will happen*."

His eyes narrowed. "Tell me of this dream, Saxon." She said nothing, merely stared up at him. Sheer, naked terror still coursed through her veins. He prompted her again sharply. "Tell me, Alana. Tell me what would frighten you so."

Alana shook her head. The breath that filled her lungs was deep and racking. "I saw death," she whispered. "I saw darkness. I saw *you*."

Chapter 9

I saw darkness . . . I saw death . . . I saw you . . .
"You raised your sword high," she gasped out. "You raised it high to . . . to strike me dead . . ."

He gave an impatient exclamation. "What nonsense is this, Saxon? I need no sword to overpower one such as you. And murderer though you think I am, I do not prey on helpless women. And you, lady, could never defend yourself against one such as me."

Still she shrank from him, as if he were the most loathsome of creatures.

Merrick's regard sharpened, as well as his mind. He recalled that very moment when he'd first laid eyes on her in the forest. She had stared at him, her features pale and stunned and almost . . . stricken.

It came to him like a sudden blow. She had been terrified of him even then.

"That first day in the forest," he said slowly. "You stared at me as if I were some apparition from Hell."

Alana shuddered, struggling to find a courage that was proving vastly elusive. She spoke haltingly, her voice barely audible. " 'Twas because I—I had seen your face before."

The sound he made was one of impatient exasperation. "Nay, that cannot be—"

"It's true, I swear by all that is holy! I-I *had* seen you before."

"Where?" he demanded. "In this dream?"

Alana stared at him. The remnants of her dream had begun to fade. The pounding of her heart was slowing. Merrick was here, aye— and oh, he demanded as fiercely and arrogantly as ever! Reality crept in slowly. Yet he did not seek to hurt her, she realized dimly.

"Aye," she agreed shakily. Her gaze fell. She went on, her voice etched with a weary bleakness. "You thought it such a great jest that the villagers call me witch. But they truly believe I *am* a witch."

His reply was swift and vehement. "And are you?"

Her emotions were a wild tempest. She ducked her head, grateful the silken fall of her hair hid her burning cheeks. But to her shame, tears glazed her eyes. "I do not know," she whispered.

He said nothing. She felt the touch of those ice-blue eyes like the prick of a dagger.

"I—I should not be here," she said suddenly. "I should be with Simon—"

"Simon's fever is gone and he is doing very well now. He can do without your care this night."

It was less an explanation than an order. Alana swallowed nervously, reluctantly lifting her gaze. A mistake, that!—for now her vision was filled with a view of an awesomely muscled chest, bare and disturbingly virile with its covering of wiry dark hairs.

He paid her no heed as he pinched out the candle. He lay back down, one strong arm tucked beneath his head. Alana quickly followed suit, sliding back beneath the furs. Embers from the fire cast out feeble fingers of a faint orange glow. Alana lay with her eyes wide open. She and Merrick touched nowhere, yet she felt his warmth like the burning blaze of a fire. The certainty that he was naked sent a flurry of alarm skidding down her spine. Yet as time marched on and he made no move to touch her, she realized he presented no threat but the one that lurked in her mind.

Beside her, Merrick turned his head. "This dream, Saxon. It comes to you often?"

Alana hesitated. "Only of late," she allowed, her voice a mere thread of sound.

"And you've had other dreams before?"

Her lips pressed together. Oh, but he was a clever one! "Aye," she said curtly.

"How long have they come to you? Always?"

"I—I cannot remember."

He persisted. "This is why the villagers call you witch? Because of these dreams?"

Though she longed to deny it, to deny him, she didn't dare. "Aye," she said again.

"I would know the nature of these dreams, Saxon. Do they foretell the future?"

She glanced at him sharply. His regard was steady, as steady as hers was reticent.

"Sometimes," she allowed.

Her reply was grudging yet he paid no heed. "And do these visions come true?"

She shivered, caught fast in a swirl of memories she'd rather not recall. "Some do," she said, her tone very low.

The mattress shifted. Alana tensed, sensing his regard. But all he said was, "Tell me."

Her lips trembled. She'd come to know him well enough to know he'd not allow her to shirk his questions. Slowly she began to speak.

"I dreamed once of the alewife, who was soon to bear a child. In my dream her babe was born with his feet turned inward."

"And was it so?"

She nodded. Her fingers linked together over her breast as she went on. "There was a cottar who once lived in the village. I dreamed I saw his son standing atop the cliffs near Brynwald, high above the sea. Then all at once"— Her voice caught; her knuckles grew white—"All at once I saw him falling, plunging toward the raging waters of the sea."

"What then?" he asked after a moment.

"The next evening he was found dead, lying on the beach below Brynwald."

She both felt and heard his surprise. "But—how?"

"The villagers whispered that I pushed him. Only my mother and Aubrey believed it could have been an accident—that the boy fell. Only they believed me innocent." She drew a deep, uneven breath. "So now you know, Norman. Now you know why they call me witch."

When he said nothing, her eyes sought his; they were but a glimmer of light in the darkness. She started when a strong hand came to cover hers where it lay atop her breast.

"Ah, but if you were a witch," she heard him say, "you'd have fled me long before now."

"Ah, but I did try—"

"Fled," he stressed flatly, "and *succeeded*."

Did he mock her? Alana could not tell. Though she clearly discerned the outline of his head, the muscled bulge of his shoulders, his features were dark and shadowed. Then all at once he turned his head. He was frowning blackly.

"Come here," he growled. "You're still shivering."

His mouth was tight. It chased through her mind that she had displeased him yet again. She started to shake her head, but before her protest could find voice, he had turned and gathered her against him, drawing her close to his side.

Alana didn't move; she didn't dare. She was all at once heartstoppingly aware that he was naked. Her hand lay curled atop the dark breadth of his chest. Her cheek lay snug against the sleek hard flesh of his shoulder.

She would never sleep, not like this, not with him beside her! Yet his warmth was like a cocoon around her, his presence a refuge.

Her mind began to swim. It wasn't right that she should feel so—so safe. Nay, it made no sense, for he was all that threatened her. Yet curiously, it was as if nothing or no one could harm her . . .

It was morning when she next awoke. She lay huddled on her side in the bed, her senses still foggy with sleep. She felt absurdly cold, for Merrick did not lie beside her.

She couldn't help but ponder the night just past—not the terrible dream that plagued her but, rather, what had followed. An elusive memory stirred—a whisper of breath across her cheek, the merest brush of a hand on her brow. Her heartbeat quickened. She had lain in Merrick's arms throughout the night and into the morn. They were strong, those arms—so very warm and strong!—yet frightening, too, in some way she couldn't define.

The door creaked. Merrick strode in, as bold as ever. Alana started to sit up only to sink back in abject horror as she realized she wore not a stitch of clothing. A wise decision, too, for at that precise instant two young lads wrestled an oval-shaped wooden tub through the door. At Merrick's direction, they placed it before the fire. Several more traipsed through the door hauling buckets of water. Hidden deep within the furs, Alana watched with wide eyes as the tub was filled with steaming hot water.

Once the procession had ended and the last youth had gone, Merrick closed the door. He turned to face her, a half-smile on his lips, one dark brow cocked at an arrogant slant. Alana glared at him, a trifle annoyed that he was fully awake—aye, and fully dressed!

She nodded at the tub. "I suppose you expect me to bathe you," she said stiffly. While she was well aware it was the custom for the lady of the manor to assist male guests with their bath, she was hardly the lady of the manor . . . and loath though she was to admit it, he was hardly a guest.

His maddening smile ripened. "The bath is not for me, Saxon."

Alana's jaw firmed. "I dislike such games, Norman. If not for you, then for whom?"

He swept a gallant hand toward the tub. "Why, who else, Saxon?"

Her glare turned to one of outright suspicion. "Surely not I—"

"And I would say again, who *else* but you?"

Oh, he did not fool her! This was naught but a trick for she knew he was well aware of her nakedness.

She shook her head wildly. "No," she said, her voice but a breath. "I-I cannot. I will not!"

His smile vanished. "You will, Saxon. Because I ask it. Nay, because I demand it."

In but the blink of an eye, all traces of amusement had fled. His features hardened. His expression grew closed and tight. There would be no arguing with him, she acknowledged dimly, just as there would be no denying him.

So it was that in the end she tugged a wide fur around her shoulders and scooted to the

edge of the bed. A slim white thigh flashed
into view as she extended a bare toe downward to the cold stone floor, then raced across
the floor. Her grip on the concealing fur didn't
lessen until the very last instant. She clam-
bered over the side of the tub. In her haste
she banged her knee and sloshed water everywhere, but Alana cared not. Quickly she sank
beneath the water.

But the sanctuary she meant to find was
simply not to be. Merrick did not leave as she
hoped—prayed! Nay, the wretch, he advanced
still closer, to tower before her at the foot of
the tub. With no shame whatsoever, he gazed
down at her. To Alana's everlasting mortifica-
tion, his regard was as bold and brash as the
man himself!

Her face burned painfully. Indeed, the whole
of her body went hot, for she was well aware he
sought to see what she would much rather he
did not! Water sloshed anew as she wrapped
her arms around her knees and hugged them
close to her breasts.

And still her torment did not end.

Slowly he moved around so that he stood
at her back. Her heart seemed to jump in
her chest when he knelt just behind her. She
twisted around, trying to see him. "Wh-what
are you doing?"

He reached for a cloth atop a nearby stool.
"Lady, I should think 'twould be obvious. You
have no maid to attend to this duty. Therefore,
I will attend you."

A maid? Oh, now he mocked her cruelly!

"I need no assistance, Norman. And I would be most appreciative were you to leave." Her resolve was firm, but her confidence had begun to waver.

And so had her voice.

She did not see the way Merrick's gaze narrowed intently. Her modesty chafed, for surely he was hardly the first man to see her naked. And indeed, his desire to see her so had scarcely been satisfied. Instead he'd been granted tantalizing glimpses of pale, perfect flesh; glimpses that were ever a temptation, a temptation that only sharpened his hunger and made it ever more difficult to put aside.

But the time was nearly at hand. Soon, he promised himself, she would be his. Soon . . .

A coarse fingertip swept a blazing path across the gleaming slope of her shoulder. "Leave?" he echoed lightly. "And deprive myself of this pleasure?"

"Pleasure! Must your pleasure always come at my humiliation?" No longer did she look at him. Her voice was low and choked.

Merrick chastened himself harshly. He must be mad to allow this to happen, for who but a fool would let such tearful protestations sway his desire—and aye, his intent! If she were spitting and angry and defiant, the match might have been well met. But as it was . . .

"So be it, Saxon. If you require no assistance then I shall offer none."

The cloth landed in the water with a loud *plop*. A wedge of soap quickly followed. Alana didn't wait to count her good fortune but set to work washing herself hurriedly. The flesh of her shoulder still burned where he had caressed her, and she scrubbed there furiously until she winced in pain. Had she been alone, the bath would have been a veritable heaven. But with Merrick present, the sooner she was finished and once again dressed, the better. With that in mind, she ducked her head under, then quickly lathered and rinsed her hair.

She wrung out the heavy tresses as best she could and tugged it into a long rope over her shoulder. It was then she saw a length of linen had been placed within reach. Merrick, she saw, stood before the window, his hands behind his back. Alana hastily assured herself that his gaze lay elsewhere, then rose. Water sluiced down her body as she stepped from the tub.

Rather clumsily she wound the cloth around her breasts and back; it hung nearly to the floor. Glistening droplets of water still clung to her shoulders and arms. She shivered, for she'd been far more concerned with seeing her body decently covered than dried. Stepping before the fire, she shook her hair loose and combed through the silken tresses with her fingers, leaning toward the heat that it might dry more quickly.

So intent was she that she didn't notice Merrick's attention was now wholly on her. His gaze was drawn to her unwillingly— unendingly. The linen cloth clung damply to her, provocatively revealing the slender shape of her—small, round breasts like firm, ripe fruit, hips that flared alluringly. The bare skin of her shoulders gleamed with the lustre of a pearl; it beckoned his touch. An odd sensation gripped his belly, like a fist drawn low and tight. He longed to strip away that wretched cloth and explore with lips and hands all that she sought to withhold from him so desperately.

Across the chamber, Alana glanced around, searching for her chemise and bliaud. From the corner of her eye she saw that Merrick no longer faced the window. She spied her clothing lying at the foot of the bed. But just as she would have reached for them, a dark hand imperiously pushed hers aside and grabbed them up.

Alana bristled. "What is this, Norman! Would you steal the very clothes from my back?"

He strode to the hearth. As if he heard nary a word, he tossed the handful of cloth into the fire. There was a pop and a hiss. Flames licked high and bright.

She gasped. "What is this? Are you mad? You burned my home. My possessions. And now you burn my clothes!"

"Saxon," he said calmly. "You are mine now. I will provide for you."

"Provide for me?" She cried her outrage. "I have naught else to wear and you know it!"

He didn't answer. Instead he went to the chair near the hearth. There he picked up a neatly folded pile that she hadn't before noticed.

She eyed him warily as he retraced his steps. "I believe you'll find these more than adequate, Saxon." One by one he displayed the articles. Alana couldn't help but stare. There was a chemise, a bliaud of dark forest green, even a pair of soft doeskin slippers.

"'Tis up to you, of course," Merrick continued. "Indeed, I harbor no objection if you choose to remain in your present state." Alana flushed as he raked her scantily clad figure from head to toe. "I find your form quite lovely, indeed, Saxon."

Alana swallowed and tore her attention from his face. Unbidden, one hand stole out to finger the chemise. It was spun of delicate cloth, finer than any she'd seen in all her days. She was completely unaware her features betrayed a wistful longing.

Her expression didn't escape Merrick. "Well, Saxon? I had thought these would meet with your approval. Was I wrong?"

Alana bit her lip. "Sybil told me most of her belongings were taken from her," she said slowly, her tone very low. "If these are hers—"

"They are not, Saxon. They are my sister Genevieve's. I brought with me some of her possessions from Normandy. Rest assured, she has no need of them." His eyes glinted. She sensed he expected her to argue.

But all at once that was the last thing on Alana's mind. When Merrick resumed his post near the window, she hurriedly slipped the chemise over her head. It was all she could do to hold back an exclamation of delight—

never had she felt anything so smooth and delicate! The bliaud came next. She had no girdle to tie at her hips, but she cared not. With her hands she smoothed the soft, thick folds. The slippers came last. Alana wiggled her toes in delight, for they were a perfect fit.

But when she looked up, a jolt went through her. Merrick stepped before her. Eyes like a sword's point slashed over her, leaving no detail of her appearance uninspected. To her shock and dismay he took her hand and brought it to his lips.

"Why, Saxon" —he smiled, his gaze never leaving hers "—you are truly a vision. Your beauty would surely vie with any—even the fairest in the land."

Alana flushed and tried to tug her hand free. His grip merely tightened. He brought her close, so close she felt trapped by his nearness, surrounded by his strength and masculinity. Her pulse raced madly. Her heartbeat quickened.

She swallowed. "Release me," she said.

He shook his head. "Nay, Saxon. Nay, for I do believe a token of your gratitude is due."

Her gaze, wide and distressed, fixed upon his rugged features. "For what?" She could scarcely force the sound past the dryness in her throat.

"Why, what else? The gown."

"The gown is your sister's, not yours," she said quickly. But her fingers, trapped securely within his, were suddenly icy cold.

"Ah, but 'tis through my generosity that you wear it. Reward my efforts."

All at once she felt ill at ease and very much the imposter dressed in such finery. After all, she was no lady. Indeed, she had no finely jeweled girdle circling her hips, nor even a wimple. Her hair tumbled over her shoulders and down her back, thick and unrestrained. No doubt his sister was very much a lady, she thought, an odd pain knotting her breast. He ridiculed her most cruelly!

Hot tears appeared without her knowing it. Her breath caught, and so did her voice. "You—you play with me, Norman."

His hands were on her shoulders now, searing her with their warmth. "Then let us play no longer," he whispered.

She made one curt, abortive movement— alas, in vain! She was caught fast within his binding hold. She had no time to twist away, nor even to think, before his mouth came down on hers.

But this was not the bruising assault she had last endured at his hands. There in her cottage he had been ruthlessly intent. Indeed, he had sought to punish, to possess her. Only now, now it was as if he sought to please instead.

His kiss was sweetness and magic, compellingly seductive. With naught but the pressure of his mouth, first here, then there, he stole the very breath from her lungs. Against all reason, all instinct, she felt herself weakening, drawn beneath his spell. His arms tightened around her. She was drawn so close she could feel the brand of his legs full and tight against her own, and all that lay between . . .

A flicker of fear shot through her, yet she could not summon the willpower to withdraw. She could only cling to him, as if she possessed no strength of her own. No *will* of her own.

From somewhere there was an odd drumming. The sound came as if from very far away. Someone was banging on the door, she realized in some dim, cobwebbed corner of her mind.

The sound came again, more demanding this time.

"My lord," a voice called.

Merrick broke away with a curse. Seconds later he wrenched the door open. One look at his thunderous expression and the soldier on the other side gave a hasty salute.

"My lord, there is a messenger belowstairs," he said quickly. "Your sister has safely made the crossing from Normandy and awaits your escort from London."

In the hall, Merrick belted his sword around his hip. From the narrow enclosure that led to the stairway, Alana saw his gaze sweep the length of the hall and back, as if searching for someone. Belatedly it occurred to her that she was the one for whom he searched. Though she tried to retreat back into the shadows, he spied her there. All too soon he stopped before her.

"I would have your word, Saxon, that you will be here upon my return."

Alana was proud of the way she faced him unflinchingly. "Would it truly matter if I were not?" she asked daringly.

His handsome features grew taut. "Aye," he stated, and she knew from the coldness of his tone that she had stirred his fury, "it would. I am your lord and conqueror, Saxon—your *Norman* conqueror. You will do as I say."

More than anything, Alana yearned to slap the bronzed plane of his cheek. If only she had the courage, she thought bitterly.

Within minutes he was riding off. Alana didn't linger to witness his departure.

In truth, she was heartily grateful that he was gone. She couldn't help it, for she shuddered to think what might have happened if not for the interruption. God in heaven, she knew not what had come over her. The sweetness of his kiss had caught her unaware. She had been perilously close to yielding to something she didn't fully understand. She knew only that to do so was to give in to *him*.

But now she would be wary. Now she would be on guard against it . . . against him.

She discovered the next morning that Merrick had given orders that a high wooden palisade be constructed around the keep. Radburn was one of those who had been chosen to help. Alana saw him one day; the chains around his wrists and ankles were gone. Though she was vastly relieved, her lip tightened as she overheard some of Merrick's men discuss his plans; it was apparently his intent to turn Brynwald into a veritable stronghold. Alana's emotions simmered and churned. The Saxons had possessed no enemies until the Normans. Until *him*. Her lips compressed. One could expect naught else but the vile Norman way . . . for he was but a vile Norman!

So it was that she had no trouble willing her mind from him whene'er it chanced to stray—a pity it displayed the annoying tendency to do so in a most persistent fashion!

The time passed more quickly than she expected, though she'd never been one to keep herself idle. She was almost certain that some vile poison had caused Simon's illness, but the morning of Merrick's departure she was amazed at how much better the boy was, though he was still obviously weak. Though he grumbled long and heartily, Alana insisted he stay abed. But on the following day the boy protested his confinement and arose to resume his duties. The morning after it was as if he'd never sickened at all.

In a blatant disregard of Merrick's orders, she resumed working in the kitchen and serving the table. At first, Sybil was tight-lipped and curt when she saw Alana's fine clothing. Though Alana had hardly forgotten the malicious words Sybil had flung at her, 'twas not in her nature to be spiteful in return, especially not to her sister. Nay, she would forgive her both now and then, for no one knew more than she how Sybil suffered. Thankfully it wasn't long before Sybil's manner began to thaw.

And indeed, she shared Sybil's distaste for serving Merrick's soldiers. Though some leered and jeered openly, others regarded her with dark suspicion. But none made a move to touch or fondle her, not even Raoul.

She was also glad of Merrick's absence for another reason. She knew he wouldn't have allowed her to visit Aubrey again, not after learning she'd intended to escape him. Though Aubrey was old, he'd always proclaimed he was well able to take care of himself. But his weariness when last she'd seen him concerned her. Alana couldn't help but worry anew.

Merrick or no Merrick, she would not be kept from seeing Aubery.

The opportunity arose early one morning, when Merrick had been gone nearly a sennight. Since she had no desire to appear his whore, she hadn't continued to sleep in his chamber. Instead she had taken a pallet next to Sybil off the hall with the other Saxons.

She awoke early. A predawn light filtered in through the shutters. Knowing that she could sleep no longer, Alana rose and wandered to the hall. There she stood at the edge of the wide arched doorway. Peering out into the early gray morn, she saw that the night watchman's chin was slumped upon his chest. He was asleep!

A glimmer of excitement gathered in the pit of her stomach. If she could sneak by him, there would be time to hurry to the village. Once she'd seen Aubrey and assured herself he was well, the whole of the keep would be awake and tending to their morning duties.

With the work on the palisade and so many others milling about, she should have no trouble sneaking back to the hall. With luck no one would even notice she was missing.

Minutes later she clasped her hands together as she stopped before Aubrey's hut—it had worked!

Aubrey, too, was already awake. His eyes lit up when she slipped inside his hut.

"Alana! Faith, girl, I wondered when I might see you again!"

She smiled shakily and embraced him. "I know," she whispered. "I won't be gone again so long, I promise."

She saw to his morning meal and stoked the fire. He appeared far better than when she'd left him last time, but he took exception to her inquiries into his health.

"Aye, I'm weary," he said with a glare. "Were your bones as ancient as mine, you would be, too, girl."

Such fire was more like the Aubrey she knew and loved so well. She left soon after, the burden on her heart a little lighter.

As she neared the keep, she lowered her vision. An eerie sensation prickled her spine. Was it her imagination, or did it seem much quieter than she expected? Her heartbeat set up a rapid tattoo. Dear God, she prayed that she'd not been missed, for Merrick would be furious if he should find out . . .

All at once there was a bloodcurdling scream.

"There she is!" someone shouted.

One of the women from the village screamed and thrust her child behind her.

"Aye, she's the one that did it!" bellowed another. "Who else would dare to do such a thing in God's house?"

Alana froze. They were all staring, she realized numbly. Staring at *her*.

Bemused, her gaze darted from one face to another and yet another. She saw not only fear, but anger, an anger she didn't understand.

"What?" she cried. "What do you mean? Why do you stare at me so?"

A burly Norman soldier planted himself squarely before her. "We are not fools, witch," he sneered. "We know what you did in the chapel!"

Alana swallowed a sickly fear, afraid of what she saw in him, what she sensed. "I've not been to the chapel! I've been to the village, to visit Aubrey!"

The soldier sneered. "So you would pretend you know nothing of how the chapel was desecrated, the holy altar ruined, statues of our Lord and his saints smashed to a thousand pieces?"

"Please, I beg of you! I-I have done nothing!"

A small crowd began to gather around. She could almost feel their hatred, as if it pulsed with a life all its own. Inside she began to shake.

"Ah, but we know what you did," someone shouted. "We know what you are, and you are a witch."

"She deserves to be punished!" another shouted. "She deserves to be whipped!"

"Aye, she deserves to be whipped," came the chant.

Someone grabbed her arm. She was whirled around so forcefully her head spun wildly. Then a hand at her back shoved her forward. She landed hard upon her hands and knees in the mud.

It happened so quickly she had no chance to prepare herself or to defend herself. She screamed as the first blow came. The bite of the lash cut cleanly through her clothing, stripping away the skin with shattering force. The second blow came, even more violent than the first. She bit her lip so fiercely she drew blood, for never had she felt such agony. The lash bit again and again. Alana crouched low, covering her head with her hands, praying it would end soon.

A hand in her hair pulled her head up. Dazed and half-numb with pain, she opened her eyes. Sybil's face swam in and out of focus. A malicious smile curled her lips, as if she hated her. A voice at her ear whispered, "Your gown is not so fine now, eh, sister?"

A blow came again. A low whimper broke from her lips. She couldn't help it. Blackness fringed the edge of her vision, threatening to engulf her.

"Bloody Christ! What goes on here?"

Pain and darkness surrounded her. She felt the thunder of footsteps, the presence of yet another. It came from a very great distance away, but she knew that voice of steel, that hand that swept across her shoulders.

She cried out, for pain sheared through her as she felt herself turned and caught up in strong arms. She gained but a fleeting glimpse of harshly relentless features, burning eyes, a mouth cast in grim lines. Just before she sank into a welcome world of oblivion, it spun through her mind that she had displeased him once more. Aye, and she'd been caught yet again by her lord and conqueror.

Her *Norman* lord and conqueror . . .

Chapter 10

Merrick and his sister Genevieve spent the night at Denham Abbey, but a few hours' ride away from Brynwald. Once a donation had been offered, the Norman guests had been assured a welcome—spartan though it was—and a place to stay for the night. Had he been alone, Merrick wouldn't have considered stopping. He would have continued on to Brynwald that very night. And though it was not Genevieve's way to complain, he knew she was tired, for he had set a breakneck pace from London these past days.

He hadn't lingered in London, though of course he'd been obliged to pay his respects to Duke William. And indeed, there was much to discuss. Merrick soon learned that Brynwald was hardly the only place where Saxon acceptance of Norman lord and law would take some time. William blustered and paced and raged, determined that England would remain his no matter what cost to the Saxons. Merrick had no doubt that the Normans would continue to reign, for indeed they already did. And Duke

William—and Normandy—would continue to stamp out whatever pockets of rebellion might crop up.

For indeed, in much the same way, Merrick felt just as possessive of Brynwald. Though William felt England was his by right of decree, Merrick had battled long and hard for the right to claim his own lands—to claim Brynwald. He would settle there in that vast fief by the sea, and it was there he would build his future.

Genevieve had chuckled at his haste to return to Brynwald, but he knew she was no less anxious to see her new home—and Simon, for he'd told her of the boy's illness. He'd hated to bear such tidings upon her arrival, for the twelvemonth since her husband Philippe had been killed had been long and difficult for her. He knew she still grieved, though she hid it well, just as she had hidden her dismay when Simon had announced his intention to remain with his uncle in England that he might hone his skills as a knight.

It was early when Merrick awoke, even before the lonely peal of a rusty bell summoned the inhabitants within the abbey to wakefulness. He quickly washed and donned his clothes, then woke Genevieve where she slept in the tiny cell across the hall. They attended mass with the monks and then were off, though dawn had yet to light the earth. Behind them one of his men drove a cart that carried her belongings.

The day was gray and cloudy, but the threat of rain did not materialize. It was early morn

when Brynwald first came into view. Atop a
small hillock, Merrick reached for the bridle of
Genevieve's mount, a small palfrey. His sister
glanced over at him questioningly.

He nodded off toward the north. "There is
Brynwald Keep." He said no more, but awaited
Genevieve's response.

In truth, he was eager to see her reaction. No
insignificant little fief was this. Three stories
high, the keep itself was huge by English
standards, and indeed by Norman as well.
High atop the bluff, with the sea at its back,
it rose tall and stark against turbulent gray
clouds. A natural fortress with a view of the
surrounding countryside, it needed but a few
relatively simple modifications—the palisade
for one—to fortify its defenses. Eventually he
would replace its timbered walls with stone,
but there was time for that later.

A feeling of pride, unbeknownst to him
before this, swelled his chest. Here he would
build his home and his future. The fief's lands
sprawled north and south and west. He longed
for the spring and summer, when the land
would run green far beyond the forest and
crops sprouted tall and fertile in the fields.
The Saxons might not accept him now, but
he was prepared to be lenient. Eventually all
would be as it was before. The land would
flourish and grow. He would prosper, and in
turn, the Saxons would prosper as well.

"Well, brother—" her voice carried a smile
"—I see why you were so anxious to return."

Merrick laughed, a rumble that came from

deep within his chest. It was a sound of both pleasure and immense satisfaction, for this was a feeling he'd never had before. This was his home. By God, *his home*.

It was inevitable, perhaps, that such a thought should take him straight to another . . .

Alana.

Would he find her here? There was a subtle hardening of his jaw. She had best have heeded his promise, for if she had fled, he would make certain she paid the price—and the price would be steep.

He frowned. 'Twas strange, how quickly he'd grown used to her, to the feel and scent of her. Indeed, he wasn't certain he liked it. Nay, indeed he was quite certain he did not . . .

He turned in the saddle and cocked a brow toward Genevieve. "Now that you've seen you will live in no hovel," he said dryly, "let us linger no longer."

Within minutes they approached the keep. He saw that the yard swarmed with Norman soldiers and Saxon villein alike. But all at once it struck him that something was not right. Just then there were shouts . . . and the unmistakable crack of a whip. It was then he saw a small form hunched over in the dirt.

"Bloody Christ! What goes on here?" The whip was jerked from the soldier's hand so fiercely the man stumbled and fell upon his back.

"She's a witch," the soldier cried. "Satan's pawn—"

Merrick whirled on him. "It's you who are Satan's pawn to do such a thing! Now get out of my sight and let me never see your face again or I will give you something to truly fear!" The crowd shrank back, frightened more by the fury reflected on their lord's features than by the girl they branded a witch.

Merrick dropped to one knee. Alana jerked as he reached out. Very carefully he gathered her in his arms. Her lashes fluttered open. She stared up at him vaguely, her eyes clouded over with pain. A low moan broke from her lips. She turned her face into his neck.

His arms tightened around his burden. As he strode into the keep and up the narrow stair, Genevieve was right at his heels.

"Who is she?" she panted, half-running as she sought to keep pace with him.

"She is Alana, the Saxon girl I told you about—Kerwain's bastard daughter." He took the last two stairs and headed toward his chamber. Seconds later he eased her onto the bed, careful to place her on her stomach.

Genevieve sucked in a sharp breath. Beneath the girl's tattered clothing, her lower back was raw and oozing. Quickly she gathered hold of herself. "Water," she commanded. "I must have warm water and clean cloths. And there is a healing salve in my chest. I will need it."

Even as she finished her command, Merrick was at the door, shouting for a servant. He didn't move until all she requested had been delivered.

At the bedside, Genevieve had already care-

fully slipped off Alana's clothing. She had discreetly tugged the linen sheet over her hips,
but her back and shoulders were bare to his
gaze. Merrick went pale as he glimpsed the
bloodied, swollen stripes left on her flesh by
the vicious lash. "Jesu," he breathed.

Genevieve glanced at him sharply. "If she is
well tended," she stated softly, "she will not
scar."

Merrick said nothing but remained near the
head of the bed, a silent sentinel.

Her hands quick and efficient, Genevieve
set to work cleansing the torn flesh. "Why is
this girl called witch?" she asked softly.

"She has dreams. Visions which oft come
true."

He dragged forward a low bench and sat.
With his fingertips he brushed a golden tangle of hair from her temple. Reaching for a
cloth, he wiped the dirt from her face. Her
eyes opened. For a heartbeat she stared at him
dazedly, then recognition dawned. She flung
out a hand.

"Nay . . . Not you . . ." Her cry was but a
feeble plea. "I don't want you to see me . . . not
you . . . not like this." Her lids closed. She slid
mercifully back into the realm of unconscious-
ness.

Merrick's jaw clenched hard but he remained
where he was, intent on his task. Soon Alana
woke yet again and cried out when she saw
Merrick.

Genevieve sighed and straightened. "It

would seem she has no liking for you, Merrick."

His voice was clipped and abrupt. "She is in pain. She knows not what she speaks."

A slender brow arched high. "Indeed," she said coolly. "Why, I could swear she knew what she said—and who she saw—quite clearly." Hands on her hips, she flicked her cloth toward him. "Away with you now, brother. Your presence disturbs her, and since I have no need of your assistance, I suggest you make yourself scarce."

Merrick's expression grew dark. "This is my chamber, sister."

Genevieve was undaunted. "Then I suggest you find yourself another," she snapped, "for you'll not be sleeping here this night. And you may as well know now, she'll be in no condition for the likes of you for many a night."

She matched his stare fearlessly, then bestowed upon him one last glare before turning back to her patient. Though Genevieve was a lady born and bred, she was scarcely ignorant of the ways of men. And she was well aware her brother possessed the same masculine urges as any other lusty male. And indeed, 'twas easy to see why Merrick so desired this one. Peasant or no, bastard or no, witch or no, Alana of Brynwald possessed a rare, golden beauty few men could ignore.

Merrick was vastly annoyed at being so dismissed, but he decided this was no time to argue. But neither did he leave, though he knew Alana was in capable hands. Instead he retreated to stand before the fire, his expression fierce as he watched his sister work over Alana.

Alana remembered little of the days that followed. She floated in and out of consciousness. In her dreamworld she was certain she had died and was now being punished, for her back burned like the fires of Hell.

But there came a time when she awoke to discover her mind was no longer fuzzy. There was still the faintest twinge of hurt as she shifted to her side, but the pain was nearly gone.

Nor was she alone. A well-dressed, small-boned woman stood before the fire, warming her hands. Beneath the snowy white of her wimple, dark hair gleamed like the wings of a raven. She turned ever so slightly, and Alana was afforded a glimpse of her face. Above full, red lips, her nose was small and straight. Her brows were slender and feminine yet bore a familiar arch.

"You are his sister," she blurted before she even realized what she was about to say. "You are Genevieve."

The woman turned, clearly startled. Then she smiled, revealing a row of small, even teeth. "And you, I am told, are Alana. I must say, 'tis good that you are finally awake."

Alana said nothing, but half-rose on an elbow.

"Would you like something to drink?"

Alana bit her lip, then nodded. Her gaze never left the other woman as she poured water from a pitcher into a small goblet. If she were wary, she couldn't help it. After all, this was Merrick's sister! And if she were at all like her brother . . .

Genevieve slipped an arm around her shoulders, helping her to rise. Alana had already discovered she'd been clad in a gown of soft linen. Genevieve's, she wondered? She drank deeply for her throat was indeed parched. When Genevieve turned away to replace the goblet on a tray, she fell back against the pillows, amazed and dismayed at how weak she was.

Genevieve smiled slightly. "No doubt you are weak from lack of food. Indeed, you must be ravenous." She didn't wait for Alana's response. She strode briskly to the doors, where she spoke in low tones to someone just outside.

Alana tried not to stare. She guessed that Genevieve was a trifle older than Merrick, though she suspected not many years separated them. Her eyes were the same clear blue, yet they were warm, not icy cold as Merrick's.

Genevieve returned to the bedside. "If you don't mind, I'd like to have a look at your wounds."

Alana's eyes flew wide. "Oh, there is no need," she said quickly. "I feel quite recovered."

Genevieve shook her head. Her tone held a mild reproof. "There is no need to be embarrassed, truly. I am the one who has tended you these past days."

Alana clutched the furs to her breast. Though she told herself such modesty was foolish, she couldn't help it. Slowly she lowered them and rolled to her stomach. Turning her face aside, she felt Genevieve step close. Her hands were immeasurably careful as she folded her bedgown up to bare her lower back. After cleaning her flesh with warm water, she rubbed a healing salve into her skin.

Alana held her breath, though her discomfort was minimal. Bits and pieces of these last days flashed into her brain. It came to her then, that her memory was not only of this woman with the gentle hands and soothing voice. Another memory welled, of another hand, a hand that possessed far more strength yet was no less gentle.

Her stomach gave an odd little flutter. Merrick, she realized. Merrick had been with her, too. Indeed, it was he who had carried her here. Dimly she recalled him bending over her. There had been something in his voice she'd not heard before. Fear? Surely not. Concern? Never!

At last Genevieve was finished. By then a tray of food had arrived. Genevieve shook out a linen cloth and laid it on her lap.

"Merrick must be very angry with me," Alana murmured.

"Angry?" Genevieve passed her a steaming bowl of fragrant stew and a wooden spoon. "Why, he scarcely left this chamber—and your bedside—though I found his presence most annoying." Genevieve withheld a smile at her startled expression. "And alas," she added lightly, " 'twould seem that you did as well. You cried out that you did not want him to see you."

Alana trembled inwardly. Now surely *that* had made him angry.

"But my brother is a most stubborn man. Why, I feared he would surely refuse when Duke William's messenger arrived requesting his presence in London once more. He was most concerned for your health, you know. Indeed, I believe he left only because I assured him you were in no danger."

Alana lowered her gaze. Genevieve was mistaken. Surely it was so. Why, Merrick despised her as surely as she despised him! "He has gone again to London?" Sweet heaven, what on earth was wrong with her? She sounded almost disappointed.

Genevieve nodded.

Alana wet her lips. "Why aren't you afraid of me?" she asked quietly. "The others—they think I am a witch, both your people and mine."

"You are no more a witch than I." Genevieve was adamant.

Alana was puzzled. "But I am a Saxon."

"And I am Norman," the other woman stated evenly. "Do you hate me for what I am? For where I was born?"

Alana was unprepared for such bluntness. She shook her head, yet she could be no less than honest with this woman. "I hate what the Normans have done. I hate what your brother has done. And yet—" She spoke haltingly.

"You had no part in what happened here." She paused. "No," she said slowly. "I do not hate you, Genevieve of Normandy."

Genevieve was pleased with her answer. Alana knew it from the way the woman smiled suddenly, the way her eyes warmed to deepest blue. Alana decided in that instant that this woman possessed a beauty not only of the flesh, but of the spirit as well.

"I, too, see no reason why we should be enemies. Indeed, I should hate that, for without you my son might not be alive." Genevieve spoke softly. "Sometimes I hate that Simon chose to be a knight like his father and uncles. But I know he will not heed the call of the Church."

A wistful sadness flitted across her lovely features. She sighed. "So while men go off to war, women are left to tend home and hearth, and I truly believe all women are kindred in the hopes and fears they share. The love they bear for their men is ever constant. But men— ah, now their allegiances are ever changing. But that's enough of men. You must eat, Alana," she went on, suddenly crisp. "For you must gather your strength."

Alana did as Genevieve bade her. Not until she'd finished did she realize how famished she'd been. Genevieve took the bowl from her with an approving nod. Alana yawned, suddenly weary beyond measure.

"Pray forgive me," she murmured with an apologetic smile. "I do not mean to be rude, truly—"

"Oh, you need not apologize." Genevieve was already drawing up the fur beneath her chin. "Sleep is the body's way of healing itself and fighting pain."

Alana glanced at her oddly. "How odd you should say that," she said slowly. "For my mother used to say the very same."

"Well, then, I do believe your mother and I would have gotten along quite well—as well as you and I shall." She squeezed Alana's fingers then left her alone.

Tired though she was, it was a while before Alana slept. Genevieve was not what she'd expected, though in truth she knew not precisely what she'd expected of Merrick's sister. She couldn't help but respond to the woman's calm serenity. Indeed, her mother had possessed much the same manner, and 'twas that which had allowed her mother to gain the trust of those she treated. Oddly, Alana felt a curious kinship with Genevieve that she had yet to experience with Sybil. The notion made her feel guilty, yet she found she couldn't help it.

It was the next day before Genevieve pronounced her fit enough to dress and walk about the keep. "We need a chemise and bliaud," she said briskly. "Where might I find them?"

Alana flushed. "Merrick burned them," she admitted, feeling supremely awkward. She had the uneasy sensation Genevieve already knew of her relationship with Merrick, though she had said nothing. "He gave me clothing of yours to wear, but I'm afraid it was ruined when . . . " She stopped. There was no need to say more.

"Well, no matter. I'll fetch another for you. I have many that I've not worn for years. And indeed, I've already given several to your sister. I admit, I was ashamed when she told me how her clothing and all her possessions had been sacked."

"Sybil?" Alana glanced up in surprise.

"Yes. Merrick took her from the kitchens to act as my maid." She smiled as if to say, *You see? He can be generous after all.*

Alana was hardly convinced. She could not say what motivated him, but most likely, 'twas hardly generosity. He'd led her to believe he might very well keep Sybil in the kitchens forever—no doubt he'd wanted to see her beg! But she was glad for Sybil. Her own fate might well hang in limbo, but at least Sybil's plight was not so bad as it had been.

The smile she managed was frugal, and solely for Genevieve's benefit. "Thank you," she murmured. "I vow I shall find some way to repay you—"

She wasn't allowed to finish. Genevieve reached for her hands. "Say no more, Alana! I owe you my son's life, and that is a debt *I* cannot repay."

She kept to her chamber those first few days. Those infrequent times she had ventured beyond the security of her chamber, Genevieve had been with her. Though no one said a word, there were many who stopped and stared—both Norman and Saxon—their gazes rife with glaring condemnation

But one afternoon she was seized by the compulsion to see for herself what they all believed her guilty of. She gave a sigh of relief that the chapel was unoccupied. Had she encountered Father Edgar, she would surely never have summoned the nerve to speak, or even look at him. She walked to the center of the nave, then stopped.

Her gaze swept wide. Her insides began to churn. On the spot where the tall stone sculpture of Christ had extended his hands to his people, naught remained but a grotesque stump. The statue of the Blessed Virgin had no head. The very sight was enough to turn her stomach.

A rustle nearby alerted her to another presence. She whirled to find Sybil just stepping up behind her.

"Sybil! Praise God 'tis only you." She reached out and embraced her. "I am so glad to see you!"

Sybil smiled slightly. Her eyes flickered over her. "And I you, Alana."

Alana smiled. "Genevieve told me you are her maid now. I am so glad that you are finally out of the kitchens!"

Sybil's full lips twisted. "I but toil in a different way, sister."

Alana's smile wavered. "Anything is better than serving the Normans. And surely Genevieve treats you far better."

Sybil shrugged. "Well enough, I suppose."

Alana frowned. She could not conceive of Genevieve being anything other than what she'd found her to be, a warm, caring woman of kindness and compassion.

Sybil gazed at her curiously. "I must confess, Alana, I am surprised to find you here. I should have thought this would be the last place you would come."

Alana bit her lip. "I—I had to see for myself," she said, her tone very low.

Sybil waved a hand. "Merrick was furious when he saw all that was done. God above, but the walls fairly trembled with his rage! Of course I assured him you could never have done such a thing and begged that he be lenient with you. 'She's been punished enough,' I told him."

Alana's hands knotted in her skirts. All at once she wished she had stayed in her chamber. But Sybil seemed oblivious to her distress.

"Oh, Alana, but you should have seen it! Soot blackened the columns near the bell tower. There was mud and dirt and dung everywhere. The floor. Even the walls. Why, never in all my days have I seen such filth—and in God's house yet!"

A sick sensation knotted Alana's belly. She needed little help to conjure up all Sybil had described. What madness, she wondered, had wrought such evil? Indeed, what wretched soul would dare to brave the wrath of God . . .

And Merrick, too.

She shook her head. "I cannot think who would do such a thing."

"Nor can I." Sybil sighed. "I had best leave you, sister. Genevieve will be wondering where I've gone off to." She patted Alana's shoulder and was gone.

Alana remained where she was, still as stone, her mind turning.

Sybil said Merrick had been furious. That she did not doubt. She shivered, for she could not help but wonder what would happen when he returned. She had been so relieved that he was gone and she didn't have to face him, for she dreaded the prospect with all her heart—and aye, now more than ever!

Did he truly believe her capable of such sacrilege? Her heart cried out, for she was not evil. She was not a witch! She feared the Lord as any other—as every other!

It came to her then . . . The air of tranquility that should have dwelled here had been violated. A curious tension descended. An eerie chill swept over her, a chill that swept to the very depth of her being. Something had indeed been here . . . Something evil . . .

She turned and ran as if she'd been caught in the midst of a wild tempest. Her legs did not stop until she ran through the door of Merrick's chamber. She slammed the portal closed, then leaned against it to catch her breath.

An eerie prickling ran up her spine.

It seemed she was not alone.

So much for the sanctuary she sought. For indeed, the very person she dreaded most in all the world stood across from her.

Alana felt as if her stomach had dropped clear to the floor and beyond. He had just unbuckled his sword belt and set it aside. Though he no longer wore the trappings of war, the aura of power and might that surrounded him was as potent as ever.

He surveyed her from head to toe. "You look well, Saxon."

Alana flushed and lowered her eyes. "I am," she murmured.

She felt his gaze upon her but could not summon the will to meet it. The silence was never-ending.

"I was most eager to return, Saxon. Why do I sense you are hardly as anxious to see me?"

Because I am not, she almost blurted. She swallowed, desperately seeking the strength to be brave.

He made an impatient sound. "Come now, Saxon. Will you not bid your lord a proper welcome?"

Her curtsy was made clumsily. She was shaking so badly she was certain she would never rise again. Breathlessly she said, "I-I would thank you for—for keeping your word and allowing Sybil to serve as maid to your sister."

He said nothing for the longest time. When at last he spoke, his words were not what she expected. "Where were you just now, Saxon?"

Reluctantly she raised her chin. His countenance was not so very grim, yet neither did he smile. She could not lie, she realized. She *dared* not lie.

With the tip of her tongue she moistened her lips. "I was . . . in the chapel."

"In the chapel. For what purpose?"

His regard was unwavering, but alas, her courage was not. "To—to see the atrocity that was done there. To see . . . why I was whipped."

He raised a brow. "I see. You did not know what was done there?"

His words were naught but a trick, she realized. "Nay!" she cried. "Indeed, I was not even aware of it until I returned that morn—"

"Returned? From where?"

Stricken, Alana stared at him. He knew. By the Cross, *he knew.*

"I would ask you again, Saxon. Where were you that morn if not here?"

His features were hard as stone, his voice harder still. Oh, but she would almost prefer to be whipped than bear the sting of his damning glare.

He expected her to lie. Somehow she knew it, but she would not give him the satisfaction. "I went to see Aubrey. Because he is old and has no one to care for him—"

He crossed his arms over his chest, his tone as unyielding as his posture. "I have continued to send one of my men with food most every day, Saxon. So do not dare to accuse me of—"

"I accuse you of nothing! But I must see it with my own eyes! Oh, I do not expect you to understand, but he is dear to my heart. I would know only that he is alive and well!"

Though his jaw tightened, he did not argue further. "And you know nothing of what happened in the chapel?"

She shook her head. "That is why I went there. To see for myself."

Merrick's eyes narrowed. "Then why did you look like a frightened hare when you returned just now? Was someone there? What did you see?"

His voice rapped out sharply. Alana shook her head, her gaze wide. "I-I saw nothing. And there was no one there but Sybil."

"Then why were you running?"

Her lips parted. "I-I do not know." She dared not tell him what she had sensed. He might think it but more proof she was a witch.

His lips, she saw, had twisted into a faint smile. "You wound me, Saxon," he murmured. "I thought mayhap you were running because you knew I had returned. Because you were eager to be alone with me."

Alana's cheeks deepened to the color of the dawn. He crossed to stand directly before her, so close she could see naught but the breadth of his chest. She swallowed, praying he wouldn't see her dismay. "You are mistaken, Norman."

Her body stiffened as he lowered his head. He touched her nowhere yet his mouth hovered but a breath above her own.

"Ah, so quickly I forget, Saxon. You find me repulsive, do you not? Oh, you claim you detest me so very thoroughly. But I'm given to wonder why I have only to kiss you to feel your body melt close to mine, to feel your heart beat wild and swift against my own."

Desperation filled her chest. "You have no heart, Norman, else you would not do this to me. I am not such a fool that I don't know what you would do. But this is naught but a way to punish me!"

His hands came down on her shoulders, disturbingly warm, disturbingly strong. And all at once it was true—the beat of her heart was wild and frenzied.

She gave a faint, choked cry. "No—"

He caught her full and tight against him. "Yes, Saxon." His whisper was as fierce as hers was tremulous. "*Yes.*"

His mouth came down on hers, hungry and devouring. She could feel the demand in his kiss, in the arms that swept tight around her back. Within but a heartbeat her bliaud lay pooled around her feet. She stood before him clad only in her chemise, so soft and sheer she might well have been naked.

She scarcely knew when he lifted his head and ripped his tunic over it in one fluid move. Her heart jumped at the sight of his chest, wide and awesome. Then once again she felt the stroke of his eyes on her body as surely as the stroke of his hand.

She wrapped her arms around her chest in an attempt to hide her body from his view. She turned her face aside for she knew he looked his fill.

A burning ache stung the back of her throat,
even as hot tears stung her eyes. He would do
as he wanted . . . whatever he wanted.

"Look at me, Saxon."

Alana did not. She *could* not. Instead she
bowed her head low.

Merrick's jaw clenched. Her shoulders were
heaving. She was crying, he noted furiously,
though she made not a sound.

A vile oath blistered the air. Hard fingers caught at her chin. She cringed visibly, her skin pale as cream. Her eyes were
huge and wounded and pleading, shimmering
with tears.

He almost hated her in that moment. Some
dark, seething emotion seized hold of him.

"By the Cross, Saxon, I have done nothing to
you that you should cower from me and weep!
Have I hurt you? Abused you? Harmed you in
any way?"

Alana shook her head. The muscles in her
throat worked convulsively, but she could neither move nor speak.

"I have given you a far better home than
your father," he said harshly. "I have fed you
far better. Given you a far warmer place to eat
and sleep. I bid my own sister tend you as
she would have her own son! You have come
to no harm at my hand. Why then do you
deny me?"

Alana curled her fingers into her palms. She
had the awful sensation that were she to make
but a single sound, the tears would fall and
never stop.

Something snapped within him. He dragged her chin up. "Answer me, Saxon! Why do you deny me?"

"I-I do not deny you." The breath she drew was deep and shuddering, the words torn from deep in her breast.

"Oh, but you do! Not with words or deed, but with this!" He swiped his thumb across her cheek. It came away damp with her tears.

Still she stood before him, trembling as if she were ill with fever. But there was something in her pose, a flash of hurt vulnerability. 'Twas then that the strangest notion flitted through his mind.

His fingers tightened on her chin. "How many men have you lain with, Saxon?"

Her voice was low and halting. "None but you have seen me . . . naked. None but you have t—touched me. I've lain with no man. No man . . . but you."

"Ah, but you've not lain with m—"

Merrick stopped. His jaw locked. He stared down at her as if he sought to see to her very soul. Nay, he thought. Surely it could not be. Surely not . . .

"God's wounds," he said tautly. "Never tell me you are a maid!"

She did not. Yet neither did she deny it.

His hands descended to her shoulders. "Answer me, Saxon. Are you?" He gave her a little shake. "Are you a virgin?"

"Aye," she said weakly. Her breath caught on a jagged half-sob. "Aye!" she said again and turned her face aside.

Sheer fury splintered through him. He dared not take her, not now, for then he would truly be the monster she believed. He was too angry, too full of resentment. Oh, not because she was a virgin. But because she cringed from him. Because her fear lay vivid in her eyes and she could not hide it. Because she looked at him as if she were utterly broken and defeated. Because she believed he was naught but a heartless beast who would use her without care. Without thought or feeling.

He released her, then snatched up his tunic from the floor. When he turned back to her, his eyes were burning.

"This changes nothing," he said fiercely. "Nothing, do you hear? You will be mine . . . as Brynwald is mine." He turned and strode from the chamber.

Alana sank down in a heap and collapsed into tears.

Chapter 11

❧

The day was endless, the night ever more so.

Alana longed for the sanctity of a place where she need never see anyone again. She had no desire to face the others. She still hadn't forgotten how they had condemned her, both Norman and Saxon alike.

You fool no one, whispered a voice in her mind. *'Twas him she had no desire to see again—Merrick.*

The hours passed in miserable dread, yet she yearned to reclaim them. Indeed, she had no doubt that the night would bring far worse . . .

Oddly, it was Genevieve who came to her rescue. She insisted that Alana come to table. But once there, she seated Alana between herself and Sybil. Merrick was already seated at the trestled table nearest the hearth. Alana braved but a single anxious glance his way. After that she dared no further, for she felt his gaze upon her like a brand of fire.

She ate and drank, she knew not what.

She spoke when prodded, though in the next breath she could have scarcely recalled what words passed from her lips. Rough male laughter rose and fell all around. Beside her, Genevieve was sweet and charming. Sybil smiled and talked and tossed her head, as if she were still indeed the lady of the manor.

Before long Genevieve excused herself. Alana was faintly troubled as she watched the woman glide smoothly across the rush-covered floor toward the bench where her brother sat, a strongly muscled leg thrust out arrogantly before him. Yet, save for the absurd notion of approaching Merrick's table herself, Alana had no way of determining what would pass between the siblings.

Across the room, with a graceful swirl, Genevieve eased down beside her brother. She leaned close. "I thought, brother, that you were anxious to return here simply because of your new home and lands. 'Twould appear I was wrong, for I do wonder about you and the Saxon girl Alana. You look at her. She looks away."

Genevieve did not doubt the truth of all she spoke. Since the instant Alana had entered the hall, Merrick's eyes had scarcely left her. His gaze was for her alone. Indeed, Genevieve decided with satisfaction, she strongly suspected Merrick had taken no other maid to his bed from the day he'd captured Brynwald.

Now he smiled at her thinly. "I would remind you I am hardly the first man to take a peasant to his bed."

Genevieve studied him. Regardless of the circumstances of Alana's birth, she was not just another lowly peasant—not in Merrick's eyes, and not in her own. Perchance Merrick was not yet fully aware of it, but in time he would be. Oh, yes, in time . . .

"Ah," she said smoothly. "But you have not taken her to your bed, have you, brother?"

Merrick nearly choked on a mouthful of ale. Smothering a curse, he lowered his horn and bestowed on her a blistering glance.

"You meddle where you should not, Genevieve."

She laughed. "Never, brother."

"Always, sister."

She laid her fingertips on his sleeve. "A word of advice, brother. Do not frighten her."

His glare burned hotter. "Frighten her! Why, I have shown the wench every care! And the same can hardly be said of her!"

Genevieve's eyes darkened. "Merrick, please. I do not speak in jest. If Alana is a maid then you must have a care—"

"I do know how 'tis done, sister! And long before you, I vow."

At this Genevieve flushed. She'd heard tales of his lusty pursuits throughout the years. "That I don't doubt." She paused, then said slowly, "Nonetheless, I pray that you will listen and heed me. For if she fears the first time, and it meets her dreaded expectations, she will fear *every* time."

He made no effort to shield the bite in his

tone. "I've had no complaints, Genevieve."

Her gaze was anxious. "But no doubt you've taken no maids to your bed. You must be gentle. You must be tender."

He scowled. "You trespass where you dare not, Genevieve! Tend to your business and I will tend to mine."

Genevieve's eyes were snapping but her tone was sweet. If he would be so blunt, then so would she! "'Tis not for my sake or even yours that I offer advice, Merrick. 'Tis for Alana, for she deserves better than to be tumbled like a common wench who will spread her legs for any and all."

From across the room, Alana gazed at the pair. Sybil had gone off with Raoul several minutes earlier. Now, Merrick drew her gaze though she willed it not, though she wanted it not! Her heart trembled as she thought of all that had passed between them; of all that was yet to come, for she was achingly aware there would be no salvation from this night. Little wonder that she was nervous. Uneasy. Sweet heaven, she was terrified!

She didn't want him to touch her, to command her. Yet she knew he would do both, for it was just as he'd once said. He was her lord and conqueror.

And she was his . . . His to command. His to possess.

Yet all within her was in turmoil. As much as she despised his control, she could not deny that never had he accused her of being a witch.

Nor had he condemned her. Nay, he had not scorned her, not for being different. For defying him, yes, but not for being different. Her heart twisted. If only he hadn't been so angry when he'd left her! The very air had seemed to thunder and pulse with his rage.

And now, again he stared at her in that piercing way he had, his jaw hewn in stone. It was as if he stripped her down to her very bones, down to her heart and soul.

There was a gentle touch on her shoulder. She glanced up, startled, as Genevieve sat down beside her.

The other woman tipped her head to the side. "Do you never smile, Alana?"

Alana could not help it. Her gaze veered straight to Merrick. Their eyes clashed endlessly, hers dark and uncertain, his steady and dauntless.

Genevieve touched her hand. "He is truly not an ogre, you know."

Alana thought of his hands, so lean and strong. The thought progressed further. She envisioned that hand on her body, ruthlessly thrusting her thighs apart that he might have his way . . .

She plucked at a fold in her skirt. "Methinks you see a different side of him than I have seen." Her tone was very low.

Genevieve smiled slightly. " 'Tis true he has little patience for those who cross him. 'Tis a trait common among men, I fear."

Alana bit her lip. "He claims I try him as no other."

Genevieve laughed, a genuine sound of merriment. "He says the very same to me, for I am very forthright. And many times Merrick dislikes it heartily." She paused. "He is not a cruel man, Alana. In battle a knight does what he must to save his life and the lives of his men. But Merrick is a man who tempers his strength. He would never crush those weaker than he."

Alana's reply was swift and unrepenting. "He crushed my father. He crushed those who opposed him here at Brynwald."

Genevieve's smile faded. " 'Twas battle, Alana, not slaughter. Had you seen men and women and children slain without cause or mercy, you would know the difference."

Alana's gaze sharpened, for there was something in her tone . . . "What?" she said faintly. "You have seen such a thing?"

"My husband Philippe was killed in just such a manner," Genevieve said quietly. "We lived in a place called Marnierre, very near Brittany. A count nearby coveted Philippe's lands. He entered our castle by trickery. And when darkness fell, his men stormed the walls and murdered all those within."

Alana frowned. "But you and Simon were spared—"

She shook her head. "Simon and I were at my father's castle in d'Aville. Had we been at Marnierre we would not have been spared." She shuddered. "Never will I forget returning home to find such butchery. Never."

Alana's heart went out to her. Genevieve was too young, too beautiful to have known such heartache. "What happened then?" she asked quietly.

She sighed. "My father and my brothers would not let Philippe's death go unavenged. They reclaimed Marnierre"— a wistful sadness entered her eyes —"but 'twas so different without Philippe! I—I found I could stay no longer. My brother Henri now holds Marnierre for Simon. When Simon is old enough to defend the lands and castle, Marnierre will be his."

All at once Alana understood. Genevieve had come here to flee old memories that haunted her still. She was suddenly just as certain Genevieve still mourned her dead husband Philippe.

Alana knew not what to say, yet she felt foolish to not speak words of comfort. Gently she touched her hand. "I-I am sorry," she said softly. "I did not know."

Genevieve smiled slightly. "Of course you didn't. How could you?"

Before long, Genevieve announced her intention to retire. Alana rose as well. Sybil was nowhere in sight, and she was reluctant to remain in the hall alone.

Across the way, Merrick's gaze was dark and brooding as it touched upon Alana. He had kept his distance from her, unwilling to test either his temper or his patience. She made him feel the beast. He found it vastly irritating she had managed to convince herself that he was little more than some foul creature dredged from the bowels of the earth.

He hadn't wanted to go to William. But one did not spurn the summons of the man who would be king. And so he'd worried about her by day, and dreamed of her by the dark of the moon . . . He chided himself scathingly. Ah, but he'd played the role of fool only too well!

In truth, he did not understand his fascination with this barefoot wench. She was haughty as a queen one minute, vulnerable as a child the next. But what he'd told Genevieve was true—he'd shown her a care he'd shown no other. He had bided his time. He'd thought to give her time to grow used to him, to his touch. Time to accept him, to accept what would happen.

His eyes tracked her progress as she mounted the stair beside Genevieve. His fingers tightened on his horn of ale. A part of him was still stunned that she was a maid. Yet mayhap 'twas not so odd after all. Indeed, if the villagers thought her a witch, perhaps they'd been afraid to touch her. Or mayhap 'twas because of her father's position. From what he had gleaned, Kerwain had readily claimed her as sprung from his seed.

Only now did he consider the implications of his startling discovery. *She was a virgin*. No man had touched her, save him. A surge of hot possessiveness shot through him, even as a slow burn ignited in his blood. It pleased him that she was a maid, he realized suddenly. Indeed, he thought derisively, there was little about the wench that did not please him . . . save her adder's tongue.

So what was he to do? Woo her? Her pride challenged him. Her beauty beckoned him. Was he to wait still longer to bed her? All that was male and primeval within him clamored against it. If he waited, the vixen would ever fight him, ever defy him!

It was then he spied the glow of slanted golden eyes beneath the bench where Alana had sat—her cat Cedric! Faith, but the wretched creature tormented him, even as his mistress tormented him! He shot to his feet. But already the animal was on his feet, arching his scrawny back. With a hiss and a yowl, the creature leaped away. An instant later, he was gone from sight.

Scowling blackly, Merrick started across the floor. Now that he was on his feet, his mind was made up, his choice made. By God, he would wait no longer.

He would have her . . . and he would have her now.

Abovestairs, Alana paced the length of the chamber and back, too nervous to sit any longer. Oh, but she'd have liked to bar the door against him—if only she dared! But alas, he came, and all too soon. Even before she heard the creak of the door, she was warned of his entrance by a prickly sensation that was all too familiar.

"It pleases me to find you still awake, Saxon."

Alana spun around from where she stood before the hearth. Merrick's presence was such that all at once the chamber seemed ridiculously small. His regard was steady and unwavering, but alas, her courage was not. Never had she felt so open, so exposed!

"Come here, Saxon."

Alana could not move. Her legs felt wooden. Her gaze strayed to the bed then back to his face.

A dark brow arched in silent query, yet still she could not move. She despised herself for her spinelessness, for he made her feel foolish and cowardly and weak.

She swallowed the tightness in her throat. "I know that you are angry," she said, her voice very low. "I have no doubt that you will chastise me. Indeed, I am prepared for it. Therefore, I ask but one thing. I care not what you do to me, but pray do not condemn Sybil because of me." She spoke hurriedly, lest her bravado forsake her. "You won't make her go back to serving your men, will you? Simply because you are angry with me—"

His eyes narrowed slightly. "Either way, I would remind you the choice is mine, Saxon."

With her eyes she pleaded with him. "Please. Please do not."

"Do you ask a boon of me, Saxon? If so, mayhap I would ask something in return."

Her mouth grew dry, her palms damp. "And what would you ask?"

Oh, foolish question, that! His gaze dropped and lingered for a disturbingly long moment on her lips.

He smiled. "Methinks you know, Saxon."

Aye, she did, and the very thought made her quiver inside. Her spine stiffened as he presented himself before her.

"So tell me, Saxon. Would you grant me this favor?"

Alana fell silent. She clasped her hands before her. How could she agree? Yet how could she refuse?

"What is it to be, Saxon? Shall I have all of you—or none of you?"

Alana's tone reflected her bitterness. "You are my lord and conqueror. Do I have a choice?"

Merrick's jaw tightened, but then he gave a short, biting laugh. "Nay, you need not answer after all. I see in your eyes that you would still refuse. And aye, you are right. I am your lord and conqueror, and you are mine."

His arrogance roused her ire. "You, Norman, are a barbarian—"

"If I were a barbarian, I'd have already had my fill of you, Saxon. I'd have lain between your thighs and vented my lust—"

Hot tears sprang to her eyes. "As you will do now!" she accused.

Merrick swore beneath his breath. Her tears would not sway him, not this time. Yet his mood was eased by the fear she could not hide. Though her chin climbed aloft, her knuckles shown white with strain.

The sound she made was half-fury, half-plea. "I—I wish you'd stayed in London and had your fill of women there!"

His smile was icily unpleasant. "Ah," he said smoothly. "But you were ever on my mind, Saxon. Why, I've lain with no other since the day I came to Brynwald. Indeed, I've *wanted* no other. And aye, I will take you, but not by fear or by force."

Alana trembled. He toyed with her, like a hunter with his prey. She averted her face. "It can be no other way!" she said desperately.

His gaze hardened. "Oh, but you are wrong, Saxon. It can be. By God, it will be."

He stepped forward. A flicker of panic raced through her like a blazing star, for his expression was one of brittle resolve. Her knees began to quaver. She recognized how useless it was to fight him.

But oddly, though his mood was harsh, his hand was not. His fingers slid beneath the fall of her hair and curled warmly around her neck. His thumb at the point of her chin, he guided her face upward.

"You have naught to fear, Saxon."

"I have everything to fear!" she cried. Jesu, even her voice was shaking.

He merely shook his head. A corded arm slid around her back. With subtle pressure he brought her resistant body flush against his. Alana inhaled sharply and then his mouth captured hers.

A tremor went through her. There was no evading his kiss. There was no evading *him*.

Aye, and angry though she was, confused as she was, the pressure of his mouth was scarcely as unpleasant as she might have wished. He kissed her endlessly, sweetly greedy, until her lids drifted shut, until her head was spinning and she knew not where one kiss ended and the next began. She was only half aware as he unlaced her bliaud and slipped it from her shoulders. Her chemise soon puddled around her feet and then his arms locked tight around her. She was borne high in the air then lowered to the bed.

Her eyes snapped open. Merrick had just divested himself of his tunic. Confronted with the hair-roughened expanse of his chest, she was all at once quiveringly aware of him as a man, of his strength and masculinity. She quickly averted her gaze and curled away from him.

But he did not stretch out beside her as she expected. The mattress dipped as he sat. An instant later he brushed his fingers lightly across the marks on her lower back.

"Does this still pain you, Saxon?"

"Nay." She stuffed her fist into her mouth to keep her lips from trembling.

"You will not scar. I am glad."

Alana bit back a sob. "I-I wish I would!"

"Why?" With his fingertips he traced the slope of her naked shoulder, down her arm and back.

She heartily longed for him to stop. Shivers played up and down her skin. "Why else? Because then you—you would not—" She stopped, unable to put into words what was about to happen.

His fingers paused. "Desire you?"

"Aye!" she said feebly.

"Oh, but I would, Saxon." There was a smile in his tone, but before she could respond, he turned her bodily toward him. Leaning low, he kissed her once. Twice. Again. And then he rose once more, his hands on his braies.

She stared helplessly, unable to look away as he stripped away the last of his clothing. Her stomach dove as his manhood sprang taut and free, swollen and erect, a blade as deadly as the other he wielded, just as fiercesome.

Some ragged sound escaped her. "Sweet Jesus . . . I've seen men before. I've seen *you*," she gasped. "Only now you are different. You—you are surely deformed . . . !"

He laughed. The wretch, he laughed!

She lurched upward, in fear or indignation, she knew not. She cared not. But alas, *he* was there. With the breadth of his chest he tumbled her back against the pillows. Alana's mind reeled at the shocking feel of his skin naked upon hers. The knotted plane of his belly pressed the softness of hers. She dare not even *think* of what lay between . . . Indeed, there was nowhere they did not touch.

She squeezed her eyes shut in abject shame, convinced a night of horror awaited her.

Merrick propped himself on his elbows to stare down at her.

Gently he brushed a tangle of golden hair

from her cheek. " 'Tis not me you fear," he said softly. " 'Tis the unknown."

Her eyes fluttered open, and she found him resting on one elbow, staring down at her.

A bitter ache wrenched at her chest. "The unknown? Nay, for I-I know what you will do." She shuddered. "I saw one of your men with Hawise, the dairyman's daughter. She screamed and screamed and he would not release her. He lay upon her and he—he would not stop. He made her bleed . . ."

Her hands had come up to jam against his shoulders. Merrick allowed it but he did not retreat.

"That is nothing like what I will do to you," he stated flatly. "And you are not so averse to me when I kiss you, Saxon."

"Aye, I am. You make me feel most odd."

Her fervent denial almost made him laugh again. "But it does not displease you when I kiss you, Saxon." When she said nothing, he prodded her again. "Does it?"

"It—it makes no difference." Alana shook her head. "When you do . . . what you want"— She felt her face flame— "then you *will* hurt me. I—I know you hate me, Norman. No doubt you—you want to hurt me!"

Merrick's eyes darkened. "I do not hate you, Saxon. And I will not hurt you lest you fight me." He eased to his side and studied her, then smiled slowly. "Indeed," he said softly, "there are things I can do to ease the way."

Alana drew a sharp breath. "You lie. This is naught but a—a trick!"

"No trick, Saxon. And I do not lie."

"Then tell me."

He said nothing. Instead he bent his head. Very deliberately he kissed the top swell of each breast.

Alana's heart was beating high in her throat. "Tell me, Norman. What . . . things?"

He raised his head, his eyes dark and unreadable. Alana was wholly unprepared for his frankness. "I will touch you here," he whispered. "With my hands, Saxon, the very tips of my fingers. With my lips and tongue I will taste you." His fingers grazed her nipple, sending a rush of sensation all through her. "And here, Saxon." Boldly he brushed the golden fleece between her thighs. "I will touch you. Caress you, until your flesh grows damp and ready. I will pleasure you, Saxon, pleasure you as never before."

Alana's ears burned. Her body grew hot. Her mind was all atumble. Nay, she thought dazedly. Surely he would not. Surely it was wicked.

His shoulders loomed dark and sleek above her, his skin like burnished copper. "Indeed"— He pressed his lips to the vulnerable place where her shoulder met her neck— " 'tis time I showed you instead."

Had she been able, Alana would have leaped from the bed. "Nay," she gasped. "Even you would not dare—"

He dared. Indeed, he did . . .

At first she was tense in his arms, so very tense, her muscles tightened against him and all he would do. But Merrick was not to be dissuaded. He gathered her close, and when he kissed her lips, she felt her own tremble beneath his as she struggled to hold back.

She was more dazed than fearful when at last he raised his head. But with a swiftly indrawn breath she sought to turn her face aside. Merrick caught her chin. His mouth hovered just above hers. "Nay," he whispered. "Do not turn away. Surrender to me, Saxon. Surrender . . ."

Wildly she shook her head.

"Then be conquered," he whispered just before his mouth claimed hers.

But he did not conquer. He seduced . . .

His hands were exquisitely tender. He explored her body at his whim and will. And all the while his mouth was sealed against hers, his kiss deep and slow and rousing. There was naught of force in his touch, though she knew he would have his way. And all too soon the battle she fought was not with him, but with herself.

The world spun madly. Her lips tentatively parted as his opened wide, his tongue ever the bold invader. Her palms slowly uncurled against his chest and now his kiss grew sweetly fierce. With one hand, he claimed the naked bounty of her breast; he filled his palm with her flesh. It seemed so strange, she thought, the warmth of his hand upon her naked skin.

Yet all too soon her breath hastened. With his fingers he stroked delicious patterns around the budding crest, teasing and circling. She was

stunned to feel her nipples grow tight and tautly straining. And when his fingers brushed one
turgid peak again and again, she couldn't deny
it—there *was* pleasure to be found in the touch
of his hand.

His mouth slid with slow heat down the
arch of her throat. He paused, and Alana's
breath came in a ragged rush. She couldn't
look away from the sight of his dark head
poised above the ivory fullness of her breast;
the contrast was stark and riveting.

Then he did what to her was the unthink-
able—his mouth descended. She looked on in
shock as his mouth replaced the hand that
toyed with her nipple. Time stood still as his
tongue joined the play, unceasing now, lash-
ing and stroking. And when he sucked full
and hard upon one deep pink circle she bit
back a low cry. A flood of sensations broke
free within her, dark and forbidden.

Merrick hid his satisfaction. He could feel
her resistance melting, for when he slid back
up to feast on her lips, her mouth clung sweetly to his. Even while her heart beat a wild
frenzy against his own, her limbs lay warm
and pliant against him.

He skimmed the hollow of her belly with
his palm. Christ, her skin was like fine silk!
He gritted his teeth, for his loins were like
steel, his shaft pounding and near to bursting
with the need to bury himself hard and deep,
driving into her core.

Boldly he tangled his fingertips within the
golden thatch at the base of her thighs.

Her eyes flew wide. Her legs clamped tight against his hand. Her nails caught at the corded hardness of his arms. He had startled her, he knew. "Let me, sweet." His voice was low and taut against her mouth . . . into it. "I do not seek to hurt you. I swear by the Cross . . ."

He kissed away her feeble protest. With his hands he swept aside her doubt. With gentle insistence he parted soft pink flesh, engaged in a tormenting foray, circling and stroking, arousing and exploring. He pleasured her until he felt her shudder; until her breath rushed past his ear, shallow and panting; until he felt the heat of her passion damp and bedewed against his skin and he was half-mad for want of her.

The beat of a drum pounded in his blood, and in his manhood. He rose above her. With the weight of his thighs he kept hers parted. For this time he would not stop. Sweet heaven, he *could* not stop . . .

Alana had but one shattering glimpse of his eyes, glittering with heat. She could feel the iron strength of his shaft rising against her, huge and pulsing against her. The rounded tip of his shaft pressed within her—into her—and she gasped at his size, certain she would be ripped asunder.

One burning thrust buried him deep—deep!—within her silken depths.

A half-strangled cry split the air. Her fingers curled into the hard flesh of his shoulders, not with passion but with pain. Her bewildered look tore into Merrick like a blade but he could no more have stopped himself than he could have halted William's invasion of England.

Hot tears stung her eyes. The shaky breath she drew only made her more aware of his shaft embedded within her, straining and thick, a spear of molten fire.

"I can't." Her voice caught on a half-sob. "Dear God, I-I cannot . . ."

Warm fingertips brushed her cheek, the fleetest of caresses. "Easy," he whispered. "Easy."

He ran his fingers gently over her face, as if to memorize its shape and texture. He lapped away the single tear that slid from her eye, kissed the curve of her cheek, and nuzzled the hollow of her throat. And all the while he did not move, allowing her to grow accustomed to the feel of him snug and full within her. The rending pain began to fade. As if he gauged her perfectly, he captured her lips with his. And as the kiss caught fire, he began to move, slowly at first, then faster and faster.

Again and again his rigid shaft pierced deep within her. But moments earlier she'd have thought it nigh impossible . . . Flames of excitement raced through her as his hips plunged almost frantically. Alana buried her face against his neck and clung to him blindly. All at once she was caught in the same wild frenzy. White-hot needles of sensation gathered tight, then suddenly exploded deep in her belly. She scarcely recognized the keening cry that burst from her throat.

Above her Merrick gave one last, desperate

lunge. His seed spilled hot and thick at the gate to her womb.

Minutes later, she still lay stunned and gasping as he slowly withdrew. He curled a possessive arm hard about her waist and brought her back against him, the curve of her back flush against the furry warmth of his chest.

The fire burned low. The night grew older. But Alana lay awake, staring into the darkness. An aching hurt enshrouded her heart.

He had beseeched her surrender—oh, and so sweetly!—yet what need was there? she reflected bitterly. This bold invader had conquered her people . . . and now her body. And aye, with pitiable ease . . .

He would not find her such an easy mark again.

Chapter 12

As was his way, Merrick woke first the next morning. A tepid sunshine slanted through the shutters, bathing the chamber in a pale circlet of light. He did not rise, but let himself savor the sensation of soft, feminine warmth cuddled against his backside. At length, he shifted, reluctant to awaken his lovely bedmate.

Drawing back the furs, his gaze wandered at will, for he knew were she to waken he'd not be so indulged. She was deliciously naked and sleek, her skin pale and unblemished, the color of cream. Idly he picked up a strand of golden hair from the graceful slope of one gleaming shoulder. He rubbed it between his fingertips, marveling at the texture. He had a sudden vision of her above him, her hair a golden tangle around her shoulders. He imagined those silken tresses brushing the taut plane of his belly; then lower still, skimming his thighs as she slid down his body, her delectable lips parted and pink and moist, so very near his . . .

He gritted his teeth and fought a potent swell

201

of desire. The image provoked an immediate and rather visible effect, and though the urge bit deep to roll her to her back and plunge hard and deep within her furrowed heat, he did not. Indeed, the night had found him replete as never before. And, he decided dryly, he was as greedy as if he were a stripling lad who had just tumbled his first maid.

She would be sore, no doubt. Though he had tried, he had not been able to stave off the seething pulse of his desire the night through. In his arrogance, he'd managed to convince himself that once he lay with her, the web of fascination that so enthralled him would be no more.

'Twas hardly so.

The breath he drew was ragged, for the memory made him stiffen still further. Indeed, 'twas all he could do to allow her to sleep at all. Twice more he had taken her. And though he sought to rein in his passion, to make love to her with lingering ardor, she had been so tight, so incredibly tight around his swollen flesh. And the last time . . .

Ah, the last time. A primitive satisfaction welled within him. He trailed a finger over the delicate slope of her jaw. She had clutched at him, not in pain, but in pleasure. Oh, no doubt the stubborn wench would never admit to such. But he had pleased her, as she had pleased him . . . and pleased him mightily.

Bending his head, he pressed his mouth to the rounded, sleep-warm flare of her shoulder. When he raised his head, it was to discover she was awake, her eyes locked upon his. The notion passed through his mind to discover how willing he might find her this morn . . . He cast it aside, for her gaze was wide and utterly wary. But seeing her so enticingly displayed in nothing at all served as a reminder . . .

In truth, Alana was stunned that he chose to leave her be. Oh, but she had dreaded the dawn of a new day. She wondered how she could ever bear to look at him without remembering all that he had done—all that she had allowed him to do!

She watched as he rose and stretched, granting her a thoroughly unhindered view of his sex, stark and bold and wantonly aroused. Her heartbeat stumbled. Her face flamed crimson.

She gave a silent prayer of thanksgiving when he washed and quickly dressed. But she was faintly puzzled when he went to his chests.

"Since your wardrobe was sadly lacking, Saxon, I brought these from London for you." He proceeded to toss ell after ell of fine woven cloth across the bed. "And this as well." He pitched a heavy woolen mantle atop the pile.

Alana sat up slowly, clutching the weaves to her breast. Overwhelmed, she could only stare, stunned at what Merrick had done. Unbidden, her hand crept out to touch the mantle—why, 'twas lined with fur!

"Well, Saxon?" Merrick watched her closely. "Does such effort warrant no word of thanks? Or would you scorn my generosity instead?"

Alana flushed, for his sarcasm was impossible to ignore. She bit her lip, wondering how she might say what was in her heart in such a way that he would not be offended.

"I—I am truly grateful," she said at last. "Indeed"—a faint wistfulness flitted across her features—"I never thought to possess anything so grand as this." Her fingers caressed the mantle's fur. She swallowed, then forced herself to meet his gaze head-on. "But there is something I would have preferred more than worldly goods. Indeed, there is something I would ask of you now."

Merrick's eyes narrowed. He folded his arms across the breadth of his chest, both furious and amazed that she would shun his gifts. "And what is that, Saxon?"

He was angry. Alana could hear it in the tautness of his voice, but it was too late to back down now. "I ask that you grant me leave to visit Aubrey."

The silence that followed stretched on forever. Alana finally braved a glance at his face only to wish she had not. His features were rigid, his eyes a veritable tempest.

"You are a fool," he stated baldly, "to think I would even consider it."

"He is an old man and I would merely see that he is well—"

"I have told you before, Saxon, he is being well cared for. You will accept my word."

Alana cried her outrage. "And what if I do not?"

"You will." He smiled, but it was a mere

travesty. His eyes, cold as a winter's sea, rested upon her. "Now come, Saxon, wish me Godspeed that I might greet the day in good humor."

He approached the bed and bent low. But Alana deliberately spurned the kiss he would have pressed upon her lips, wrenching her face aside.

Merrick straightened. "Ah, but I should have known. 'Tis the way of women to withhold their bodies as it pleases them, to bargain for what they do or do not want. But this will not lessen my desire, Saxon."

Alana matched his cool stare with one of her own. "Indeed," she stated icily. "Well, according to you, Norman, my body is not my own."

"You are learning, Saxon." An arrogant smile curled his lips. "That pleases me. That pleases me greatly." With that he spun around and departed the chamber.

Alana's nails dug into her palms. 'Twas only through sheer effort of will that she stopped herself from bursting into angry, bitter tears. Oh, but he was hateful! Yet in truth, little wonder that he was so well pleased with her—and with himself! Oh, if only she had not been so weak—and so foolish, for he had been right. She had been afraid of the unknown, of what he would do. And in her weakness he found his triumph, for he took from her all that he sought—and she had let him!

A furious resolve hardened in her breast. Not again, she vowed fiercely. Never again would she partake of pleasure at his hand. She had surrendered once—*once*—but never again would he claim victory so easily.

Just then there came a knock upon the door. "My lord ordered us to fetch water for your bath," called a servant. "He bade us hurry that it would not grow cold."

It was on the tip of Alana's tongue to refuse, for she was in no mood to countenance his edicts. But in the end she decided against it, and moments later she was heartily glad she had not. She winced a little as she lowered her bottom into the steaming waters, for she was decidedly tender there between her thighs.

She had just finished dressing when the door opened. Alana whirled, her heart leaping for she was certain it was Merrick—who else would enter unannounced? But it was only Sybil, who breezed into the chamber as if it were her own.

"Alana, I've come to retrive the needles you borrowed from Genevieve—" She stopped short when she spied the mound of cloth still heaped upon the bed. Her pretty mouth pinched together in a way that suddenly reminded Alana of Rowena, her mother. Without preamble, Sybil swept a hand toward the pile then whirled toward Alana.

"What is this?" she demanded.

Alana bit her lip. What might she say that Sybil would not be angry or jealous? There was nothing, she realized, and so she could only offer truth.

"Merrick brought it with him from London," she murmured.

"For you, Alana?"

Her tone was petty and shrewish. Alana paused, then said lightly, "Oh, I'm sure 'tis meant for the both of us. Indeed, I would hardly know what to do with so many gowns." She smiled slightly. "Father always said you were very skilled with the needle, and I am hardly so blessed. So please, Sybil, take what you will."

Sybil's eyes gleamed. "My thanks, Alana. I do believe I shall do just that." With that she plucked four lengths of cloth from the pile, one a bold, vivid blue that Alana secretly thought just lovely . . . She scolded herself firmly. Envy was the curse of the devil, or so her mother had always said.

Sybil breezed through the door a moment later, arms laden with her selections. She had no sooner departed than Genevieve stepped within, an odd expression on her face.

"Alana," she said, "I do believe Merrick meant the cloth for you alone."

Alana started. She hadn't realized Genevieve was near, but it appeared she had overheard the exchange with Sybil. She shook her head, then said softly, "I know. But in truth, she is no less in need of a new bliaud than I." There was a small pause. "Sybil lost much when the Normans came. All her possessions. Both father *and* mother. It has not been easy for her to suddenly find herself a servant when all her life she has been a lady. And I would not begrudge my sister such small pleasures as she might find."

For a moment an uncomfortable silence hung in the air. For a time she thought Genevieve might disagree, yet in the end, the other woman smiled. " 'Tis rare to find one so unselfish as you, Alana."

Alana flushed but said nothing. Genevieve was looking at her rather intensely, she realized. Shame flooded her, for all at once she had the feeling that Genevieve knew very well what had passed between herself and Merrick last eve.

But if she did, she did not speak of it. Instead she tipped her head to the side. "I came to see if you would accompany me to the village just south of here. The day is warm and clear for winter, and one of the maids told me of the village market in Fengate, and I should like to browse among the wares there. What do you say?"

Alana wasn't certain that Merrick would approve, and that alone prompted her agreement. And indeed, a surge of defiance rose fast and swift when she and Genevieve arrived outside in the yard. Merrick was there with a group of his soldiers and a number of Saxon men who had taken a respite from their work on the palisade. His dark head swung around when he spied his sister and Alana. Alana stiffened when he immediately started toward them.

He addressed himself to his sister. "Did you need my assistance, Genevieve?"

"Why, no." Genevieve smiled at him sweetly. "But since you are here, would you order a cart brought round? Alana and I have decided to visit the village market in Fengate just south of here."

Merrick scowled. "I have no time to escort you—"

"And we would not think to trouble you," Genevieve said briskly. "If you could but spare one of the Saxons, a man who may be trusted to protect us and one who knows the countryside." Alana nearly gasped when Genevieve pointed at Radburn. "That one," she announced. "Is he a trustworthy man, Alana?"

Alana's chin tipped high. All at once she knew a perverse satisfaction that for once Merrick might not have his say. "*Most* trustworthy," she stressed clearly, knowing full well that Merrick's expression had gone dark as a demon's.

He gestured for Radburn to come forward. "I am not so convinced as my sister," he said tightly, "but I will allow her to have her way in this. You will take these two to Fengate market and remain with them at all times. A warning, however—if you are ever to earn my trust, you must prove it, so were I you, I'd not consider this a chance to flee. And were I you, I'd make certain no harm comes to this pair."

Alana held her breath, for all at once a sizzling tension charged the air. Radburn's features were as stormy as Merrick's and for one frozen instant she feared Radburn might lash out at the Norman. Instead he inclined his head, his lips twisting slightly as he said, "As you wish, my lord."

Merrick gave him a long, slow look then strode away.

A short time later they were clambering onto the seat of the cart. Radburn took the reins, while Genevieve sat between him and Alana. As they left Brynwald behind, the skin at her nape prickled eerily. Unable to stop herself, she craned her neck and glanced back over her shoulder.

Merrick stared at them from near the entrance to the keep. Even from here, Alana keenly sensed his displeasure. Whether it was aimed at her, Genevieve, or Radburn, she didn't know—in truth, perhaps 'twas all of them.

As the cart weaved down the rutted roadway, Genevieve made idle chatter, asking questions of both her and Radburn, occasionally chatting about her family. At first Radburn's responses were subdued and restrained. Alana knew he was suspicious of the Norman widow. But Genevieve did not speak down to him as if he were a slave or even a servant, though 'twas obvious from his speech and manner that he was no common villein, despite his tattered and filthy clothing. Instead, Genevieve spoke to him as if he were an equal, and Alana's admiration for her grew ever more. Indeed, Genevieve's charm and frankness were such that before long the tautness had eased from Radburn's shoulders.

Before she knew it, her own worries fled as well, at least for the moment. Though the air was damp and cool, the sun was bright and the sky clear as a warm spring day.

In Fengate they wandered on foot down narrow, crooked streets of damp, packed earth, browsing through the various booths of spices, fabrics, and goods of every kind. Radburn trailed slightly behind them. Genevieve wrinkled her nose as they passed a pen of oxen but Alana merely laughed.

By late afternoon Alana's stomach rumbled hungrily. At Genevieve's insistence, the three shared a loaf of fresh-baked bread and a length of hot, spicy sausage. A short time later, her stomach comfortably full, Alana stood back as Genevieve haggled with a merchant over the price of an elegantly braided girdle of white and gold. At last Genevieve turned away, her face wreathed in smiles. She held up her prize with a squeal of joy.

"Oh, Alana, it's lovely, is it not? It reminds me of one I had when I was just a girl—"

She got no further. A meaty hand closed around her upper arm and spun her around. Alana straightened only to suffer a similar fate—a hard hand at her back thrust her forward so that she almost knocked into Genevieve.

A guttural laugh rushed past her ear. "One is as fetching as the other, eh, Etienne?"

Alana's blood froze. *Etienne*. Normans, she realized in dread. By now three of them surrounded her and Genevieve, huge and burly. They stank of sweat and ale. She glanced around frantically. Sweet heaven, where was Radburn? Surely he had not deserted them! It flitted through her mind that perhaps Merrick had been right after all. Perhaps he had seen this as an opportunity to flee . . .

"A pity there is not another." The burliest of the three grinned, displaying dingy, yellowed teeth with a wide gap in the front. "But no matter." He gestured at Genevieve. "I'll jump the wench and thump her and then one of you can have a turn while I take the other." He leered at Alana, who blanched visibly.

Genevieve went pale as well. "Leave us be," she ordered, yet even she could not keep the quaver from her voice. "If you do not, you shall regret it, for my brother is Merrick—"

"What I regret," interrupted another, "is that we did not see the pair of you earlier. But let us not waste any more time, eh—"

He got no further. A dark form leaped out from behind them, knocking the one nearest Genevieve to the ground. Genevieve screamed and grabbed at Alana, pulling her out of harm's way. Only then did Alana recognize their rescuer as Radburn.

She uttered a stricken cry. "Dear God! He is unarmed. And there are three of them!"

And indeed, the remaining two had whirled on Radburn. One grinned as if he relished the prospect of slaying yet another Saxon. The sound of steel being whisked from a scabbard filled the air, even as his companion tugged a long, wicked looking dagger from a sheath at his waist.

Though the Normans' actions were slowed by drink, they were nonetheless deadly. Slowly they began to circle Radburn. Both women gasped as Radburn leaped aside to evade a vicious slice of the dagger; he did not escape unscathed, for the blade rent diagonally through his tunic. Alana's stomach plunged as a thin line of blood welled swift and sure.

But Radburn was not beaten by any means. One foot flashed high and outward; the sword clattered to the ground. Radburn's fists shot out, landing a fierce blow to Norman's jaw. Were the circumstances not so very dire, Alana might have laughed at the Norman's dumbstruck expression before he slumped to the ground.

But the instant when Radburn had turned away from the remaining Norman cost him dearly. This time it was Alana who screamed when the burly Norman plunged his dagger deep into Radburn's back. Radburn arched in pain but recovered swiftly. He gouged his elbow deep into the Norman's belly. The Norman doubled over then straightened with a snarl of rage.

Suddenly the pair was rolling and twisting over the ground, over and over in a flurry of motion. Someone was screaming, her or Genevieve, she knew not. Terror clogged her throat as she glimpsed the flash of a dagger arcing downward. Once. Twice . . . Thrice.

The Norman slumped over Radburn. Then all was quiet.

Beside her Genevieve was sobbing. Alana's knees sagged. Through a haze she saw Radburn stagger to his feet and start toward them. She hugged Genevieve, then rushed forward.

But Radburn advanced no more than a single step. He was alive . . . but he was far from unhurt.

Once they were back in the yard at Brynwald, Genevieve clapped her hands swiftly. "You there! And you and you! Carry this man up to the chamber next to mine . . . nay, gently, now, and heed his wounds, man, else you'll start him bleeding again!"

Radburn was carried away, barely conscious. Abovestairs, Genevieve peeled away his bloody tunic while Alana ran for her mother's herbs and medicines. She inhaled sharply when the extent of his injuries was revealed. Besides the puncture near his shoulderblade, there was a gaping tear in the front of the opposite shoulder, and a ragged gash near his ribs. Quickly she mixed a potion to help him sleep, for two of the three were deep and she knew they would require stitching to close the jagged flesh. The prospect made her insides tighten, for though she'd seen her mother perform the very same task countless times before, she had never done it herself.

Perspiration beaded on her forehead as she worked as quickly as possible. Her stomach was knotted in two by the time she finished.

She snipped and tied the last thread, then released a long pent-up breath.

Genevieve glanced at the neat rows of stitches. "A fine job," she praised.

Alana dipped a cloth in clean water, then swiped at Radburn's brow. Frowning, she laid the back of her fingers over his forehead. "He is not feverish, but he is pale as linen," she said with a shake of her head. She bit her lip. Now that the ordeal was over, the magnitude of all that had nearly happened—and *did* happen— seemed suddenly overwhelming.

"This is all my fault. I—I only said what I did so that he might come, for I knew Merrick did not wish him to." Dread clutched at her heart. "Dear God, what if he should die?" She swayed dizzily.

Genevieve shoved a stool behind her knees. A hand at Alana's shoulder, she pressed her down. "Alana! My knowledge is not nearly so vast as yours, but look! Even now he rests easier."

Alana stared down at the man before her. He lay so still, it was almost as if he . . . Nay, she thought. *Nay!* She dare not even think such a thing.

"The wound must be tended properly," she said, her voice very low. "Especially these first days. He must rest, and the wounds must be bound with clean cloth at least once a day lest poisons set in."

"He will not die," Genevieve said firmly. "You have the knowledge to heal him should he sicken."

Alana tipped her head to the side. "You are so trusting," she said slowly. "Why? The others are not. Even my own people . . ."

Neither woman was aware that Merrick lurked near the door. Some strange emotion blustered and raged inside him, an emotion he could not control. Of a certainty he did not begrudge this man his life; he begrudged no man the chance to test his fate. Radburn's wounds were grave, but he was strong and would no doubt prevail. Indeed, Merrick reflected, he himself had suffered worse and survived. But there was a part of him that resented Radburn's success in claiming Alana's attention so very thoroughly . . . and, aye, as *he* had not.

He was vastly irritated with himself—and with Alana.

In his heart he was appalled at himself, for such pettiness was unlike him. He scoffed at the thought he might be jealous of this handsome Saxon. Yet he could hardly deny the obvious. He heartily disliked seeing Alana with this man, her hand so small and white against his brow, her expression anxious and distressed as it had never been with him—in truth, he admitted blackly, it would never be so, for he was well aware she despised him as no other.

He crossed the floor to the two women. Standing beside Alana, he stared down at Radburn, his expression impassive. "He will not die?"

He didn't miss the way Alana's shoulders

stiffened abruptly the very instant he came near. It was Genevieve who answered. "The prospect seems unlikely, praise God. And he is resting comfortably, thanks to Alana."

"Then her presence is no longer required here." He retreated once more to the doorway. "Come, Saxon."

Alana's spine had gone rigid. She continued to bathe Radburn's face, as though she'd heard not a single word.

"Saxon!"

Alana made no answer. Her features were as mutinous as Merrick's were incensed.

Genevieve stole a backward glance at her brother—one look at his stony jaw was all she needed. She laid a reassuring hand on Alana's shoulder.

"'Tis all right. I will stay with Radburn through the night. If I should need your assistance, I will come for you, I promise."

Alana did not even blink. "There is no need to trouble yourself, Genevieve. I will stay with him."

"Saxon, I'll not tell you again!"

Genevieve grew desperate. She bent low. "Alana, I beg of you, please go!" she whispered. "My brother tolerates much from me, and even I would not dare cross him right now."

Alana pressed her lips together, then gave a tiny, reluctant nod. She would honor Genevieve's wishes, but, by God, Merrick could rot in hell for all she cared. Her chin high, she rose and swept by him with nary a glance nor a word.

Merrick was but a breath behind her the entire length of the corridor. As soon as the door to his chamber clicked shut, she whirled on him and let loose her fury.

"Have you no compassion? No kindness or mercy?"

Merrick's eyes glinted. "Were I you, Saxon, I would tread with care. My mood is not easy this night."

Her glare was blistering. "Nor is mine, Norman!"

He ignored her. Instead he discarded his sword belt and pulled off his tunic. At the sight of his broad, hair-matted chest, Alana's stomach seemed to tip precariously. Bared from the waist up, he seemed more dangerous than ever. She swallowed. Her gaze swung from his naked torso to the bed and back again.

A dangerous smile lurked on his lips.

Alana dug her nails into her palms. The pain gave her sorely needed courage. "You are selfish," she charged, her tone very low. "A man lies injured, and you think only of your own pleasure!"

"And you are foolish if you think to win this battle, Saxon. Had you not defied me, I might have let you be. But not now. Nay, you bring this on yourself. And so I would know, Saxon . . . what is it to be? Will you lie with me willingly?"

Her gaze was blistering. "Never," she vowed. "Never will I lie with you willingly."

He was before her in an instant. His smile had vanished. "A pity then," he said tightly. "For you *will* lie with me."

With his eyes he damned her. With his hands he stripped the clothes from her body. Alana was left gasping, her mind reeling. Even as a protest hovered in her throat, he tumbled her back on the bed.

His mouth was fiercely devouring, his kiss but a stamp of unyielding dominion. His tongue stabbed into her mouth again and again, even as his body would stab into hers. His body lay heavy and hard over hers.

Panic erupted within her, panic and an anger beyond any she had ever known. Somehow she managed to tear her mouth away. Furious beyond words, she was all at once beyond caution, beyond reason.

"Nay," she cried. "*Nay*! I will not let you do this! I hate you, do you hear? I hate you!"

Above her, Merrick swore. She was made for a man's hands. *His* hands. She was made for pleasure. *His* pleasure.

Their eyes clashed, fiery green with steely blue. "So this is how it is to be," he said fiercely. "Well, curse you, Saxon. You would have me take by force what can be otherwise won. Ah, but you tempt me, you tempt me mightily! But methinks I would find more enjoyment in a horn of ale than with you this night."

He climbed off her, then stood staring down at her, tight-lipped and stony. "You had best remember, Saxon, for next time you'll not be so lucky. You will serve me. In any way. In every way. Your duty is to please me. You would do well to remember it."

Once again, he stormed from the chamber.

Chapter 13

While Radburn's condition was no better the next day, neither was it any worse. Nor did he show any signs of fever. Alana cautiously interpreted all this as a good sign, though she warned Genevieve it was too early to predict what course his recovery might take.

In the morning she showed Genevieve how to clean the wounds and apply a healing poultice. It was while they worked that Genevieve discreetly inquired as to her fate last eve.

Alana hesitated. "He was angry," she admitted, feeling distinctly uncomfortable. "Where he slept I—I do not know."

A faint smile appeared on Genevieve's lips. "He is jealous, Alana. Faith, he is jealous!"

Why Genevieve should sound so pleased, she did not know. Though she said nothing, Alana was hardly convinced. Indeed, she decided bitterly, Merrick considered her naught but a possession—a pawn—and no doubt 'twas only that which had precipitated his anger.

221

Later she peered in to check on both Radburn and Genevieve. Radburn was sleeping—and so was Genevieve. Seated on a stool beside the bed, her head was tilted at an angle that looked most uncomfortable.

Gently Alana jostled her shoulder. Genevieve blinked sleepily up at her. Alana shook her head and scolded her gently. "You've had no sleep at all, have you?"

Genevieve's sheepish smile was answer enough.

Alana pointed her toward the door. "Go to your own chamber and rest," she said firmly. "I'll stay with Radburn until you return."

Genevieve rose, then impulsively slipped an arm around Alana's shoulders. "You have the heart of an angel," she said softly.

Genevieve departed, and Alana took the stool near the head of the bed. It was inevitable, perhaps, that her mind should stray to Merrick . . . She'd not seen him since he left last eve. What if Merrick should find her here? The thought had no more than vaulted through her mind than he was there in the room, so tall his dark head nearly touched the crosstimber. Alana scrambled to her feet, despairing of the guilty flush that immediately heated her cheeks.

"Genevieve had no rest at all," she said quickly. "I bade her sleep for a time."

Their eyes locked. Whatever he might have said, she would never know, for all at once Simon was there as well. The boy's features were both harried and grave.

"Uncle, there is a knight called Gervase belowstairs. The knight slain in Fenwald was one of his own. He knows the Saxon Radburn still lives, and he demands we give him over that justice may be done."

Alana inhaled sharply.

Merrick paid her no heed. "See that he is brought food and wine, Simon. I will greet him shortly." Simon nodded and hurried away.

Merrick betrayed no hint of his intentions. His expression was just as unreadable. Lean fingers stroked the squareness of his jaw. Alana had the sensation he had forgotten her. With nary a glance her way, he spun around and departed.

Alana ran after him. Halfway down the corridor, she caught at his sleeve.

Merrick whirled on her. "Leave me be, Saxon."

"Nay! Merrick, please! You can't give Radburn over to them! He is sick!"

Merrick's eyes narrowed. "You said last eve his life would likely be in no danger."

"And it is not—not at this moment! But that might easily change were he thrown in some filthy prison!"

"Prison?" He gave a biting laugh. "If they take him, Saxon, he will not last that long."

She blanched. "What?" she inquired faintly. "You mean he will be slain?"

"Executed," Merrick clarified curtly. "I thought this might happen, for he is a Saxon, a Saxon who killed a Norman soldier."

Alana's breath dammed in her throat. "You cannot let that happen!"

"This is not your affair, Saxon."

"It is! Radburn did nothing wrong! You told him to let no harm come to us, to Genevieve and me. Those men . . . they would have raped us, both of us. Radburn merely protected us and did your bidding!"

"Do not interfere, Saxon."

She gave a half-sob of anguish. "Sweet Mother Mary, what manner of man are you? Would you give him over only to—to spite me?"

Merrick was suddenly furious. "Does he mean so much to you then, this love of yours?"

"Oh, stop! He is not my love, and you know better than any he has never been my lover!"

"Would you plead for him, Saxon?"

"Aye," she cried desperately. "If that's what it takes to save him, aye!"

"If I do this, Saxon, I would expect much in return. What would you give then?"

"'Tis not what I would give but what I owe. He saved my life. I must do what I must to save his." She spoke with the fervency of a prayer. "And so I would give you anything—anything you wish."

Merrick caught her against him, his arm hard about her waist. Both his words and his stare were brutally frank. "You know what I would have, Saxon. You. You in my bed. I would have you come to me and not turn away from my hand, for you make me feel the lowliest beast for daring to touch you. I would have you give yourself to me and not fight me at every turn."

The very thought made her feel all hot and strange inside. For all that he was commanding and arrogant, he was not cruel. Her pride had been stung, for she 'deeply resented her helplessness. But in truth, laying with him had not been the ordeal she feared. He had not hurt her, beyond that initial tearing pain; indeed, he had taken every care with her. Now, she had no choice, she realized. No choice but to cast aside her pride for the sake of another's life.

With quavering heart and trembling limbs, she forced herself to meet his challenge straight-on. "I—I am yours, Norman." She faltered, her voice but a thread of sound. "Yours to command. Yours to—to do with what you will."

There was no mistaking the triumph that flashed across his features. For an instant Alana almost hated herself for giving in.

"So be it then, Saxon. I accept your bargain." He put her from him and strode away.

Alana's gaze trailed him until he disappeared from sight. She returned to Radburn, who still slept peacefully. But she was too nervous to sit, and before she knew it, she'd crept down the tower stair. She sat upon the last step, her ears straining, her pulse pounding madly. From here she caught just a glimpse of a knight she didn't recognize, no doubt the Norman Gervase.

Fat and balding, he sat across the table from Merrick. His cheeks were red with fury and his eyes were snapping.

" . . . the wretch killed one of my men-at-arms!" he was saying. "I demand you turn him over to me!"

Though she could not see Merrick's face, she saw him lift one broad shoulder. "Were you not aware your men attacked two women?"

Gervase scoffed. "One was a Saxon wench! Surely you would not protect her!"

Merrick's voice went cold. "She is a Saxon I hold dearly."

Dearly. If he held her dear, 'twas only for the pleasure her body brought to him!

"The other," Merrick went on in tones of steel, "was my sister. And I will not stand for any man—Norman or otherwise—who attempts to defile those near to me. And do not pretend to misunderstand your men's intentions, Gervase, for they were hardly honorable. In my mind, the Saxon Radburn merely protected what is mine. I will not turn him over to you, now or ever. Indeed, those two men who escaped should consider themselves fortunate, for had I been there, they would lie as dead as their friend. But I am prepared to be fair, and so I will offer you a reasonable compensation for the loss of a knight."

She saw him extend a pouch fat with coin. Gervase did not hesitate, but grasped it at once. They spoke further, but Alana did not wait to hear. Her heart was pounding so she could scarcely think. Merrick had done what he'd promised.

And now . . . now it was up to her to fulfill *hers*.

Alana stayed with Genevieve and Radburn for the remainder of the day. Unfortunately, as night fell, Radburn's temperature began to rise. But when it came time for the evening meal, Genevieve shooed her away, assuring her that she had nursed the sick before and was fully capable of tending his fever. Alana did not doubt her, for she knew Radburn was in good hands.

Belowstairs in the hall, there was no sign of Merrick, thought she scoured the assemblage searching for him. Still, she had no doubt it would not be long before he appeared, a prospect that had her insides tied in knots. So it was that she started at the touch of a hand on her shoulder.

But it was only Simon. In his hand he held a tray heaped full with food and drink. "I have food and wine for you and my lord," he said softly. "He asks that you accompany me."

Alana gave a terse nod. If Simon noted her plodding steps as they ascended the stairs, he said nothing. Dread climbed its way up her spine even as her feet climbed the stairs.

Simon opened the door and stepped back that she might precede him. Alana stepped past him, feeling as though she were on her way to the hangman's noose. Simon deposited the tray atop the table and quietly withdrew.

Merrick had apparently just finished his bath. Naked from the waist up, he wore naught but his braies. His hair was still damp, slicked back from his broad forehead. Amid the dark fur on his chest, droplets of water glistened like tiny diamonds. His shoulders were sleek and bronzed, like oiled wood. All at once she felt curiously deprived of breath.

He gestured her forward. "Come and sit, Saxon."

Alana obliged, her gaze lowered, praying he'd not glimpse her distress. He heaped a trencher full of food. Their fingers brushed as she accepted it; the contact went through her like a blaze of lightning. He paid her no heed as he ate and drank, his appetite as keen as hers was frail. Her stomach was roiling so she could eat no more than a few bites of the richly spiced herring. Unbidden, her gaze strayed to his face again and again. But alas, she could discern naught of either his mood or his thoughts.

At last he leaned back, one strong hand curled lazily around his chalice. The gaze he bestowed on her was openly appraising. Alana wished frantically that she were as composed as he. Why must he always make her feel as though she were at a disadvantage? Oh, foolish thought, that! Mayhap because he ever saw to it that she was!

She hid her fingers in her skirts, seeking to match his even stare and failing miserably.

"Must you look at me so?" She was unable to bridle her irritation.

He smiled, a smile that did not echo in his eyes. "I merely ponder your sacrifice, Saxon. Indeed, I hope your young swain is appreciative." He watched her closely. "You must care about him greatly."

Her lips parted. "Not in the way that you think—"

"How then, Saxon? Do you love him?"

In truth, Alana was stunned at his vehemence. Could it be that Genevieve was right—that he was jealous? She bit her lip, unaware that her uncertainty lay vivid in her eyes. "Mayhap I did once," she said faintly. "But I was young, and he was a man full grown. I-I knew nothing of the ways of men and women."

She bowed her head. "He is the son of a lord in the southern climes of England," she said, her voice very low. "I soon came to realize such a knight would never woo the daughter of a peasant, lest he wished to pursue a dalliance alone. His—his future would have been ruined. I knew that he must bind himself to a lady—and not to a bastard."

As she spoke, he traced the rim of his chalice with a roughened fingertip. Merrick was pleased that she was not given to wantonness. Aye, he was mightily pleased. Radburn had been a fool to overlook such beauty as hers, but he could not stop the turn of his mind . . . Did she secretly long for him still?

He rose, moving to stand before the fire. At length he turned back to her.

"I would know, Saxon. Did you dream of him when you lay with me?"

Alana gasped. "Nay!" Too late she realized had she answered differently, she might have been spared this night and many others . . .

His relentless regard was disconcerting. "You paid a heavy price for his freedom, Saxon. You stand to gain nothing from it."

"I would see no man harmed because of me. Indeed, I would have the same concern over any man sick and wounded."

"Then you swear Radburn means nothing to you?"

She flushed but did not flinch from either his question or his gaze. "Aye."

"And you will come to me willingly?"

To her horror she found she couldn't tear her eyes away from his. She nodded, unable to do more.

"Then come to me now."

Alana's heart began to pound. His eyes were all aglitter, burning torches of silver. He waited, his legs spread wide apart, the tilt of his head supremely arrogant.

Her throat grew dry as tinder. On trembling legs she arose. She had made a bargain, and now she must abide by it. Her legs carried her forward slowly, until at last she stood before him.

An odd little tremor seized her. She was torn inside as never before. So near to him, he seemed bigger than ever. She was resigned to her fate, yet inside she wondered why he affected her so—and he a man she despised with all her being! He had only to look at her and she felt as if a tempest roiled within her. And when he touched her . . .

His hand slipped beneath the fall of her hair. Shivers raced all through her as pleasantly rough fingertips brushed across her nape.

"You tremble, Saxon. Do you find me so repulsive then?"

"Nay," she said quickly. " 'Tis just that I—I know not what you would have me do."

Merrick's imagination ran wild, along with his senses. Her nearness never failed to stir him to a painful state of arousal. He wanted to feel her small hands on his body, stroking and discovering, her mouth hot on his naked skin.

His fingers weaved into the unbound glory of her hair, then tightened slightly, slowly tilting her face to his.

His gaze impaled her. His voice was low and taut. "I would ask that you not deny me this night—or yourself, Saxon. I would have you share my bed, and all the pleasures therein, with no thoughts of refusal. With no thoughts of regret. If you cannot do this—if you *will* not, then mayhap you should leave now, Saxon."

Her eyes clung to his. Never had she been so shaken, so confused! She had entered this chamber so very certain that he truly did not want her, that he merely sought to tame her to his hand. Yet she could detect no trace of either mockery or triumph in his features, only a brooding heat that set her pulse to thrumming madly.

She swallowed. Her fingers grazed the center of his chest. Heat stormed all through her. Though the impulse to snatch it back was strong, she did not. It spun through her mind that her hand looked small and white there amid the dark forest on his chest.

"I will not forsake the bargain we made," she whispered. She gave a tiny shake of her head. "I-I will not leave, Norman."

His eyes darkened. "So be it then," he muttered, "for I can wait no longer."

His mouth captured hers. Alana surrendered her lips with a low moan. Her spine felt as if it had turned to water. She locked her arms tightly around his neck. The pressure of his mouth was sweetly fierce, but she reveled in it. She could taste the hunger in his embrace, in the way his arms clamped tight and urgent around her back, but her own was just as wild.

Deny him? she thought in amazement. Sweet Mother Mary, she could not. Nor could she deny her own traitorous need for him.

Not once did he break the searing fusion of their lips, not even when he eased her down upon the bed and shifted to lie beside her. Her clothes were swept from her body. Only then did he raise his head. She flushed at the stroke of glittering blue eyes warm upon her naked flesh, but she did not turn away.

He rose next to the bed, his shoulders wide and awesome in the glow of the fire, his torso strong and muscular. He cast away his braies so that he was as naked as she.

Her gaze touched the knotted muscles of his arms, then strayed helplessly lower. Her breath slammed to a halt. He was aroused, and wantonly so, the rigid thickness of his manhood brazenly implicit. She tore her gaze from his rigid arousal and back to his face, only to find he knew of her scrutiny. Heat flooded her face. She was horribly embarrassed to have been caught staring at him so.

He stretched out beside her. His whisper rushed past her ear. "I cannot hide my passion for you, Saxon. But I do not mind that you stare. Indeed, I enjoy it"—he gave an odd laugh—"though not as much as I would enjoy the feel of your hand curled tight around that part of me that yearns for you so."

Her head jerked up. Why, surely he did not mean that he would have her touch him *there* . . . surely he would not dare . . .

Sweet heaven, he did.

She gasped as he tugged her hands against his chest. Of their own volition, her palms slid back and forth over the bristly dark mat on his chest. Hard fingers caught at hers. Her knuckles grazed the ridged plane of his belly. His hand engulfed hers, guiding her down—down!—until her hand was filled with him, with his power and essence.

A strange dark thrill ran through her. His very size and breadth made her shiver, for her palm could hold but half of him. Her fingertips skimmed daintily in a shy, tentative quest. He was hot—so very hot! She was amazed at his blistering heat and hardness, the satin texture of the sleek round crown that seemed to swell still further. Her pulse thundered wildly in her ears. She felt the muscles of his belly tighten. Then once again his hand clamped around hers as he wordlessly showed her the motion that would please him most.

It was torment—sheer, sweet torment. Yet Merrick would not have given up this moment for all the glory in Christendom. He cast his head back, his powerful neck arched, his eyes half-closed. He gritted his teeth, for her innocent caress drove him half-mad. He bore it until he could stand no more, certain he would spill himself at any moment.

His hand on her shoulders, he eased her gently to her back. Greedy fingers boldly charted warm, feminine flesh that lay open to sight and touch. She was exquisite, her breasts small and firm, tipped with delicate nipples the color of roses. He bent and touched one perfect pink circle with his tongue, then drew her deep into his mouth. He wet her nipples with curling strokes, first one and then the other until they thrust taut and stiff against his tongue. Her fingers dug into his shoulders. The sound of her breath, quick and ragged, inflamed him almost past bearing.

Slowly he raised his head. The heel of his hand slid with unerring intent down the hollow of her belly. His fingers weaved through dark gold curls to find her damp and sweetly wet. He nearly moaned. His heart was pounding so that he could scarcely breathe. His shaft was throbbing so that he thought he might burst, but he was not yet ready to claim her.

Boldly he found what he sought. Her entire body jerked as he brushed the very pearl of sensation, hidden there within sleek pink folds. It spun through his mind to deepen her pleasure still further, but he sensed she was not yet ready. He felt her stiffen when with one long, strong finger he dipped within the cleft of her womanhood, taunting and teasing. But she did not deny him, and in the next breath her thighs parted of their own will. Her head thrashed back and forth on the pillow. She gasped, her lips were damp and parted. He stared down at her, the rhythm of his hand now blatantly erotic. Wanton sounds of pleasure burst from her throat.

Only then did he lever himself over her, fiercely compelling her to share this pleasure. Palm to palm, he weaved his fingers through hers. The sleek, round crown of his manhood parted damp, golden fleece. Alana gasped anew at the slow slide of his body inside hers, the unyielding pressure. She couldn't look away as she took him in, all of him; he filled her until there was no more of him to give. His blood pounded with a primitive beat, there where he lay planted so solidly within her.

His whisper was taut and ragged. "I do not hurt you, do I, sweet?"

That he could yet speak was a marvel. It was all he could do not to thrust hot and wild in her clinging heat. The feel of his shaft imbedded hot and deep in the tight silken prison of her flesh tore at his control. She was so small he knew he'd have hurt her were she not sweetly damp and ready for him.

Alana's breath tumbled out in a rush. Her body stretched to the limit for he filled her completely, yet there was no pain. She shook her head, unable to tear her gaze from his face. His features were taut and strained, his eyes burning like embers.

She nearly cried out as he withdrew, all hard and sleek and glistening. And then he was inside her again, deeper than she thought possible.

His hands slid down to cup her buttocks. Her own slid around to his back. Her nails dug into his skin. A coil of heat gathered there in the place he possessed so fully. She breathed his name, and then again as a piercing delight shot through her. "Merrick . . . *Merrick*."

It was as if something snapped deep within him. He crushed her to him, catching her cry with his mouth. His kiss was wildly devouring. He plunged again and again, mindlessly hungry. Guided by instinct alone, the churning of her hips met his in perfect tempo, faster and faster. Then suddenly sparks seemed to burst, showering all through her. At the same instant, he exploded within her, scalding her with his seed.

Time spun adrift. She was scarcely aware as Merrick eased his body from hers. He pulled her tight against his side, tugging the furs over her shoulders. Utterly spent, Alana released a long pent-up sigh, feeling as if her very bones had melted. A curious peace settled over them, a peace she was reluctant to break.

Instead it was Merrick who broke it. With a muffled curse, he propped himself up on an elbow. Alana frowned up at him sleepily. "What is it?" she murmured.

He gave an impatient exclamation. " 'Tis that accursed cat! Has he been here all the while?"

"You mean Cedric?" She raised her head, following his gaze. She smothered a smile, for it was indeed Cedric. He sat in the corner, leisurely licking one paw. As if he sensed their scrutiny, he raised his head and peered across at them with glowing yellow eyes. He padded across the floor, his tail curling lazily in the air. Alana patted the space beside her. Cedric leaped up, nuzzling his head beneath her hand. Chuckling, she buried her fingertips in his fur, petting him lazily along his spine.

Merrick's mouth turned down. "Wretched creature!" he muttered. "Only yesterday I bid Simon take him out to the forest and release him."

Alana looked up. "Ah, but he has nowhere else to go. Like me, would you not say, my lord? Ah, but I forget. I dare not complain, for I have a warm bed and food aplenty."

The mildness of her tone did not rob her query of its bite. "Do not mock me," he growled.

"Why, surely I would not dare," she stated sweetly. "After all, you are my lord and conqueror, are you not?"

"Aye, that I am." A slow smile claimed his lips. He leaned close. "So tell me, Saxon. Did your lord and conqueror please you?"

Oh, but the glint in his eye should have given her fair warning . . . "I wonder that you should ask after my pleasure and not your own," she snapped.

His laughter was low and husky. Alana glanced at him sharply. Her heart fluttered strangely, for she could have sworn there was something of tenderness in his expression . . .

Cedric slipped away to settle at the foot of the bed. Alana shivered as a lone fingertip traced the delicate slope of one bare shoulder. "If you pleased me any more, Saxon, the whole of Brynwald would know it."

Alana's cheeks flared crimson. She hid her face in his shoulder before he could see it. But all at once he rolled so that she lay atop him. Stunned, Alana blinked down at him in confusion.

His hand caressed the tumbled glory of her hair. "Aye," he said again, his gaze on her lips. "You pleased me, Saxon . . . and no doubt will yet again this night."

And alas, she did.

The pair were not the only ones to find little sleep that night. Genevieve watched over her charge, as vigilant as a mother tending her babe. Radburn's fever climbed ever higher, but she did not want to awaken Alana, for it was just as she'd said—such things as fever were not beyond her realm of experience.

First she filled a basin with tepid water. She dipped a linen cloth in the water, then drew it slowly over his naked torso. His legs thrashed; he kicked away the sheet. Beneath the feeble covering he wore only his braies.

Deep in her breast, her pulse began to clamor. Of a certainty she was no stranger to the sight of a man's naked chest, though this man's was most impressive. Her gaze wandered at will; she felt herself blush at the sight of him.

No doubt he was a knight well-skilled with lance and sword, she mused. The muscles of his chest, shoulders and arms were cleanly defined, round and sculpted. Genevieve swallowed. Her eyes flitted to his face.

His hair was dark as midnight, long and tousled on his forehead. His lashes were dark and curved, his chin square and strong, his nostrils long and flaring. But it was his mouth that captured her attention for endless moments. Carved in harshly beautiful lines, she could not prevent herself from staring.

Her stomach fluttered. She felt curiously breathless. Her thoughts ran wild. The Saxon named Radburn was very handsome . . . Her hand stilled. A pang rent her breast. Indeed, she'd not thought of any man as handsome since Philippe had died . . .

God in heaven, his eyes were wide open—and dwelled full upon her! To her shock—and then dismay—he sat up.

She tried to press him back. "Nay, Radburn!" she cried. "You must not rise yet! You are too ill!"

A strange bright light flared in the eyes that roved her face. "You are a beauty, lady," he murmured. "Aye, a beauty beyond price." His voice was raspy as dry tinder, yet strangely pleasing.

It flitted through her mind that he was not himself, that he did not know her. Her hands fluttered against his shoulders. She was acutely aware of the feel of his skin, hot as fire, yet sleek and resilient beneath her fingertips.

An odd shiver raced through her. She raised her face to his. "I beg you," she implored. "Please, Radburn, you must lie back, else surely you will harm yourself!"

His gaze had settled on her mouth. "A kiss," he said hoarsely. "A kiss and I will do as you say."

He gave her no chance to argue. His head descended. His mouth came down on hers. Genevieve's eyes flew wide. She yielded with a low moan. Unbidden, her arms slid around his neck, even as his own clamped her hard and tight against his naked chest.

And she cared not. It was wanton; it was wicked, but she was unable to summon the will to deny him. Her lips trembled, then parted beneath the demanding pressure of his. Her heart cried out, even as a thrill shot through her. She'd felt no desire for a man since Philippe had been gone, but faith! it felt so good to be held fast against a man's breast.

To be kissed and to feel passion burst into flames inside her.

Why it should happen now, with this fierce Saxon knight, she did not know. She knew only that it seemed somehow right . . .

Her head was spinning by the time Radburn raised his own. Genevieve struggled for composure, for she knew not what madness had possessed her.

She could feel his gaze on her face, hot and burning. Somehow she found the courage to lift her eyes to his. "Please," she said shakily. "Please, Radburn, you must rest." Trembling hands urged him back. For a moment she feared he might argue. Then all at once he leaned back, as if he were exhausted. His lids half-closed, then all at once he flung out a hand, groping for hers.

Strong fingers weaved through hers. "Stay with me, beauty," came his raspy voice. "Stay . . ."

Soon he slept. Genevieve kept vigil the night through, caressing his brow, soothing with gentle whispers when he restlessly tossed and turned.

She gave a fervent prayer of thanksgiving, for by morning, his fever had broken . . .

Her fingers were still twined with his.

Chapter 14

❦

The following morn Merrick told Alana he would allow her to visit Aubrey—but only with Simon as escort.

Not that Alana minded. His change of heart was wholly unexpected ... yet undeniably pleasing. Nay, she dared not question his decision for fear he would change his mind.

The days grew short, the nights long and dark. She spent as much time as possible with Aubrey, for his frail condition worried her. Soon winter spread its chill across the land, freezing lakes and rivers, blanketing hills and forest with glistening frost and snow.

Though neither she nor Merrick spoke of it, little by little the days wrought a subtle change in their relationship.

Life with Merrick of Normandy was not the unbearable struggle she had feared. Nay, no longer did she look upon him with fear and outrage.

By day a state of wary caution prevailed. No longer did they seek to wound one another with words and wit. And the nights ... the

242

nights were spent in a blaze of passion, wrapped in each other's arms.

Merrick had only to glance at her to kindle a soul-deep yearning unlike anything she'd ever felt before. Bleakly she despaired her weakness. She had made a vow that she would not do battle with him, and so she did not. But many was the night she sought to hold herself aloof, ever distant that he might claim her body and ne'er her heart. But Merrick was not a man to be denied.

And God save her soul, she possessed not the strength to deny him.

Yet trust did not come easy for either of them.

She watched him oft when he held manor court in the hall, resolving the grievances of those he now ruled. Mayhap she expected to find fault with his judgment, yet she could not do so.

On this particular day in early February, she stood near the winding stairs, quietly listening to Merrick pass judgment.

"Two drunken Norman soldiers seized every sack of grain in my hut!" complained a peasant named Filbert from the village. "They cut them open and scattered the grain to the wind. I have five hungry mouths to feed, my lord. But now I have naught to feed them!"

Merrick sat upon his chair, stroking his chin. "Do you know the identities of these two Norman soldiers?"

"I do," Filbert proclaimed stoutly. "'Tis the

pair there, my lord!" He pointed to two soldiers along the wall who had been laughing to each other while the villein spoke. As Merrick's gaze swiveled to them, their laughter ceased abruptly.

"Armand. Marcel. What have you to say to this man's charges?"

The one called Armand opened his mouth, yet no words were forthcoming. Marcel said quickly, "Why, of course the man is mad, my lord."

Filbert shook his head. "Mad, am I? The others said I was surely mad to bring this matter before you. But I told them you were a man to bring justice fairly, even against your own men! And I saw them with my own eyes, and so did my wife!"

Merrick glanced at his soldiers. His voice took on a note of steel. "I would have the truth now, Armand. Marcel. Did you steal this man's grain?"

This time it was Armand who stepped forward. "We did, my lord," he muttered.

Merrick transferred his gaze to the villein. "I will replace the grain you lost from Brynwald's stores." He gestured to one of his men. "Jean, take him to the grainery and see that it is done. As for you, Armand and Marcel, when spring arrives you will perform seven days' labor in Filbert's fields."

As the next case was called, Alana turned away, her expression thoughtful. In truth, Merrick administered justice fairly and without bias to both Norman and Saxon alike. It was then . . . then that Alana came to admit the veriest truth of all . . .

Merrick of Normandy was scarcely the monster she had once accused him of being. He was a man such as her father had been, strong but honorable, both fair and prudent.

Yet her heart lent her no ease. Never had she been so torn! Torn between loyalty to her father's memory and her fledgling feelings for Merrick.

She dare not love him. She *did* not love him. For despite all, he would ever remain her lord and conqueror . . .

Sybil was less than pleased about the turn of events. She watched the pair as they watched each other—Merrick with dark, burning eyes and Alana with vague unease. At table Alana was nearly always at his side or at his knee. And many was the night when Merrick stood, silently extending a hand to her.

Her generous mouth slid down at the corners. *Bah!* It was beyond imagination why Merrick had taken her pale, skinny sister to his bed—more astounding yet that he had yet to replace her with another! Castle gossip was such that it seemed he fancied no other. Surely her own body was far more pleasing, Sybil decided with disdain. She ran an approving hand over the mounds of her breasts, then smiled slyly. Alana was not half so generously endowed. And her hips were wide and ample as well, well able to accommodate a man the size of Merrick. The very thought of coupling with a knight such as he made her hot and wet.

And surely Merrick would be a virile, demanding lover. Her smile withered. Of a certainty the silly wench Alana possessed far less knowledge of what might please such a man than she! She scowled as she rounded a corner of the passageway.

Her foul mood did not last long. Raoul stood there at the far end of the corridor. His eyes agleam, he beckoned to her.

Her fanciful musings vanished. While Merrick might be her chosen one, Sybil had no qualms about taking her pleasures where she might find them. And Raoul was a most satisfying lover. Indeed, she'd never known a man who could please her for hours on end.

It did not take long for the pair to find what they sought—an empty chamber.

Within seconds she stood naked before him. "You have neglected me, my lusty Norman prince." She cupped her breasts in her hands as if to offer them for his approval. As she knew full well it would, his breathing grew rough and his rod swelled full and erect before her very eyes.

He gave a hoarse laugh. "Not for long, my pet." With his hands he squeezed both breasts, then bent to suck both turgid nipples. Sybil whimpered her pleasure and wantonly arched herself into him. His head came up and he ravaged her mouth with his tongue. He pulled her roughly toward him, his hands on her hips, grinding himself against her mound.

Sybil gasped and opened her thighs. With her nails she raked at his tunic until she encountered naked skin. But she was not content with that for long. Her hands dipped boldly into his braies, shoving them down his thighs until she found what she sought. His prick jutted forth, thick and heavy and distended in her palm.

Smiling, she wet her lips with her tongue. With the pressure of his hands on her shoulders, he thrust her down before him. Before long, a guttural moan ripped from deep in his chest.

In their haste to grapple with the other, neither realized they'd failed to fully close the heavy oaken portal.

Outside in the passageway, Alana was on her way to Genevieve's chamber. On hearing the sounds of movement within an unoccupied chamber, she stopped, her gaze puzzled. It was then she noticed the door ajar. Moving nearer, she peered through the narrow opening.

For the space of a heartbeat, she was convinced her eyes deceived her. Her jaw sagged. A strangled sound of disbelief caught in her throat. Little did she realize she was backing away until she collided with a tall hard form.

Merrick caught her elbow. He took in at a glance her horrified expression. "Alana! What is amiss?"

Alana could only shake her head wildly. "Raoul," she gasped. "Sybil . . ."

Just then there arose a series of short, shrill

feminine cries, followed by an ever-increasing hammering.

Alana went pale. "Sweet Jesus," she breathed. She fought like a creature of the wild when Merrick snagged her arm and proceeded to drag her in the opposite direction.

She jerked her arm free. "Stop! I cannot leave Sybil there with him—"

"What is between those two is best left unheard by others, Saxon."

The sight of Raoul, his hands tangled in Sybil's hair, burned through her mind. "You did not see what I did!" she cried.

By now they were alone in their chamber. He folded his arms across his chest and arched a brow. "What, then, did you see?"

Alana's cheeks flamed. "I-I cannot tell you," she stammered.

"Aye, but you can, Saxon."

He was insistent. Determined. He prodded and probed until—little by little—the scene she had witnessed came out all in a rush.

But Merrick did not have a shred of sympathy for Sybil. Indeed, his lips were twitching, as if he found the incident vastly amusing.

Alana's ire spiraled. She did not find Sybil's plight so amusing. She straightened indignantly. "You are cruel!" she accused. "Raoul is a beast. Why, 'tis surely some Norman perversion—"

"I assure you, Saxon, it is not. Why, I'll wager he's done the very same to her."

Alana blanched. Did he seek to make her appear the simpleton—or, God in heaven, was it true? "Nay," she said faintly. "Such things cannot be . . ." She spun around, unable to face him any longer. All at once she felt immensely foolish and naive.

Merrick was sorely tempted to laugh again, for her eyes were enormous, her face the color of fire.

His arms stole around her from behind. He pulled her back against the solid wall of his chest, then rested his chin on the shining cap of her hair.

Warm breath rushed past her ear. "There are some who say 'tis a feast of the senses . . . the most wondrous sensation a man and woman can bestow on each other."

He turned her so that her hands were splayed on his chest. Beneath her fingertips she could feel the rasp of dense, dark fur. There was a familiar tightening low in her belly. Still, she felt compelled to say, "But you heard Sybil scream . . . Raoul was hurting her . . ."

"All screams are not screams of pain, sweet." He nuzzled the baby-soft skin behind her ear. "Need I remind you?" Slowly he turned her in his arms. All traces of laughter left his features. A finger beneath her chin, he raised her face to his.

"'Twould be my very great pleasure to show you, Saxon," he said quietly.

And God above, he did.

He undressed her slowly, his features solemnly intent. Then he shed his own clothing and carried her to the bed. There was a melting sweetness to his lovemaking that robbed her of breath. His hands were everywhere. She trembled as he feasted greedily on the achingly sensitive tips of her breasts, suckling and tugging.

His head moved lower, his lips skimming the hollow of her belly. Her breath snagged deep in her throat. In one smooth move he dragged her legs over his shoulders, and then what feeble protests she might have made died on her lips. All thought fled her mind.

His breath touched her first, warm and damp. And then he was there between her thighs, with the lapping stroke of his tongue, darting and teasing. A jolt of sheer delight shot through her, for he was right. It was wondrous. She closed her eyes and arched against him, searching for the elusive torment of his tongue, until at last she felt it there; *there* at the very heat and heart of her core. Her hands twisted into the sheets. But he was insistent. Determined. Her teeth dug into her lower lip as she sought to withhold a cry of pleasure.

Her breath was ragged and her chest heaved when at last he raised himself above her; Merrick's eyes were fiercely aglow. She couldn't look away as he bound his hips to hers. He came inside her slowly, plunging until he had no more to give, driving them both half-mad. Filled with the rigid thickness of his manhood, she clutched at his arms.

He bent his dark head to hers. "Your ferocious little beast once left his marks on my back," he said against her lips. "But I'd not mind if you did the same, sweet."

With that he began to move, so very slowly at first, then faster and faster until he was thrusting almost wildly, out of control. But Alana did not care. The friction of his body on hers—*in* hers—was more than she could bear. Pleasure, heady and dark, swirled all around her. Caught up in the same mindless frenzy as he, her nails dug into the smoothness of his shoulders, then slid down to capture his wildly churning buttocks. All at once, rapture burst inside her. Overwhelmed with an abandon she'd not known she possessed, broken cries of sheer bliss tore from her lips. Above her she felt a shudder wrack his entire body. The scalding heat of his seed erupted inside her, again and again, his climax as powerful and torrid as hers.

She drifted back to awareness slowly. Only then did she realize how very wanton she had been. Caught snug against his side, a muscled arm wrapped tight about her back, she ducked her head against his shoulder.

"'Tis wicked," she whispered, "the things you do . . . the way you make me feel, Norman."

Beneath her cheek, she felt his chest vibrate in a rare chuckle. He caught a length of golden hair and wrapped it round his fist.

"Wicked, eh?" This time a laugh full-blown emerged. "Faith, how could anyone believe you a witch? You are an innocent."

Aye, it took but a single burning caress to rob the very breath from her lungs. Alana was not proud of the way her body betrayed her anew every time they came together. She could withhold nothing, and her lack of control was frightening.

It was that very truth that weighed heavy on her mind the night through and into the next afternoon. She trudged along next to Simon as they approached the village to visit Aubrey. Merrick had gone to York. Though the day was unusually sunny, the snow bright and glistening, it was unearthly cold. The fur-lined mantle Merrick had brought her from London lay heavy and snug around her shoulders, yet still a chill seeped through. But so intent were her thoughts on Merrick that she didn't realize Simon had stopped until he sharply called her name.

They were not alone.

A small group of men mounted on horses had halted just ahead of them.

"Ho, there!" one of them called. "I would ask a boon of you, mistress."

Alana hesitated. She recognized the man as Saxon by his speech and by his garb. His tone was pleasant enough, yet there was a lean, hungry air to the lot of them that lent her no ease. Their tunics were ragged and filthy. Beside her, she felt Simon stiffen as well.

It was the boy who answered. "What boon would you ask, sir?"

The man rubbed his bewhiskered cheek. "There was a fork in the road a fair distance back. I fear we lost our way. Which will take us to London?"

Simon raised a hand and pointed back over

their shoulders. "If you go back whence you came, the road to the left will take you south to London. The ride will take you some three or four days."

The man doffed his coif. "Our thanks, lad."

An instant later they whirled their horses and were off. Alana sent a fervent prayer heavenward, heartily glad they were gone. Giving a nod to Simon, they hurried on their way.

Tucked in her pouch were several honey cakes for which Aubrey had displayed a particular fondness. He was pleased with her gift, as she'd known he would be. It was near dusk when she finally arose to take her leave of him. She hated to go, for it seemed that only with Aubrey could she truly be herself. With Merrick she must be ever on guard, ever alert to keep her feelings in check.

Though Alana urged him to stay seated, Aubrey walked with her to the door of the hut. He grasped his staff, tottering a bit as he stood there. Blessed Virgin, but the winter had not been kind to him. He seemed so old, she thought with a pang. Fear struck her heart like the shaft of an arrow; it was then she was struck by a fleeting sensation . . . How many times would she see him thus again? She hugged him fiercely, and for so long he cleared his throat.

"Faith, child, you dare not dally any longer! Darkness comes soon and I would have you and the boy back at Brynwald before then. I hear tell that rebel bands of Saxons prowl about, robbing and thieving, men who care nary a whit whom they hurt."

Alana laid a hand on his arm. "We will be back at the keep long before dark," she assured him. Her mind was not on his warning, however, but rather on the strange feeling she'd had. Yet his wave was hearty and stout as he bid them Godspeed. Mayhap, she decided cautiously as they left the village behind, her imagination had become overzealous.

But her mind was soon to turn to other matters. They were scarcely out of the village when Simon grabbed her elbow.

By the time she glanced up, she and Simon were surrounded . . . by none other than the ragged, filthy men they'd encountered earlier.

Beside her Simon's eyes flashed. "Stand aside that we may pass," he ordered sharply.

"I think not, lad." The man who had addressed them earlier—their leader, it seemed—gave a wheezing laugh. "Nay, I think not."

Alana's insides seemed to freeze. Nonetheless, she faced them boldly. "We have done nothing to you," she stated clearly. "We are on our way back to Brynwald Keep—"

"Ah, lassie, that we know." He grinned, displaying a wide gap-toothed smile. " 'Tis amazing what can be learned by asking the right questions."

Her heart seemed to stop. Her lips barely moved as she spoke. "What do you want of us? We have no jewels, no coin—"

"'Tis not what we want of you, but what we would have of the lord of Brynwald. But never fear, lass, if all goes well we'll have the both of you back within a fortnight."

A cold lump of dread settled like a stone in the pit of her belly. "What," she said faintly. "Surely you cannot mean to abduct us—"

The man leered. "A quick one, ain't she, lads?"

"Nay, you cannot do this! I am Saxon, as Saxon as you—"

"But a Norman's prize—and one he obviously favors from the look of that mantle of yours." He grinned slyly. "No doubt he would pay a king's ransom for ye, and aye, for his nephew, there, too."

Terror raced through her. By now four of the others had dismounted. Both she and Simon began to back away, but alas, two of the men had already seized hold of them. The two of them twisted and kicked and struggled mightily, but there was no help for it; they were soon trussed up tight as piglets and thrown on the back of a horse.

At a signal from their leader, the Saxons tore off wildly toward the forest with their bounty. But one thought crowded her mind as they left Brynwald behind.

Merrick would surely think she had tried to flee him . . . yet again.

In that, she was right.

Merrick was furious when he arrived back from York, only to discover Alana had not returned from the village. He had immediately searched out Simon, but the boy was missing as well.

Now he turned burning eyes toward the old man Aubrey's hut. The old man swore that naught was amiss when Alana had left shortly before eventide; he was adamant that she had departed with Simon.

Merrick smote his fist against his palm. Ah, but he should have known better than to trust her . . . those lips that were ever so sweet and pliant would ever lie and deceive him! He despised the thought that leaped to his mind, yet he had no choice. It seemed the wench had escaped him yet again!

Yet why was Simon with her? It made no sense. Had she forced the boy into leaving with her? Simon scarcely possessed the strength of a man, yet he was a wiry, muscled youth well able to defend himself against a woman—especially one so slight as Alana.

Even as he stood there, snow began to drift from the sky. Within seconds it was like a fine white curtain before his eyes. He cursed long and foully. He could accomplish little in the darkness. And if the snow did not cease soon, whatever tracks she might have made would be covered by morn.

His jaw clenched. But he would find her, he vowed blackly. By the Virgin, he would find her. And then . . . then she would learn she had played him for a fool for the last time.

Chapter 15

Never in all her days had she been so frightened. They rode for hours, ever deeper into the darkness of the forest. It was well into the next day before they stopped at a spacious forest glade. Alana was numb with cold and fatigue and hunger by then.

Their leader's name was Bramwell. He jerked Alana down from where she'd sat behind him on his mount. As her feet touched the ground, her legs protested her weight after so many hours in the saddle. She staggered and nearly fell, biting back a cry of pain.

He untied her hands that she might attend her personal needs, and she did so quickly. Returning from the bushes, she could not help but overhear a low-voiced conversation.

She started when a hand touched her elbow. But it was only Simon. He beckoned and they retreated slightly.

"Could you hear them?" he whispered.

She nodded. "Bramwell has sent a man back to Brynwald with a demand for ransom."

He would have spoken further, but his teeth began to clack so that she could scarcely understand him. One of Bramwell's men had stolen his mantle, still another his heavy woolen tunic, leaving him clad in only a thin linen shirt, chausses and boots.

Without hesitation she whipped her own mantle off and placed it about his thin shoulders.

His eyes conveyed his protest. "There is no need," he began.

"There is every need, Simon." Her eyes flashed warningly. "You shiver with cold. I am far more used to the chill than you," she lied. "What if you should sicken as you did not so very long ago? Your mother would ne'er forgive me. I would ne'er forgive myself."

He bit his lip, his gaze reluctant as it met hers. Some silent message passed between them in that instant, something that had not been there before.

He touched her arm with his bound hands. "I am in your debt," he said solemnly.

Alana pretended to watch the snow sift down from the treetops, but her throat was achingly tight. She and Simon had spent much time together, but there always had been an elusive barrier between them. Only now—now she had the curious sensation that such was not the case at all . . .

Her attention was not to dwell for long on the boy. She gasped as one of Bramwell's men suddenly dragged her forward, nearly wrenching her arm from its socket. Dirty and unsavory, his hair hung in clumps nearly to his shoulders. His beard was ragged and unkempt. There was no doubt what he intended. His eyes, afire with lust, lingered on her breasts. Though terror lay in a cold hard lump in her belly, Alana sought to jerk her arm back, but he was not to be denied. He rounded on her with a feral snarl.

Simon's voice rang out clearly. "If she is harmed, you may be certain Merrick will pay no ransom. He prizes her greatly."

Bramwell, off with another of his men, suddenly turned. "Ewert!" he shouted. "The boy is right. Tie the wench once more and come here!"

The Saxon Ewert retrieved the leather thongs that had bound her wrists. But as he straightened, Simon sneered. "What, Bramwell! Do you so fear a mere woman that you must bind her?"

Again Bramwell's head swiveled toward them. Alana held her breath, for the Saxon's expression was fierce to behold.

He approached them. "You are a noisy one, Norman. And methinks I would like it better if I did not have to listen to your drivel." He stroked his beard and smiled slyly. "Aye, I should like it even better if I were no longer forced to gaze upon your Norman face and form."

An awful fear gripped Alana's heart, for she was certain they meant to kill the boy. Bramwell turned away and gestured to one of the others. They spoke in low-voiced whispers; she strained to hear.

" . . . take him north to the place where the river meets the sea . . . keep him there at the camp . . . Nay . . . Nay! We must have a care, for 'tis said Merrick of Normandy is as deadly a warrior as any of the Danes! And 'tis his coin we covet, not his vengeance . . . wait there until you have word from me . . . when their ransom is in hand we will kill them, both of them . . ."

Alana's blood turned to ice in her veins. Sweet heaven, they would *kill* them . . .

Her shoulders slumped as she watched Simon taken away, mounted behind his captor. Her heart cried out. She could only pray that God would keep him safe, if only for now.

A long time later, she stared into the firelight. She feared what Merrick would think, afraid of what he would not. She had no doubt he would pay whatever ransom Bramwell demanded for Simon, but what about her? Her heart twisted. Indeed, there was every chance he would refuse to part with his coin for the sake of her safety. No doubt he would think himself well rid of her.

But indeed, what did it matter if he paid the ransom or no? Bramwell would kill them either way.

On and on her mind twisted and turned. Bramwell threw her a fur and offered her a hunk of dried meat but she could scarce eat a bite. The snow had stopped long ago. The circle of the moon rose high in a night-dark sky. The Saxons swilled eagerly from several horns of ale. Alana sat huddled against the trunk of an oak tree, unable to rest, unable to still the wanderings of her mind.

From whence the idea came, she didn't know. Nor did she care, for she suddenly realized . . . One by one, the Saxons had dropped off into a noisy sleep. Snores rose and fell all around her. Indeed, there was no one to see what she did or did not do . . . No one to stop her from doing what she would . . . *going* where she would. No doubt morning would be nigh before these drunken louts awakened.

A full moon shone down from the heavens, spilling its milky glow through the tree branches. Excitement gathered in the pit of her stomach. She rose, her muscles stiff and cramped from the cold. Little by little she crept forward, watchful for any signs of stirring from the Saxons.

Her heart was thudding so wildly that she feared they could surely hear it. She scattered the horses, save for one, a gentle palfrey. With no mounts, the Saxons would be unable to give flight after her except on foot.

Moments later horse and rider vanished into the night.

It was purely a hunch that prompted Merrick to lead his men northward into the forest. As he'd suspected, last eve's snow had covered all trace of footsteps. But near midday, near a fallen tree trunk he spied the unmistakable signs that horses had passed through.

He forged on, more determined than ever.

Not long after, there was a shout from one of his men. "My lord, look!"

Merrick's eyes followed his finger. A small, bedraggled figure atop a small palfrey plodded toward them. He gave a sharp exclamation and dug his spurs into the sides of his destrier.

It was Alana.

The instant he drew near, he was off his horse and grabbing for the reins. Her hands were wrapped in cloth torn from her skirts. Her face was so pale her eyes stood out like vivid jewels. The tattered fur draped over her shoulders looked half-frozen. Her lips formed his name but no sound emerged.

Weary beyond measure, chilled to the marrow of her bones, she sought to focus both mind and sight. Indeed, Alana wondered if the sight of Merrick before her was perchance but a dream.

It took all her strength to hold herself upright in the saddle. She pressed a hand to her forehead. Why was she so dizzy? Yet deep in some far distant corner of her brain she realized she had made it.

"Simon," she said hoarsely. It hurt to speak, to move, even to breathe. "You must find . . . Simon. They took him . . ."

"Who, Saxon?" It was Merrick. His voice washed over her like a flood of reality. "Who took him? And where is he?"

Strong arms caught her as she leaned forward. She was dimly aware of being pulled from the horse, then being held, of staring

upward into searing gray eyes. He was angry,
she thought vaguely, his scowl as black as
she'd yet to see it. Her heart wrenched. Why?
her heart cried. Why must he ever and always
be angry with her . . . ?

Spots danced before her eyes. Merrick's features drew near, then seemed to fade. She
shivered violently, unaware of the arms that
tightened about her.

"Saxons," she managed. "One named Bramwell sought to ransom him . . . they took him
north . . . to a place where the river meets the
sea . . ." Her eyes filled with tears. "You must
hurry. You must help him . . ."

Above her, Merrick rapped out orders. A
dark void seemed to swirl all about her, tugging at her, as if to pull her in.

She remembered no more.

When next she woke, she was warm and
dry, tucked snugly into bed at Brynwald.
Memory surfaced, swift and merciless, and
she heard herself cry out Simon's name. Above
her, someone murmured reassuringly, laying
a soft, feminine hand on her brow.

It was Genevieve. Alana opened her eyes
to find Merrick's sister bending over her, the
smoothness of her brow furrowed with worry.
With a gasp she tried to sit up.

"Nay, be still," Genevieve said firmly. "You
are not yet ready to rise."

Alas, it was true. Alana felt as if she'd
been bruised and beaten over every part of
her body. "How did I come to be here?" she
asked weakly.

"Merrick sent one of his men-at-arms back with you, then went on to find Simon."

"They have not yet returned?"

Genevieve shook her head no.

Try though she might, Alana could not withhold the anxious fear that flitted across her features. Oddly, it was Genevieve who reassured her, patting her hand where it lay atop the edge of the furs.

"Do not fear, Alana. My brother would spare naught to protect those he loves. He will find Simon before he comes to any harm." She smiled, then said softly, "Indeed, 'twas you who gave me a fright such as I have never known. Faith, but when I saw you lying so still and pale and silent . . . ! You slept the day and night through." She tipped her head to the side. "You must surely be starving." She moved to the door and called for food.

Once a tray was before her, Alana discovered she was indeed ravenous. She ate every last crumb of the cheese and bread.

Genevieve laughed delightedly. "Would you like more?" Already she'd begun to move toward the door.

"Aye—" Alana started to say, then all at once stopped. She flung her legs from the bed, clamped her hand over her mouth and fought to control the sudden heaving of her stomach. It took but one glimpse of her startled eyes and lack of color and Genevieve ran for a basin.

Alana fell to her knees and retched violently there and then. Her skin was clammy and sweating. She was so weak Genevieve had to half-lift, half-push her back into the bed. There she collapsed weakly against the pillows.

Genevieve sat beside her and bathed her face with a wet cloth.

Alana's smile was feeble. "You must forgive me," she murmured. " 'Tis unlike me to be so sickly. But I am ashamed to say that seems to be happening oft of late."

Genevieve spoke slowly. "This is not the first time?"

Alana shook her head, startled when Genevieve bit her lip. Her expression grew troubled. Alana's smile withered, for she didn't understand why Genevieve should peer at her so oddly.

"What," she said faintly. "Genevieve, what is it? Tell me."

For an instant it appeared she would not. Then all at once she blurted, "Oh, but I do hate to say such, but . . . you are so slender, Alana. As I undressed you I couldn't help but note that your waist has thickened." She hesitated. "How long has it been since your last course?"

Alana blanched visibly. Her mind searched frantically backward. What with the drastic changes her life had seen of late, she'd paid no heed . . . "Not since I came to the keep," she said shakily. "Early December mayhap."

"Alana, I've rarely been wrong about these things, but . . . 'tis my guess that you are with child."

Alana's hand slid to her belly. God in heaven, there was a slight roundness that hadn't been there before. "Nay," she said faintly. "Nay, it cannot be."

One look at her stricken expression and Genevieve was at her side, a comforting arm around her shoulder. "There now," she soothed. "Do not be distressed! Surely Merrick will—"

"Merrick!" Alana clutched at Genevieve. "Nay, you cannot tell him! I beg of you, do not tell him!"

Genevieve bit her lip, clearly in doubt. Alana pleaded and wept until at last she agreed. The girl was so distraught Genevieve could do little else. She managed to calm her, settling her back into bed and drawing the covers up about her chin.

But there was no rest for Alana.

She laced her arms about her knees and stared sightlessly across the chamber, her eyes so dry they hurt. Genevieve had whispered this babe would be a blessing. A shroud of despair crept around her heart. A child was a possibility she had not foreseen—and oh, she'd been so foolish not to! All at once she was terrified of what the future might hold, not only for herself, but for her child.

For she had no doubt that Merrick would be less than pleased when he discovered her condition.

She remained in her chamber throughout the remainder of the day. A soft, purple haze of twilight crept between the shutters when there was suddenly a loud commotion outside in the yard.

She hastened to the window. A group of

riders had just entered the keep. Even as she watched, Simon leaped to the ground. The relief that flooded her was immense, yet she could scarcely focus on anything other than Merrick as he swung to the ground. Genevieve ran out from the hall just then. As mother embraced son, Alana looked on, a curious catch in her heart. Genevieve wept freely. Merrick stepped up, and laid a strong hand on the back of the boy's head, a gesture that bespoke a familiar affection.

There was an odd tightening in her chest. Would Merrick treat his own son so? She was unable to stop her mind from straying where it would. Indeed, 'twas hardly likely Merrick would even claim her babe as his own. A melancholy sadness seemed to grab hold of her heart and squeeze. Never had she felt so very alone! As if she did not belong . . .

As indeed she did not.

Some while later there was a knock on the door. Alana hesitated, then called, "Enter." Her muscles relaxed as she saw it was Genevieve. In her hands she carried the fur-lined mantle Merrick had brought her from London. Smiling, she laid it on the bed.

"Simon thanks you," she said softly, "as I thank you."

Alana smiled slightly. "They stole his mantle and tunic. I was greatly afraid he would sicken again."

Genevieve nodded. "They prepare a celebration in the hall soon. I pray you, come join us."

Alana could not help it. Her thoughts sped straight to Merrick. It spun through her mind that he had only to look at her to know . . . She chided herself for her foolishness. How could he possibly suspect, when she'd had no inkling herself until Genevieve suggested the possibility this very day?

Her hesitation was her undoing. Genevieve took her hands and gazed at her steadily. "You cannot avoid him, Alana. He expects you and—and I would have you share my joy." She squeezed her fingers. " 'Twould please me greatly."

Stupid, foolish tears burned the back of Alana's throat. Yet again, it struck her how much closer she felt to this woman than her own sister. How could she refuse? She could not. She did not, though it took every shred of courage she possessed to take her place in the hall that night.

She had no further glimpse of Merrick till then, for he didn't return to their chamber. Alana was secretly glad; for she dreaded seeing him again with all that she possessed.

He stood near the head of the table, dark and striking and so very handsome he stole the very breath from her lungs—a feeling that was utterly terrifying.

Some hours had passed before he made his way toward her.

His expression betrayed no hint of his thoughts. "You are quite recovered?" His tone was cool.

She nodded. Unbidden, her eyes flitted toward Genevieve, who quickly glanced away. Genevieve had kept her promise and said nothing, though many was the time when Alana saw her eyes travel again and again between herself and Merrick.

"The Saxons did you no harm?"

"Nay," she said, her tone very low. "Simon told them you would pay no ransom if we were hurt. But the leader said he would kill us both once the ransom was in hand." She shivered. " 'Twas fortunate indeed that you were able to find him so quickly."

"Indeed," he echoed. "He tells me he might have perished from cold if not for you. It seems I owe you much, Saxon."

Alana knew not what to say, and so she said nothing. But he stared at her so long and so hard, she grew uneasy.

Something was wrong. Something was very, very wrong. As the ringing silence grew ever stronger, so did her certainty.

She laced her hands before her and nervously moistened her lips. "What is it? Why do you look at me so?"

"I find it disturbing, Saxon, that you claim the Saxon Bramwell sent a man to demand a ransom of me. Yet no such demand was made—"

Alana's chin came up. "You were not here!"

"Nonetheless, my soldiers were, along with my sister. No Saxon appeared to demand a ransom, and so I wonder what you have to say for yourself now."

Alana clamped her jaw tight. "I cannot

pretend to know the reason why," she told him curtly. "Mayhap the man lost his way. Mayhap your men are mistaken—"

"And mayhap you lie, Saxon. Indeed, you once said you would ally yourself with the devil in order to escape me. I merely find myself curious . . . did you ally yourself with your fellow Saxons instead? Did you seize opportunity by the throat and plot my demise?"

His tone was as cutting as his eyes. Alana's mind blurred. For one heart-stopping moment she felt perilously near tears. Did he truly believe she sought to plot against him?

Bitterness blotted her soul. She had saved his nephew's life twice now. Yet still he was always so quick to condemn her without reason or cause, to believe the very worst of her.

Temper flared, hot as fire. She could no more curb her tongue than she could the blaze of her anger.

"Your gratitude overwhelms me, my lord . . . ah, but I forget . . . my lord conqueror! You would thank me, then condemn me, and nearly all in the very same breath!" She glared her ire. "You may be certain I'll not make the same mistake again!"

With that she whirled and ran, weaving and darting through the crowded hall. Behind her she heard a mighty crash and a vicious curse. Her steps quickened until she was running full tilt. Her breath came in panting spurts. Footsteps pounded behind her . . . or was it merely the thunder of her heart?

She had just cleared the top of the winding stair when he caught her. He whirled her around, the bite of his fingers in her arm like iron manacles.

"Damn you, Saxon! Do you run because you are guilty? Because you betrayed my generosity? Will you not even deny it?"

She wrenched herself from his hold, but the hold of his eyes was no less harsh. "Why do you ask?" she cried. "You will believe what you will and it matters little what I say or do not say! But I will tell you this. I've done nothing that you should so accuse me!"

Glittering light from the torch mounted on the wall cast flickering shadows across his face. "Then mayhap I was wrong. But I am not wrong about this," he said fiercely. "I watched you tonight, Saxon. You were distraught. Your dismay at my presence was plain for all to see. So tell me, sweet. Did you not expect that I would return to Brynwald? Did you hope that I would not?"

Alana's delicate jaw locked tight. Oh, that he could think so little of her! He knew naught of her—he cared naught *about* her. Her feelings. Her pride. Her soul cried out the injustice. He spoke of betrayal, yet whose was the greater betrayal? He did not trust her. To him she was naught but a possession.

Steeling herself against him, she pressed her lips together and matched his stare with her own.

His temper exploded. He seized her by the

shoulders. "Answer me, Saxon!"

Alana was suddenly so angry she was shaking with it. She flung back her head and met his demand with a fire equal to his.

"And what if I did? I despise you," she hissed. "You put the torch to my home. You and your men killed my father and took him from me. You made me your slave and my sister as well! I weep for the day you and your vile Norman bastards stormed our shores, and I long for the day you will leave—or fall beneath a Saxon blade! Indeed, I will rejoice! You talk as if I owe you loyalty, but I owe you no allegiance. I owe you nothing!"

A blistering curse split the air. He shook her so that her head fell back like a fragile blossom. Shocked, she stared at him, dazed. "By God," he said through his teeth, "you owe me your very life!"

Neither realized that Genevieve had given chase as well. She surged around the corner at that very instant. With a sharp cry she lunged forward, dragging at her brother's arm.

"Merrick! My God, man, have a care! She is with child!"

Chapter 16

In all truth, Merrick could not explain the dark shadow that slipped over him, the doubt eating away at his insides. She had cried for Simon, when she had feared for his life. Yet were her tears real or but a trick? Ah, but how easily she might have plotted with the Saxons to seize the boy, a plot to lure him from Brynwald and kill him.

He gritted his teeth. Not an hour passed that he did not think of her, whether he willed it or no! He thought of how she melted against him in the heat of passion, how her lips tasted, damp and bedewed with the moist heat of his, and how wildly her hips churned beneath his. And still he wondered . . . did he stir her desire as she stirred his? Did she give herself over to him merely to deceive him?

I weep for the day you and your vile Norman bastards stormed our shores, and I long for the day you will leave. Indeed, I will rejoice!

Her angry cry echoed in the chambers of his mind. Nay, he thought blackly. She would not put aside her hatred of the Normans so easily.

He would do well to be wary of her.

All this . . . all this and more ran through his mind in that mind-splitting instant. So it was that he raked her with a glance as searing as his tone.

"Is it mine, Saxon? Or will you boast an English sire?"

To Alana he might well have struck her. Her throat worked. For the space of a heartbeat, words eluded her. Then she flung at him all the seething emotion that burned in her soul.

"I hate you, Norman. God, but I hate you!"

She pushed her way past him and into their chamber, slamming the portal shut behind her. A curse on his lips, Merrick started after her, only to have Genevieve plant herself squarely in his path.

"You are a fool," she said without preamble.

"And you are in my way," he growled.

Her chin tipped mutinously. "Faith, but you are cruel." Low as her tone was, it vibrated with her fury. "Cruel to accuse her of such a thing when you are well aware she's known the touch of no man but you. Cruel to even *think* she sought to plot your demise with the Saxons. Her people condemn her for being a witch, while you condemn her for things that simply bear no truth!"

His features were a mask of stone. "Cruel, am I? She is not the innocent you believe, Genevieve. Once before she sought to escape me. And you were in the hall tonight. Her distress was vivid for all to see—she wanted no part of me!"

"She was scarcely anxious to see you again, aye, but not for the reason you think! She knew not how to tell you she was with child. And you, brute that you are, gave her the very reaction she feared!" She confronted him in righteous indignation. "You know the ways of the world far better than she, brother. If you had no wish to get her with child then you should never have taken her to your bed. So if you would blame her—"

"I blame no one!" he exploded. " 'Tis just that I did not expect it!"

Slender brows arched high. "If you plow the field the seed will flourish, brother."

Merrick glared at her, trying to thrust aside a twinge of guilt. But an inner voice inside would not be silenced. *She is right*, taunted the voice. *I should have suspected the possibility long since.*

"If you are wise you will let her be, brother. This is a trying time and—"

"And once again you interfere where you should not. It has become a most annoying habit of late, Genevieve. Now stand aside, if you please."

Despite the pretense of manners it was nary a request and she knew it. His purpose was plainly writ in the intensity of his expression. Genevieve surrendered with a tiny nod. Her gaze was troubled as he swept by her. As the door swung closed, she directed a fervent prayer heavenward.

Alana's shoulders went rigid as he stepped within the chamber. It took all the courage she possessed to turn and face him.

Time stood still. The silence seemed to engulf them both. Then at last he spoke. "It seems we must talk, Saxon."

Her chin climbed high. "I have naught to say to you, Norman."

Merrick curbed the biting retort that rose to his lips. Behind her, the firelight bathed her form in golden silhouette. She stood before him, her eyes huge, so very pale but calm, small hands linked together before her. A rush of some nameless emotion struck him like a blow. Never had she been more desirable. Never more beautiful. And to his mounting irritation, never more unapproachable!

"I should not have spoken as I did. Of a certainty the child is mine." His tone was curt. "I spoke rashly, though you have many times provoked me."

"Provoked you? Why, I said nary a word!" To her horror, her voice wobbled traitorously. "And I do not understand why you are so angry. 'Tis hardly my fault!"

"I did not say that it was. But I am curious, Saxon. Does it please you that you carry my babe?"

His jaw was tense; it revealed the lie in his words. All at once the strain of the past days was too much to bear. Though she hated herself for such weakness, her gaze faltered beneath the unyielding demand in his.

A mask of icy coldness descended. The sound he made was one of disgust. "I should

have known you would scarcely be pleased."
He paused, then said harshly, "Go to bed. We
will talk more on the morrow." With that he
presented his back to her.

Alana needed no further urging. She slipped
out of her clothes and crawled into bed, clad
only in her chemise. Drawing the furs around
her, Alana's eyes strayed to Merrick. He stood
facing the hearth, his hands linked behind his
back, his posture rigid.

Time marched onward. There was no sound
but the crackling and hiss of the fire. Unable
to stand the horrible silence, Alana shifted to
her side, curling her knees to her chest. Never
in all her days had she been so miserable.

In time, she heard the rustle of his clothing
as it dropped to the floor. He blew out the
candle and slipped in the bed beside her. She
squeezed her eyes shut and feigned sleep.

But there would be no sleep for her this
night. How long she lay there, in the dim light
and silence, she knew not. Though surely no
more than the span of a hand separated them,
the distance seemed immense. He did not
touch her, and oh! it made no sense, but all
at once that was all she longed for. To feel
his arms hard and tight around her back, the
beat of his heart steady and strong beneath
her ear.

Desperation filled her chest. What was
wrong with her? Not an hour since, she'd
sworn she hated him and meant it with all
of her being. Now all she yearned for was
to banish the hurtful words and pretend they

had never been. But such was not possible, and now there loomed before them an even greater hurdle.

His reaction was all that she had known it would be—feared it would be. He had been so—so coldly enraged and the knowledge was like a thorn in her heart. Despair seized her breast like a clamp, until she could hardly breathe. Her throat clogged with emotion as she fought to hold back tears. Thinking that Merrick now slept, she could no longer withhold a dry, choked sob.

Merrick's head turned sharply. Beside her, he raised himself on an elbow to peer at her. She lay huddled in a tight little ball, a small, closed fist at her breast. Her head was bowed low. There was something very forlorn in her pose just then, a glimpse of hurt vulnerability he could scarcely ignore.

She jerked as his hand brushed her shoulder. Undaunted, he brushed her hair away that he might see her face, bathed in firelight.

"What is this, Saxon! Why do you cry? Are you ill?" he exclaimed impatiently.

Alana shook her head. But alas, now the tears began to flow in earnest.

Unswayed by nothing, he turned her so that he could see her. When she stringently sought to avoid his gaze by lowering her lashes, he caught her chin in hand.

"Tell me," he demanded. "Why do you weep?"

A half-sob escaped and then everything was tumbling out in a rush. "You think that I plotted with the Saxons, but I swear I did not . . . Then you asked if I was pleased. In all truth, I—I know not what I feel! But you, 'tis plain that you are the one who is displeased, you who are angry—"

"If I am angry, Saxon, 'tis because I learned from my sister the news that should have been mine to hear first—and, I might remind you, from your lips rather than hers. Why did you not tell me?"

Calm though he was, his voice still carried a hint of bite. Alana floundered, all at once feeling absurdly guilty. "I—I only just discovered it myself this morn. Indeed, 'twas Genevieve who guessed." She hesitated, then continued in a tear-choked voice. "I—I understand that surely you no longer want me. That you do not want my babe . . ."

She was not allowed to finish. "You forget, this babe is mine as well. And you are wrong, for I do want you."

Her lungs burned as she fought to hold back the tears. "You wanted a—a slave. A whore. Not a child."

He clenched his jaw. His fingers dropped from her chin. He scowled blackly. "You are neither a slave nor a whore, Saxon."

She trembled, for she could feel his piercing regard like the tip of a knife. "I—I will be a burden. A burden you will soon grow tired of." She couldn't stop the betraying catch in her voice. "My babe will be a burden."

"A burden! By all that is holy . . . surely you did not think I would send you away?" Merrick swore foully. "You did, didn't you?"

She hung her head, for that very thought hung high aloft in her mind throughout the day.

"I cannot let you go, Saxon. I will not. Now come here." Though his voice was harsh, his hand was not. Without a word, he rearranged her body so that the slender length of her back rested flush against his naked chest. A dark hand curled against the swell of her hip. Silence drifted between them, yet it was not an uncomfortable silence. She shivered a little, and he drew her closer still.

"Have you been ill?" he murmured.

"Some mornings," she admitted. " 'Twas foolish of me to have been so blind, yet I—I was."

Mayhap 'twas not so much blindness as fear—fear of the truth. But this observation Merrick kept to himself. For a time they did not speak. He winced a little, caught in a haze of conflicting emotions. Her nearness tempted him, tempted him greatly! The part of him that desired her most lay cradled between the softness of her buttocks. He gritted his teeth with every slight movement she made, for he ached with the need to lay her back, strip away her shift and make her forget all else but the passion that raged between them. Yet he did not, for oddly, she seemed so very young just then, though she carried a child curled deep in her womb.

His child, he thought with a swell of pride, and it was then that the full import of this revelation dawned full and rich.

He felt her tense as his hand first moved, gently exploring. With his palm he traced the thrusting fullness of her breasts, then ventured further downward in discovery. His fingers splayed wide against the slight roundness of her belly.

"I can feel the changes in you," he said softly. "I should have known, too, Saxon."

She flushed. Though he could no longer see her face, he could feel the heat flare beneath her skin. A surge of fierce possessiveness shot through him. God, but she was sweet!

He pressed his mouth to the delicate sweep of her shoulder, inhaling the soft, womanly scent of her. "When do you expect the child?"

His voice was a warm rush of air against her ear. Her pulse seemed to stumble. An odd pain knotted in her breast. She yearned to believe he spoke the truth—that he was not angry— for the thought he might not want his child was not to be endured. Yet she detected no hardness in him just then, and so she clung to a fragile tendril of hope.

Her mind traveled fleetingly back in time. It must have happened that very first time . . . "I am not certain," she murmured. "But I think at summer's end, shortly before Michaelmas."

"Michaelmas." A note of satisfaction echoed in his tone. "Brynwald will reap the fruits of harvest, while I will reap the fruits of a cold winter night's pleasure."

She gave a shocked gasp at his bluntness, and he gave a low, vibrating laugh, then drew her back against him more tightly. He weaved his fingers through hers, then let them rest snug against her belly.

Alana could not help it. Simple though the gesture was, tears stung her eyes anew. But this time they were tears of gladness. Oh, mayhap it made no sense, but there was comfort—a world of it—in his nearness. She did not mind the heaviness of his arm hard about her waist. Against her back she could feel the steady tattoo of his heart. Content despite the turmoil of the day, her lids began to droop. Gradually the tension seeped from her limbs. Soon she slept, deeply and dreamlessly.

By the next day, her condition was hardly a secret.

Someone—she knew not who—had apparently heard the exchange abovestairs that night. The news that she was with child spread like a blazing fire. Within but a few days, the whole of the keep knew she carried Merrick's babe. And alas, with each passing day, the doubts that had plagued her that eve returned a hundredfold . . .

And never more so than the day she encountered Sybil alone in Genevieve's chamber.

She had gone there to borrow some thread from Genevieve's vast supply. Sybil glanced up from where she was straightening the bed.

"She has gone to see the village alewife, sister." Alana murmured her thanks and began to withdraw, but Sybil rounded the bed and called out, "Do not leave! I would have a word with you."

Alana did not venture within, but remained there near the entrance.

Sybil presented herself before her, hands on her hips. She nodded toward Alana's middle. " 'Twas foolish of you to be so careless, sister."

Alana was too taken aback to reply.

"How far gone are you?" she inquired.

"In a fortnight it will be some four months," Alana said slowly.

"Four months. Why, soon you will be fat as a sow!"

Alana's hand moved instinctively to her belly. In her bath this morn she had noticed how her waist had thickened, how her stomach had begun to swell and soften and grow. Even her breasts were heavy and tender.

Sybil went on boldly, "No doubt 'twill not be long before Merrick turns you out, you know."

Pride came to her rescue at last. "You sound jealous, Sybil."

Sybil threw back her head and chuckled heartily. "I am hardly jealous, Alana." She winked at her. "Raoul sees to it that I have no time to spare for other men."

Alana's lips tightened in disapproval. How Sybil countenanced Raoul was beyond comprehension.

"Besides," Sybil added knowingly, " 'tis common for a man to stray when his woman is near term. An enormous belly is unsightly and ungainly—scarcely pleasing to the eye—and it hampers his pleasure, if you know what I mean. And indeed, Merrick has no reason to be faithful, since you are hardly his wife."

Alana caught her breath. The thought of Merrick with another . . . Pain dragged upon her breast like a fallen timber.

Sybil pursed her lips. "Indeed," she continued matter-of-factly, " 'tis likely the babe will be born with your curse."

Alana's eyes met hers in horror. "Nay," she said brokenly. "Nay!"

Gleaming dark eyes fastened on her. "There are ways to end the possibility of such, you know." When Alana gazed back at her blankly, Sybil heaved an impatient sigh. "Come now, Alana! Surely your mother knew a potion to get rid of an unwanted babe!"

Alana stared at her in shocked, frozen silence. Mayhap Sybil only meant to help, but she could tolerate no more. She spun around and ran.

She was completely unaware of the tight-lipped scrutiny locked on her form from just down the passageway.

In her chamber, she collapsed before the fire. She took her evening meal there that eve, but there was no peace for her wayward mind. What if Sybil was right? Merrick desired her now, but what would happen when she grew round and full and heavy with her burden? Perhaps Sybil was right and he would cast her aside.

Ah, but isn't that the very thing you sought from the beginning? needled an intrusive little voice inside. *To be free of him forever?*

Her heart constricted. She did not know . . . God in heaven, she did not know!

Merrick entered shortly thereafter. He stood in the doorway, tall and lean and so handsome it stole the very breath from her. But did her imagination run wild—or was there a hint of brooding darkness in those eyes that chanced to light upon her?

She rose, uncertain of his mood, just as uncertain how to proceed. Some strange emotion caught at her heart. His hair was tousled, she noticed, as if he'd run his fingers through it time and again. It struck her then that he appeared incredibly tired. There were deep grooves etched beside the stark masculine beauty of his mouth.

"You look weary," she murmured. "Mayhap a hot bath would be to your liking." She did not await his answer, but glided past him to the door, where she called for buckets of hot water.

A short time later, he climbed into the round wooden tub, paying no mind to his nudity. Alana disrobed and slipped into bed naked. Her gaze strayed helplessly to him again and again as he bathed. He had not asked her assistance, and oh! how she wished he had!

Against the flickering flow of the firelight, his profile was arresting and noble and proud. With her eyes she traced the jutting strength of his nose, the lean squareness of his jaw. His arms and shoulders were wet and sleek, like oiled wood, his biceps cleanly defined. Her fingers fairly ached with the need to skim her hands over the binding tautness of his arms and shoulders, to savor the feel of muscle sheathed in skin.

She found she couldn't look away as he arose, water rolling off his body. Droplets glistened like tiny jewels in the dark mat of hair on his chest. Her treacherous gaze slipped helplessly lower. His legs were long and bulging and sinewed. And his manhood, even unaroused, was of a size that made her cheeks heat anew.

He dried himself with a length of linen, then climbed into bed beside her. He lay with one hand tucked under his head, his eyes on the ceiling. He had yet to speak, and she was both puzzled and wary, for he seemed so very distant!

It was she who broke the silence, her tone tentative. "You are very quiet tonight, Norman."

At last he turned. Their eyes tangled for an immeasurably long moment before he spoke. "I have much on my mind this night, Saxon."

A pang shot through her. He'd claimed last eve he would not let her go. Had he changed his mind so soon then?

All at once the need to be close to him was too strong, too powerful to be denied. She wanted to feel him hard and straining and full inside her, clear to her womb, for only then would she know he still desired her.

"A troubling day?" Her voice was but a breath. She did not want him to turn away from her. God help her, but she did not . . .

He shifted so that he was sitting, staring down at her. The furs fell down around his hips, but he paid no heed. "That it was," he said slowly. "That it was."

Her heart skipped a beat, for his gaze had dropped to her mouth.

"And now a question for you, Saxon. Would you ease my troubles if you could? Would you make me forget all but my need for you?" Reaching out, he ran his thumb across the swelling fullness of her lower lip.

Alana caught his palm to her cheek, a touch that surprised them both. Her heart was pounding so that her blood rushed in her ears. The breath she drew was deep and unsteady. "If it were within my power" —she heard herself, as if from a very great distance— "so I would."

His eyes darkened. He caught her by the waist and pulled her upright, holding her arms lightly at her sides that he might look his fill. Modesty compelled she cover herself, for she was still shy about appearing naked and bare before him, especially now that her shape was changing. But the hot swell of desire coursing through her dictated otherwise. His regard was slow and unhurried, as potent as any caress. Her breasts seemed to swell and quiver; the budding crests grew all tight and aching. She yearned for the brush of his finger-tips against the very tips, the wanton lash of his mouth on her nipples, tugging hot and sweet and wet.

A finger beneath her chin, he guided her eyes to his. "Then show me, Saxon." His whisper was low and vibrating, so intense she trembled anew. "Show me . . ."

Her fingers twisted in the springy dark hair on his chest. She wanted to please him, to drive him as wild as he drove her. But suddenly a faint distress flitted across her features. She bit her lip, feeling all at once confused and unsure. "I want to," she confided all in a rush. "But I—I know not what you would have me do."

His eyes sheared directly into hers. "I would have you touch me, Saxon. With your hands. With your lips. Wherever you wish. In whatever *way* you wish."

His declaration was stark and shattering. A quivering excitement ran the length of her spine. Emboldened by the glittering heat in his eyes, she wound slender arms around his neck. With hesitant heart, she raised her tremulous lips to his.

His mouth captured hers. She tasted urgency in his kiss, a raw hunger, and something almost desperately seeking.

It was all the invitation she needed. She clung to him blindly, arching eagerly against him, molding strength to softness, crushing her breasts against the unyielding breadth of his chest.

He cupped the weight of her breasts in each hand, then bent low to avail himself of the fruit of first one taut nipple, and then the other, teasing and taunting. Her heart plunged into a frenzy. She recalled what he'd said that very first night . . . *I will take you, not by fear or by force.* Nor had he. Even as her heart and mind fought to resist, he had only to touch her and her body responded with a will of its own. Yet ever and always, he gave of himself unselfishly, seeing to her pleasure long before his own.

A reckless abandon washed through her. She could not deny the magic that flared between them in the dark splendor of the night. Many was the time she'd longed to explore his body as he explored hers, but she'd been so afraid of giving her all—afraid Merrick would see her surrender as still another victory. But now . . . now she longed to bestow on him just a measure of the rapturous delight he'd given her time after time.

She broke off his kiss, gently easing him back from his taunting play with her breasts. She glimpsed the faint puzzlement that flitted across his features, and gave a slight shake of her head. He went very still, his hands dropping to his sides.

Slowly she knelt between his thighs.

Shaking, praying he wouldn't guess her uncertainty, she combed her fingers through the dark pelt on his chest, skimming nipples she discovered were as sensitive as hers. His breath caught and her courage bloomed, ripe and full. With her mouth she tasted his skin, traveling down . . . down over the grid of his belly.

Merrick's breath came fast then slow. There was no thought of stopping her. Sweet Lord, this was the moment he'd awaited forever, it seemed . . . the first time she'd touched him of her own free will. A nagging shadow surfaced deep in his consciousness. Ruthlessly he thrust it aside, greedy to take all she offered.

The muscles of his belly clenched. Small hands delicately paved the way for the touch of lips as soft as summer rose petals.

Her hair feathered over his thighs, just as it had a hundred times in his dreams. Her tongue swept over his navel, down the crease of his hips. He gritted his teeth. Blood rushed to his loins, swelling him hot and full and rigidly erect. He stared down at her and nearly groaned. God above, would she never . . .

Her fingers touched him first, cool against his burning flesh. Her breath, warm and damp, wafted across the most achingly sensitive part of him. And then she was there, her tongue swirling around the boldly arching tip of him, a searing, molten caress that ripped the very air from his lungs and caused a massive shudder to sweep the whole of his body.

His hands slid into her hair. It was beyond his most wildly erotic imaginings. His breath was harsh and scraping. He cast his head back, the cords of his neck taut, unable to withhold a deep, ragged groan. Immersed in an agony of pleasure, he bore her daintily shy exploration as long as he dared, until he was certain he would splinter into a thousand tiny shards.

"Sweet Jesus," he said thickly. "I can take no more . . . enough, sweet! Enough or I will have naught left to give you."

He caught her beneath the arms and dragged her up against him, his embrace almost frighteningly strong. Alana did not care. She felt sotted and dizzy with the knowledge that she had pleased him beyond measure. Feeling him quiver beneath her had but kindled her own desire to fever pitch.

But her eyes flew wide when his hands slid around to cup her buttocks. A soft cry of confusion hovered on her lips. Instinct warned he meant to take her. Yet how on this earth . . . ?

"Wrap your legs around my waist," he directed hoarsely.

She needed no further urging. A thrill shot through her as she glimpsed the blistering passion reflected on his hard features.

She did as he asked, exhaling a ragged rush of air. Her nails dug into the knotted strength of his shoulders. She felt herself lifted and impaled, her passage slowly stretched and filled by the turgid length of his shaft. She gasped, certain she could take no more of him and yet she did, all that he had to give, until at last she felt him fully imbedded within her.

Time spun endlessly. For the space of a heartbeat he did not move. He kissed her then, with aching tenderness, his breath mingling with hers. Alana moaned and clung to him all the more tightly, seeking to tell him all that she felt, for the words ever failed her.

Something seemed to give way deep inside him then. His fingers dug into her hips. She almost cried out her loss when she felt herself lifted away, but then he was straining and driving, a sword of molten steel within her. His arms bulged as he brought her down over his pulsing hardness . . . lifting . . . lowering . . . again and again.

Never had it been like this, their emotions a wanton tempest. Scalding pleasure carried her higher, ever higher. Her breath was jagged, almost sobbing, the sound pushing them both over the edge. He plunged wildly within her, reaching her heart, her very soul. She felt the heat of his seed burst within her, again and again.

They collapsed in a tangle of limbs and furs. A strong arm curled hard about her waist, he drew her tight to his side. Her hand curled naturally there in the midst of his hairy chest, looking small and impossibly pale. Unconsciously seeking, she nestled closer, as close as she could be.

A finger beneath her chin, he raised her face and kissed her mouth, the contact long and lingering.

When at last he released her, she tucked her head against his chest. She pressed her mouth to the hollow of his shoulder, the veriest kiss. "My lord," she whispered. "My lord conqueror."

Chapter 17

For once it was Alana who awakened first. She lay pressed against Merrick's side, curled tight against him for warmth. There was a certain contentment in awaking so, and she remained very still, reluctant to move. He was naked, his chest awesomely broad and masculine. The furs lay tangled about his hips, scarcely covering that part of him that lay flaccid and undemanding now against the plane of his belly. Her mind ran wild as she recalled anew all that passed between them throughout the night. Her entire body flooded crimson, for now in the cold light of day, she was mortified to think how very wanton she had behaved! And yet, God save her soul, she could not regret it. Nay, not a bit, for Merrick had whispered again and again how she pleased him.

Slowly her eyes traced the ruggedness of his profile. In sleep he no longer appeared the fierce warrior. The lines of his face were smoothed, his harshness blunted. Mayhap now, with his mood eased, he might be inclined to allow her to visit Aubrey once more. She lay quietly a while longer, then slipped out of bed, careful not to disturb him.

After tending to the call of nature, she quickly washed and dressed and tended the fire. She straightened and turned. It gave her a jolt to see that Merrick's eyes were fixed upon her. Her heart skipped a beat. How long had he been awake . . . and watching her? As usual, his features provided no hint of his thoughts. Yet she could not rid herself of the sense that he seemed rather brooding.

"You are awake early, Saxon."

"I could sleep no longer," she murmured, feeling all at once inexplicably shy.

A dark brow arose. "Have you plans for the day?"

His scrutiny was unwavering. She felt distinctly uneasy. "Aye," she admitted.

"Indeed." Was it her imagination—or had his gaze sharpened? "Mayhap, sweet, you would care to share them with me."

Alana floundered. Why must he always make her feel so guilty? She laced her fingers together to still their trembling, then summoned all her courage. "I would ask your leave to visit Aubrey. I—I've not seen him for some days."

For a moment Merrick could scarcely believe he'd heard aright. Everything inside him grew hard and brittle as bone. By the Virgin, now he knew why she'd been so sweetly obliging, so determined to please. Ah, but he should have known! he decided scathingly. Last eve had been naught but a woman's deception, a display of feminine wiles. She had sought to bargain her favors for his, but he would *not* play the fool so easily . . .

And it was time she learned it.

"I think not, Saxon."

Too late Alana noticed the tightness about his mouth. In the space of a heartbeat, everything changed. It was as if a frigid wind swept in from the sea. The set of his mouth was grim, so very grim. *Damn him*! she thought brokenly. *Damn his soul to eternal hell! Why must he be so cold? So heartless?*

"Why? Is it because you still believe I plotted with the Saxons?" Her cry was torn from deep in her breast. "I swear on the grave of my father, I did not!"

"'Tis not that, Saxon." His eyes were as cold as the northern seas. The passionate lover of the night before might never have been. In his place was the cold, ruthless knight who had laid siege to Brynwald. He rose and began to gather up his clothes.

Alana stared at him, unaware that her heartache lay bleeding and vivid in her eyes. The breath she drew was painful and racking. "What then?" She slammed her hands flat on the table in fury and frustration. "*What?*"

He turned, fully dressed now, tall and straight as an arrow . . . and just as deadly. "You carry a child," he stated flatly, "a child that is mine as well as yours. Despite your feelings toward me, I will not tolerate any attempts to rid yourself of it."

Alana inhaled sharply. A staggering horror caught her in its grasp. She stared at him, her face bloodless. "Dear God," she said faintly. "Never say you heard Sybil . . ."

"Aye, that I did. She said that surely your mother knew a potion that would rid a woman of an unwanted babe. And I did not hear any denial spring from your lips, Saxon."

She had seen him angry before, but not like this. His hands were fisted at his sides. His rage boiled over into his voice.

She shook her head wildly. Oh, if only this were but a dream! "Surely you cannot think that I . . . God above, I could not . . . I *would* not!"

"No? 'Tis my flesh you carry, Saxon. And you bespoke your hatred of me only last eve."

Her face was wild and anguished, her eyes full of angry hurt. He still did not trust her. But Mother of God, surely he could not think she would murder her babe . . . The knowledge pierced her heart as keenly as a blade.

"I spoke in the heat of the moment! And after you accused me of lying with another! Why are you allowed to change your mind as the wind changes and not I?"

She gave him no chance to answer but went on, her emotions as raw as her voice. "Once . . . *once* I sought to escape you, Norman, and it seems I must forever pay the price. You ask for truth and I give it. But you must ever choose not to believe me, ever and always. And I would remind you that Aubrey will be the one to suffer here. He does not deserve this, for he is innocent—"

"But you, Saxon, are not!" Merrick remained as unyielding as ever. "And I would remind you that it takes but one deed to undo all others. Were I you, I should keep that in mind."

Seized by an unbridled rage, Alana was suddenly so furious she was shaking with it. "You are cruel, Norman. Cruel to deny me the one thing I ask of you—what you know will wound me most." Each word grew more bitter than the last and came out without thought. "Damn you! Why can't you let me go? You want this babe no more than I!"

It was the wrong thing to say. She knew it as soon as it was out. Only then it was too late, for his face, his every muscle had gone rigid and stiff.

He moved so quickly she cried out. His hands shot out. He encircled her wrists in a merciless grip and dragged her close—so close his breath pelted her cheeks like the lash of a whip. Above her his eyes were cutting. He spoke through lips that barely moved.

"A word of warning, Saxon. If you do anything to harm this child, or yourself, I promise you will pay the price. And if I am convinced you would dare to try such a deed, I vow I will lock you in this chamber until this babe is born."

Their eyes locked endlessly. The very air seemed to pulse with the fever of his fury. Alana shrank back, stunned and numb, for his utter control was almost terrifying. His expression as frigid as the northern seas, he dropped her wrists as if he found her suddenly abhorrent. Without a backward glance, he whirled and strode away, slamming the door so hard the floor vibrated beneath her feet.

Alana pressed the back of her hand to trembling lips. Tears scalded her throat, tears that ripped her heart to shreds. And alas, now that Merrick was gone, her last vestige of control shattered. She slumped to the floor and burst into deep, wracking sobs.

That was how Genevieve found her.

And it was Genevieve who wiped the tears from her cheeks, who stroked her brow, who held her and rocked her as if she were a child . . . Genevieve who nodded and listened while she poured out her heart and soul, her hatred and anger, her doubts . . . and her fears.

A long time later Alana sat huddled before the hearth. She stared into shooting flames of amber and gold, her features pale and tear-stained. But when she spoke, her voice was curiously hollow.

"He can be merciful to others, but not to me. Never to me."

Genevieve shook her head. "I cannot believe he truly thinks you capable of harming your own babe. I do not defend him, only to say that he is a suspicious man by nature and by necessity. This will pass, I promise you." She hesitated, wondering if she dare speak what she had known for some time now. "Alana, I—I know my brother well. I see in his eyes that which I have never seen for any other woman. He cares for you—"

"He cares naught for me!" Alana raised her head, unable to contain her bitterness. "I was a convenient wench for him to bed. And now I am merely the vessel that carries his child."

Genevieve was undaunted. "You must trust in yourself, Alana. And you must trust in him."

"Trust!" Alana cried out her frustration. "If he will not trust in me, why should I trust in him? He killed my father, Genevieve!"

Genevieve laid her hand on her head. "Nay, Alana," she said gently. "War killed your father."

"He made me his prisoner! And now he would do so again!" *Nay*, whispered a voice deep within her. *Her heart made her prisoner.* But what that meant, she dare not speak. She dare not even *think* of such . . .

Reaching out, she clasped Genevieve's hands lightly in hers. "If Merrick cannot give his trust to me, then he will have none of mine." Pain flitted across her features, but then her expression softened. "But I trust in you, Genevieve. Indeed, I would do anything in my power to help you. And so I can only pray that you would do the same for me." With words she beseeched her. With her eyes she pleaded mutely.

Genevieve squeezed her fingers. "What is it you wish of me?"

Alana took a deep breath, marveling that this woman she'd known for so little time knew her so well. "I know that Merrick sees that Aubrey is well fed." She bit her lip. "But he is old, and there is a need for food of the spirit and soul as well. I—I do not think that Merrick understands that." She smiled wistfully. "Indeed, Aubrey himself would hardly admit to such. But I know that already he has grown fond of you. And if you could talk with him from time to time, walk with him if he so desires . . . It need not be each and every day, but—"

Genevieve pressed a finger to her lips. "Alana, say no more. I will tell him that you will be with him as soon as you are able. And I will strive to be the comfort to him that you are."

Alana's smile was shaky. "Then I can ask no more." Her smile faded. "Someday God will cast his blessings upon you, Genevieve. I pray it will be soon."

Genevieve smiled in return, but deep in her breast was a rending ache. She had Simon, and she loved him dearly. And while a corner of her heart would be solely Philippe's, the gnawing emptiness inside her had sharpened of late. She was still a woman, and not so very old that she did not yearn for the closeness of a strong male body in the cold of the night . . . A vision flashed into her mind, a vision of tousled dark hair, tattered clothing and angry, flashing eyes . . . She relinquished it quickly, for such a thing was most improbable . . . nay, impossible!

Moods were unsettled indeed in the days that followed. Genevieve was Alana's only link with Aubrey, and though she was forever in Genevieve's debt, it near broke her heart. Though she fretted and fumed, argued and pleaded, Merrick was not to be dissuaded. Saxon will battled Norman pride time and again.

But if he was stubborn, so was she. No longer was she captive to his whim and will. Many was the night she kept her lips closed tight against his kiss . . . against him! Oh, in the end, he wore down her defenses and conquered her resistance, yet his victory was not so easy as before. Then, alas! one night they lay together side by side, a smothering silence all that existed between them. All at once, Merrick arose, a violent oath upon his lips. He snatched his clothing from the floor and stormed from the chamber . . . and their bed.

He had not returned.

Nearly a sennight had passed since then. Oh, Alana told herself she cared not where he slept . . . or with whom! Yet one day, she spied Sybil smiling up at him, her hand on his arm. Quickly she turned away, a hot ache closing her throat.

There was a seething tension whenever he was near . . . a wrenching heartache whene'er he was not.

Never had she been so torn! She bitterly resented him for what he had done, and while the anger soon faded, the hurt did not. Yet still there was a part of her that longed for him with all of her being. She woke in the darkness, yearning to be held fast in his strong embrace, to wake in the morn with her head on his shoulder. She did not understand why it was so, for he was her enemy, and would ever be so!

In all her days, never had she been so miserable . . . or so lonely.

Her nerves were ever ajumble. Sleep proved elusive until well into the night. Plagued by a nagging restlessness, she stretched out upon the bed after noontide one day, numb and exhausted beyond measure. Eventually she fell into a fitful sleep.

But it was a sleep plagued by dreams . . .

She was there in the darkness, a darkness that encompassed all else. The ever-present sense of evil was all around, smothering her, seeking to snatch her within its grasp. The wind howled. Lightning crashed. And there in the distance was Merrick, astride his great black steed, his sword raised high aloft . . .

Then all at once, everything changed. The darkness faded. Light shimmered all around. A figure appeared before her, stoop-shouldered and thin, his hair flowing like silver about his shoulders.

Aubrey.

Gnarled fingers stretched toward her. "Alana," came his whisper. *"Come to me, child. Come to me now . . ."*

She jerked upright with a jagged cry. She pressed shaking fingers to her forehead. Something was wrong. Something was horribly, horribly wrong. She flung the furs away and ran from the chamber.

She did not stop, not in the hall, nor in the yard. She paid no heed to the puzzled glances flung her way as she bolted toward the gate. She was nearly there when a hand of steel caught her arm and whirled her around.

It was Merrick. "Saxon! What the devil—" He stopped cold when he glimpsed her expression, wild-eyed and stricken. "What is it?" he said quickly. Strong hands grasped her shoulders. He gave her a little shake. "Tell me, Saxon. What is amiss?"

Her vision misted by tears, she shook her head. "Aubrey!" she choked out. "I must see him . . . I must!"

He turned and gestured. In an instant his steed was before them. He swung up cleanly into the saddle, then lifted Alana before him.

A cloud of dust spiraled behind them all the way to the village.

When they neared Aubrey's hut, she leaped to the ground even before he'd reined to a halt.

Genevieve stepped outside just as she reached the door. Tears stood high and bright in the Norman woman's eyes as she spied Alana. "Alana!" She seized her hands. "Oh, praise God you are here! I was just about to send a man for you."

Alana searched the other woman's features and saw all she had sensed in the dream—all she feared. Her heart seemed to wither in her breast. "Dear God. Never tell me he is—"

"Nay," Genevieve spoke hurriedly. "But you must go to him. Quickly now, Alana!"

Alana squeezed Genevieve's fingers then ducked within the hut. When Merrick made as if to follow her, Genevieve laid a beseeching hand on his arm and gave an imploring shake of her head.

Within the hut, Alana saw that Aubrey lay on his pallet in the corner. But he was so still that in the moment between one breath and the next, she was certain Genevieve was wrong, that the worst had descended even now. But then Aubrey opened his eyes. He stretched out his arm and beckoned. "Come to me, child," came his rasping voice, just as in her dream. "Come to me now."

Alana crossed to him, then knelt down next to his pallet. Blinking away the mist that blurred her vision, she bent low and kissed his wizened cheek. Drawing back, she clasped his hand within hers. "I am here, Aubrey. And I will not leave you."

He smiled, a smile as feeble as his body. "I knew you would come. I knew it."

Throughout the hours that followed, she stood vigil at his side. At times he slept. At times they spoke of all things past . . . and things yet to come.

His voice boomed suddenly. "You will bear a son, Alana. A son of Norman strength and boldness, a son of Saxon spirit and pride. His hair will be dark as his sire's, but his eyes will be green as yonder fields in spring . . . *your* eyes, Alana."

For a moment Alana could not speak. She had not been aware that he knew of the babe she was to bear.

She clutched his hand to her breast and held it fast, as if to will the life from her being into his. "Aubrey, I beg you . . . I would have you see my son . . . you must fight this so you will be well again . . . you must . . ."

"I cannot fight the will of God." The breath he drew was deep and rattling. "I am old. 'Tis my time. I accept this. So must you."

She dashed away the tears that threatened. "I cannot," she said brokenly. "I cannot bear it—"

"You will be all right, child. I feel it here." With his free hand, he thumped his barreled chest. "And now . . . now I fear it is I who must leave you. But I would see you one last time . . ." His gaze roved her features. Eventually, his eyes drifted shut, as if he were incredibly weary. The hand clasped tight within hers grew limp. And she knew . . .

Aubrey had departed this world for the next.

Chapter 18

How long she stayed there, on her knees in the dirt, she knew not. As if in a daze, she staggered to her feet. Grief wrapped around her like a shroud. Numbly she moved toward the door. She was only dimly aware of Genevieve hovering nearby.

Outside, Merrick turned from where he'd been standing. It took but a heartbeat to grasp that the old man had died. Alana's eyes were two endless pools of anguish. But when she would have passed by with nary a word, nary a glance at him, he laid a hand on her shoulder.

She whirled on him, her eyes shooting sparks of fire. "Do not touch me!" she spat.

Stunned, he released her. "Alana—"

"I should have been with him," she accused. "All these days, he was alone. He was alone, for you would not let me near him! May the devil take you, Norman! May you burn in Hell forever!"

Merrick had gone utterly still. His conscience stabbed at him. He had denied them both this time together, and all at once it seemed monstrously cruel.

It was wrong. He had been wrong. And only now did he acknowledge his mistake . . . now when it was too late . . .

He swallowed, his own throat tight, for the agony he glimpsed on her face rent him in two. "You are right," he said with quiet dignity. "I should never have denied you." He hesitated, then extended a hand toward her. "Alana, I will make it up to you—"

She knocked his hand away with stunning force. "*Now* you are prepared to be kind. *Now* you are prepared to be generous! Well, I hate you, Norman. I hate you as I will never hate another! I shall pray to God that I never set eyes on you again! Do you hear? I never want to see you again!"

His lips tightened. He caught her by the shoulders when she tried to rush past him, but once again she whirled on him, kicking and screaming, pounding his chest, fighting him with all her strength.

"Alana! Calm yourself, sweet—"

"Let me pass!" she screamed. "Let me pass!" Somehow she managed to wrench herself free. She grabbed her skirts and ran. Merrick swore and would have started after her, but all at once Genevieve was there, dragging at his elbow.

"Nay, Merrick! Do not stop her! Not this time!"

He rounded on her, his features taut and white. "Do not stop her?! Woman, are you mad!"

"Merrick, I know her. She will come back—"

"She will not! Did you not hear? She despises me! Surely you know this far better than any!"

"I know far better than any that she does *not* hate you."

His gaze narrowed. "How do you know this? Has she said—"

"Nay." Genevieve shook her head. "She does not speak of it, not to me." She took a deep breath and poured out all that was in her mind—and prayed it was so! "She is confused, Merrick. She feels trapped between her feelings for you and her love for her land and her people."

"Feelings!" He scoffed. "She has no feelings for me save one—hatred!"

Again Genevieve laid beseeching fingers on his sleeve. His arm was rigid beneath her fingertips. "I beg of you, Merrick, give her this time alone. Trust in her," she entreated. "Aye, she is angry with you now. But it will pass. I know it will!"

His expression was grim. "She will never turn to me," he said tightly. "Even now, with the old man gone, she must ever turn away from me."

In that moment, Genevieve ached for him as never before. "I know, Merrick. But you must trust in her to return to you."

His gaze lifted, then fixed on the place where he'd last seen Alana, tearing off into the forest. "I will grant your wish, Genevieve." His tone was curt. "But only because 'tis you who ask it of me. But I tell you this—if Alana has not returned by twilight I will go after her."

So it was that he waited . . . and waited. Indeed, he waited until he could wait no longer.

A pale purple haze hovered above the treetops as he ordered his destrier saddled once more. He searched far and away, through the forest and fields, but he did not find her.

Anger burned through his veins that she would take advantage of his weakness to escape him yet again. Yet there was fear as well, a fear that soon crowded out his anger.

He was just outside the newly built palisade when he saw it . . . the yellow cat, Cedric. The feline sat squarely on his haunches in the middle of the rutted roadway. Twitching his ratted tail, he lifted his neck as if to confront him boldly, as proud and haughty as his mistress! Merrick reined his horse to a halt, one dark brow aslant as Cedric rose to all fours.

For a heartbeat, a curious tension hummed between the two. Yet the animal did not hiss and run off as Merrick expected. He remained where he was, his tail still swishing the air.

Merrick's jaw firmed. By all the saints, he could almost believe the wretched creature awaited him . . . He lifted the reins and urged his horse forward. As he drew within a swordlength, Cedric turned and padded lightly away. Merrick followed, drawn by some nameless force he did not understand, unable—nay, unwilling!—to ignore it. He and his destrier kept pace behind Cedric as the cat

led them down a narrow, twisting trail that
descended down the cliffs to the sea.

At first Merrick was convinced the wide
stretch of beach was deserted. The breeze
carried with it the scent of brine, sharp and
tangy. High atop the bluff, Brynwald rose in
noble majesty.

And then he spied her. She stood near the
base of a huge rock, still as a statue but for
the wind whipping the silken glory of her hair,
tossing it wildly behind her like a banner of
silver and gold. Her gaze was fixed far out
upon the wild, churning waters of the sea.
Boiling waves crashed upon the rocky shore,
leaping high and spraying mist heavenward,
and still she did not move. The air was cold
and wet. Merrick paused, caught squarely
betwixt two very different—and conflicting—
urges.

Genevieve's warning rang in his ears. Should
he retreat and leave her be? His mind urged
that Genevieve had been right. Alana neither
wanted him, nor needed him. Yet the urge to
hold her, to feel her soft and warm in his arms,
was suddenly overwhelming.

Again he urged his destrier forward. As the
distance between them decreased, an odd little
twinge nipped his heart. Her profile was stark
and lonely, as lonely as the wind.

At last he stopped. The narrow set of her
shoulders went up. She was aware of his presence and obviously did not like it. The cast of
his mouth grim, he remained in his saddle and
said nothing.

She did not look at him as she spoke. "How did you find me?"

The corner of his mouth drew up in a faint smile. "Cedric led me to you."

She turned then, unable to hide her startled surprise. "Cedric! Oh, but I should have known! He does not always choose to show himself yet he always lurks near!" Her lashes lowered again, swiftly veiling her eyes, concealing her thoughts. To Merrick it was as if all the life had gone out of her, for in that instant before she glanced back to sea again, all that she felt lay naked and open to him. Inside he bled for her, for never in his life had he seen such barren emptiness!

He clenched the reins in his fists. He had to fight to keep from leaping down and gathering her close, pulling her tight against his breast.

Quietly he called to her. "Saxon."

Silence.

He dismounted and walked to her, placing his hands lightly on her shoulders. As she stiffened beneath his grasp, he stifled his frustration.

At length he spoke. "It grows cold and damp here, Saxon, viciously cold. You must have a care for yourself—and the babe." He brushed his lips across the tangled cloud of her hair. "Come back with me."

She bowed low her head. She gave no answer, yet he sensed no resistance as he guided her to his destrier and lifted her before him into the saddle.

Back in their chamber at Brynwald, she partook meagerly of the meal he had brought to them. Later she stood before the window, watching as the circlet of the moon rose high in a night-dark sky. Her listlessness worried him, for it was so unlike her. His expression somber, he crossed to her.

She started as he came up behind her. He caught her elbows and turned her to him. With his knuckles he brushed the curve of her cheek.

"Genevieve said that I should give you this time alone," he said softly. "And so I held back. I left you alone, for I thought she knew best. But this is not what you need, Saxon." The pitch of his voice grew lower still. "You grieve for Aubrey. So why do you not weep?"

Alana caught her breath, for in truth she had not expected such bluntness. But to her horror, tears sprang to her eyes, tears she dare not shed. She stuffed her fist in her mouth and bit down hard, praying the pain would give her the strength to keep herself from sobbing aloud. But Merrick would not allow her to turn from him. He caught her hands in his and pulled them to his chest.

The breath she drew was deep and shuddering. "When I weep, you ask me why. And when I do not, you still ask me why!"

He searched her face. "Do you fear I will think you weak?"

Her eyes grazed his, then slid quickly away. "I—I know you do!"

The merest of smiles grazed his lips. "You have no sword and shield and you battle me, Saxon—a battle it seems I cannot win." His smile withered. "I wish it could have been different," he said, very low. "That Aubrey had not died. I know you think me cruel, and mayhap I was. I would not allow you to be with him, and now I realize how much I hurt you."

His eyes darkened. His voice was low and taut with strain. "If I could set this aright, I would. If I could take away your pain, Saxon, I would. But I cannot, and so I would offer what comfort I may, if only you will let me."

Alana's mouth grew tremulous. She didn't want him to be gentle—to be tender—for then it was so hard to hate him! And yet . . . as much as she wanted to hate him she could not. She *did* not.

An immense wave of pain broke over her. She twisted her fingers into his tunic. "First my mother died," she said in a half-stifled voice. "Then my father. Now Aubrey. Don't you see? . . . Now I have no one . . . now I have no one!" A dry, jagged sound escaped, then another, and it was like a well bursting inside her. She began to sob. Helplessly. Uncontrollably.

Merrick bent and gathered her in his arms. He bore her to the bed. He ached for her, for he could scarcely remain unmoved by the depth of her despair. A fierce surge of protectiveness swept through him, for she clutched at him feebly. Cradling her shaking body close, he smoothed her hair and kissed away the endless flow of tears, his heart in knots. And when she had finished, he undressed them both and drew her once more against his length, tucking her head into the hollow of his shoulder. She lay against him, limp and exhausted, her emotions bled dry.

Darkness flowed all around them. For once there were no barriers between them, nothing but the starkness of emotions laid naked and bare between them.

Idly he sifted his fingers through the tangled skein of her hair. Low and deep, his voice fell into the silence. "You loved him very much, didn't you, Saxon?"

She released a long, pent-up breath, still thready with tears, then nodded. Damp, spiky lashes brushed the skin stretched taut across his collarbone. The arm about her shoulders tightened ever so slightly.

"I—I do not know how to explain," she said, her tone very low. "But . . . many times Aubrey was more my father than my own. He was there to guide me—to help me—when my father was not."

Merrick frowned. "I thought Kerwain claimed you as his seed."

"Aye, he did. But my mother was a peasant. He loved her but he would not marry beneath him. Instead he married Sybil's mother Rowena, for she brought him lands aplenty and a fortune as well. Aubrey felt my mother should have gone to another village to live her life anew. But she would not . . ."

She swallowed. "I—I loved my father dearly. He gave to us what time he could, what coin he dared, but 'twas difficult for Rowena despised us both, both me and my mother. Yet God forgive me, there were times I hated him—hated him for what he did to my mother. Many was the time he rode into the village with Rowena. Yet if he passed by my mother, he spared her nary a glance or a word." A faint bitterness crept into her voice. "I saw how it wounded her, how it hurt her. I heard her weep into the wee hours of the morn. He wanted my mother. But he prized what lands and fortunes Rowena could bring him far more."

There was more, far more. Merrick's heart went out to her—and to the woman who bore her—for all they had suffered. The hardships, the ridicule, the innocent child called bastard and witch, the woman called whore. He listened, and for the first time, he began to truly comprehend all that she was, all that she had endured.

Oddly, the humiliation Alana thought to feel was simply not to be. From her own lips he knew all. Her secrets. Her deepest shame and heartache. Yet there was no contempt, no condemnation. He held her tight in the warmth of his arms, and never had she felt so sheltered and safe, as if no harm might ever befall her.

In time, peace settled around her, luring her into slumber.

Instead it was Merrick who lay awake long into the night. At length, he turned her in his arms. He kissed the swell of her belly, the downy curve of her cheek, the softness of her lips. Inhaling the sweetness of her breath as if it were his lifeblood, he sighed.

"Ah, Saxon," he whispered, "You think you have no one, but you are wrong, for you have me. And I have strength enough for both of us. I would share it, if only you would let me."

Chapter 19

Spring came to Brynwald in a burst of warmth and sunshine. The days slipped by, one into another. The seas calmed. The land grew wild and green and vivid color adorned hill and vale.

Even as flowers bloomed and flourished, so did the babe within Alana's womb. Her hand crept frequently to the mound of her belly, for the child who dwelled there moved often now. Merrick seemed just as fascinated. At night he splayed his palms wide upon the curve of her belly and there was no stopping him. She was relieved beyond measure that he displayed no reticence in claiming fatherhood, yet there was a part of her that was so very afraid to hope.

Since the night of Aubrey's death, there had been an unspoken truce between them. Alana was only too glad of it, for she was tired of the enmity that had raged between them, weary of the distance and tension. She welcomed the tentative peace that existed . . . a peace she dared not shatter.

For Merrick, it was the time he'd awaited—

the dream he had envisioned. He was tired of
battle, tired of plunder and war. He had come
to England to build his future, and Brynwald
was a fief worthy of pride—worthy of whatever sacrifice it took to see it thrive. His days
were long and hard, but he did not mind. Now
Norman and Saxon alike worked side by side
for a common goal—to see the fields tilled and
seed sown; to reap the rewards of harvest in
fruitful abundance that all might feed home
and family without worry or care.

But all was not placid or serene. Nay, there
was evil afoot . . .

It happened one fine day in late spring. Alana
had been busy gathering herbs and roots in the
forest. Merrick had at last relaxed his guard,
and given his leave for her to come and go
from the keep as she wished. Most often she
was accompanied by Genevieve, but on this
particular day, she was alone.

She was on the outskirts of the village when
she saw a group of villagers gathered in a
circle near the pasture. Shrill voices raised in
shock reached her ears.

"Mother of Christ, its eyes have been cut
out!"

"Merciful God on high," quavered a voice.
"Who would do such a thing?"

An odd prickling trickled up her spine. Not
certain she wanted to see, yet unable to stop
herself, she stopped near a young boy. The
boy's eyes flew wide. He latched onto his
mother's skirts with a wail.

"'Tis her! 'Tis the witch!"

The crowd fell away. Alana did not hear the gasp that went up. She could only stare in shocked, stunned horror, for there on the muddied ground lay a small white lamb, bloodied and lifeless.

A sick sensation curdled her stomach. Alas, they were right. The lamb's eyes had been cut out. But it was the gaping hole in its tiny chest that chilled her to the bone . . .

Its heart had been cut out.

The warm sunshine seemed suddenly obscene. She swayed, feeling as if the earth were giving way beneath her feet. It was then Alana became aware of the frightened murmurings rising all around her. Only then did she realize the villagers had withdrawn, and even now backed away, crossing themselves, their features white with fright.

She stood there, alone . . . in spirit and in deed. Never had she felt so . . . so mistrusted. So misunderstood. As if she were the vilest of beings flung from the dregs of the earth . . .

A thousand layers of hurt descended. Her heart squeezed. This was too much. More than her wounded soul could take right now.

With a cry she wrenched away. Blindly she ran, frantic in her haste to escape. She did not hear the hoarse male voice shouting her name. Desperate and stricken, she was beyond seeing, beyond hearing. She ran until her breath came in jagged sobs, her throat raw and scraping; she ran until she had no strength left within her. Her legs gave out and she sprawled heavily to her knees.

Her stomach heaved. The world spun crazily. Spots danced before her eyes. She retched violently, horribly sick then and there.

She didn't hear the footsteps pounding along behind her. But when at last she raised her head, Merrick was there on his knees beside her. A supportive arm slid around her waist. He drew her close to his side.

Alana was afraid to look at him, afraid what she would see, what she might not. "Did you see?" she whispered, the words but a breath.

"I did," was all he said.

Alana's fingers curled into the front of his tunic. "They think I am responsible, don't they?"

Merrick said nothing. His expression was lined and drawn.

"Don't they?" she screamed, the sound rooted in pain.

He hesitated, then nodded, the line of his lips thin.

To Alana it was the final blow. She felt as if every bone in her body had been broken. *Always*, she thought helplessly. Always they judged her. Always they condemned her.

She lurched upright. His hands were there to help steady her, but she did not notice. Her breath was like fire in her lungs, threatening to choke her. "God!" she cried, a broken, tearing sound. "I've lived all my life among them. Why can't they see what I am . . . what I am not! I am not a witch. *I am not!*"

Merrick's insides twisted. Something caught in his chest, something that made him hurt as she was hurting. She had spent her life in the shadows, an outcast. Aye, and therein lay the heartache, for she had been branded different . . . yet she was not so very different at all.

His arms engulfed her. Never had he felt so helpless in his life, and he knew not how to overcome it. "They fear what they do not understand. Alana, calm yourself. Surely 'twas some prank by some foolish lad." She shook her head, over and over. When he gathered her closer still, she clung to him, held fast within the binding tightness of his embrace. Tears slid down her cheeks, hot and slow, wetting the hollow of his throat. But she made nary a sound, all the way back to Brynwald.

When next the moon rose high and bright, it happened again . . . this time with a young calf.

Merrick rode to the village to view the carcass discovered in the pasture. One by one the villagers began to gather round, their faces somber and unsmiling.

A villein shouted out to him. "You know, my lord, there is only one capable of doing such a terrible deed as this."

Merrick turned burning eyes toward the farmer. He spoke but one word. "Who?"

"Why, who else? The witch. The witch Alana."

Merrick's jaw clenched hard. "Do not dare to lay this at her door. She has scarcely left the keep of late, and when she did she was with my sister." His lip curled. "Why you so accuse her, I do not know. What harm has she brought to you that you would be so cruel?"

The man said nothing. Merrick turned to a woman clutching a small child. "And you, mistress? What harm has she done to you?"

The woman flushed and stammered. "N-none, my lord."

The sweep of his gaze took in the others. No one said a word, unwilling to test the patience of their Norman lord. But at last one brave soul ventured to speak.

"But who then, my lord, if not her?" he asked.

"I do not know. But I would tell you this. Look among yourselves instead for one so weak he must blame another, or lacks the courage to claim his deeds."

"But why would anyone do such a thing?"

"Find the one responsible and you will find the answer," said Merrick.

The villein who had first shouted nudged his way forward. "You are wrong, my lord. We need look no further than the maid Alana. We know she is the one, for we all know—"

Merrick found himself possessed by a fury to rival the tempest of the sea. He seized the fellow by the throat of his tunic and lifted him clear off his feet. "You know nothing," he said fiercely. "You pretend she has done all manner of evil when in truth she has done nothing—nothing!" He shook the man as if he were a cur. "By the Virgin, I will hear no more accusations against her. Or I swear I will cut out your tongue—you or any other who dares speak such lies!"

He released the man, who scrambled back as if he'd been burned.

Yet again within the next few weeks, the butchery continued. Rumors of witchcraft abounded, though all heeded Merrick's warning—naught was said in his presence, though some whispered that Alana had cast some witch's spell over him that he might aid her in her cause.

Alana floundered anew. Indeed, to a heart so battered and bruised, this was worse than any of her dreams. How she could survive the coming days and keep her sanity, she didn't know. She rarely took her meals in the hall anymore, for more oft than not, the moment she entered, the hall would fall quiet and hushed. Genevieve was her only friend . . .

And Merrick her only hope.

Merrick wanted his child—that she no longer doubted. But to him she was a possession, a pawn, she reflected bitterly. Aye, he kept her now. Aye, he was tender and sweet, for he would have his child from her. Never had he said he loved her—never, in the heat of all the blistering passion that raged between them.

And Alana longed desperately to hear those very words, for only then could she admit what her heart had told her long, long ago.

Nay . . . *Nay!* She dare not love him. She *did* not, for never must she forget he was a warrior to the very marrow of his bones. He would command her surrender. Conquer her heart . . .

Indeed, he'd already done so.

She walked often on the beach, for the forest held too many memories of Aubrey. But on this day, despair was a heavy weight on her breast. Mayhap 'twas due to those horrible mutilations, but the future preyed ever on her mind.

Oft as she had grown to womanhood, Alana had pondered long and hard as to why her mother had chosen to remain at Brynwald, there in the shadow of another . . . a wife. Aye, her mother had loved her father. But it was a love that had only brought anguish. A love that hurt all of them—a love that did not heal.

And now she, too, was to bear a child, a child of the lord of Brynwald, a man not her husband . . . a man who would *never* be her husband. Aye, her father had not deigned to marry beneath him.

Nor would Merrick.

So while Alana strived oft to cling to a frail tendril of hope that he might someday come to care for her—to love her—on this day she did not. She feared she was like her mother. Blind to her fate. Resigned to her future, a future that could only lead to heartache.

She thought of her child, who kicked strongly in her womb. Would his hair be dark as a raven's wing, like his father's? Or would his hair be as hers, pale as the moon? She thought often of Aubrey's last words—his prediction that she would bear Merrick a son. She prayed

Aubrey was right, for he had seemed so certain! And indeed, she had come to think of the babe as a boy as well.

Her heart clamped down in misery. She could not bear to think of Merrick with another . . . with a *wife*. Her mind wandered where it would, and there was no leashing it. What would happen when he married, as surely he would? *What then?* How could she stand to leave, never to see him again? Yet how could she stay?

And what of her babe? Her son would be of no more consequence than she had been. He would be . . . the lord's *bastard*. A stark pain wrenched her breast. She wanted for her son all that had never been hers. She could not bear to think her child must endure the secret shame that had always been hers . . .

All these things and more circled through her mind, over and over. Though the summer sun shone down in showery rays of golden splendor, a melancholy bleakness enshrouded her. Her head down, she plodded onward through the sand, paying no heed to the surf that dampened her boots from time to time. So engrossed was she in her troubles that she didn't see the figure that stopped squarely in her path—alas, until it was too late and she had collided full tilt with a hard male chest.

It was Raoul. Rough hands came out to steady her, but she wrenched herself away, loath to feel his touch.

He laughed softly. "Greetings, Alana."

Alana said nothing, but inclined her chin to

show she would not stand meekly before him. Once again he stretched out a hand but she quickly retreated a step.

"What, Alana! Do you scorn me?"

"Aye," she responded curtly, "for it seems you are without sight or even wits. I am scarcely in need of your assistance, Norman, now or ever."

He smiled at her coolness. "Your sister is hardly so averse to my attentions."

My sister and I have little in common, she almost snapped. She didn't, and was heartily glad she held her tongue, for it would have seemed petty and mean.

He ran his eye over her with practiced ease, lingering long on the generous swell of her breasts beneath her bliaud. Alana's face burned painfully.

"Indeed," he said suddenly. "I would not speak so hastily were I you, Alana. For you may well be wrong—and far more in need of my attentions than you think." He laughed, a sound that made her skin crawl. "Aye, and far sooner than you think."

Alana's eyes narrowed. "What do you mean?"

That mocking smile continued to play about his lips. He spread his hands wide. "Only this, my lovely. I fully understand why Merrick was so captivated with one so lovely as you. But 'tis scarcely his way to remain so for long. And so I fear I must tell you, it cannot last."

Alana inhaled sharply. A part of her was well aware Raoul sought deliberately to wound her.

But that he voiced her every fear lent no ease to her troubled mind.

But by God, she would not let him know it. She squared her shoulders and looked him straight in the eye. "And I fear I must tell you, Raoul, to tend to your own affairs and leave well off mine."

Still he smiled. He moved closer. "And I vow, lady, the time will come when you will turn to me." He laughed, a sound that sent a chill the length of her spine. "Should you please me well enough, I might even be persuaded to marry you."

Alana's eyes flamed. "Never would I turn to you—never!"

His smile vanished. A hand shot out and he snared her wrist, his hold so tight she gasped aloud. "You shun me now, lady. But where will you be without him?" he sneered. "The time will come when you will not spurn me. I told you once my blade would please you far better than his—"

"And if you value that blade of which you speak so proudly, I should let the lady go lest I decide you'll have no further need of it."

Merrick had appeared behind Raoul. His eyes were pale and glittering, his features a mask of stone. The color had drained from Raoul's face. There was no doubt Merrick meant what he said, for the blade of a dagger even now lay snug against the side of Raoul's throat.

Raoul released her so suddenly she stumbled back. "There is no need to draw your weapon against me," he said stiffly.

Merrick's teeth flashed white. "No? It seems the lady still does not favor you, Raoul—a fact that still escapes you." The blade pressed harder, until a drop of blood shone fat and red. "I cannot think why."

Raoul had gone utterly still. Beads of sweat popped out on his brow. "Nor can I, Merrick. I would seek your forgiveness, if . . . if only you allow it."

"The lady is mine," Merrick stated flatly, "and what is mine, I hold. Twice now I have warned you what will happen should you touch her again. I vow I'll not be so considerate again."

He lowered the blade. Raoul gave a nod and stepped back, clearly anxious to depart. When he had gone, Merrick turned to Alana.

Slipping his knuckles beneath her chin, he guided her eyes to his. "Did he harm you?"

Alana's heart had lodged in her throat. Only now did she consider what could have been her fate had Merrick not come along. Merrick had said he'd once warned Raoul against touching her; mayhap Raoul had sought only to frighten her. Indeed, Merrick was not a man of idle threats. And surely Raoul was not so unwise as to risk Merrick's wrath.

Wordlessly she shook her head.

His grip on her chin fell away. "You should not walk alone," he chided gruffly. When Alana kept silent, he frowned. "What is it? Never tell me he has done this before!"

Alana swallowed. "Nay," she said, her voice scarcely audible.

His expression had grown dark as a moonless night. "Would you have told if he had?"

She made no answer.

His scowl deepened. "Alana!"

Slowly she raised her head. "Would you have cared?"

His jaw clenched hard. "I cannot believe you would ask such a thing, Saxon! Did you not hear what I told Raoul? I will allow no man to claim what is mine!"

Her face wiped clean of all expression, she lifted her gaze. "Aye," she said clearly. "Forgive me, my lord conqueror, but I did forget. I have food aplenty in my belly. A roof over my head far better than any I have known."

He crossed his arms over his chest and glared at her. "Do you denounce my treatment of you?" If he was affronted, he couldn't help it. "By the saints, woman, I've cared for you as I have cared for no other!"

"And will you discard me like all the others before me?"

Merrick was angered by her accusations, puzzled by her behavior, which was most peculiar. "By the Cross, woman, what madness is this? I've lain with no other since the day we met. I've wanted no other and you've no cause to believe otherwise!" He cursed vilely. "Is Raoul responsible for this? Did he seek to fill your head with lies about me?"

Alana struggled to maintain her composure. All at once she felt as if the world were shattering all around her. "Do not blame him. He said nothing. Nothing but the truth. Nothing but what I have known all along."

"And what is that?" he demanded.

She made no response but instead asked a question of her own. "What will happen to me when my babe is born?"

Merrick stared at her. Her words made no sense. *She* made no sense.

"Will you take him from me?"

"Nay!" he exploded, though some of his tension fled. Was this what was behind the strangeness of her moods of late—the fear that he would separate her from her child? A part of him was angry that she still thought so little of him, but he sought to reassure her.

"You need not worry, Saxon. All will be as it is now. You will remain here with me— and our babe—at Brynwald." He started to reach for her, yet he sensed a curious distance in her manner. She regarded him unblinkingly.

"So," she said at last. "All will be as it was. I will remain your whore."

"Bedamned!" he swore. "You are not a whore!"

Alana could not look at him. She did not dare, for she was terrified the pain in her heart would show in her eyes.

Merrick's hands came down on her shoulders. He drew her to him, his embrace warm and comforting. "Saxon! Look at me!"

Slowly her head came up. Her eyes grazed his. He spoke quickly.

"Alana, you need not worry. You will be

the mother of my child. I will care for you always."

Tears glazed the beautiful emerald of her eyes, tears that cut his insides like a knife.

"What is wrong, sweet? I do not understand this—this melancholy sadness! You should be filled with joy, for you will bear a fine Norman son—"

She made a faint, choked sound. "Nay," she said tonelessly. "I will bear a bastard."

Chapter 20

I will bear a bastard.

Long into the night, those words haunted Merrick. Alana's mood remained bleak, and when at last she lapsed into sleep, Merrick slid from their bed. He dressed and made his way belowstairs.

The hall was deserted, which suited him well. He took his place alone at the trestled table, and there nursed a hearty cup of ale.

I will bear a bastard.

Alana's speech lent him no ease. The words resounded in his head, over and over. He felt guilty, though he knew not why. She shared his home, his hearth. She would bear his son, and share his life, and he would have it no other way! How could she not know this? He'd thought it mattered little to her that they were not wed. Surely she knew that he would take no other to his bed. Surely she knew he cherished her as he had cherished no other woman in all his days!

In truth, he'd given little regard to the fact their child would not be legitimate. After all,

Duke William was a bastard . . . and now he was king of all England!

Such was the bent of his mind as he chanced to glance up and find his sister before him. No sign of a welcoming smile broke his lips, for he suspected she was ever ready to stir trouble anew.

He stiffened at the touch of a gentle hand warm upon his shoulder. "What is wrong, brother? Can you not sleep?"

"There is much I must think on," he said gruffly.

"What! Can you not think clearly with Alana beside you?"

Curling his fingers around his cup, he glared at her. She merely laughed, rousing his frustration even further.

"Why do you laugh? You find me so amusing?"

"What I find amusing is that a knight, so strong and so bold as you, is all adither because of one beauteous Saxon maid."

He snorted. "A beauty she may be, sister. But she is hardly a maid—"

"Thanks to you, brother."

His jaw clamped shut. "I am scarcely adither. I merely have much on my mind, and I would thank you to leave me to my business."

Genevieve's smile withered. She stated without preamble, "Marry her, Merrick."

His eyes flickered. But he made no reply. He stared at her, his expression stormy.

The soft line of Genevieve's lips tightened. "Why will you not consider it?"

"I did not say I would not consider it!"

"You will be a father before you are a husband. Does this not trouble you?"

He swore. "Genevieve, once again you trespass where you should not!"

"And you tarry when you should not!" she said sharply. "Is it not enough that her people call her witch? Must they call her wanton as well? Must they call her whore?"

His fist landed atop the table, sending a spray of ale spouting high in the air. "She is not wanton. Nor is she a whore," Merrick exploded, "and I would kill any man who dares to call her one!"

Genevieve watched him closely. "Tell me, brother," she said suddenly. "Would you take her to your bed and not your heart?"

His features had turned brooding. Holding her breath, Genevieve pressed on. "What of the child, Merrick? Will you claim this babe as your own?"

"Aye!" Merrick was furious that she might think otherwise. "I will. By God, I have!"

Genevieve nodded her approval. "If you would have others treat Alana as an equal," she observed calmly, "then so must you. Aye, her mother was a peasant. But she is also the by-blow of a lord. And she has as much pride as you, brother."

Merrick directed his gaze heavenward. "Blessed be," he muttered. "Do you think I do not know that?"

Genevieve paid no heed. "Would you do to your son or daughter what Kerwain did to her?" she demanded.

I will bear a bastard.

Merrick's features were stormy. He had gone very still. Nay, he thought. He could not. He *would* not.

I will bear a bastard.

He wanted his son to grow to manhood here at Brynwald. To take his rightful place. Genevieve was right. He did not want his child to spend his life ever the outsider . . . ever the outcast.

Something twisted inside him. The circumstances of her birth were scarcely her fault, yet still she suffered . . . Not long ago he had watched her . . . as she had watched the villagers indulge in games and dancing one eve. A faint wistfulness marring the smooth skin of her brow, she had stood from afar. Ever distant. Ever lonely. Ever apart . . .

Ever his.

Resolve flowed through his veins. By God, she *was* his. His alone. And so she would remain. Yet still . . .

He spoke without knowing it. "She despises all things Norman—the saints forbid that she should take a Norman husband." He shook his head. "God above! What if she will not have me?"

"Your child grows plumper with every day that passes, Merrick. Alas, this child may well be half-grown before you would take Alana to wife." She gave a shaky laugh. "And then, my lord, I do believe she would not have you!"

She hesitated, then added quietly, "Alana has said naught to me, Merrick. Aye, she may have hated you once, but no more. This I believe with all my soul. And if we Normans would make our lives here—if we would be one with the land, then we must be one with the people as well." She bent and kissed his brow, her expression soft. "I will say no more, brother. Instead I will do as you ask, and leave you alone to ponder this matter."

Merrick remained where he was, but in truth, there was little need to ponder long and hard.

He'd thought himself so much better than her people. But was he guilty of judging her as well? One question led to another. Had she been a lady born and true, would he have taken her as he had? He did not know. God help him, but he did not. So mayhap Genevieve was right. Mayhap he was no better than those who judged her so harshly.

But he could not set her free. Indeed, he could scarcely imagine his days without her. Aye, she roused his temper. But she also brought him pleasure as no other ever had . . . as no other ever *would*.

He wanted her trust, he realized. Her love. Her very heart . . . for she'd already captured his own.

And indeed, it seemed he need ask himself no more.

It was very late when Alana woke the next morning. She heard the shutters clack open, then brilliant sunshine poured into the chamber, bathing all with a golden yellow glow.

Genevieve flashed across her line of vision. When she saw that Alana was awake, she clapped her hands. "Up with you, Alana!" she said crisply. "So come now, and hurry, for your bath is ready."

Alana gingerly propped herself on an elbow. 'Twas hardly Genevieve's habit to wake her, let alone tend to her bath.

Genevieve was busy pouring a generous stream of oil from a small jar into the bath. The sweet, fragrant scent of roses wafted from the steaming water. "There, now!" she pronounced. "Doesn't that smell heavenly? I adore this scent, don't you? 'Tis my favorite!"

Alana frowned. Her eyes never left Genevieve as she flitted around the chamber. Was it her imagination? Or was there an air of joy about the Norman that could scarcely be ignored.

Genevieve continued to chatter. "The day is a glorious one, is it not? Why, I vow it shall prove most unforgettable! Aye, 'tis a fine day for . . ." She broke off abruptly, then smiled—ah, and verily! a most secret smile, Alana decided.

"A fine day for what, Genevieve?" Alana made the query slowly, more puzzled than ill at ease. Were it possible to be suspicious of the Norman woman, mayhap she was. For indeed, 'twas hardly like Genevieve to be anything but forthright.

"Oh, for just about anything, I should say." Genevieve's laughter rang out, light and tinkling. "For hunting. For riding. For dancing and feasting and celebrating all the world has brought us." She seized Alana's hands and pulled her up. "Hurry now! Your bath grows cold!"

Alana allowed Genevieve to help her undress, then she slipped into the huge wooden tub. She prodded and probed as to why Genevieve seemed to find this day different from all others, but Genevieve merely laughed and laughed. Clearly she was pleased with herself and the world in general. And alas, Alana could scarcely begrudge her that.

At last she arose, a length of linen wrapped around her body. Genevieve held up a gown of deep, rich purple. "What do you think of this one, Alana?" Alana had no chance to answer, for already Genevieve was nodding her approval. "Aye, this is the one! Why, 'tis fit for . . ."

Alana glanced at her sharply, for again Genevieve's words dangled—and again there was that unexplained smile. Indeed, her eyes were fairly sparkling.

"Genevieve," she said slowly. "You must tell me. What is amiss? Why do you act so strangely?"

"Strangely! Alana, I am merely filled with gladness! Now come and dress," she said briskly.

Alana sighed. She had learned long ago that there was little point in arguing with Genevieve once her mind was made up. She gave herself over into the other woman's hands. Genevieve brushed her hair until it shone like a silvery waterfall down her back.

She did not bind it but left it loose and flowing gently around her shoulders and hips. Alana said nothing, but protested mightily when Genevieve draped an intricately spun silver girdle around her hips.

"Genevieve! Whatever are you thinking . . . I cannot wear this! 'Tis yours and—"

"And I will hear no more, Alana." Genevieve pressed a fingertip against her lips, stifling her speech. "Wear it this day. Wear it and . . . well, you shall see."

Genevieve would say no more, shaking her head as she draped a sheer wimple over Alana's hair. By all the saints, Alana did not know why Genevieve should take such care with her appearance—nor did she understand why Genevieve insisted she wear her girdle— and such a fine one yet!

At last, Genevieve circled around her, then stopped. She clapped her hands with delight. "Oh, Alana, you are truly a vision. Truly!"

It was Alana's turn to shake her head. "Genevieve—" she began, her eyes beseeching.

Genevieve grasped her elbow. "Come," she said crisply. "Else all below will think you intend to laze abed until noontide."

Alana sighed. By now she'd deduced there was little point in pursuing the matter further. And indeed, why should this day be different from any other?

Her mind thus preoccupied, Alana descended the winding stair next to Genevieve. When at last she raised her head, a frown knit the smooth skin of her brow. The instant she stepped within the hall, a sudden quiet descended. All eyes came to rest upon her, and it spun through her mind that the others present were also dressed in their finest. Even the kitchen boys stood like small soldiers, their faces scrubbed clean as could be.

Merrick stood before the hearth, dark and striking, his shoulders as wide as the horizon. And it was Merrick who commanded her attention as no other . . . Merrick . . . and the man who stood beside him.

Father Edgar.

Her gaze skipped back to Merrick's, and then she couldn't tear her eyes from his. Behind her, Genevieve gave her a gentle shove. "Go," she whispered.

Alana's heart skipped a beat. Then another, and still another. Bold as you please—bold as ever!—Merrick crossed to stand directly before her. The breadth of his chest eclipsed her view of the others.

All at once she was trembling like a leaf in a storm. Nay, she thought dazedly. This could not be what it appeared. She was afraid to hope. Sweet Jesus, afraid to even dare think!

Her lips would not work properly. "Merrick—" She spoke, though the sound seemed to come from a very great distance away.

He extended a hand. "Methinks we need a priest, Saxon."

A priest. Alana stared as if struck dumb. Her knees went weak. How she remained upright, she knew not. 'Twas surely a dream, but of a certainty one she did not fear or dread.

Her breast felt near to bursting, yet the sound that escaped was not what she expected. "Why?" she heard herself say. "Why would you do this?" Her hand came to rest unknowingly on the swell of her belly. "Because of this? Because of the babe?"

He had yet to withdraw his hand. "Aye, I want my son." He paused for the space of a heartbeat. "But I also want you, Saxon."

Alana felt like weeping with relief. She could scarcely speak for the huge lump in her throat. "And you would . . . marry me?" Her voice was but a breath. She had to hear it aloud, for only then would she know this was real, and not some desperate dream conjured up from the depths of her being . . .

A half-smile lurked about his lips, but his eyes were solemn. "I would," he vowed softly. "I would have you as my wife. This day. By God, this night and every other."

She searched his features . . . the very depths of her heart, which knocked so wildly in her breast. This was what she wanted. Above all else, she longed for her babe to bear his father's name. It no longer mattered that Merrick was Norman. He would not forsake her. Indeed, he had believed in her when no one else did.

But it still seemed so unreal. She closed her eyes, drawing in a deep, fortifying breath. When they opened, Merrick was still there before her, tall and strong, as handsome as ever.

"'Tis not my way to beg or plead, Saxon, and so I would ask . . . Will you wed me?"

Alana quivered. Ah, but it was just like him to do this! True, he did not ask or plead, but commanded, as if it were his due! And then he did the one thing she did not expect.

"The choice is yours, Saxon." His tone was gruff but his eyes were tender. "Say aye or nay, but say it now."

Her mind was all awhirl. Sweet heaven, he wanted her to marry him . . . !

She could do no less, she realized. And alas, she could *ask* for no more . . .

"Aye," she said breathlessly. "Aye, I will marry you, Norman."

Shyly she placed her hand in his. His palm, callused and strong, engulfed hers. Then she was tugged near and caught up against his side. He turned and started across the hall.

Now that the time was nigh upon them, Father Edgar had grown nervous. When Merrick beckoned to him, he approached. His eyes darted between Merrick and Alana. He leaned close and whispered, "Forgive my boldness, my lord. But are you certain this is what you wish to do?" His gaze slid to Alana, a reflection of his disapproval.

Beside him, Alana stiffened. Merrick felt it and glanced at her sharply. She had lowered her gaze but not before he saw the sudden glaze in her eyes.

Father Edgar pursed his lips. "This woman—"

His eyes bulged as he abruptly found himself seized by the throat of his coarse woolen robe. "Will soon be my wife and the lady of Brynwald," Merrick said from between his teeth. "So say no more, lest you forever regret it until the end of your days—which may be far sooner than you wish, Father." His glare bespoke his displeasure as keenly as the cutting edge of his tone.

Father Edgar paled. "As you wish, my lord," he stammered. "As you wish."

By the time they reached the chapel, Alana's mind was all awhirl. The assemblage followed; all grew quiet as the people of Brynwald filed in behind them and stood, shoulder to shoulder. Alana fought a choking panic. Did they come to see the lord of Brynwald wed? Or did they come to stare at *her*?

Clearing his throat, Father Edgar took his place before the altar. Merrick knelt, then tugged her down beside him on the smooth wooden floor. From that moment on Alana was aware of little else. At last Father Edgar made the sign of the cross, and bestowed on them the final blessing. Then Merrick was drawing her up beside him. Alana stood dumbly. It was over, she realized.

Her gaze strayed to Merrick. An odd smile curled his lips, but his eyes spoke only to her. A rush of emotion squeezed her chest, so intense it was almost painful. Merciful heaven, he was her husband . . . her *husband*. Unbeknownst to her, a slow-growing smile etched across her lips, a smile so sweet the man beside her caught his breath for never had he seen such blinding radiance.

Her hand held high and clasped tight within

his, Merrick turned. "The lady of Brynwald," he announced.

The crush of people closed in on them. Alana pressed close to Merrick's side, for she knew not what to expect. But there were no scathing denunciations; there was only much hearty laughter and boisterous congratulations. Alana felt her hands clasped by first one, then another and another. She turned, and Sybil's pale face swam before her. Such black rage dwelled there that for a mind-splitting instant it was as if she'd been dealt a stunning blow to the head. But then it was gone and Alana was convinced it was naught but her imagination.

Sybil pressed a kiss upon her cheek. "You have done well for yourself, sister," she whispered.

Genevieve came next. She hugged her fiercely. "I am so pleased for you, Alana. You will be happy, all of you. I know it. I feel it with all that I am."

The people of Brynwald were ever ready to put aside their work, to feast and dance, and the wedding of the lord seemed as fine an occasion as any to do so. Wine and ale flowed freely throughout the day and evening. Then at last came time for the newly wedded couple to retire. Amidst much laughter and bawdy shouting, Alana fled up the stair with Genevieve but a step behind her.

It was Genevieve who helped her from her clothes and slipped a gown of sheer white linen over her head, whisking it into place.

She brushed her hair until it crackled and shone, then helped her into bed. Alana settled back against the pillows, awaiting whatever the night would bring.

It seemed Genevieve had scarcely left her alone than Merrick appeared. He closed the wide oaken portal, then paused there near the entrance. In that moment, he seemed as tall as the heavens, his chest as wide as the sea, as powerful and strong as some ancient god.

A tremor seized her. Her nerves were all amuddle. Never had he been so handsome—never had she been so afraid! Her emotions were a hopeless tangle. She told herself she'd awaited him so many countless nights before . . .

But never as his wife.

And now, in a never-ending moment, she felt the weight of his regard like a stone upon her breast. The sweep of his gaze dwelled long and intently upon her lips, the swell of her breasts, the rounding of her belly.

All at once Alana despaired as never before. She wished this night could have been different. That she could have come to him lithe and slim and proud . . . A pang rent her breast. Instead she was swollen and misshapen, and growing more so with every day that passed!

Such was not the case with Merrick.

His gaze traced slowly over her. Firelight played upon her hair, turning it to silken ripples of gold and silver, framing the exquisiteness of her features and tumbling around her shoulders. She appeared very young, draped in sheer white linen, and something caught in his chest.

A powerful tide of emotion swelled within him. He'd been right to bind her to him in this way . . . in every way. He remembered how she had looked up at him when she came to realize he sought to marry her—her eyes huge and shining, her lovely features dazed and sweet. And now she was his wife. By God, his wife. She was soon to bear his child—God willing, there would be others. She shared his home. She would share his life, in this and every way . . .

But something was wrong. Her eyes grazed his, then slid away. Her fingers wound together on an upraised knee, so tightly her knuckles showed white. He frowned, for she appeared as timid and uncertain as a doe in the presence of some great, fearsome beast.

The mattress dipped as he sat on the edge of the bed. Reaching out, he clasped her hand lightly within his. "This night is no different than many others we have spent together."

"Nay," she blurted. "It is different!"

He studied her a moment. "How so?"

"We were not wed," she said wildly.

"And now we are. Does that not please you?"

"Aye, but—" She struggled to free her hand but he would not allow it. His fingers tightened ever so slightly around hers.

"No," he commanded softly. "Do not turn away, Saxon. I would know what distresses you so."

Never in her life had she felt so helpless—
so utterly foolish! She floundered, wondering
if she dare speak the truth. And then she realized she must, for Merrick would have it from
her no matter what!

Her lips quivered. "'Tis different because . . . we are wed . . . and . . . and I wish
that I could come to you as a bride
should . . . untouched and . . . and slender . . ."
Sybil's accusation tumbled in her brain, even
as the words stumbled from her lips. "But I
cannot for I am fat as a—a sow . . . and oh,
how I wish I were not!"

She thought he would agree—at the very
least, that he would laugh and chide her, mayhap even mock her. But to her horror he cast
the furs away and tugged her onto his lap.

The warmth of his whisper brushed her
cheek. "You are untouched by any but me,
Saxon. That pleases me as nothing else could."
She felt his fingers, spanned wide across her
belly, the gentlest caress. "I have no way to tell
you the satisfaction I feel, knowing 'tis my child
that rounds your belly, sweet. But know this—
that, too, pleases me as nothing else could. To
me you are more alluring and desirable than
ever. You possess a beauty unequaled by any
other. I want no woman save you. I will *have*
no woman save you."

Solemnly intent, his expression made her
throat ache. The words he spoke were the very
words she needed so desperately to hear.

With a stifled sob of relief, she locked her
arms around his neck and clung, burying

her face in the hollow of his shoulder. For
a time he merely held her, until her shaking
ceased. Sweeping away a shining lock of hair,
he bared her nape and brushed his mouth
across the smoothness of her flesh. He kissed
the quivering lips she offered so shyly, a kiss so
infinitely sweet it brought tears to her eyes.

At last he drew back, a finger beneath her
chin so he could see her face. Her eyes wide
and glistening and overbright. But the veriest
smile grazed the curve of her lips . . .

One thought stood high in his mind . . . *Mine*,
he thought in amazement, and then with stark
possessiveness. *She is mine* . . . Passion soared,
swift and hot and bright.

With a groan he crushed her to him. He
kissed her over and over, then rose to discard
his clothes impatiently. He made short work
of hers as well, with far more care but just as
much haste.

At last they stretched out together, naked
and unashamed. She blushed fiercely as his
eyes roamed where they would, but made no
effort to shield herself. Nay, for the heat in
his eyes was scorching. His hunger for her
was thrilling. The evidence of his desire for
her rose wantonly proud and erect before her
very eyes.

Never had he made love to her so tenderly.
He kissed the place where their child slept so
peacefully, laughing a little as the babe stirred
within her. With his fingertips and tongue he
toyed with the dark, straining centers of her
breasts, circling and teasing, his touch mad-

deningly elusive. Boldly he sought the furrowed cove between her thighs, stroking and tormenting until she was twisting beneath him and his name was a wanton plea upon her lips.

"Merrick," she cried. "*Merrick*!"

His chest heaving, his shaft near to bursting, he levered himself above her. He braced himself on his arms above her, ever mindful of his greater weight and the precious burden she carried.

Alana ran her fingers over the bulging tightness of his arms, loving the sleek feel of corded muscle smoothly sheathed in skin. Her hands climbed higher, curling and uncurling against his shoulders.

She gasped his name anew. "Please, Merrick. Oh, please . . ."

He came inside her then. With a groan his lips sealed hers. His breath filled her mouth. His shaft filled her body, so deep he touched her womb, her very soul . . .

It was a union unlike any other. They were linked by a force more powerful than a joining of the flesh, a bond of spirit and soul.

Husband . . . and wife.

Lord . . . and lady.

I love him, she thought helplessly. *I love him so*. The certainty seared her very breast, even as the words hovered on her lips. Above her, Merrick gave one last, piercing lunge. Feeling his seed throb and burst within her, her pleasure reached its zenith. Release came in a blinding shimmer of blazing sensation.

She was only vaguely aware of Merrick turning her. She smiled, for she did not mind as his arm came hard around her and he tugged her close, his torso warm and furry against the arch of her back and bottom. Merrick chuckled and brushed a kiss across the downy softness of her cheek. Just so, they fell asleep, her small hand trapped beneath his and resting squarely atop the hard mound of her belly.

Chapter 21

⸎

The days passed and summer waned. Her babe ripened within her; her belly grew round and distended.

For Alana, it was a time to face a bittersweet truth. Merrick was ever obliging, ever attentive, ever tender and considerate of her every wish. Indeed, his arms provided a sheltering haven from the turmoil all around, for but a sennight past, there had been yet another mutilation of a wee, tiny lamb.

And they had yet to discover the reason for the killings. She hated the whispers, the wary glances cast her way when they thought she was not looking. One day in the yard she chanced to hear a stableboy whisper to another.

"My mum says 'tis she who butchers the animals. She says we'd best watch out lest one of us comes next."

Alana had cringed inside, and hurried away. She hadn't realized that Merrick had overheard as well. Later, a beaming Genevieve disclosed how Merrick had plucked up the lad by the scruff of his collar, warning the boy sharply that he would hear naught said against his wife.

'Twas odd, she reflected as she lay wrapped in Merrick's arms later that night, that this man who had once vowed to be her lord and conqueror should in truth have become her staunchest defender . . .

Nay, no longer could she hide the truth from herself.

She loved him. She loved him wildly. Endlessly. Forever and ever . . .

The thought that he might never return her love was devastating. Aye, he whispered of his passion, his pleasure. But she was terribly afraid that it would ever be so—that Merrick would give of his body but not his heart . . . never his heart.

And alas, her dreams had returned to haunt her—and taunt her—as well. Many was the night she bolted upright, a garbled scream wedged in her throat, the vision of Merrick looming above her, his sword held high aloft, the sense of danger so acrid she could taste it.

But on this night the dream was different, for Sybil was there, hands perched on her hips, dark eyes agleam. And she could see herself lying abed, a small bundle wrapped in swaddling nestled against her breast.

"It matters little that he married you," Sybil sneered. "Your babe will still be called bastard. Aye, bastard like his mother."

"Nay," Alana whispered. "Nay!"

"Yes, Alana, yes! Indeed, 'tis likely the babe will be born with your curse," she jeered as she had once before. *She leaned close and hissed. "There are ways to end the possibility of such, you know. I could show you—"*

Alana saw herself as if from a very great distance away. "Nay!" she heard herself shriek. "You will not touch my babe. You will not touch him!"

Sybil just laughed. And laughed and laughed and laughed . . . And then she reached for the babe . . .

"Alana! Sweet God above, you will harm yourself! Do not fight me so! Do you hear? You must not fight me!"

Her eyes snapped open. She stared into Merrick's features, dark and taut above her. Only then was she aware that she'd been twisting and thrashing wildly. Feeling Merrick's hands warm and strong upon her shoulders, she sank back against the pillows. Her hand had crept to her belly. The babe was alive and well; he rolled strongly within her. Giving a silent prayer of thanks, she tried to summon a smile but failed abominably.

Merrick's breath stirred the fine hairs on her temple. " 'Twas just a dream, Saxon. A dream you've had these many months that still has yet to pass. Indeed, 'twill never come to pass, for you are my wife, sweet. My wife, and never could I harm you."

Softly though he spoke, the intensity of his passion made her heart turn over. She prayed anew that he was right, for she could not bear to think she loved the man who would ultimately slay her! Merrick was right, she sought to assure herself. Such a thing could not be. Nay, surely not . . . Despite all, she shivered.

Strong arms immediately swept her close. Held tight against his chest, she released a long, uneven breath.

"Alana!" he chided. "Why do you tremble? You must believe me. I would never raise my hand against you—never!"

Her fingers curled in the springy dark hair on his chest. "I know," she said haltingly. "And truly, 'tis not that I fear *you*." She stopped, unable to go on.

Merrick probed gently. "What then? Tell me, sweet."

Alana blinked back a hot rush of tears. Her time would be soon, she knew, for the babe had settled uncomfortably low within her. She longed for the day she would hold her child in her arms, yet she could not banish her secret dread so easily. How could she tell him of all she held within her?

"I am . . . afraid."

"Of what?"

Sybil's face swam afresh in her mind. Her cruel warning tolled through her mind until Alana longed to clamp her hands over her ears.

"Tell me, Saxon."

He was not to be dissuaded and she knew it. "Sybil says this babe may well be born with my curse." She turned her cheek into the hollow of his shoulder. Her voice emerged scarcely more than a breath of air.

Above her, Merrick swore a vile oath. "Were she not your sister, I would see her banished from this keep, for she is ever ready to brew trouble for you. By all that is holy, the wench has a tongue of which I should dearly like to deprive her. And as for you, Saxon, you have no curse, save that of having one such as her for a sister!"

Alana's throat grew achingly tight. That he would defend her so tied her heart in knots. Alas, if only he loved her. If only . . .

In time, she slept again, curled against his side, her head pillowed trustingly on his chest. She roused slightly when he arose at dawn. She was only half-aware as he brushed a feathery kiss upon her lips, but she slept again with the memory of that caress seared into her consciousness. She woke some time later, wincing a little as she struggled to rise. The dull ache in the small of her back that had plagued her these last days had not lessened.

She had just finished plaiting her hair and donning her bliaud when she heard a loud rumbling belowstairs. Hurrying as best she was able, she entered the hall in time to see everyone rushing toward the chapel. An eerie prickling raised the hair on the back of her nape. Drawn by some force she could not control, she trailed the others.

Just then came the piercing shrill of a scream. "He is dead," someone wailed. "May God have mercy, Father Edgar is dead!"

"Murdered!" came the cry. "He has been murdered!"

Alana had reached the entrance to the chapel. Her heart pounding, she edged forward numbly, as if in a trance. Several men-at-arms stepped aside, affording her an unobstructed view of the chapel.

An icy jolt tore through her. God above, it was true. Father Edgar lay sprawled near the altar . . . face down in a crimson pool of blood.

The world tilted all around her. Her head swam giddily. Her face bleached of all color, Alana pressed the back of her hand to her mouth. "It cannot be," she whispered. "It cannot be."

One by one all those present turned. To Alana it was as if the whole of Christendom stared at her. Their expressions ranged from furiously accusing to frankly terrified.

"Who would dare to kill one of God's own?" The whisper began to spread.

A figure near the body raised his fist high and shook it, then pointed to Alana. "She did it!" he cried. "She killed Father Edgar because he did not wish to see her married to Merrick!"

"Aye," shouted another. "The devil's hand she is!"

"'Twas she who killed our animals—a sacrifice to the devil!"

Alana began to shake.

Merrick shoved his way into the fray. " 'Tis foolishness you spout, the lot of you!" he said fiercely. "She was with me the night through. Last eve and all others before it, so cease your accusations."

Behind him, a sudden stab of pain tore through Alana's belly. Still another came, this one more violent than the first. With a low moan she sank to her knees, clutching her belly.

Genevieve had been standing nearby, stunned and dismayed by all that went on before her. But then she chanced to glimpse Alana's distress. In but an instant she was at her side.

She came down beside Alana, her features frantic. "Alana, what is wrong? Is it your time?"

Frightened eyes met hers. "I—I do not know," she gasped. "But I—I think it may well be."

Genevieve hugged her. "There now, do not worry," she soothed. "I've delivered many a young one into this world and you may be very certain I am as anxious to see this one as you," she teased.

Merrick was there, his features as frantic as his sister's had been. "What is amiss? The babe?"

Alana nodded and sought to summon a smile, a smile that quickly transformed to a grimace of pain.

Without another word, Merrick swung his wife high in his arms and bore her to their chamber.

As Alana soon discovered, having a babe was no simple task. Indeed, she reflected hours later, it was sheer torture, for her pains did not start slowly, as Genevieve had assured her was wont to happen. The dull ache moved around to the front, cramping her womb with ever increasing intensity.

Then all at once, they stopped. For some few hours, the pains ceased; Alana was both relieved and frustrated. Now that the time was upon her, she wanted nothing more than to hold her child in her arms. Then, alas, just when she thought she was destined to wait she knew not how long, her labor began anew.

And now it was stronger and harder than before. Alana could not stifle the scream that broke from her lips, for the pressure within her swelled until she was certain she would be torn asunder.

Hearing her cry, Merrick burst into the chamber. Genevieve straightened from where she stood near the end of the bed.

"Merrick!" She proclaimed her displeasure aloud. "You cannot be here!"

"Why not?"

"Because—because 'tis simply not done! This is women's work and—"

She broke off abruptly, for Merrick paid her no heed. Instead he barreled straight to the side of the bed where his wife lay, pale and gasping as an especially strong contraction ebbed at last.

Though Genevieve clucked and muttered beneath her breath and cast dark glances at the unwelcome visitor, Merrick cared not. Shaken to the core of his being, his attention was solely on his wife. He sat beside her, her hands

locked tightly within his. An awful dread
unleashed its claws within him. Sweet Mother
Mary, if he should lose her now . . . nay. *Nay!*
He refused to consider that such a thing might
happen.

Yet his heart lurched again and again as
spasm after spasm tightened her womb. Her
efforts to expel his child wrenched at his
insides, for never had he seen her so pale
and weak. Faith! He would gladly take her
pain unto him to spare her own, but alas! he
could not. He could only stand by and offer
what comfort he could.

Just when he was convinced she could stand
no more, Genevieve gave a half-laugh. "Oh,
there, it will not be long now, I promise you!
Push, Alana, push now!"

Alana propped herself on her elbows. She
strained mightily, then fell back, exhausted.
Tears glistened in her eyes. "I cannot," she
moaned. "God help me, I can stand no more!"

Merrick leaned forward. Fingers that were
incredibly gentle smoothed a wild tangle of
hair from her cheek. Though his face was ash-
en, he spoke sharply. "What is this, woman?
I did not marry you that you might give up
before I see my son! Come, are you Saxons
truly so feeble?"

A spark of life flared in her eyes. She drew
a breath and prepared to deliver a scathing
denouncement when the pressure within her
soared once more. She clutched at his hand so
tightly her nails carved furrows in his palm.

Genevieve gave an excited cry. "Yes, Alana,

yes! Oh, I can see the head! Oh, so much hair there is, love, and I believe . . . yes, dark as night, it is!"

Battling and anxious now, convinced the time she'd awaited so long was near, Alana arched her back so that the cords in her neck stood taut. Gritting her teeth, she summoned her last vestige of strength and pushed.

The babe slid from her in a tremendous rush. A thin, mewling cry filled the air. Alana sank back, relieved and dazed.

Merrick framed her face in his palms and kissed her lips. " 'Tis over, Saxon. 'Tis over and we have a fine son to show for it. Aye, and 'tis just as I predicted—a fine Norman son, sweet."

Alana's eyes opened. She fixed him with a glare as best she was able, but again there was no refuting him. Merrick laughed heartily and bestowed on her lips another long, lingering kiss.

Soon Genevieve was busily cleaning the slippery little body. The babe squalled, loudly venting his dislike of the task. Merrick stood watch, anxiously scrutinizing this tiny new being.

Genevieve turned. An odd smile crossed her lips as she spied him standing there, a faint longing in his eyes, a longing that he was aware he displayed so vividly.

His heart caught as his sister laid the now tightly swaddled bundle in his arms. He swallowed, stricken by humble pride. Dark hair was slicked tight to the babe's scalp; the child carried his Norman coloring, but the slant of his brows and the pucker of his mouth were his mother's.

A rush of emotion shot through him, nearly sending him to his knees, for this moment was far more than he could have ever imagined. He was sire to a fine, healthy babe, husband to a beauty that he did not doubt would someday make him the envy of half the kingdom.

Alana . . . his life.

Alana . . . his love.

She would share his life, bear his children. She roused a hunger in him unmatched by any other. He would have it no other way— by God, it would *be* no other way! She was his and would ever be so. Yet even as pride swelled his chest, a bitter despair seared his soul. Bleakly he wondered if she had truly put aside her hatred of him. Would she ever come to care for him? Would she ever *love* him?

He handed the babe back to Genevieve, then moved to the bedside. He knelt, reaching for Alana's hand. He whispered her name.

Her lashes fluttered open. Cool fingers curled around his. She smiled, a sweet, serene smile that sent a whole new pulse of emotion sweeping through him. Her lashes closed, and he knew from the deep, even rise and fall of her breast that she slept. He kissed her fingers, the fullness of her lips, before he rose and stepped from the chamber.

It was early evening when Alana woke again. The last fading rays of sunlight trickled into the chamber. The wail of an infant came from the corner, and Alana turned toward the sound eagerly. Genevieve was there already, plucking the infant from his cradle. With deft, sure hands she changed his swaddling. Alana looked on, carefully counting fingers and toes from afar. The babe's cries had lessened, but when he was lifted high in Genevieve's arms, he began to fuss and squirm once more.

"An impatient mother," Genevieve teased as she approached. "And an impatient young lord." She lowered the bundle down into Alana's waiting arms. "There, now, lamb, now you shall both have what you want."

Holding her son for the first time, Alana flashed a beaming smile, abrim with joy. With Genevieve's assistance, her gown was eased from her shoulder to offer her breast. The babe clamped down hard on her nipple with a ferocity that rounded his mother's eyes, but then she smiled.

With the tip of her finger, she traced the arch of splendidly shaped brows, then pressed her lips to the fine dark fuzz that covered his head. Her eyes grew soft and she was filled with an incredible gladness.

Her son had been born to the lord Brynwald as she had not been, yet naught could have pleased her more. Indeed, she could not bear to think this innocent babe might face the same hardship and struggle she had endured. He would someday take his place as the lord of Brynwald. He would be tall and strong and just, like his grandsire—and aye! his father. Norman and Saxon alike would come to revere and respect him . . .

She was roused from her musings by the sound of a deep, male voice—Merrick. She spied him there in the doorway but he did not remain there, as she thought he might. Instead he ventured within and perched beside her. Alana flushed a vibrant shade of rose. The ivory fullness of her breast lay plump and naked and exposed, for in truth she'd not expected to be disturbed. Only then did she realize that Genevieve had quietly withdrawn, leaving the new family alone.

She was all at once struck by the notion that something was different. His manner was easier. No longer did he appear the cold, ruthless warrior who had seized her in the forest. Indeed, there was something almost tender in the eyes that roved her upturned features, something that made her pulse pound and her heart beat a rapid tattoo.

His gaze upon her lips, he murmured, "I would thank you for my son, Saxon."

Wide eyes searched his face. Alana bit her lip. "You are . . . pleased with him?" she whispered, her voice but a breath.

Something flashed in the back of his eyes, something that made her pulse run wild. His hand slid beneath the thick curtain of her hair, warmly cupping her nape. His head lowered. His mouth touched hers, gentle and infinitely sweet, yet the heat of his kiss went through her like a brand. Alana's free hand came up to twist in the front of his tunic, so that their hearts pressed together as one . . .

A loud squalling startled them both. They

drew apart sharply, then laughed shakily when
they saw that the babe had lost that which
he coveted so highly! Though Alana was still
shy and uncertain about Merrick seeing her
thus bared, she did not want him to leave.
She switched the babe to the other breast as
Genevieve had instructed her; he latched on
with avid hunger.

Her attention focused on her son, Alana
stroked one tiny cheek. "Aubrey told me I
carried a boy," she murmured.

She felt rather than saw Merrick's surprise.
"You did not tell me Aubrey was one such as
you—"

"He was not," she said quickly. "Yet he was
so certain I could not believe he was wrong.
Indeed, I—I felt that he was right."

"That he was," Merrick observed with a
faint smile. "And now, sweet, I would remind
you we must choose a name for this young
one." His gaze held hers. "I thought mayhap . . . Geoffrey."

Now it was he who hesitantly questioned.

Alana smiled, a smile of such blinding sweetness he was robbed of breath. "Geoffrey it shall
be."

But alas, it was over far too soon. The newly
christened Geoffrey had fallen asleep at her
breast. Merrick eased the babe from her and
gently placed him in his cradle. Returning to
the bedside, he frowned when he glimpsed the
cloudiness in her gaze.

"What is it, sweet? Are you unwell?"

"I am fine," she answered, her voice half-strangled. "But I cannot help but think of Father Edgar. Merrick, I must know . . . how did he die?"

Merrick imprisoned her hand tightly within his. For a time it seemed he would not answer. Then he said quietly, "A dagger through the heart."

She stared down at the frailty of her hand nestled so trustingly within his. An elusive hurt twisted her insides. She was now the lady of Brynwald. But in truth, nothing had changed.

"How can they think I would do such a thing?" Her voice was half-choked. "Never have I harmed a soul in my life—never!"

She trembled against him. With a muffled exclamation, he turned to her. "Alana, you must not worry!"

She ducked her head against his shoulder. "I fear I cannot help it. Merrick, I—I am frightened! Why would anyone do such—such terrible things! And to slay a priest . . ."

Powerful arms wrapped her tight and close. "I will let nothing happen to you—nor to Geoffrey," he vowed. He held her until her shaking subsided, until she, too, had fallen asleep in his embrace.

But his mind was as troubled as Alana's. He thought of the bloodied animal carcasses lying limp and mutilated on the ground. What twisted mind had conceived of such torture? What hand could willingly perform such deeds?

An eerie chill ran the length of his spine. For indeed, he reflected grimly, the veriest question was not simply why . . .

But who.

Chapter 22

While the fields reaped the summer's bounty, Alana discovered the joys of becoming a mother, for indeed, the birth of a babe was a thing of beauty and wonder. From the instant she first held her son in her arms, she was seized by a thrill unlike any other. Indeed, she did not mind that the babe woke often for his feedings. She could imagine naught more precious than cradling her son close and watching him nurse, his tiny fist curled against the swell of her breast.

The days turned, one into the next. Soon a month had passed since Geoffrey's birth. While Alana regained her strength and slimness, the babe grew strong and lusty, his cheeks and belly round and plump.

Merrick was no less proud of his son. In some faraway corner of her being, a part of her had secretly feared Merrick would exhibit little interest in their son. But it was oft Merrick who brought Geoffrey to their bed in the dark of the night, and returned him to his cradle. Her throat tightened at the sight of such strength displaying such gentleness, his hands so big and Geoffrey so small.

Genevieve, too, was a doting aunt, as smitten with the babe as were both his parents. Geoffrey had only to let out the slightest wail than he was almost instantly snatched high in someone's arms.

Yet Alana could hardly deny the tension that lingered within the walls of the keep. Merrick had ordered more guards to keep watch in the night, but still the people of Brynwald appraised her with wary eyes . . . and each other as well. For the identity of Father Edgar's murderer remained a secret.

To all but the murderer.

So it was that a shroud of uncertainty hung over Brynwald, an ominous shadow of all things past . . .

And all yet to come.

Soon the weather turned gray and threatening as well, chill and wet and blustery. The seas churned wildly, crashing high upon the rocky shore. Storm clouds gathered dark and forbidding across the sky, unleashing on the world below a torrent of rain and wind.

It was on just such a day that the muffled sound of weeping reached Alana's ears. She had just nursed Geoffrey and was in the midst of soothing him to sleep. A hasty glance revealed a frothy bubble of milk at his lips, his lashes a dark crescent on his cheeks. Dropping a light kiss on his scalp, she laid him in his cradle and tiptoed across the floor.

In the passageway, she tipped her head first

one way and then the other. The sound came again, from the direction of Genevieve's chamber. With a frown she hurried forth.

Standing before Genevieve's room, she knocked lightly upon the broad wooden panel and called her name. "Genevieve? 'Tis Alana."

No answer was forthcoming. Alana hesitated, then pushed the door open and stepped within.

Genevieve sat upon her bed. She raised her head, apparently startled by the disruption.

Alana halted in her tracks, both embarrassed and concerned. "Forgive me the intrusion," she murmured. "But I did knock . . ."

"I—I did not hear." Genevieve swiped at her eyes, as embarrassed as Alana. She sought to summon a bright smile but failed miserably.

Alana hesitated but an instant. In a thrice she was across the floor and kneeling before Genevieve.

"Genevieve," she said gently. "You must tell me what distresses you so."

Genevieve refused to meet her gaze. "I—I do not know if I can!"

Alana grasped Genevieve's hands lightly within hers. She gazed at her steadily. "I'll understand if you choose not to. But mayhap 'twould ease your mind if you were to talk of what troubles you."

Genevieve bit her lip. "You will tell no one?"

"I will tell no one," Alana vowed solemnly.

"Not even Merrick?"

"Not if you do not wish me to." Alana squeezed her fingers. "Genevieve, I would help you, if only I could."

Genevieve's eyes filled with tears. "There is naught you can do," she said painfully. "'Tis—'tis Radburn, you see."

"Radburn?" Alana was confused.

Suddenly all was spilling out, and all in a rush. "I—I came here that I might be with Simon," Genevieve confided, her tone half-choked. "Never did I expect to fall in love!"

Alana caught her breath. "Radburn? You are in love with Radburn?"

Genevieve nodded.

Alana was still stunned. "When did this happen?"

"It—it began when I cared for him after he was injured in the village. The second night, his fever rose. He awoke and he was not himself." Color rose brightly in Genevieve's cheeks. "Alana, he called me beauty and he—he kissed me. I—I did not stop him. Indeed, 'twas a—a wondrous thing, for he awoke in me a longing I could not deny!"

Alana gently encouraged her. "What happened then?"

Genevieve took a breath. "I—I tried to forget what he'd done, but I could not. I found myself remembering that moment—and wishing for it to happen again! And, oh . . . 'tis silly, but I would go out of my way to catch the merest glimpse of him. Then one day we chanced to meet when no one else was about. It happened several more times, and soon he confided that he *did* remember that kiss. And then it was happening all over again . . . I—I could not fight it," she confided helplessly. "Nor could he.

Never did I expect to spare a thought for any other man after Philippe," Genevieve went on. "Yet with Radburn, I could not stop myself from feeling . . . oh, so many things I never thought to feel again. Alana, we—we have been meeting each other behind the cook-house each evening."

Alana's mind was all awhirl. "But why is this such a terrible thing?" A sudden thought occurred and she straightened her spine indignantly. "Did he spurn you? Oh, the wretch—"

"Nay." Genevieve denied it quickly, but her mouth was tremulous. "But Radburn—I saw him this morn. Alana, he says that it must end and I cannot bear the thought."

"But why? If you love him—"

"I do!" Genevieve gave a half-sob. "And he loves me. But he is convinced there is no hope for us."

"But why?"

"Because he is no longer a knight. Because he has naught to offer me. He is a man of honor and principle, Alana. He says he will not sully me should I wish to marry again."

Only then did Alana begin to understand. Once Radburn might have felt equal to this lady from across the Channel, but alas! no more. A faint bitterness seeped into her soul. The Normans had wrested from the English their homes and lands . . . and Radburn? He had lost both his station and his dignity.

Yet of a certainty Alana could harbor no malice against Genevieve. She had come to love her as a sister and she couldn't bear to see Genevieve so unhappy.

She squeezed Genevieve's fingers. "Do not despair. Radburn may yet change his mind."

Genevieve shook her head. "A man's pride is his greatest strength—as well as his greatest enemy," she said sadly. Her eyes darkened. "And 'twould do no good even if he did. Merrick would never allow such a match."

"Why? Because Radburn is a Saxon?" Alana's reply was heated. "*He* married a Saxon! Why should you be condemned for doing the same as he?"

"'Tis different for a man, Alana. He may do as he wishes with no one to please but himself—and mayhap Duke William." She rose and walked to the shuttered window. Alana's heart went out to her, for the set of her shoulders was not quite so straight as before.

And alas, she was unable to let the matter rest. When she chanced to see Radburn alone the next day near the herb garden, she quickly made her way toward him. Perchance he might have known what she was about, for he would have turned away had she not called out to him.

"Radburn, wait! I would speak with you."

Slowly he turned. "Indeed," he stated coolly.

"Aye," Alana said quietly. "About Genevieve."

He stiffened.

Alana bit her lip, for only now did she realize her task might well be in vain. His expression was stony, and she suspected he would not welcome her intrusion.

She straightened her shoulders. "No doubt you will think I meddle where I should not. But Genevieve is very dear to my heart, and I would not see her hurt."

Radburn's fingers tightened on the handle of the scythe he held. "So she told you."

Alana nodded. "I have but one question, Radburn. Do you love her?"

"Aye," he said with no hesitation.

"Then why do you not do all within your power that you might be together?"

"All within my power?" His laugh was grating. "I need not remind you, Alana, I am a slave—a slave to your husband."

A frisson of guilt shot through her. "And what if that were to change?" she asked slowly.

"It will not. I've had word that my father is dead, and all that was his is now in the hands of the Normans. I am not free to make my way as I once was. I am bound to Merrick, even as you are bound to him. I no longer carry a sword in my hand but the tools of a—a farmer!" His lips twisted. "I am no longer chained but I am a slave nonetheless. I am not a man of honor but a man of the fields."

Alana shook her head. "Radburn, do not persist in this folly, for you will surely break her heart! She lost the man she loved once before. Would you see her suffer the same heartache?"

His jaw thrust out. "Were I able, I would give Genevieve all that I have. But my coffers are empty, you see—stolen by the Normans. So what would you have me do? Offer her my straw pallet in the stable? I think not. And I think you will understand, lady, that I simply do what is best for Genevieve."

Alana's heart was bleeding. So much had been taken from him. The chances that might have been his. His hopes and dreams . . .

She gazed up at him, quietly beseeching. "You told me once, Radburn, that we must accept the Normans, for we cannot beat them. I have accepted that, and so must you. But that does not mean all will remain as it is now. Perchance you might serve Merrick in another way—"

He was adamant. "Merrick will never grant me my freedom, and I will not see Genevieve dragged to her knees as I have been. I would have her on my feet as a man, not as a mud-spattered slave to her Norman brother."

Alana replied swiftly. "Genevieve does not give a care about worldly possessions—surely you know this! You say you would offer all that you have. But she would have you offer all that you are." Her eyes softened. She laid her fingertips on his forearm and spoke imploringly. "Do not forget this, Radburn, for all is not lost. I beg of you, do not give up." Leaning forward, she brushed her lips across his hardened cheek, then retraced her steps into the keep.

The matter weighed heavily on Alana's mind throughout the rest of the day, yet the notion persisted . . . *what if Radburn were to regain all that he had lost. His honor. His pride.*

Alas, she could think of only one way.

Merrick had been absent throughout the day, supervising the work in the fields. Alana spied him in the yard as he returned, handing his reins to a stableboy. She held her breath as he mounted the stairs into the hall. She'd asked a maid to convey a message that she wished to dine alone with him above stairs. To that end, she'd ordered a hot bath and a quiet meal for him in their chamber.

Now, as she heard his approaching footsteps, she smoothed the folds of her bliaud. Of palest mauve, it clung enticingly to the fullness of her breasts and slender hips. She'd combed her hair till it shone and left it loose and flowing down her back.

The door was flung wide. Alana rose. In that instant before he swept the door closed, she noted he looked tired. Summoning a smile, she stepped forward.

"You look as weary as I expected, my lord. Your bath awaits, and I've ordered food and wine when you've finished." Her voice emerged breathlessly. Sweet Mother Mary, she prayed she didn't appear as nervous as she sounded!

A dark brow climbed high. "Indeed, Saxon, it seems you've anticipated my every need."

Alana's laugh was rather airy. Geoffrey lay sleeping in the corner, and she watched as Merrick pressed a kiss on the babe's head, then he disrobed and lowered himself into the steaming waters. Her gaze traced lovingly across the clean, spare lines of his shoulders, sleek and damp. Her mouth grew dry as sweet hunger blossomed within her.

Thus was the bend of her mind as Merrick partook of his meal. It had been weeks since he'd made love to her. Only yesterday Genevieve had hinted that she was well enough that they might resume the pleasures of the marriage bed. Her heartbeat quickened at the possibility it might be this very night. Of a certainty she was hardly averse to such an undertaking. The thought of feeling him hard and full within her, planting his seed deep at the very gates of her womb made a quivering heat storm through her veins.

At last he leaned back in his chair. His eyes were fixed on hers, so keenly appraising she was abruptly jarred from her musings.

"I have the feeling, Saxon, that you wish something of me. If so, come out with it."

Foolish tears stung her eyes. Alana lowered her lashes lest he could see. She cried out inside. What was wrong? Why was he being so cold? It had been so long since he'd been like this and she hated it! This was not what she'd planned, and for an instant she floundered, uncertain how to proceed. But there was no help for it. She must do as he said and simply come out with it.

"I crave a boon, my lord," she said levelly. "I would ask that you take Radburn from the fields and count him among your men-at-arms."

His voice came, almost deathly quiet. "You would have me put a sword in his hands."

Her nod was jerky. "I believe he would serve you well."

A mantle of silence descended. Powerful hands atop the table, Merrick pushed himself to his feet. Alana couldn't tear her gaze from his. There was a painful catch in the region of her heart, for she could almost feel the blistering heat rise between them.

And she knew . . . she *knew* that he was filled with a rage as black as any she'd yet seen.

And so he was. For he'd seen her, his lovely wife, the way her hand fluttered on the Saxon's arm . . . the way her lips dwelled oh-so-sweetly on his cheek.

Slowly he walked around her. "Sweet heaven, I cannot believe it!" he burst out. "You would have me put a sword in his hand. Aye, and no doubt I'd soon find a dagger in my back! But that would suit you, eh, Saxon?"

Alana's hands twisted in her lap. She was dangerously close to tears, and she hated both herself and him for bringing about such weakness.

"Of course not! Oh, why can't you see? Radburn has given you no trouble these many months, but he was not meant to labor in the fields. He was trained to be a knight, as you were. And—and that is what he should be!"

Merrick's lip curled. "You champion him well, Saxon. Dare I ask why? Dare I ask the nature of the kiss you shared?"

For a mind-splitting instant, Alana could

only gape. Then she protested heartily. "We shared naught—"

"Ah, but you did." The twist of his lips resembled a snarl more than a smile. "I saw your hand on his arm, sweet. Your lips on his cheek."

Alana despised the flush that even now heated her cheeks. "I but comforted him—"

"What need has he of comfort? *Your* comfort, I would add?"

The truth nearly spilled from her lips, but she had promised Genevieve she would not betray her secret. Even as a burning ache seared her breast, she was filled with a stinging resentment that he could think so little of her.

Bravely she raised her chin. "You refuse? You will keep him in the fields?"

Merrick's jaw snapped shut. "Aye!"

Alana's eyes were smoldering. "You refuse only because *I* ask it," she cried.

"I refuse because I am lord here, Saxon. I would remember that were I you. And a word of warning," he said fiercely. "If I should see you with Radburn, both of you will regret it. This I promise. By God, this I vow."

Sheer outrage brought her to her feet. "Oh, how foolish of me to forget! My duty is to please you, is it not?"

He stopped before her. "Your duty—and aye, your affections!—are to me, your lord and husband. And it seems you need a reminder, Saxon."

Strong hands caught at her arms, brought her close, so close she could feel the unyielding breadth of his body. She opened her mouth to cry out, but there was no chance. She had but one glimpse of glowing heated eyes before his mouth trapped hers.

Her cry was smothered deep in her throat. His kiss was not the sweet caress she knew him capable of, but a punishment. Though he did not hurt her, she could feel the anger in his touch. Struggling to be free, she tore her mouth from his and shoved at his chest.

"Nay," she gasped. "Nay!"

Slowly he raised his head. His tone was as grim as his tightly drawn features. "What! Do you deny me yet again, Saxon?"

A suffocating tightness seemed to wrap around her chest. "Aye," she stated with aching heart and tear-choked voice. "I would *not* deny the man who is my husband, the father of my son. But I would deny the man who proclaims himself my lord and conqueror."

He snatched her against him with a force that wrenched the breath from her lungs. His fingers bit into the tender flesh of her arms. A low, strangled moan broke from her throat even as his head dipped low.

But the hurtful kiss she expected to bear was not to be. For one long, paralyzing moment their eyes met and clashed, his dark with some nameless emotion, hers bright and sparkling with tears. With a muffled oath he flung himself away . . .

Then there was only the sound of her heartbeat drumming in her ears.

The tension sapped her courage and

strength. She sank to the floor in a heap, awash with a blinding despair.

Nothing had changed, she realized with stark, wrenching clarity. She was Merrick's wife—his *wife*—but still he did not trust her. And alas, he was still her lord and conqueror . . .

She meant nothing to him, nothing at all.

Chapter 23

◦━◦◯◯◦━◦

Perchance it was inevitable. Later she was certain it was so, for Merrick did not return to their chamber . . . and her dream returned that very night.

The same . . . yet different.

All around loomed shadows and darkness, an endless sea of black. The stench of blood lay thick in the air. Bloodcurdling screams pierced the night. Then all at once thunder and lightning broke the sky wide open. As if from above, she saw herself, frozen there amidst the terror and the evil. Then she was within herself once more. Her feet began to move. Her heart pounded with stark, frantic terror. She was running . . . from something . . . nay, someone.

Bodies lay strewn all about. Normans. Saxons . . . and men from the North.

Her eyes snapped open. She bolted upright and pressed her fingertips into her forehead. A sick sense of dread churned in her belly, for all at once she knew . . .

"Danes," she whispered, and then again: "Danes."

A figure screeched shrilly and backed away—the maid who had just crept in to wake her mistress.

"Nay," Alana cried wildly. "Do not be afraid of me. Oh, don't you see? 'Tis the Danes! The Danes will come here . . . to Brynwald! They will attack and—"

With a shriek the woman darted from the chamber.

By eveningtide it was the talk of the keep— how Alana had been visited by another vision and was convinced that Danes would attack.

Within a sennight, all thought her mad.

Merrick was more furious than ever.

And much to her despair, all was as it had been before. Alana was heartsick, for Merrick's manner with her was cold and remote. He returned to their bed but they lay ever apart, ever distant. No tender words were whispered in her ear; he made no move to renew the passion that had once flared so brightly between them. Her nerves were scraped raw, for whene'er they were together, the air between them was charged with the fury of a thunderbolt.

She lay on her side late one morn, nursing Geoffrey, alone in the chamber. With a fingertip she tenderly traced the curl of one tiny ear. The slightest smile touched her lips. Already he resembled his father greatly—aye, and in temperament as well, for when he was hungry, he was demanding and would ever have his way. But surely he would grow to be handsome and strong and brave and proud . . .

A sound nearby alerted her to another presence. Merrick stood there in the doorway, so tall and commanding he stole her breath. Yet an empty despair encircled her heart, for never had he appeared more aloof than at this moment. Instinctively she tugged the sheet over the bareness of her breast, for with his manner so distant she was shy about displaying herself so before him. She did not see the way his expression tightened.

He wasted no time stating his business. "I plan to spend the day hawking, Saxon. I suggest you spend yours packing your chest, for I am sending you and Geoffrey to London on the morrow."

Stunned, Alana stared at him. "London," she echoed. "Will you be going?"

"Nay."

An awful tightness lay heavy in her breast. "Then . . . why would you send me away?"

He gestured impatiently. "The villeins fear you, Alana. I would assure your safety from them."

"My safety! You—you lie, Merrick! You would be rid of me!" Her cry was a mixture of outrage and fear. She started to raise up, only to remember Geoffrey.

"You will not be alone," he told her, his eyes pure ice. "Genevieve may accompany you." There was an awful finality to his tone. He spun around and left.

But Alana would not be so meekly accepting. Quickly she rose and put Geoffrey in his cradle. The babe wailed loudly, but she raced after Merrick as if Satan himself were at her heels.

She caught up with him in the yard, just as he would have mounted his horse. Panting, she seized his elbow. "Merrick, what of the Danes? You must believe me, for I know it will happen—and soon! You must prepare the keep for battle—"

He whirled on her, his expression as fierce as she'd ever seen it. "Cease this display, Alana! You make a fool of yourself!"

From behind her came a sneer. "Pay her no heed, my lord, for 'tis but a trick. She would blind us to the truth—that she murdered Father Edgar. And now she seeks to gain favor by crying that the Danes will come."

Alana turned in rage. "Scoff if you like, all of you, but I tell you they will come! And you will be sorry you were not ready!"

"Mad, she is," proclaimed the lout beside the first. "A mad witch!"

Merrick stepped forward. "Enough!" he shouted. "I will hear no more!" He leveled on the pair a glare so blistering they paled and fell back a step. His jaw clenched and he turned back to Alana, snaring her arm and urging her into the hall where they might speak in private.

She placed her hand on his forearm. "Merrick, I beg of you," she implored. "Do not do this. Do not send me to London."

He gazed down at her dispassionately. Beneath her fingertips his arm was rigid. "You plead so prettily, sweet, but I would know . . . Why are you so determined to stay? Is it because you cannot stand to be parted from me—or from your handsome young Saxon?"

She stiffened. *Damn you!* she thought. *Damn you to hell!* In that instant, she almost hated him. His arrogance. His power over her fate. "You are wrong about me," she said feelingly. "And you are wrong about Radburn. Indeed, you forget he fought for your sister—"

Merrick's jaw locked anew. "And he fought for you, too, sweet. Let us not forget that."

Her fingers locked convulsively around his forearm. Her heart cried out. *How can you do this?* she screamed silently. *It's always been you . . . only you . . . Oh, don't you know that I love you?*

But all that seared her breast would never be spoken. She would neither cry, nor beg nor plead, for there was little point. Merrick did not love her, she realized with heartbreaking candor. He would never believe that she loved him.

And it seemed he did not want *her*.

Tears burned the back of Alana's throat. Gathering what little of her dignity remained, she raised her chin. "I can offer no more assurance than what I have done, Merrick. I have been faithful to you in every way, in every deed. Never have I betrayed you, though I know you think otherwise. So I would ask you once more. Do not send me to London!"

His mouth tightened. " 'Tis you I think of, Saxon. The people distrust you. Matters are still unsettled here and feelings still run high against you."

"And what of you? Do you believe I killed Father Edgar?"

For the space of a heartbeat she fear he would not answer—or perhaps she feared he might. At last he said, "Nay. I do not."

Through some miracle she did not retreat from his regard. "Then tell me this. The others think me mad. Is that what you think as well? That I am mad? A mad witch?"

He remained brutally silent, and in that silence she read a bitter truth. 'Twas then she saw the one thing she'd not thought to see in his eyes . . . the one thing she could not bear to see. A glimmer of doubt.

His posture was inflexible, yet when he spoke, it was not what she expected. "Mayhap you are," he said harshly. "God help me, I do not know anymore! I know only that these dreams of yours have come to naught."

When she would have protested, he shook his head. "Nay, Saxon! Need I remind you of your foolishness? You dreamed I raised my sword high to strike you dead. Yet never have I hurt you, never! You've come to no harm at my hand, nor will you!" His lip curled. "If I can hold no store in your dreams, 'tis little wonder."

His scathing denunciation cut her to ribbons. Ever conscious of his thin-lipped scrutiny, she drew a sharp, painful breath and swallowed her heartache. "No matter what you think of me, Merrick, I tell you my dream will come to pass. Brynwald is in danger of attack from the Danes. Do not disregard this!"

He did not turn away as she thought he would. "We will talk more on this when I return, Saxon. For now, I suggest you ready yourself for your journey."

Her hand fell away from his arm. So it was true. He thought her mad, as mad as the others believed her to be. A corner of her heart seemed to shatter, then another and another. How she stopped herself from sobbing aloud, she knew not. She could bear such condemnation from the others for she had known it all her life, but not from Merrick . . . never from him.

He spun around. Not once did he deign to look back. She was left alone . . . alone as never before.

Raoul was mayhap the only one who did not doubt Alana's claim that the Danes would soon attack. Concealed behind a corner, he grinned as he listened to the heated exchange between Alana and Merrick. Rubbing his hands together with glee, he recalled the moment just a few days past when he'd first conceived his plan.

Merrick had dispatched him to carry a message to Robert, a fellow Norman who ruled a large fief to the north of Brynwald. He'd spent the night at an alehouse upon his return. It was while he supped that he noticed a youth across from him. He wore a cap and boots and leggings of a fur Raoul did not recognize. Even as he watched, the youth sidled closer to the Norman men-at-arms who occupied the bench behind him. The youth's head cocked to and fro; he semed to be listening intently.

Such behavior was quick to arouse Raoul's suspicions. When the youth slipped out the door a few moments later, Raoul quickly rose and followed him.

"Hold there, boy!" he shouted once he was outside.

The youth stopped, then slowly turned.

Raoul stepped before him. "Who are you?" he demanded.

The youth's eyes flickered, but he said nothing.

"I saw you listening to those soldiers," he barked. "Now answer me, boy!" When the boy again said nothing, Raoul snarled and snatched the cap from his head. Hair the color of straw stuck out in every direction. Raoul swore. "Bedamned! Are you one of the Danes?"

The youth's eyes flickered. When he would have remained silent, Raoul seized his arm and twisted it behind his back. "If you value your life, you will tell me who you are," he said between his teeth. "And do not pretend you do not understand me, for I know you do or you would not be here!"

The youth was bent nearly double. "I am Dagnor," he gasped, "son of Rasmus the Fair."

Raoul did not lessen his grip. "And why are you here? To spy?"

"Y—Yes!" the youth stammered. "My father sent me to discover what rich fiefs lie near."

Raoul's eyes began to gleam. He allowed the

Dane to straighten but kept a bruising grip on his arm. "So," he mused. "You return to your father now?"

The youth nodded.

Raoul allowed the boy to straighten but kept a bruising grip on his arm. "I would have you take me to him, boy."

Dagnor gaped. "Why?"

Raoul laughed. "Because I can help him with what he seeks. A rich fief . . . and your life, boy."

Recalling that night roused a potent satisfaction. A slow smile crept across his lips. All he had dreamed of was within his gasp. Brynwald . . . and Alana.

Indeed, 'twould be his this very day.

Even as the sun rose high in the sky Alana's spirits dipped low. At Genevieve's urging, she spent most of the day making ready for the journey. Though a part of her longed to blatantly defy her husband, she decided bitterly that Merrick would have his way, no matter what her wishes.

Late in the afternoon after feeding Geoffrey, she laid him in his cradle and summoned a maid to stay with him. Needing solace from the world that battered her, she sought refuge where she had found it so often before—along the rocky beach below the cliffs.

There, as a lonely wind whipped her hair and skirts and stung her cheeks, she railed against herself and Merrick. For all that lay between them . . .

For all that would not.

The sound of her name being called roused her from her despair. Thinking it was perhaps Merrick, she flung up her head. But alas, it was not.

Instead it was Raoul. He stood before her, his hands braced on his hips, his demeanor one of supreme and utter arrogance.

Beneath her mantle, Alana straightened her shoulders. "Let me pass," she said quietly.

"I think not, my love."

Her glare burned hot as fire. "I am not your love," she snapped.

"Ah, but you will be." His smile was feral.

An icy tingle of foreboding ran down Alana's spine. But before she could say a word, Raoul's smile widened.

"Unfortunately, I fear your prediction was not quite right, my love. For you see, the Danes will not be coming after all. Indeed," he went on softly, "they are already here."

One by one, a half-dozen men filed out behind Raoul. Their hair was shaggy and unkempt as the beards that obscured their faces. Clad in rough, furry animal skins, to Alana's startled eyes they appeared as massive giants.

Held fast in the grip of a staggering horror, her mind screamed silently. If only her dreams had deceived her. If only her eyes did as well. For God above, Raoul did not lie . . .

They were Danes.

*   *   *

Though Merrick heartily enjoyed hawking, he could summon little enthusiasm for such sport this day. In truth, he was sorely vexed by the fiery Saxon he'd taken to wife, for she strained his temper and his patience as no other.

It was then he was forced to acknowledge the truth—'twas not Alana with whom he was angry. 'Twas himself, for he could not forget her wounded expression, her eyes wide and shimmering with tears. His accusation hammered in his skull, again and again.

Mayhap you are mad.

A bitter self-loathing blackened his heart. His conscience stabbed at him. He had hurt her, hurt her immensely. God's blood, he didn't know what had come over him! His mood had been black as sin; some devil within seized hold of him and would not let go.

He should never have taken her into his home. Into his bed. He should never have touched her. Loved her . . . Yet he could not imagine no other in his life.

In his heart.

A wrenching pain clawed at his insides. They shared a son, a son that would bind them through all eternity. He did not doubt that she loved Geoffrey . . . but did she secretly wish the babe's sire were a certain handsome young Saxon? He scowled, glad that Simon had ridden off to retrieve the rabbit he'd killed.

He despised the doubt that plagued him, for he could not bear to think of her with Radburn. Bitterness seeped deep onto his soul. Did she regret all that had brought her into his arms—and his bed? He was reminded how her lips flowered sweetly beneath his, how her hips churned wildly in the heat of passion. Surely she could not respond so ardently while she longed for another man . . . surely not!

Shifting in his saddle, he stared broodingly off into the distance, where the cliffs dropped off into the wild sea. A hearty breeze carried with it the scent of brine. Alana's prediction nagged at him. Invasions from the Danes were scarcely unheard of along the northern shores of England, but surely none would be so foolish as to brave the seas with winter's onset so very close.

Simon approached then, triumphantly displaying his prize. 'Twas then that the oddest sensation came over him . . . Something was wrong, he thought vaguely. Something was very, very wrong . . .

His heart seemed to stand still. "Brynwald," he said urgently. He grabbed Simon's reins. "Simon, we must return to Brynwald!"

Simon took one look at his wild expression and nodded. A cloud of dust spiraled in their wake.

His eyes scoured the horizon. Darkness would soon veil the earth. It was his most fervent wish that he was wrong. As they rapidly neared the keep, he prayed that all would be as before. The maids would be preparing to serve the evening meal. Alana would no doubt be in their chamber, Geoffrey nursing greedily at her breast.

But he did not find what he expected at Brynwald. Indeed, chaos reigned supreme. A crush of people scattered in every direction. Merrick leaped from his mount, quick to glean the air of frenzy.

A dairyman from the village fell to his knees before him. "My lord," he cried. "My son spied Danish longboats beached just to the north. We must defend ourselves!"

"Aye!" cried another. "We should have listened to your lady, for she was right, God save her soul!"

"Aye," piped up a young maid. "If she were a witch, she would mean to do us evil. Instead she sought to warn us—to save us!"

"Indeed," spoke up the laundress, "I've thought long and hard on what my lord once said. The lady Alana had done me no harm, nor anyone I know. Methinks we have wronged her sorely!"

Merrick head them, but his mind was otherwise occupied. For the space of a heartbeat, his gaze veered straight to Radburn standing near the bake-house. Was this invasion merely a ruse? A Saxon ploy to trick the Norman conquerors?

Nay, he thought. Every instinct within him said they did not lie. And they were right. The Danes did not come in peace. They came to plunder and wage war.

He raised an arm and beckoned to one of his men. "You, there, ready the horses!" He continued to bark out orders, but all the while his mind worked frantically and his eyes scanned the assemblage, everything within him cried out for Alana.

Where was she? Blood of Christ, where was she?

A hand caught his elbow. It was Genevieve.

"Genevieve! Where is Alana? Have you seen her?"

Her eyes were dark with fright. "Nay! I've searched for her everywhere. She left Geoffrey with a maid ages ago to walk along the beach. But I sent a man after her and there was no sign of her!" She gave a half-sob. "Oh, Merrick, she would not leave Geoffrey for so long! Something is wrong, I know it!"

Merrick was unable to give voice to his deepest fear—that Alana had fallen into the hands of the Danes. He squeezed Genevieve's fingers. "I will find her, I promise. Now go inside where you will be safe."

She swung around in a whirl of skirts. Merrick did not see the long, speaking look she exchanged with Radburn. When next he turned, Radburn stood before him, bold and tall.

Radburn stared him straight in the eye. "Give me a sword, man. I would fight—for Brynwald. For England. For all of us. And so will the others here." He gestured to where a group of grim-visaged Saxons gathered behind him. "We are as worthy soldiers as any of your men. If we combine our strength, we can surely defeat the Danes."

Merrick's decision was made in an instant. He beckoned Simon forward. "See that this man is armed," he ordered. "And the rest of these Saxons as well."

From somewhere came a shout. "They come! The Danish heathens come!"

For a heartbeat, everything ceased; the whole of the world seemed to hold its breath. It came then, carried on the wind, a bloodcurdling cry of war.

Even as he raised his sword high, an acrid fear sped along his veins. He chanted a silent litany over and over in his mind. He prayed that Alana was alive and safe and unharmed.

He prayed as never before.

The clash that erupted was vicious and bloody. For a time it appeared the fates were against Merrick. As one Danish attacker fell, still another took his place.

But the Normans—aye, and the Saxons— were determined not to succumb to the wild invaders from the North. The night air was filled with the sounds of battle. Harsh, guttural cries torn from the throats of all who fought added to the relentless din of clashing swords, spears, and battle-axes.

The night grew old and eventually there came a lull in the skirmish. Outcries grew fewer. Norman and Saxon pride swelled and strength was renewed. Atop his destrier, Merrick wiped the sweat from his brow.

Beneath his helm, his dark gaze scanned the fray. Victory was imminent. He could feel it in his very bones.

Closing his eyes, he let his mind take hold of his senses. As if some unknown force guided him from afar, he opened his eyes and turned his head.

It was just as it had been once before. Cedric sat on his haunches a short distance away, twitching his tail, as proud and haughty as ever!

Caught fast in the snare of some strange, unknown force, Merrick nudged his destrier into a walk. Not an arm's length away from the cat, he halted, leaning on his forearm to bow low.

"Cedric," he said softly. "Take me to your mistress."

Merrick could have sworn some silent message passed between them. Even as he watched, Cedric rose daintily to his feet. An instant later, the cat leaped around and darted toward the cliffs.

Merrick was right on his heels.

The hours since Alana's capture had taken their toll. After tying her wrists with hemp, Raoul had deposited her in a tiny, dark cave with a huge, hulking Dane standing guard. He and the others had left and had yet to return. That Raoul had allied himself with the heathens made her long to retch. But far surpassing her hatred for Raoul was her fear for those she loved.

Even now the sounds of battle still raged overhead.

Numb and chilled to the bone, Alana fought the very depths of despair. The fighting had gone on for so long now! She trembled to think of those who had fallen beneath the thrust of a sword, the blade of a battle-ax. Was Geoffrey safe? And what of Genevieve and Sybil? Her heart wrenched. Genevieve would be crushed should any harm befall Simon.

And Merrick. Did he still live? Her heart cried out. *Please, God. Oh, please . . .*

"Did you think I'd forgotten you?"

Raoul had returned. He stood there in the gloom, a careless smile twisting his lips. Alana glared her distaste.

"Come now. Let us remove these bonds."

He knelt before her. Alana suffered his touch but welcomed the surge of anger that warmed her veins. "You led the Danes to Brynwald, didn't you?"

"Oh, of a certainty 'tis to my advantage that they should come now. Though I admit, when I encountered their leader Rasmus a few days past, I was most successful in persuading him Brynwald was worthy of his attention."

The hemp fell free. Alana rubbed the chafed skin of her wrists. "What can you possibly hope to gain?"

His laugh was hearty. "Oh, a great deal, love. A great deal indeed."

"You would betray your own people," she accused. She was suddenly so angry her voice shook with it. "The Danes are barbarians. They will spare no one. They will set fire to any and all—"

"Nay, love. They will not."

Her eyes narrowed. "What bargain did you strike with them?"

His laugh was chilling. "Rasmus will do what I dare not—see Merrick dead at his feet. Indeed, he may already be so. Then they will plunder and loot as they wish, but no matter. They are easily satisfied. Indeed, the Danes are far more interested in bloodlust than treasures. They will take a few baubles and be on their way."

Her eyes sparked. "And leave bloodshed in their wake!"

He shrugged and went on as if she hadn't spoken. "And when they are gone, Brynwald will be mine." A finger came up to stroke her cheek. He smiled. "And so will you, love."

Alana wrenched her head away. "You are a cur," she spat. "A vile dog that will burn in hell—"

"Say no more!" he hissed. "I will do no more than Merrick did to your father, what William did to England. Take what the weak cannot hold for their own." He leaped to his feet, jerking her along with him. "And now I think the time has come for us to join the victory."

He dragged her along behind him. Alana tripped and nearly fell time and again as they traversed the rocky trail up the cliffs.

The smell of rain was ripe in the air. The winds began to rise and dark clouds raced overhead. Thunder rumbled across the earth.

Raoul did not stop until they reached a grassy hillock just outside the gates. The battle had spread beyond the outer wall of the keep. Alana sank to the ground—and her heart did as well—for bodies lay like sticks fallen in a storm.

Raoul stood several paces before her, enthralled with the grisly scene spread out below. Bile rose in her throat and she battled a sense of helplessness, cringing with every scream that rent the air.

All at once something leaped into her lap— a ball of matted yellow fur. Cedric! Slanted yellow eyes gleamed up at her. 'Twas odd, but a sizzle of something seemed to kindle between them. Cedric bounded from her lap and ran off, then paused and looked back, as if summoning her to follow.

Her heart beating like a captured doe's, she rose. Slowly she began to retreat, her legs shaking, her gaze never leaving the broadness of Raoul's back. When she deemed herself a far enough distance away that he would not hear, she spun around and began to flee, as if beset by demons.

And perhaps she was, for alas! she had misjudged Raoul. Behind her came a furious shout. Glancing over her shoulder, she saw him raise a fist high; with his other hand he ripped his sword from its scabbard.

Sheer terror consumed her. For a timeless moment, she stood as if frozen . . .

All around was a darkness such as she had never known. Blacker than the deepest pits of Hell. Shadows shifted and loomed, darting back and forth, in and out, as if to snatch at her with greedy, grasping fingers.

She could feel . . . something. Something evil . . . *Raoul*. A sense of danger that loomed all around, as heavy and thick and depthless as the shadows.

The wind rose in fury, wailing and howling. Lightning crashed across the heavens, a blaze of rending light. Thunder roared across the land, shaking the very ground beneath her feet. Great pools of blood splotched the earth. The air was rife with the sickening stench of gore and destruction.

Then she was running. Over the shriek of the wind, her blood roared in her ears. Footsteps trampled the earth, just behind her.

Blindly she ran, besieged by darkness. Beset by danger. By those horrible shadows that lurked all around. The specter of death loomed close at hand. Pressing in on her. Smothering her so that she could scarcely breathe . . .

But all at once there arose before her a hulking shadow. From out of the shadows they came . . . Man and beast. Knight and destrier.

He sat atop the great black steed, armed and mailed. For one single, frozen moment, he was dark and faceless, his features hidden behind a cone-shaped helmet. Behind him, lightning ripped the sky apart; it was as if he were cast in silver.

Slowly he raised his helm. A jolt tore through her. His expression was utterly fierce, pale and glittering and cold as frost; it stabbed into her like the point of a spear. Then slowly he raised his arm. Clasped in one gauntleted hand was a gleaming sword. He raised it high, his weapon poised for the space of a heartbeat.

Merrick. Her love. Her life.

It was then she realized . . . This was her dream. Her dream come to stark, vivid life . . .

An utter certainty came over her. She marveled that she had been so foolish—and so blind! For Merrick had come, not as her enemy . . .

But her savior.

Chapter 24

Raoul was still behind her. As Merrick rode past her, Raoul leaped toward Merrick with a bellow of rage, blood in his eyes and murder clearly writ in his heart.

Merrick's sword sliced down . . . down to pierce Raoul's breast . . .

Her eyes squeezed shut. She turned her face away and swayed unsteadily, certain her legs would give out at any moment. When next she opened them, Merrick towered above her, his face streaked with dirt and sweat.

With a strangled sob she collapsed against his chest. His arms closed around her. He bent her face into his shoulder that she might not see the mangled body.

"He's dead?" she choked out.

His fingers stroked the tangled cloud of her hair. "Aye," he murmured.

She raised her head. Her fingers curled and uncurled on his chest. "Merrick, he brought the Danes here. He planned for them to attack Brynwald. The Danes' leader was to kill *you*. When they left, Raoul sought to claim Brynwald for his own."

"I suspected some such thing when I realized Raoul was not among my men." Merrick's tone was grim.

Tears she was unaware she had shed glistened on her cheeks. "Merrick, it was just as in my dream. You came from out of the darkness, your sword raised high. You must forgive me, for all this time I thought it was me you meant to slay . . . " Emotion clogged her throat. She could say no more.

Merrick stripped away his glove. With the tips of his fingers, he skimmed away her tears, his touch infinitely gentle. When he'd finished, he clasped both hands around hers and brought them to his heart.

"'Tis I who must beg your forgiveness, for you were right about the Danes," he said quietly. "I doubted you, and I was a fool to do so." His gaze never wavered from hers. "I'll not make the same mistake again, sweet."

Alana stared. She could have sworn a wealth of tenderness dwelled in the eyes that lingered upon her upturned face, tenderness and something she was half-afraid to name. A finger beneath her chin, he lifted her lips to his.

The kiss they shared was long and sweet. Alana cared not that his mail dug into her breasts; she reveled in the way his arms tightened hard and strong about her back, as if he would never let her go. By the time he released her mouth, she felt she was soaring, like a falcon among the clouds.

Only then did they realize the sounds of fighting were all but gone. Merrick mounted his destrier, then lifted her before him on the saddle. Alana leaned back against the breadth of his chest, wrapped in his loose embrace. Long before they approached the gates, the last of the Danes had fled.

The people of Brynwald wasted no time in declaring their revelry. Shouts of triumph and victory were long and hearty. A cheer was heard as Merrick rode in with his bride.

"She lives!" came the call, and then another: "Praise God, our lady is safe and well!"

A boisterous cry went up. Alana's jaw went slack. She twisted in the saddle, her surprise keenly evident. "Sweet Mother Mary," she muttered, "they must be ill!"

A possessive hand tightened on her belly. Merrick smiled crookedly. "I told you, sweet. You were right about the Danes. And at last they have come to realize that while you are different, you are not to be feared or scorned."

He reined to a halt before the great hall. Alana was still numb with amazement as he lifted her down. He gave an unexpected chuckle and pressed a lingering kiss upon her mouth. Alana's head was still reeling as he escorted her inside the hall.

But they were scarcely within than he stopped abruptly. Beside her, she felt him stiffen. With a swift, sidelong glance, she saw his gaze trained directly across from them. Alana followed the direction of his gaze, then caught her breath.

Genevieve was wrapped in Radburn's arms.

Alana could almost feel the jolt of anger that went through Merrick. "By God," he swore hotly, "I will see the wretch in hell first—"

She cried out sharply when his hand went for his sword. "Merrick, no!" She tugged at his forearm. "She loves him! Do you hear me? Genevieve loves him! And he loves her!"

Merrick's jaw clenched. "Nay! Such a thing is not possible—"

"Oh, but it is, brother." Genevieve had finally noted their entrance. She hugged Alana fiercely, then turned once more to her brother. Radburn remained where he was, his expression wary but watchful.

"I suggest you explain yourself, Genevieve." Merrick said curtly.

Ever dignified, Genevieve lifted her chin. "There is little to explain," she stated. "I love Radburn and he has declared his love for me. He would ask for my hand but stubborn pride forbids it. Indeed" —her tone was cutting— "now that you are lord here, brother, he is no better than a peasant."

"What!" Merrick exploded. "And you would marry the man? My sister with a Saxon husband? Nay, I say!"

Genevieve's temper began to smolder. "You have a Saxon wife," she pointed out icily. "Besides, the decision is scarcely yours to make."

While Merrick glared, she went on daringly, "I once asked if you would take Alana to your bed and not your heart. And now I would ask you much the same . . . Would you rather I took this man I love to my bed and not my heart?"

Merrick did not answer. Instead his gaze swung to his wife. "Did you know of this?" he demanded.

Alana bit her lip. "Aye," she said weakly.

Genevieve spoke up once more. "Radburn is worthy of my love, brother. He is also worthy of your respect, for he fought long and hard this night that the rest of us might live. And if I have my way, he *will* be my husband."

Merrick threw up his hands. "So be it, then! You will do as you please no matter what I say!"

"Aye," she said sweetly. "That I will." She turned back to Radburn, all at once transformed. The happiness that radiated from her as she reclaimed her place in his arms was like a burst of sunshine.

But before Alana could say a word, there was a piercing shriek from just behind them.

"Nay! This cannot be. He swore he would kill you . . . *he swore he would kill you!*"

It was Sybil. She and Merrick whirled around to find Sybil on the threshold, her expression wild.

In the instant between one breath and the next, something pieced together in Alana's mind. Sybil and Raoul. Raoul and Sybil. Merciful God, *Raoul and Sybil*.

Every drop of blood drained from her face. "Nay," she said faintly. "Oh, Sybil, no . . ."

Beside her, Merrick was rigid. Apparently he had guessed as well. "Who?" he demanded.

"Was it Raoul? You and Raoul planned to see Alana slain as well?"

"Yes," Sybil hissed.

"Raoul is dead," Merrick said tautly. "He died beneath my sword." He would have said more, but Alana drew a deep, wracking breath.

"Sybil," she whispered. "Oh, Sybil, you are my sister! How could you wish me ill?"

Sybil's eyes burned like fiery embers. "How could I not!" she spat. "Always you have claimed what should have been mine, Alana, just like your mother claimed what should have been *my* mother's! You, his bastard daughter, were always Father's favorite. Faith, but I hated the way he would ever tell me I should grow to be gentle and sweet like you—how I've despised you all these years! Then when the Normans came, I thought you would be put in your place—serving me!—while at last I took my rightful place as the lady of Brynwald!"

Her gaze raked over Merrick. "You were no different than my father!" she sneered. "You took this slut to your bed when you could have had me! But I vowed I would not suffer the same shame as my mother, knowing that the man I would have was claimed by one such as her!" With a lift of her chin she disdainfully indicated Alana. "But I knew you would not want her if you believed her a witch!"

Alana blanched. A horrible thought had formed, one she could not bear to think might be true.

Alas, it was.

Sybil's features had turned purely malevolent. "Oh, but it was so easy, and you were all so stupid! *I* butchered the animals, and everyone was convinced it was Alana!" She threw back her head and let out a wild laugh.

Merrick's fury was barely suppressed. "Father Edgar. You murdered him, too, didn't you?"

"Aye!" she boasted. "It wasn't so very different from slitting the throat of an animal. Indeed, he gave me far less trouble than those beastly creatures!"

Sybil's smile was gloating. Her eyes glittered. Alana's stomach heaved. She shrank back, for the woman before her was a stranger, an evil, horrible stranger.

Sybil's gaze fastened on Alana. "Raoul might be dead, but I am not. And now, dear sister, it's your turn!"

It was so quick, Alana was never quite certain how it happened. Sybil's hand darted inside her sleeve. There was a flash of silver, the gleam of a blade. Merrick lurched forward, even as he pushed Alana out of the realm of danger. A powerful hand closed around Sybil's wrist.

Sybil's eyes bulged. Merrick's grip was merciless. He squeezed until the dagger clattered to the floor. A vile oath spewed from Sybil's lips. But just when he would have kicked the dagger aside, Sybil dove to the floor.

Alana saw it all through a haze. With a cry Sybil raised the dagger high, then plunged it deep in her breast.

Without a sound she slumped to the floor.

* * *

It was a night filled with many emotions. Terror. Relief. Gladness. Pain. Alana's heart was in shambles. Merrick held her tight against his breast while she cried, saddened by Sybil's death, devastated by her hatred and betrayal, overwhelmed by all that had happened this day. Merrick had startled everyone by gruffly announcing that should Radburn be willing to swear fealty to William, he in turn would speak to William about granting Radburn and his Norman bride a small fief. Indeed, there was one not so very far to the west . . .

And there was more yet to come.

The night was nearly spent when at last they sought their bed. Merrick insisted on carrying her up the stairs; Alana was too tired to protest. Once the door of their chamber was bolted, he lowered her to the floor. But when she would have stepped away, his arms closed more tightly about her.

Fingertips placed lightly on his chest, she glanced up at him questioningly.

His eyes found hers. "There was a time this night when I feared I might never hold you again, sweet." He smiled slightly. "I find I am loath to let you go."

"I—I felt the same," she confided shyly. "I was terrified I would never see you and Geoffrey again . . ." To her shame—and Merrick's confusion—sudden, startling tears glazed her vision.

"Alana, sweet, what is it?"

"I have always thought my dreams a curse,

for I had no wish to see the future. But now
I wish that I could, only I cannot . . . nor can I
see what's in your heart . . . and, oh, Merrick,
I wish that I could . . . I—I wish you loved me
the way I love you . . ." The words broke free
of her heart—and her lips.

She would have buried her face in the hair-
roughened hollow of his throat but he wouldn't
allow it. A finger beneath her jaw, he guided
her face to his.

His gaze was riveted to hers. "I do," he said
softly. His head bowed low. And then it came
again, a dark, velvet whisper that touched her
very soul, this time against her lips.

"I do love you, sweet. I feel it with all that
I am, with every beat of my heart. I love
you . . ."

Her heart squeezed. Everything inside her
went from dark to light. She cried anew, but
this time with joy.

Her arms slid around his neck. Their lips
clung. Merrick carried her to the bed, and there
with body and breath, proceeded to prove the
truth of his words.

It was dawn before passion's fires had
cooled. Drowsy and content, Alana lay with
her head pillowed on his chest. Merrick idly
stroked the ivory slope of her shoulder.

"Do you recall that first day in the forest?"
His voice was a low murmur. "The day I
came upon you and Aubrey surrounded by
my men?"

A slender brow arched high. "Indeed, I could
hardly forget," she teased. "You demanded

that I surrender. And you proclaimed yourself my lord and conqueror, my *Norman* lord and conqueror."

"That I did." He laughed, but then his eyes grew tender. "But now, sweet, now I am your sword and protector. And I love you, my sweet Saxon witch. I will love you forever."

So he said . . . and so it was.

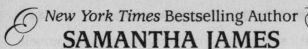